The Twenty-Nine

By J.M. Richardson

Winter Goose
PUBLISHING
where words take flight
wintergoosepublishing.com

Copyright

Winter Goose Publishing

2701 Del Paso Road, 130-92

Sacramento, CA 95835

www.wintergoosepublishing.com

Contact Information: info@wintergoosepublishing.com

The Twenty-Nine

First Edition, September, 2011

ISBN: 978-0-9836764-2-3

Cover Art by Winter Goose Publishing
Typeset by Victoriakumar Yallamelli for
Winter Goose Publishing

Published in the United States of America

Dedication

To my beautiful, supportive wife Melissa and to my wonderful children Audrey and Elle.

Chapter 1

The midday sun was finally beginning to peek from behind the clouds as they shifted to the southeast, heating the concrete and pavement to send billows of steam into the air. This was supposedly a cold front, but this did not mean much in mid-June in Carrollton, Texas. The only break from the stifling heat was during the cloud cover and actual rain. Once the clouds moved out and the sun began beating down on north Texas, it was once again unbearable, adding intense amounts of moisture and mugginess to the already hot day.

With the rain gone, there was finally movement down the quiet residential street. Through the steam rising between the rows of driveways, pristine yards and gardens blooming with color, and nice middle-class homes, boot-clad feet scurried down the pavement, splashing in the shallow puddles left from the summer downpour. It was a cow-town stampede of various shades of gray and blued metal that moved hastily from one residential block to the next and paused briefly at each intersecting street—streets with cliché names such as Pine Hollow Drive and Park Meadow Court.

The sky behind the concise line of gray clouds moving south above downtown Dallas was a brilliant shade of blue, with not one puff of cloud to blemish its perfection. The leaves of the large pin oak and Bradford pear trees in each yard rustled gently in the slight breeze that coursed through the air. Everything was green. Everything was fresh. The lawns were well-manicured, as if the neighborhood were immune to the events that plagued the land.

No doubt they're in there, Derek thought as he peered into his periphery at the quality brick homes, all lined with the distinctive Texas flags and the twenty-nine-star red flag of the Republic. *They're in there cowering under their tables. Red bastards should've thought twice before messing with Uncle Sam's war wagon.*

Derek Putnam was bitter, and for good reason. At the tender age of twenty-two, he had already seen far more horrors and atrocities than any man should in his entire life. He could not understand why all of this had to happen. The American people had weathered turbulent times in the past, and come through them to once again shine bright as a beacon of hope and prosperity to the rest of the world. All of these thoughts rolled and churned through his head every day, and especially at moments like this, forming a callus impenetrable by compassion and humanity, and a blazing hatred within that he could not easily escape.

Ahead, the street led out of the quiet residential neighborhood, and into a more commercially-zoned area. Derek and the rest of the men could see the overpasses of the extensive and complex Metroplex highway system, which was engulfed by parking lots and large retail home improvement stores, sporting-goods outfitters, banks, and strip malls, all of which were completely empty.

Abruptly, the lead man stopped, signaled for the rest to do the same, and then crouched down close to the rapidly-heating asphalt. No one said a word as they followed suit, but everyone looked around at one another as they crouched, holding tight to their assault rifles. There were a variety of expressions on the faces of the predominantly young band of men. There were looks of confusion and anxiety, but mostly looks of sheer terror, except the face of Derek Putnam. His face revealed coldness, anger, and even malice. He clearly had his game face on. He had seen this before, as most of the other young men had not. He was ready to go.

The platoon leader turned his head back to his men, scanning them over and taking in all of the expressions of emotion that emanated from them. He knew they were frightened. Not one of these soldiers had thoughts that were outside of the realm of death. Their lives had only begun, and it was unfortunate that their prime had to come in such horrible times that threatened their short lives. Some of them would die. But he knew that they all were prepared to do so. They knew exactly what they were getting themselves into when they signed on that dotted line, and allowed their patriotism to carry them into their country's service. Now is the time they would put their lives on the line, as did their ancestors.

He motioned for his men to move in close to him with a quick wave of his hand, and the hard, black rubber soles of the combat boots they wore clapped on the pavement as the soldiers rushed in and huddled around the lieutenant like he was a quarterback. There they all crouched around him holding tight to their rifles and resting their forearms on their knees, attentive to their commander, but keeping a watchful eye on their surrounding environment. Adrenaline was coursing through their blood vessels causing their pupils to dilate and their heart rates to increase as they waited for wisdom from this battle-hardened man they all trusted.

Lieutenant Jacobi was a strapping, leather-faced man. He was tall and bulky, which was heightened by the urban camouflage fatigues and Kevlar helmet. This was his element, and it showed. Everyone knew he had been in quite a few combat zones, and he had the scars to prove it, the most prominent one being the perfectly circular one on his left cheek. It was confidence-inspiring to the men to know that they had a competent, tested, and knowledgeable commander to follow into battle.

"Okay, fellas," he looked briskly around from face to face, sweat pouring over his cheek. "The eyes in the skies indicate that they're going to try and hold us off here. They're trying to keep the fight out of the residential areas and away from civilians, and that's what we're going to do. So we're on our own—no tanks; no air support."

"Why, Lieutenant?" Derek squawked angrily. "All these traitors deserve to die."

"Look, Putnam," he fired back, "we're here to take control of Dallas—a military operation. I understand and appreciate your intensity and patriotism, but let the government figure out what to do with the civilian Reds after the job is done." Derek shook his head in frustration. If it were left to him, he would call in an air strike and level the whole area. The way he saw it, they were all rebels and traitors, and treason is punishable by death.

"Now look," Lt. Jacobi continued, pointing to the east and west, "Foxtrot and Romeo Companies are out farther east, while India secures Irving, Hotel and Zulu Companies take Arlington, and Bravo Company comes up from the south. The object is to secure the suburbs from the Reds and keep reinforcements and supplies from coming in from the outside—just like Houston."

"So it's a siege," one young soldier chimed in.

"Exactly," Lt. Jacobi responded. "Tighten the noose around Dallas and Fort Worth. Dallas is a major commercial and financial center of the Republic. We're going to starve them out, and hopefully this will all be over soon."

"What can we expect right here, Lieutenant?" a young, green soldier asked with a tremble in his voice.

"Bellingham," he paused and looked down to the pavement, "I'm not going to bullshit you. They're going to give us hell. Dallas is a major objective and the Reds need it. They will defend it fiercely. Plus, these are mostly Texans, not men brought in from other states—shit-kickers and good ole boys. They're especially bad-ass. Back before all of this, they already kind of thought of themselves as a separate country. But remember your training, stay alert, and hit these shit-kickers hard."

"Hoorah!" the rest of the men uttered in unison and waited for further orders.

About half of a mile south of their position, another young man trembled, his assault rifle quivering as sweat dripped from his chin to the concrete below. It had begun to pool between his boots, and though he was crouched beneath this storefront overhang in the shade, it was still like an oven out there. He could feel the sweat beginning to soak into his socks and trickle down his back beneath the solid black fatigues and flack jacket. It was seeping from his palms onto the weapon he held in his hands.

Inward, he was also a mess. Fear and doubt swelled within him as he watched his hands and his rifle continue to shake. He swung his head around to scan his surroundings. To his right was an empty parking lot, veiled in a thin layer of steam rising upward. To his left was a window behind which stood bright signs that advertised low prices on the newest footwear. Kyle couldn't help but fantasize over how much cooler and more comfortable his aching feet would be. Behind his position crouched a dozen other men like him, all in single file along the storefront windows and walls. These were only a small handful of men in the immediate vicinity waiting for the enemy to inevitably strike.

He was loyal and intended to perform his duty, but he had no malice for the Blues just a short distance away. He simply wished they would leave well enough alone. This was a free state apart from a nation of other free states. Personally, he wished the split had never happened. At the age of nineteen, he would have had far more important things to worry about, like girls and working on his vintage '77 Corvette Stingray. He wasn't concerned with the politics and finger-pointing.

He was, however, concerned about his family just a short distance away. Many of these Blues were fanatics, capable of all sorts of vengeance in the name of the United States government. He worried about how his mother and father were doing and if the Blues had made it there or not. He worried that his younger brother was leaning toward joining the Republican Guard. Survival and defense was what kept him going, and it was the only thing that kept him from spiraling into a complete breakdown in this moment.

He peered down to his tactical watch with his blue-green eyes, and wiped the sweat from his smooth, baby face with the cloth over his right shoulder. It was nearing one o'clock, not that it really meant anything. There was no intelligence that indicated a strike time, but looking at his watch somehow provided some sort of calming effect, like keeping track of the time was the only thing he had a handle on.

The briefing that morning was exactly that—brief. There was no intelligence on the exact plan of action on the part of the Blues, but it was pretty simple and clear as to what they were attempting to do. Months before, this battalion had been moved into the Metroplex to defend it from probable attack. Dallas was the last stronghold. They were clearly going to tighten the noose.

No amount of briefing or training could prepare him and the other men for this moment. He had never been on the front lines. He was positioned deep into Dallas County, but he had heard the reports of carnage and casualties from the area south of Dallas earlier in the week. Texas in general had been relatively untouched in this conflict until the last couple of months. It was a huge state with enormous amounts of military bases but carried little personnel. But Texas had a fighting spirit and pride unparalleled in most of the other twenty-nine. They had saved one of the toughest objectives for last.

But now he was about to see the fight first-hand, and it could come at any moment, as could his death. His heart began to beat more rapidly as the thought crossed his mind. He was sweating more profusely and his body trembled more violently until he felt a hand on his shoulder.

He slowly turned his head to the right to see the friendly face of his superior officer smiling in excitement. Sergeant Williams was one of those fervently devoted patriots of the Republic that gave the cause hope. As much of a hard-ass as he was, he had been there for Kyle from the beginning, guiding him since basic training into the cold, unforgiving realities of active duty in a war zone.

"Ready, son?" the sergeant smiled enthusiastically as he patted the young man's back, causing him to nearly lose balance.

"Yes, sir," he nodded and trembled. Williams knew that deep within; this kid was scared out of his mind.

"Good," he nodded and smiled back. "'Cause you're gonna keep your mama and daddy in mind and defend their lives and rights, and all those other people up in them houses up there too," he continued in his heavy Texas drawl. "Think about all your buddies dead—the ones you went to boot camp with! Think about them Blue sons of bitches tearin' up your house and beatin' on your kid brother! Get mad! And let's properly welcome them Commie Blue bastards to fuckin' Texas!"

"Yes sir!" he raised his voice in a new-found confidence.

"Good boy," he smiled as he suddenly reacted to sporadic gunfire nearby. "Let's go, son."

They both moved briskly to the corner of the storefront and shouldered their rifles in the direction of the enemy. Every corner was the same with men trying their best to maintain some level of cover, yet lay down cover fire so that another team of men could move up to head off the Blues.

The automatic rifle fire was deafening, ringing into Kyle's ears to the point that he thought they were going to bleed. Even in training he had not heard this much gunfire at once. It echoed from building to building like a violent symphony of death as Kyle watched enemy soldiers fall to the ground with spurts of crimson mist exiting their bodies. He continued to fire his weapon in the direction of the audacious and bold enemy attack, wondering if any of his own bullets were finding their mark. He liked to think that maybe he hadn't taken anyone's life. Most were young men around his age and with similar interests. They may have been friends in another setting, punching each other in the arm and telling dirty jokes. So perhaps his bullets were only wounding them and stopping them from moving further.

Yet he knew this wasn't the case. This was a kill zone. He watched one of his own men take two shots in the chest, and saw yet another Blue soldier lose part of his head. As much as he tried to still maintain some level of humanity, adrenaline took over. His animal survival instinct was taking precedence and in this moment, it was kill or be killed.

Derek Putnam found a shield behind one of the huge concrete posts supporting the highway overpass. He could hear the enemy bullets striking and ricocheting off of the post before him. His heart was racing as he tried to determine the correct time to move forward. If he and his men stayed behind their shields, no progress could be made. He had to move, especially to inspire the other young men who were so inexperienced.

He peeked around the edge of the support post briefly a couple of times, rattling off a few short bursts to hopefully persuade the enemy defenders to take shelter for a moment. He then sprinted from behind his shield, running as fast as he could into the barrage, and dove into a ditch before him. He could hear the bullets whizzing overhead just like back in basic and just like he had experienced in Mobile and New Orleans. Dirt and grass began to pile upon his helmet as it erupted from the soil above the ditch.

His heart felt as if it would leap from his chest and his breathing was labored and raspy. Only a few minutes into the advance, he was already exhausted, but the rush of combat kept him sharp and focused. He lifted his weapon above his head, parallel to the ground, and without lifting his head he squeezed the trigger, releasing short bursts and hoping he was thinning out the enemy personnel.

In his head, he weighed the feelings of compassion for fellow man and the extreme hatred he had for these traitors. It did not matter now. He was deep into the battle lines and he had to survive. More importantly, he had to do his duty and further the objective. He knew he had to get up and move again. He again fired a few short bursts before lifting himself to his feet and readying himself to move forward to the garbage dumpster about seventy-five yards in front of him. This was going to be a tough one. This one might get him killed, but he had to try because someone needed to.

He was blind. He could not see. What was this? Was it some sort of new weapon—a flash-bang of sorts? Yet everyone was blinded, at least momentarily. The gunfire stopped as every soldier from either side dropped his rifle, and instinctively covered his eyes, rubbing and shielding them from a flash that seemed to last forever, yet was only momentary.

Derek suddenly felt a rush of wind that pushed him back a few feet, but not to the ground. Kyle felt his body slammed into the stucco façade of the store as if someone pushed him. Men all over the killing field fell over and lay squirming on the ground in disorientation, but not hurt. Was this the Valkyrie of Germanic lore? Had the angels of death come to collect their souls and cart them off to the afterlife?

As quickly as the first rush of air forced its way across the strip mall, breaking windows and pushing grown men to the ground, another wind reversed the direction, pushing over any remaining on their feet, or those who had just pulled themselves from the ground.

Every man tried to pull himself together; to find his equilibrium, regain his balance, and begin to finally see colors and shapes, rather than just white nothing. And as this sight began to come back slowly and the men stood tall, they all looked at one another in confusion. One man, and then another sharply turned his attention to the southern sky to witness a spectacle that neither of them, nor their grandparents ever thought that they would see in their lifetimes.

The cloud of dust, debris, and smoke billowing in the distance was filled with fire within and was shaped into its iconic mushroom form by the rush of oxygen fueling the intense heat that was undoubtedly incinerating downtown Dallas a mere fifteen miles away. It stood miles tall, its menacing shape and sound stood hulking over the Metroplex like an angry giant ready to squash and destroy all buildings and people in the vicinity.

No one spoke. Men from both armies stood side-by-side only looking in amazement at the giant and briefly at one another. Their differences became secondary and mundane. Their cause was dwarfed by this new monster. It was huge and it was violent.

The questions began rolling though their heads. Why did this happen? We're all equally shocked, so if neither side did it, then who? How many people are dead? And how did it come to this?

Chapter 2

September, Twenty-one months earlier

The early morning sunlight flooded the bustling kitchen, bathing the tall, white cabinets and tan granite countertops in warm, nourishing rays. Everything in the kitchen was neat and tidy with fine cooking utensils sprouting from a black ceramic bin like flowers, a crystal bowl filled with fresh apples, oranges, and kiwi, and various small appliances all neatly placed along the earthy beige backsplash tile beneath the upper cabinets. The large kitchen's centerpiece was an island topped with matching granite with a stainless steel five-burner range beneath an enormous stainless vent that matched the rest of the small and large stainless appliances.

The sound of bacon sizzling in a cast iron skillet dominated all sounds in the house and its salty aroma crept and cornered into every room in the two-story north Texas home. The coffee maker gurgled as it brewed the morning's must into the large container below, its smell combining with that of the bacon to ensure that everyone in the house awoke happy. Scrambled eggs were being stirred in another skillet, mixed with sliced honey-cured ham, and topped with mild cheddar cheese. On yet another of the burners simmered a large pot of homemade grits, steaming and swirling with real butter. In the oven, from-scratch biscuits were plumping and browning, ready for consumption with butter and jelly.

"Kyle! Dylan!" the gracefully aging woman yelled from before her position behind the stove. "Breakfast!"

For a woman in her mid-forties, Angela Perkins still looked every bit the trophy wife that she did in her early twenties, except that she never really was a trophy wife. The term trophy wife implies that she has no brain, but is beautiful in every square inch of her being. She was quite the latter with shoulder-length blond hair that she dared not tell a soul she had begun to dye away the gray, graceful fine lines near the eyes, a wonderful light tan, and a figure that remained appealing, despite birthing two boys. She also held a bachelor's degree in literature from TCU, and was well-cultured, well-read, and well-traveled. In fact, when she and her husband first met, this was far more attractive than her dazzling looks.

Angela poured her husband a tall mug of coffee, adding nothing to it just as he liked it, and then carefully walked it slowly to the butcher-block-style table in the glass-surrounded breakfast nook, setting the steaming brew before him. He looked up from his morning newspaper, smiled lovingly, and received a deep-suction kiss from his wife.

Drew was dressed as he usually was for another workday. His black business suit was nice and moderately priced, but altered to accentuate his fit, yet increasingly flabby body. It was fine for the office, but it wasn't Wall Street. But he didn't need to be. A civil engineer with a reputable Fort Worth construction firm, he usually removed the jacket as soon as he shuffled into his office, only to slip his arms back into it for meetings. Otherwise, he maintained his appearance quite well. He never looked as though his clean-cut hair needed a trim, his face was always closely-shaven, and he tried to make it to the gym at least twice a week.

"Breakfast, boys!" Angela yelled again as she prepared her loving husband a plate of home-cooked goodness.

Upstairs, a baby-faced young man walked out of the bathroom, still brushing his teeth, yet freshly showered and fully dressed. His short, brown hair naturally spiked a little in its dampness, and the smell of soap, shampoo, deodorant, and minty toothpaste combined for a refreshing and oddly energizing scent.

He traversed the hallway into his younger brother's bedroom, which upon entering, appeared to have been tossed and robbed. Yet beneath the rubble was a bed, within which still slept Dylan, who was three years his junior.

"Get up, douchebag," he mumbled with a mouthful of toothpaste and saliva. He quickly looked for somewhere to discharge the load in his mouth, and found an old soda can that very well may have been sitting there for upward of a month.

Within the light blue walls, clad with posters of rock bands and half-naked women, one could barely see any of the beige carpet below. There was a heaping pile of dirty laundry in the center of the room with other articles of clothing draped over the cluttered dresser and sparsely utilized desk. Dotting the widespread dirty laundry were scattered bits of trash such as candy bar wrappers, empty soda cans, balled-up paper, and an electric guitar that had barely been used.

"Get up, dude," Kyle spoke a little more forcefully. "You're gonna be late for school."

Dylan did not budge. He continued to lie in his bed, which had not been made in a year, with his arm draped over his eyes and forehead, his shaggy, blond hair peeking from beneath. He simply snorted and smacked, while gyrating his body subtly and mumbling from some place between dreaming and waking.

"Come on, asshole!" Kyle yelled, picking up a dirty t-shirt and hurling it into Dylan's head region.

"Dude," he finally rolled over, burying his head into his dingy pillow.

"Boys!" their mother's voice floated distantly from the kitchen downstairs.

"Alright, I'll let Mom come up and get you," Kyle turned around. "I know she'd love to talk to you about this room."

"Okay," he rolled lazily out of bed, "I'm up. I'm up."

"You need to clean this shit up."

"Yeah, yeah. Get out of my room," he swiftly bypassed his brother and narrowly avoided the waiting noogie. He ducked into the bathroom, and slammed the door with a level of disregard, attitude, and angst that was typical of him.

Kyle descended the staircase upbeat and ready to start the day. He continued past the formal living room and formal dining room, which had always been off-limits. Mom had always kept those rooms pristine. The fine tan leather furniture seemed that it had never known the warmth of someone's rear end, while the hardwood and blue and red floor rugs looked as though no one had ever trod on them.

He followed his nose past the kitchen to the breakfast nook and plates loaded with eggs, bacon, and grits, all set neatly upon the placemats. His father sat transfixed upon the newspaper in his left hand, while he sipped his strong, black coffee with the right. He had barely touched his food, which was typical. He set his mug on the table, and used the freed hand to pick up a strip of bacon, and lay it on the fourteen by fourteen white tile floor for the family Weimaraner to scoop up, devouring it in just a few short chomps.

The Weimaraner was a beautiful dog, her short, shiny gray coat accented by light green eyes. Though bred from two quite large parents, she remained a bit smaller, despite being three years old and full-grown. It was clear that she was not the runt of the litter of seven, yet she was small for her age and breed. She did not, however, escape from the typical Weimaraner quirks and demeanor. Though sweet and friendly, even to strangers, she was extremely high-strung and full of energy. Without a sufficiently large back yard in which to run and play, it would have been nearly inhumane to keep this breed. Inside, however, she remained docile, typically lounging on the family room furniture when she had the chance. Peculiarly, she sat on her cropped tail like a human, rather than on her hind legs, and looked around at everyone as if she were about to speak. Kyle and Dylan were convinced that if she were to someday utter a few words, she would likely possess a British dialect. Despite being hyper and neurotic, she was a great family dog.

"Morning," Kyle greeted his parents as he sat down to the breakfast table, and began shoveling eggs into his mouth.

"Morning," his mother replied, still milling around in the kitchen. "Orange juice?"

"Um," he paused to think of his options, "yeah. That's cool."

"Cindy Chandler is leading in the polls again," Drew spoke up from behind his newspaper. "She's way up. She's going to end up winning this election," he folded up the paper, and tossed it to the side in bitter disregard.

"So what if she does?" his wife said, never deviating her eyes from the skillets and pots she was cleaning in the kitchen. "Maybe she's just what we need in the White House to shake things up a little. Have you seen her in the debates?"

"Yeah, she's a bitch."

"Why, Drew?" she turned to him in annoyance. "Because she's a strong-willed, motivated woman?"

"No," he defended. "She just comes off as a bitch. But that's the problem. This is just why she's going to win. She'll already inherit the black vote just for being a Democrat, she's loose on immigration, so she'll get the Hispanics, and then she'll get all of the females. You'll all be in the streets burning your bras like it's 1972! Hail Cindy Chandler!"

"No, I like her because she's well-spoken and educated," she replied.

"Hitler was well-spoken, too. Besides, what basis is that to be qualified to run the country? Our current president went to an Ivy League school, and he's an idiot. I've seen these reporters interviewing people outside her rallies and speeches, asking them why they like her. And that's all I keep hearing. She's smart. She speaks well. Nobody has a clue why they are voting for her. There should be a test you have to pass on the issues and platforms of each candidate before you're allowed to vote."

"Well," she paused, "we're in a recession. We need someone in office that will make some changes."

"Like what?" he began to get frustrated. "Make the government bigger? Socialize everything from the financial system to health care?"

"If that's what we need," she took on a tone of worry. "Drew, Pam told me that her husband Jim got laid off last week. He's been with his company for twenty years!"

"Angela, these things happen, and..." he stopped, interrupted by his wife.

"All the Republicans in congress want to do is bail out the corporations. Let's give these greedy idiots more money while common people like Jim and Pam suffer! What about their kids? What about their house? What if they lose their house?" Her expression became one of terror in an instant. "Are you in danger of losing *your* job?"

"No, no, no," he shook his head and winced in a way to imply that what she suggested was ridiculous. "I've been there a long time. Hell, I play golf with the CEO twice a month. I'm a big-wig, and besides, as long as there is such a thing as infrastructure, they'll need someone like me to design more."

The conversation went silent, but not as if the conversation was over. Both Drew and Angela stared at each other with looks of concern and frustration as tension in the kitchen and breakfast nook began to mount. They were not angry with each other, but they obviously had a difference of opinion, and Kyle sat looking from his father to his mother and back, too uneasy to even eat.

"Kyle, what do you think about Senator Chandler?" Drew broke the silence. "Would you support her or Byron Davenport?"

"Um," he paused to think and chew. His eyes grew wider, hesitant to answer the question, for fear of fierce rebuttal. "I don't know, Dad. I haven't really kept up with it. I won't be eighteen until April anyway, so it doesn't matter."

"Well of course it matters!" he exclaimed. "It makes no difference how old you are. Taking interest and an active part in your country's affairs is your civil duty. You've got to stay informed, and don't just believe everything these idiots and candidates say on TV. Inform yourself."

"Well, there is a mock election coming up at school. We have to fill out registration cards and they're going set up computerized polling stations in the lunch room. We're all going—actually all of the high schools in the district are going to vote about a week before the real election."

"Well there you go!" his father seemed happy. "They're teaching you kids right. The earlier they get you active, the better."

"But it's not a real election," Kyle shrugged. "It's not going to make any difference. They don't count our votes."

"Yeah, but you'll know what to do during the next one," he took another sip of his coffee.

Kyle stuffed the last few morsels of his hearty breakfast into his already full mouth, cutting the conversation short, and carried his plate into the kitchen where his mother stood ready to receive and clean it. He lightly jogged over to the staircase, where his younger brother was just making his way to the first level of the house, his wardrobe thrown together without much regard for style or appearance. Both boys lifted their backpacks, hoisting them over one shoulder, and made their way to the front door.

"Dylan," Angela yelled from the kitchen, "you didn't eat any breakfast!"

"Not hungry, Mom!" he yelled back without turning to her.

"Alright," she shook her head as she walked over to pick up his full plate of food, and scrape the eggs and bacon into the dog's food bowl. "Have a good day at school."

The two brothers exited the house through the front door, the bright morning sun causing their pupils to contract and their hands to instinctively shade their eyes. Kyle spotted his friend Ryan at the end of the driveway waiting as he always did, and began jogging toward him, leaving Dylan lagging sluggishly.

Ryan was a short and skinny seventeen-year-old, significantly smaller than Kyle, and as usual, he was wearing his baggy, faded jeans, tattered and frayed at the bottom of the legs, and a black t-shirt. He was not goth or angst in style, but preferred simple and almost over-comfortable clothing. He peered down with is dark brown eyes transfixed upon the screen of his cell phone, reading and punching keys as if in a trance. The already building September heat caused a bit of sweat to bead on his forehead, which he wiped with his shirt sleeve, the fabric irritating his moderate teen acne. He then ran his hands through is shaggy brown hair, wiping sweat onto his jeans.

Kyle jogged past a car in the driveway, covered with a tarp, spare parts partially protruding from beneath. He gazed at it for a moment in disappointment. He had been able to work on it a little over the summer, but with school back in session and the building homework load and activities piling up, he was again neglecting his car.

"Is that Shelley?" Kyle tried to take a peek at the screen of the phone.

"Yeah," he continued to text message his girlfriend.

"When are you guys gonna do it? You walk around school like you're so in love—everyone already thinks you're having sex."

"Whatever," Ryan smiled mockingly. "Mister sex expert who's only gotten a girl to touch his dick once."

"Twice, okay," he smiled back. "And Ashley let me finger her on the Ferris wheel at the state fair last year."

"Ashley Dykes? No shit?" he seemed surprised. "You never told me that!"

"She told me not to," he shrugged.

"So why are you telling me now?"

"She ditched me, so screw her."

They both laughed as Kyle turned his head to the rear to make sure his brother was actually coming to school. He watched as Dylan trudged along staring at his feet, periodically looking up at all of the large, well-maintained homes that lined the quiet residential street. It was not that he was a bad kid or mischievous; that would have taken effort. Dylan Perkins was simply lethargic and unmotivated. No one had quite found a way to reach the child and spark his interests outside of the realm of sleep and goofing off.

"When are you gonna get the Corvette running?" Ryan gestured toward the covered vehicle in the driveway behind them.

"Dunno," he shrugged. "Dad's supposed to help me with it, but he's always working."

"Dude, why didn't you just take all that money you saved up and get something that runs?"

"Three thousand bucks doesn't get you much on the used car lot," he leered at his friend. "Besides, it's a classic. It's in good shape, it just doesn't run. And once it does, Ashley is gonna regret just letting me use my finger!" he smiled deviously.

"So anyway," Ryan changed the subject. "What took you so long this morning? I was waiting for, like, ten minutes."

"Oh, you know, another political discussion with Dad."

"Oh yeah? What was it this time?" he smiled.

"He wanted to know what I thought about Cindy Chandler."

"Oh shit," Ryan knew what that meant.

"Yeah, he went off on a rant about how 'that woman will destroy this country'," he mocked his father's voice. "And of course Mom disagreed with him and things got tense. So then he wanted to know what my take was."

"Which is?"

"I don't know. I don't really give a shit."

"Yeah, my Dad's a big Davenport supporter, and I guess I agree with him," Ryan shrugged.

"You don't have your own opinion?"

"No," he shook his head. "Not really. Like you said, I don't really care."

"Yeah, dude. I just want to focus on getting out of high school, and go to college somewhere."

"Any idea where?"

"No, not really. I was thinking A & M or Tech," Kyle said.

"I put in my application to North Texas a couple of weeks ago."

"Cool, is that where you want to go?"

"Not really, but I don't have the grades you do, so my options are limited," Ryan admitted.

The boys continued their usual morning conversations as they approached the giant two-story edifice a couple of blocks away. This was the newer high school in the district, completely covered outwardly with red and dark gray brick, and sprawling over the area of about seven acres. It cost the school district approximately $90 million to build, fully furnished with the newest equipment and technology and surrounded by tennis courts, a practice football field, a field house, and a baseball diamond. They continued toward the school with nothing in particular on their minds that morning, Dylan lagging behind them as always.

Chapter 3

Derek Putnam didn't bother shaving the day-old hair from his face as he stared into the small medicine-cabinet mirror of his bathroom and brushed his teeth violently. It occurred to him that he would not mind if he never shaved again, if only women liked big, bushy facial 'fros that made them feel like they were burying their faces into an armpit. It did not matter whether or not he shaved for his job anyway. He was not negotiating multi-million-dollar deals for a living.

He spouted the gigantic load of toothpaste saliva into the sink, while simultaneously ratcheting the outdated steel faucet to wash the concoction down. He then cupped his right hand, filling it with the heavily chlorinated city water, and slurping it into his mouth to rinse and spit.

He looked up and into the mirror again, giving himself another assessment. He did not look terrible, but he did look blue collar. His stubble was thick, as if it were painted onto his face, and it matched the color of his dark brown hair, which was kept relatively short and neat. His brown eyes were in sharp contrast with the white that surrounded them, a feature for which he was frequently complemented. He turned his face from one side to another, giving himself one more quick look before swiftly zipping up his stained blue jumpsuit and turning to leave for work.

He stepped out into the hallway from the plain white linoleum floors of the bathroom and onto the 1970s brown and beige shag carpet. There were a few pictures hanging on the eggshell walls between the darkly stained pine baseboards and the popcorn ceilings. Derek always stopped momentarily to reminisce at the sight of him, his two older sisters, and his parents enjoying some random outing in the park. It was a happier time. It was a time before worry.

He could not remember the last time he had seen his father. His mother had said once that he went to work in shipping on the Great

Lakes, but ended up never coming back. When he was a child, he thought that meant he had died in some accident; maybe falling overboard or something of that nature. He then, however, came to realize that he had simply deserted his family, never to return home. He remembers getting a birthday card once when he was about ten years old, but since then, neither he nor his mother had any idea where his father was or if he were alive.

As for his older sisters, they began down a dark path as far back as junior high. The identical twins developed physically at an early age, and with the curves came the clothing to match it. The combination of an early puberty and long, flowing blond hair made them popular with the boys, and by the time they reached high school, they had already gained a reputation for being the most promiscuous girls in school. Low self-esteem followed, which led to drug and alcohol use, and by senior year, they were ready to drop out. The last Derek had heard, they were somewhere on the east coast dancing at strip clubs to feed their habits.

Derek shook his head, trying to pull his mind from the abyss of broken promises and lost dreams, and moved past the memories into the family room, if anyone could call it that. His mother sat in a trance in her easy chair, watching the television, an increasingly frequent sight in the mornings the past few weeks. The dark brown easy chair was stained beyond recovery, much like the woman that sat in it. Times had become hard with the economy slowing. People bought less, so demand was less, and therefore supply lowered. The only way to make up profits was to downsize, and with Sherry's age and declining health, she was an easy short-term target. With no job prospects in a failing economy and no skills beyond the work she did in the textile mill, she spent her mornings smoking her long, thin cigarettes in her easy chair watching the news networks and praying that things would get better.

The family room was too small for Sherry's chair, the love seat, and the sofa. The small, antiquated television set sat atop an old coffee table sitting flush against the far wall. There were no pictures or decorations in this room, but the eggshell walls were beginning to turn yellow near the ceiling beneath an almost permanent cloud of cigarette smoke. There was a small end table next to the easy chair topped with a large, glass ashtray and a cup of coffee, but otherwise, the room was as plain as plain can get.

Sherry was completely transfixed upon the television, which was turned up much too loud for the comfort of most people. Her hearing was failing along with much of the rest of her body. Her skin color was beginning to pale from too much time indoors and she had nearly doubled her smoking habit with so much time on her hands, despite rising taxes and price per pack. She had also begun to drink more than usual, something that reminded Derek of his father far too much. These new developments were all in addition to growing health problems like hypoglycemia, gout, and thyroid issues.

"Chandler is once again on top of the polls," the classy blonde anchor spouted almost proudly on the news network Sherry was watching, "and with only about two months left to Election Day, many analysts are speculating, and even predicting that the Democrats will not only retake the White House, but even regain control of the House and Senate. Let's go to our panel. Do you think America is ready for its first female president?"

As a panel of pundits and analysts contemplated and commented on the news anchor's question beyond Derek's interest at the moment, he rifled through the nearly empty pantry and cabinets for something that he could take as an improvised breakfast for his ride to work. His infamous temper was rising quickly as his furious search through the tiny kitchen yielded few prospects for some kind of nutrition.

"Mom," he raised his voice a bit without yelling, "there's nothing to eat. What happened to those grain-fruit bar thingies?"

He was not angry at his mother for the lack of food in the house. She could not be faulted in losing her job. He was frustrated that the household was once again back to a single income. Not only was it difficult for him to feed the two of them with his meager wages, he was beginning to worry about paying utilities and the house note. He was a twenty-year-old forced to grow up way before his time.

"We ate them all, Derek," she responded without deviating her glare from the news.

"Mom, I've got to eat something before work," he pled.

"I think there are some Little Debbie cakes or something in the junk food cabinet."

He sighed at the thought of sweets and snack food for breakfast. He needed something less sweet than a sugar-coated snack cake packed with empty calories and trans fat.

"It'll have to do," he quickly swung open the cabinet door, grabbing two of the white and black-striped cakes and shoving them into the pocket of his blue jump suit.

He briskly walked from the kitchen, past the outdated white bar countertop with its faux marble swirls and silver glitter, and into the family room where Sherry had just lit another cigarette, sucking it feverishly, inhaling deeply, and letting the smoke exit in a thick cloud across the room. Derek coughed somewhat as he moved into the toxic mist until he reached the armchair, leaning over to kiss her on her deeply lined, leathery forehead.

"Love you, Mom," he stood again erect while she affectionately hugged and patted his right arm, a smile of love and appreciation crossing her badly aging face.

"Love you, too, sweetheart," she finally released his arm to allow him to rapidly move for the front door. "Have a great day," he coughed as he twisted the tarnished knob, pulled the door open, and exited the house, slamming the door behind him.

"Come on!" a slightly older man yelled and motioned with is arm from the drivers' side window of a beat-up, baby blue mid-seventies sedan. "We're gonna be late, man!"

Derek made no haste, despite the commands of his co-worker. He looked around at the chipping white paint falling from the beams and posts of the rickety front porch. A once homey two-person swing sat motionless and rotting on the decking of the porch, the chains piled onto the seat. The once quaint and happy street was now deteriorating around him. Most of the leaves had begun to turn a medley of browns and oranges, and the overcast morning was bathing the neighborhood in gray. It made the scene seem so much gloomier. Surrounding the Putnam home were other crumbling homes inhabited by mostly simple factory workers, many out of work. The lawns were largely overgrown and ill-kept, accented by older model cars in the driveways and along the curbs, many of them broken down.

He shrugged, trying to shake the depressing imagery around him, and removed one of the snack cakes from his pocket. He tugged and pulled at the clear cellophane until he was able to retrieve the cake, and then sink his teeth into a large bite of it. He began to make his way down the creaking, failing steps, high stepping with energy as if the sugary breakfast had immediately sent him a jolt.

He trotted down to the curb where his friend's vehicle idled high, causing it to shake and rattle slightly. He rounded the front end, running his right hand lightly over the fading paint before yanking on the silver metallic handle, and causing it to squeal open. Derek plopped down on the vinyl seat, the material squeaking beneath his body weight as he finished his first Little Debbie cake.

"Breakfast of champions, huh, buddy?" Jake smirked at his new passenger, gripping tightly to the steering wheel with his right hand and brushing the poorly groomed brown curls from his oily forehead.

"It's all that was in the house," he replied, while keeping his eyes on the endless crumbling homes flying by him. "Trust me. If Mom had made eggs Benedict, I would have invited you in," his words dripped with sarcasm.

"Well hell," he fired back, "she's got enough time on her hands."

Derek simply glared at him with disdain. He did not have to utter a word. His brown eyes beamed with a heat that threatened to remove every bit of hair from his curly head and seldom-shaved face. Jake looked at his friend momentarily, before returning to the road, but during the initial glance, he caught sight of the look he was receiving. He returned his eyes to Derek twice more, each time losing the smirk from his face.

"Dude," he half giggled, "I'm sorry. Okay, I know that was a bad joke. I know she can't help it."

Derek turned his head back to the road and toward the passenger side window, but still said nothing. It was a sore subject for him in that he was angry with the factory that laid his mother off. He was angry about the amount of responsibility that had become his to own. He was angry with the way the government was mishandling the recession.

"Dude," Jake spouted again. "I said I was sorry. God, you don't have to get so pissed off. What's the difference between that and a few 'yo mama' jokes over beers?"

"You just don't fucking say that, okay?" he snapped his head back toward the driver. "Jesus, a 'yo mama' joke is just some ridiculous bullshit that has no truth. My mom getting laid off is serious shit!"

"Okay, like I said, I'm sorry."

An all too inevitable awkward silence entered the cab of the sedan. Jake knew that he had offended his friend, and in retrospect, should not have joked about Derek's mom. From that point, he was not sure that there was anything else that he could say to ease the tension. He had already tried everything he could, so he was at a loss. Derek was, as well, unsure whether to audibly forgive, continue into a rant, or just let the discomfort intensify, before slowly fading.

"She doing alright?" Jake broke the silence.

"Um," he nodded sluggishly, "yeah, I guess. All she does is sit around the goddamned house smoking and watching *Golden Girls* reruns."

"I love the *Golden Girls,*" he nodded, watching the road. "Blanche was hot. Cougar woman."

"I was always a big fan of *Bewitched* reruns," Derek giggled back. "In fact, my first wet dream was having sex with Elizabeth Montgomery in a gigantic pair of overalls."

Jake unleashed a monstrous flood of laughter that brought the mood within the aging sedan a full one hundred and eighty degrees from the tension just a couple of minutes earlier. Both men rode the wave of laughter until the inertia ran out, and it came gradually back to a pair of grins. Silence followed with Jake keeping a keen eye to the road, stopping at red lights and making turns through the decaying suburb of Cleveland. Derek still grinned with the lingering images and humor of his adolescent dream, his fingernail resting between his front teeth.

"You ever think about doing anything else?" Derek broke the silence.

"What do you mean?"

"The garage," he clarified. "You ever think about being something other than a grease monkey?"

"Shit, man," Jake shrugged. "It was all I was ever going to be. My old man was a mechanic and my two older brothers. I grew up holding the flashlight for Pop while he ripped out carburetors and pumped the brake pedals to help him bleed the lines. It's the only thing I'm good at."

"Okay, but was there ever anything else you wanted to be?"

"Like buy into all that bullshit my third grade teacher said about 'you can be president'?"

"Not necessarily. Anything. A dream? Ever want to be a rock star or something other than a working stiff with permanently oil-stained hands?" Derek pried.

"I used to think I wanted to be an airline pilot," he admitted, almost cautiously.

"No shit," Derek nodded. "How come?"

"Well, pilots get to fly all over the world," he droned as if he thought it sounded corny, "and they make pretty good money. It just seemed like a cool job."

"What happened?"

"Well as it turns out, most airline pilots flew in the military, and the military just wasn't my thing. They have to get up early and make up their beds so you can bounce a quarter off of it and shit. Then you've got to run, like, five miles a day. Damn that!"

"See, that's what I'm talking about," Derek interjected.

"What?"

"I don't think I'd mind going into the military," he began to get excited.

"Why?" Jake didn't seem to understand.

"I don't know," he shook his head as if to doubt that it was a good idea. "At least it's not the garage."

"What's wrong with the garage?"

"Nothing," he shrugged. "I'm just getting tired; I feel stuck. I feel like I have something else I can do—like I have more purpose to fulfill."

"That has to be the corniest thing I've ever heard," he smiled. "But go for it. You're young."

"That's the thing," Derek began to look pessimistic. "I can't. I've got to take care of Mom. I mean, what would happen to her? She'd lose the house, she'd be homeless, she's sick..."

"Dude, you'll make money in the army," Jake spouted back. "Hell, Uncle Sam probably pays better than Dickie pays you at the shop! Then they've got that GI thing..."

"The GI Bill," he corrected.

"Yeah, the GI Bill. You can go to college on that, and then really make a good living for you and your mom."

"Nah," Derek scoffed, "I'm not college material. I made average grades, but classrooms and books—not my thing. I did much better in shop and automotive. I like working with my hands."

"Well I'm sure the military can teach you to kill one of them raghead jihadists with your bare hands," Jake chuckled.

"See, that's one of the main problems I have with the military," he pondered aloud. "I don't know that I have it in me to kill a man. I mean, maybe if I were really pissed off or if it were 'kill or be killed', maybe."

"Shit, man," Jake said. "We're pretty much out of the Middle East already. You probably won't even have to go overseas or kill anybody," he commented as he pulled into the parking lot next to the garage.

It was a small, independently run full-service shop that took care of all manner of problems from engine issues and brakes to the aesthetic tinting and body work. It wasn't much to look at. A nationwide franchise it was not. Instead, it was the kind of place that one might expect to see a drug deal taking place in the shadows in the wee hours of the morning. It was a long, steel building with the ever-typical garage doors lining the exterior wall. The white paint was showing signs of deterioration as the elements were beginning to take their toll in bringing the oxidation and rust to the surface. Along the outer walls were various canisters and fifty-five gallon drums, no doubt filled with old oil products. The residue was seeping from beneath the lids and staining the concrete beneath the scrap metal, old discarded parts, and short stacks of tires.

Jake eased into the parking spot, shifted into park, and killed the engine, retracting the key from the ignition in one motion. He unhooked the seat belt, as did Derek, both men stepping out of the vehicle with a sluggishness that spoke volumes of how badly they did not want to be at work. As they turned their bodies toward the garage bustling with men still yawning and drinking thermos bottles filled with coffee, they could see a short, rotund man approaching, trying to fix the comb-over atop his severely balding head. He rapidly moved his short, fat legs in a way that the vertically challenged did, unable to take longer strides to cover more distance. He was sweating as he always was, whether it was hot or cold, and wiping the beads from his face and forehead with the sleeve of his blue jumpsuit.

"Oh shit," Derek uttered at the sight of his boss. "Dickie looks pissed!"

"You're late," he snapped with a dialect that sounded, perhaps, more native to Brooklyn. "Get your asses inside!"

"It's his fault," Jake motioned toward his friend "I had to wait…"

"I don't give a shit whose fault it is," he interrupted, stopping abruptly in front of their slow advance and lifting up a clipboard. "We've got a brake job due at ten, and you jerk-offs haven't even started on it," he violently tapped at the sheet on the clipboard.

"We're on it, Dickie," Derek nodded as his boss, who shot them a frustrated look, turned sharply, and then scurried off toward the garage ahead of them. Derek rolled his eyes, grinning at his friend. "Yeah, I've gotta find something else to do."

Chapter 4

October, Twenty months before the bomb

"Mom," Derek called as he pushed through the badly creaking doorway.

It was almost as dark inside the house as it was beginning to get outdoors. The last rays of the sun were beaming across the darkening blue sky and turning a few lazily moving clouds a pastel pink color. The crickets were chirping as the country was dimming, and he was just arriving home, sweaty, oil-stained, and radiating odor.

"Mom," he called again, still with no response.

Beyond the bare, yet dim single bulb, faintly illuminating the sorely outdated kitchen, it was darkness, save for the flickering glow of the television in the pitch black family room. Derek could see his mother's face and torso rising from above the lower regions of the armchair in between the brightness and darkening of the light emanating from the set. Each time the light filled the room, he could see the swirls of translucent cigarette smoke circulating around the occasional orange glow of a drag being taken.

"Mom," he tried again.

"Dinner is on the counter," she did not move her eyes from the screen.

Derek did not see a single pot or skillet on the stove, nor a casserole dish upon the countertop. In fact, it appeared as though the kitchen had not been in full use in years. He scanned the dated space for a hint of food, and brought his gaze to rest upon the quintessential Chinese take-out container. It had been sitting in its location for long enough that some of the oils and grease had begun to seep through the folds and creases in the paper.

"Got you Kung Pao Chicken—your favorite," she added.

"Great," he winced in secret at the sight of the cold, leftover-grade

Chinese food. "Hey, I've got something…" he pulled a wrinkled and damaged pamphlet from his back pocket.

"The debate is on," she interrupted.

Derek said nothing as he opened the silverware drawer, and then pushed it shut in frustration when he saw that it held no forks. He laid the sweat-damaged pamphlet on the counter near the sink as he rummaged through endless soiled dishes and silverware piling up in the white porcelain-lined sink, selecting a fork that seemed to be the cleanest. He then lifted the dingy green sponge at the top right ledge near the faucet, and began scrubbing the utensil and rinsing it thoroughly.

"Mom, I've been thinking…" he was interrupted again.

"This debate is on," she did not even acknowledge that her son was speaking. Her eyes were transfixed on the TV screen. "It's the last one before the election next month."

The young man was disappointed and frustrated that his mother had become such a zombie, that she barely listened to him. She was wearing the same baby blue night gown that she had awoken in that morning. The ashtray was filled with a heap of squeezed and wrinkled cigarette butts. Derek was angry, yet attempting to not allow his mother to see that. It was not as though she was paying attention anyway. He simply tossed the Marine Corps pamphlet onto the counter in disregard, sighing and rolling his eyes as he picked up the take-out container and made his way to his spot on the couch.

The blonde journalist moderating the debate had just begun outlining the rules of this classic Lincoln-Douglas style argument. She sternly explained to the two candidates what order the questions would be asked, to whom, and how long each had to respond and rebut. Derek did not know who the woman was, but he was pretty sure he had decided that she was a bitch.

The royal blue carpet on the lower and upper tiers of the platform glowed in the stage lights of the theater. Upon the top tier, the Republican and Democratic candidates stood confidently behind their respective wooden podiums. The backdrop was a giant projection screen displaying a full-screen, computer-generated flying U.S. flag, attempting to instill patriotism and pride in one's country.

"Senator Chandler. Senator Davenport. If you're prepared, let's begin," she looked down at the desk behind which she was seated, shuffling around some pages. "The first question goes to Senator Chandler, and this one is about terrorism. In the time that has passed since the withdrawal of American troops from terrorist haven countries around the world, the threats from Muslim fundamentalist groups, particularly based in Pakistan, have increased by nearly sixty percent. How would your administration handle the task of responding to threats and securing our country against attack? Two minutes to you, senator."

"Let me first begin by saying that it's a pleasure to be here and be back in good old New York City," she revealed a big toothy smile framed by her gracefully aging skin while pushing her light brown hair over the shoulders of her expensive women's skirt suit. "We've come a long way with the way we think about terrorism since the attacks of September 11, so many years ago. We've come a long way since the archaic generalized stance that 'we don't negotiate with terrorists.' Every situation is unique and must be dealt with in a unique fashion. We must remember that terror is not something that we can wage war on. It is a tactic, and as long as we allow it, it will inspire terror amongst our people. That being said, we can't send troops into foreign countries to fight an invisible foe, because as we've learned in the past, it drags on forever and costs thousands of American lives, as well as billions of taxpayer dollars. We must work together with haven countries to help them eradicate these groups from their lands, while using our intelligence agencies to track and monitor terrorist activities. But under the Chandler administration, most of the preparation will be done right here at home. We will continue to secure our seaports and airports, while relying upon Homeland Security and the NSA to stop attacks from happening."

Derek watched attentively as the woman on the television screen offered her view on military issues, something that was materializing in a very real way within his mind. He wondered often if when he enlisted, there would be a sudden conflict half way around the world, and he would have to ship out to fight in a war. He was almost having second thoughts about this. He was a mechanic. He was barely out of high school. He didn't want to end up with a gunshot wound in his skull.

"Thank you Senator Chandler," the blonde smiled slightly, and then turned to the other candidate. "Senator Davenport, two minutes."

"Well, thank you all for the opportunity to be here today," he smiled even bigger than his opponent.

He seemed larger than life; ten feet tall, though only about five feet and eleven inches. He carried himself with such charisma and commanded such attention that even when he spoke softly, his voice resonated throughout the entire room.

"Ladies and gentlemen, I've served this country in the armed forces, so you can rest assured that I know how to command the military, I know tactics and strategy, and I know how to defend our people. And you can't do that solely from behind our borders and from behind our desks. You have to stop these guys BEFORE they bring the fight to our soil. Why would we wait for another potential Manhattan high rise to come down? If we have real intel that a terrorist group is in a particular place, planning an attack of some sort, we'd have to have troops ready to go. Pakistan is a nuclear country. If it falls to terrorist groups, anti-American fundamentalists will have access to a nuclear arsenal. And under my administration, we will have small contingencies of soldiers in place in strategic areas, rather than a large occupying force, while using our intelligence and security agencies on the home front and abroad."

"Would you be open to having a small contingency of foreign troops sitting around in our country in case they wanted to eradicate a group within our population, Senator Davenport? Maybe they'd like to get rid of the Boy Scouts." Chandler snapped politely before waiting for the go-ahead from the blonde.

"Well, I..." he was interrupted before the opportunity to speak.

"I'm sure you do not, and neither do the citizens of Afghanistan or Pakistan. All they know is when the Americans show up, their children get caught in the crossfire. Even they, often, don't know who's a terrorist or not, so how are we supposed to expect our troops to know who to shoot? It's like the Viet Cong all over again."

"These people are oppressed!" he began to get excited, all the while displaying the big businessman smile. "They would like nothing better than to get rid of the Taliban and go about living a normal life!"

"And that's our responsibility?" she responded. "Our responsibility is to secure our own freedom, not someone else's. If we have a unique opportunity to wipe out a terrorist force, then so be it, but as far as liberating a group of people, that should be the job of that country's government. I will waste no American lives on ideological quests about 'securing democracy for the world'," she cut at him deeply.

"We're out of time, candidates..." the blonde interjected.

"Wow," Derek sat wide-eyed, staring at the TV and looking at his virtually unresponsive mother. "She's got some spunk! I kind of like her."

"The next topic is immigration. Tens of millions of undocumented aliens are estimated to live within the United States. What will you do to secure borders and how will you deal with existing aliens? Senator Davenport, two minutes," the blonde motioned toward the Republican candidate.

"Well," he brushed his forehead and grinned smugly, "this is a no-brainer. We absolutely *must* secure the borders, first and foremost. I'm for beefing up the border patrol and possibly stationing National Guardsmen at the borders to provide some extra security. But the most delicate of issues is with existing illegals. We must identify them, round them up, and send them back to where they came from. If you break our laws, there must be a consequence. We can't just say, 'Oh, it's okay. You can stay, and we'll start enforcing the law for everyone else.' We have to send them home, and then they can apply for citizenship legally. My plan would offer tax incentives for businesses who refuse to use illegal workers and to people who successfully report the whereabouts of undocumented aliens. In such terrible economic times, a tax break, if only a little bit, would be very attractive to businesses and U.S. citizens. Furthermore, we must crack down on so-called 'haven cities' who look the other way while illegal workers steal the jobs of legal citizens and take advantage of our Constitutional rights and government programs, yet don't pay taxes or contribute to the system. We have to get tough on this issue."

"But let's get real, shall we?" Chandler glanced in the direction of her opponent ever so slightly to let him know she was addressing him as much as she was addressing the nation. "When we talk about people living in our country illegally, we're not talking about French people or Scandinavian people. We're not talking about the Koreans or Canadians. We're talking about Mexicans. That's the only group we ever seem to worry about. So this becomes a much more sensitive issue than Senator Davenport seems to acknowledge. We run the risk of appearing racist, though ninety-three percent of the undocumented workers are, indeed, Mexican. I'm not opposed to the idea of increasing the number of border patrol agents, but where the senator and I differ in opinion is what to do with existing aliens. I don't believe that we can just round everyone up and send them home. It's difficult and I don't think the tax incentive will work because of the amount of money these employers already save in not having to pay someone minimum wage. Not to mention, if we keep giving so many tax breaks so freely, how are we ever going to balance the budget? I say we offer them the chance to apply for citizenship within the US, and anyone who's ever seen the test that applicants have to take would say that most natural-born citizens could barely pass it. So this isn't the 'soft' way to deal with it. If you can't pass, you get sent home, but I at least think that they should have the opportunity to achieve the same better standard of living that our ancestors sought when they came to this great country."

"But at least our forefathers signed in at Ellis Island, or wherever they came in through. At least they were documented," he was now leering directly at Chandler with a look that implied that she had lost her mind. "You're talking about amnesty. Amnesty! The fact is, they broke the law. They crossed illegally, and they must face the consequences," he seemed annoyed.

"No one said anything about amnesty," Chandler fired back. "We're not talking about a total and unconditional acceptance of existing illegals. I'm saying that they would be given a *chance* to become legal citizens, and otherwise *will* be deported. Do you have any idea how long it takes to apply for and become a citizen of this country? It's sometimes ten years, when they've already been contributing to the economy and raising their families with a much better life than in their home country."

"Yes," he nodded in an exaggerated fashion, "I do know that it takes a long time to become a citizen. And it's wrong to allow the illegals that jumped ahead in line to stay at the front ahead of those who sought to do it legally. Remember in school when you cut in line, and the teacher or lunch lady made you go to the end of the line? The same should apply to immigration," he drove his point home. One could detect in his glowing facial expression that he knew he had won this topic, although Cindy Chandler was still willing to fight.

"But…" she was interrupted by the bitchy blonde at the moderator's desk.

"That's all the time we have for this topic. We move to the economy—the one everyone's been waiting for," she smiled to a reciprocating pair of candidates behind their podiums.

"Bring it on," Chandler smiled and chanted enthusiastically to the laughter of the audience.

"Senator Chandler," she began, "unemployment is at the highest point since the early 1980s, consumer spending is down, foreclosures are up, while our nation now operates at a deficit in the tens of trillions. We keep borrowing money from foreign banks or just print more and more money to try to remedy the problem. What is your plan to try to get the U.S. back on its feet economically in the wake of this recession?" she looked up at the senator, awaiting response.

"It is a complex problem with businesses suffering on one end and unable to keep their full amount of employees, but more importantly, *people* are suffering. You can't hug a business. A business doesn't cry on your shoulders and tell you how hard it is to work three jobs and still not be able to feed her children on some days. But people do. So that is why we have to focus on how we help *people*. I propose we cut taxes for the poor and middle classes by at least $1000 per year, while making it up in raising taxes on the wealthy, particularly those who make upward of five million dollars per year. This will be a start. Perhaps our people can start regaining some faith in the system and have a little more money to spend. You have to get money flowing through the economy. Businesses have to start making money again so they can pay employees, put money in their pockets, and have them spend it all over again. Without that, the economy will remain stale. I also plan to institute a stimulus package that will inject the economy with some cash flow and possibly millions of new jobs. We would allocate the money to the states for spending in areas like our crumbling infrastructure, education, and healthcare. Providing jobs and a sense of security to our people is the key to getting through this."

"And how do you propose we pay for that?" Davenport immediately chimed in. "Print more money? Borrow it? We can't mortgage our future with a flimsy stimulus plan that may not work. It's irresponsible. I agree that cash flow in the system must happen, but there are more responsible ways. I won't stand for a socialist method of stealing from the rich and giving to the poor. We have to give employers the ability, once again, to hire employees and put money into the pockets of our citizens by giving tax breaks to businesses and corporations. Revising the income tax system won't fix this. We can't afford it. It's also not fair to penalize the rich for all their hard work. It should be a flat tax across the board. But if we give employers the ability to pay salaries, that will translate into income tax dollars, which will help balance the budget and fix infrastructure."

"Yeah," she scoffed, "trickle-down fiscal policy. I seem to remember Hoover trying that at the beginning of the Great Depression. I also seem to remember him going down in history as perhaps the worst president we've ever had, simply because he was perceived as only willing to help the rich CEOs and not the common man. But FDR went the other way, and now he's on the dime!"

"Holy shit!" Derek gawked, a huge smile on his face.

"And my plan is *not* socialist," she continued. "You have to remember that our government's policies on economy and public service are already slightly socialist, anyway. If you're so hung up on socialism, maybe we should try completely privatizing the military and defense. Or what if we just allowed families to pay for their children's schooling? I think the future of math and science programs would greatly be hurt—something you champion greatly, if I remember, senator. But we're not fully socialist, and my plan would not *make* us socialist. Besides, don't you think it's time to do away with this old, archaic Cold War mentality that socialism equals communism, or that socialism equals totalitarianism? Is it really that evil of a thing?"

"Yeah, it is," he nodded rapidly. "It starts with policies like this, and before you know it, we're paying fifty percent of our income in taxes to support people that refuse to work, and salary caps are placed on those who work hard to become successful and wealthy. It's un-American!"

"If that were going to happen, don't you think it would have happened in the years following the Great Depression—a time of some of the most socialist legislation in U.S. history? No, it worked for the time period and situation that was at hand, and then it faded as America got back on its feet. And by the way, my tax system would not penalize the rich. It's not fair to tax the lesser-earning people as much as the rich. It further widens the gaps and promotes animosity between the poor and rich. And if you're so worried about people living off government welfare programs, maybe we can revamp the system to where you don't get a check unless you work. Give them all jobs working as janitors in government buildings and such—earn their keep."

Derek smiled as widely as he possibly could. He liked Senator Chandler. She was fiery, charismatic, and to his mind, kind of cute for her age. It all seemed to fall into place for him. She seemed to be the champion of the downtrodden and victims of the recession, willing to give people such as himself a chance to dig themselves from an ever-deepening hole of despair and depression. She also did not seem like the type of president that would so readily send a future Marine such as himself thousands of miles away to likely die in the scorching sands of some distant desert. Perhaps she was the turn-around that the country needed. Derek had never been one to take much interest in politics, typical of his age group, but times were different now. The state of the nation seemed dire, and everyone felt sucked into the issues that affected the poorest of the paupers and the most regal of the wealthy.

He turned his head slowly to the left, eyeing his mother in sorrow, pity, and perhaps a bit of disdain as she peered motionlessly into the screen before her. She did not move, except to light another cigarette and to ash in the tray beside her. She was emotionless and almost inanimate. It was as if she had become a statue or some brainless zombie with nothing that flowed within her that resembled life. He knew he had to take care of her, but he could not wait to leave.

This election would be the first time in his life that he could make his voice heard. He knew he had an opportunity to make something of his life, and he had found a Commander in Chief that he could serve. He stood from his chair, stretching his back and legs, walked over to the counter, picking up the Marine Corps pamphlet, and headed down the hallway entering his room and shutting the door behind him.

Chapter 5

The Portland, Oregon apartment was a separate world and season, it seemed. Outside, fall hung on the cool breath of some ancient pagan winter-bringing god. Centuries ago, people would have started to become feverish and die painfully in their beds. But today, it simply prompted a light jacket and a flu shot. But inside the moderately-sized apartment, it was as Independence Day. The walls were strobed with frequent flashes of varying intensity. They switched brightness sporadically with no real pattern, briefly illuminating the bachelor décor of the living area before again plunging it into darkness.

It was the lair of a single man with the light touch of a woman. The sofa and love seat were used and mismatched, yet clean and nicely arranged. The coffee table was free of old beer cans and pizza boxes. On one wall hung an illuminated old neon beer sign stolen from a bar while in college, the only décor that donned the walls.

The space sprawled widely beneath a low ceiling, the majority of which was designated as the living area. The sofa and love seat, positioned in a complimentary ninety-degree angle was the only separation of the living area from the kitchen, foyer, and single hallway leading to the bathroom and bedroom. The kitchen was simple, and equipped with slightly out-dated, cheap appliances. Yet it was organized and clean considering the occupant.

The focal point of the room was clearly the television. A young, single man will take handed-down old furniture from his parents. He will sleep on a rigged mattress atop a box spring. He will live on microwaved noodles and take-out, and re-wear clothing that smelled okay. Yet he will spare no expense in personal entertainment. The refrigerator was stocked with beer and his exceedingly large flat-panel television was of the highest technological order. Perched upon a black lacquer stand, its high-definition picture was complimented by a five-piece stereo sound system, receiver, and gaming console. It was a shrine of digital entertainment.

And sacrificing time and attention upon the altar of media was Grayson Moore. The flashing images of the two presidential hopefuls on his screen gave his khaki shorts and beige Hawaiian button-down shirt a neon effect. The small rectangular eyeglasses resting on the bridge of his nose reflected the images and their every change and flicker. He lounged in his usual place on the sofa, a bottle of some obscure microbrewery's latest brown ale in his left hand, his right leg propped upon the other, and his other arm resting around the shoulders of his cute brunette girlfriend. They watched as the audience cheered in the auditorium where the debate was held. The two candidates exited the stage, and Grayson's girlfriend Jeannie began to stir from her cozy nook under his arm.

"Want me to stay over tonight?" she looked up at him with a stretch and a tired little grin.

"You know you can," he kept his eyes on the television, staring at it for a long while before changing the subject. "God, I hope this idiot Davenport doesn't win," he swigged his beer and shook his head.

"Most of the polls have Chandler ahead," Jeannie played along. "I'm sure she'll do fine."

"I just don't know," he shook his head, pessimistic. "There are some just retarded and ignorant people out there that are going to vote for this asshole. We're in a recession. We have never had a higher national debt or a higher deficit in the government budget, and he wants to actually give more tax breaks to the wealthiest Americans."

"It doesn't make any sense," she added, tiredly yawning, almost uninterested in the conversation, but she played along because she knew how passionate her boyfriend was. "Reaganomics and 'trickle down' have never worked the way they said it was going to."

"Exactly," he said. "So why do they still do this? I'll tell you why," he never gave her the chance to answer. It was strictly rhetorical—a preparation for a rant that she just let him go with. "The Republicans are a business party. They have always claimed to be the party of the common man," he became more animated, swinging his hand with emphasis. "But they screw the common man out of more and more money every year. They take money that should stay in the middle and lower classes and hand it to the richest five percent, like they need it or something. And the average Joe friggin' falls for it every time. All the party has to say is something like, 'Why raise taxes on the rich? That's penalizing hard work and success.' Meanwhile, harder-working and sometimes higher-educated middle and lower-class people get screwed on taxes, health care, and inflation, all while having to work five times as hard as they used to, and for a worse standard of living. And the corporate CEOs get to take home an average of three hundred and forty times the pay of their employees. And they're the ones who get the tax breaks? But feed the people a line of bullshit that leads them to believe it's okay to do this because it's the American dream, and one day they can gain that kind of success, too. That's the trick! The common man supports exaltation of the rich and powerful because they somehow think they can be that successful too. The GOP is stealing the middle class and creating a new feudalism and it's all okay because they promise the people they will uphold traditional values like protecting the Second Amendment, deporting all of the Mexicans, and keeping those godless fags from getting married," he shook his head in disgust.

Jeannie was still, unable to respond and unsure she wanted to look up at him. She simply kept her eyes forward and remained under his arm. She had never quite heard him rant like that before. Perhaps the election drawing so near and the seriousness of the outcome were getting to him. She began to worry a bit, but she did not let him know of her concern.

"All you can do is vote—do your civil duty and hope others see the light, too," she finally responded.

"I don't think so," he winced, shaking his head slowly. "I think we're past that. I have no confidence in the people. I wish there was something that could be done."

"Like what?" she sat up and looked him in the eye. "The people vote and that's it. The people choose their president and the rest is history."

"Bullshit," his eyes widened. "The people haven't chosen a president on their own since maybe Eisenhower. Nineteen-sixty was the first TV debate—Nixon versus Kennedy. Kennedy was attractive."

"Yes he was," Jeannie smiled in delight, almost licking her lips. "And Nixon was sweaty. So let me guess. The people voted for the attractive one."

"Exactly. The media had an effect. Did you know that most people in the thirties and forties didn't know FDR was in a wheelchair?"

"I think there are more than a few people today that don't know that," she replied.

"Do you think people would have voted a cripple to four terms during the worst economic disaster in history and a war to end all wars?" he drove his point home. "Shit, no! Mass media wasn't as massive then, and even news photographers back then had more respect for the presidency than to print a bunch of photos of him in his wheelchair. The media has influenced every election since nineteen-sixty. If it's not just the showing of their faces, and the people picking the pretty one, the biased news companies get ahold of some insignificant, private aspect of a candidate's life and they blow him out of the water."

He cooled his tongue, letting the awkward silence set in as he watched the debate become a panel of journalists and pundits analyzing their score cards. Grayson thought, shaking his head and watching, but not really listening to, the pundits give their opinions of the candidates' responses. Then his eyes widened and his neck straightened. He leaned forward, forcing Jeannie to move somewhat.

"That's it," he said.

"What's it?"

"The media takes something about a candidate and just exploits it," he smiled. "I wonder if there's any dirt on Davenport that no one has dug up yet."

"I'm sure they've tried," Jeannie said. "What, you're going to be the one that dug up dirt where the mass media has failed?"

"I'm sure they've looked into his public records and such," he smiled. "But what about the stuff they can't access?"

"I don't know if I like where this is going," she lowered her eyebrow and backed her head away.

Grayson leapt to his feet, banging his shin on the coffee table as he carelessly passed it, but without an audible or visible display of pain. He was now on a mission. She had seen him do this before, but usually in a video game store searching for the newest fantasy computer game. He rounded the loveseat, exiting the living area for the desk tucked inconspicuously into a dark corner of the room. He hunched over, lifting the top of his notebook computer and bringing its screen to life with a sudden flash of organized ones and zeros.

"You know who I work for?" he smiled, logging into his work server. "I work for Infodrive—the world's largest internet company."

"Anyone can just go onto the web and run a search for Senator Davenport," she shook her head, smiling in ridicule. "I'm sure somebody has already thought of that."

"True," he continued to smile, finally sitting down to begin his search. "But first off, they may not know where to look. There's a lot of information out there on Davenport. Hell, there's a lot of info out there on you and I. Most people don't feel like digging deep enough for it. It's buried under all of the other crap on the net, but it's out there. You see, Infodrive is the most innovative technology company in a decade. We're always three steps ahead of the competition. And one of the ways we did this is through cookies."

"Mmm, oatmeal raisin," Jeannie joked.

"No, you know what I mean—the little files we send to your computer when you use our site," he continued. "Well, they help us determine things like your location and we combine that with previous searches so the site already kind of knows what you want. It's more efficient service. So next time you search for your favorite restaurant, we automatically give you results in your area, complete with our map results, driving directions, menus, reviews—you name it."

"So wait," she paused for a moment to take in the statement. "You guys basically gather up as much information on people as you can?"

"Yes," he smiled deviously. "We retain every search you make for months, and we tie it to your IP address. Restaurants, symptoms of prostate cancer, porno—we know everything you searched. And it's all in the interest of serving you better. If you use our internet browser, we really know everything you're looking at. Anytime you use our products or services, we have another record of your imprint on the net. And since we own half the popular sites on the web now, we can find anything we want to know on you."

"Jesus," Jeannie sneered. "I thought the government was 'Big Brother.' So wait," she paused in hesitation, "what are you planning to do?"

He did not answer for several minutes. His very spirit seemed to be drawn into the screen through his eyes any time she saw him before a computer. He was immersed, and she knew that he would not return from the trance until he had found what he was looking for. She just watched him. So many times, she had just walked away and awaited his return. She knew this was what he was. Who was she to change him? It was one of those little things about someone that you just accepted as a quirk in his personality and being. Yet this time, she was worried, unsure of what he was planning to do. She watched and waited, finally hearing him speak after several minutes.

"Oh yeah," he smiled and nodded into the screen. "He has an e-mail account with us and this is just what I was looking for!"

"What?"

"People really should read the terms and conditions section before using Infodrive," he smiled. "Here's a guy sending dirty e-mails to his mistress and he doesn't think somebody at our company is going to read it?"

"Shut up!" her mouth gaped as she jumped up and hurried to the desk. "Seriously?" she arrived at the computer and began reading the senator's messages to some woman. "This is like a bad romance novel. Pretty kinky shit!"

"I bet his wife of thirty-one years would like to see this, not to mention the liberal media!" he looked at his girlfriend with a deviant giddiness. "Look at this! E-mails to an investment bank CEO about his campaign contribution! He actually said 'I'll scratch your back when the time comes'! I wonder if I can find a video of him in drag or something."

"You're actually going to send this to the media?" she folded her arms. "Is releasing this stuff even legal?"

"Freedom of Information Act," he smiled. "He's working in public cyberspace, regardless of Infodrive being a private company or not. It would be like me witnessing him leaving a hotel—a private business—with his mistress. It wouldn't be illegal for me to report that."

"Okay, what about your job?" she grew more concerned. "Can't you get fired for this?" she watched him search for contact information within the more liberal television news networks.

"I guess so," he said. "But who's going to find out?"

"If you're able to look up Davenport's information, can't your supervisors trace who accessed his files?"

"Yes, but even if they do, the founders are all liberal computer nerds like me," Grayson shrugged. "They'll be glad I did it," he attached files to his e-mail, addressed to several journalists.

"And Davenport's family that you're about to wreck?" she stared somberly.

"He should have thought of that before he screwed around on his wife," Grayson briefly looked up at her and then clicked *send.*

Chapter 6

The two presidential candidates beamed with congeniality, smiling widely and happily as they moved from behind the wooden podiums. They naturally gravitated toward each other, glancing into the audience and waving to their respective constituents. They glided across the stage confidently, embracing the hand of one another. Chandler smiled upwardly at the towering man before her as she smiled into his grin, each of them chatting inaudibly as the audience roared with applause that almost seemed palpable in the air of the theatre.

They each strolled into the backdrop of the stage, fading into the shadows and through the backstage entrance, where they separated to walk down the hallway opposite of one another. There was not another word spoken between the two, and staff members of each rushed to their sides carrying clipboards and papers.

Senator Chandler crossed the threshold of her changing room, taking a seat before the brightly-lit vanity of the backstage room and releasing a sigh that threatened to blow over the makeup and beauty products upon the vanity table. Her facial expression simultaneously morphed from that of alertness and posture to one of fatigue and relief in an instant.

"God, I'm glad that's over," she slumped forward, and then arched backwards to stretch her back muscles. "What an asshole!" she turned to her chief campaign advisor, Sandra. "Did you hear that tone? Did you see the way he looked at me? He looked like an abusive husband about to slap his wife for ruining the pot roast."

"Yeah, I know," Sandra pulled her long, silky blonde hair back into a ponytail, and began flipping through papers and agendas. "And he's goofy looking. Like Mr. Rogers if Mr. Rogers were a condescending prick. But you're gonna hit him where it hurts—the polls."

"You think?" she turned her head to the side. "You think I did okay?"

"Yeah," she shrugged. "He's tough, you've got to admit. I think he debated you well on things like immigration, but you blew him out of the water on issues that are most important like the recession."

"I guess only the polls will tell. This isn't going to be an easy race."

"Well you're already ahead in the latest polls. But pundits are predicting this race to have the highest voter turnout in history and to be the closest election in history."

"There's my girl," a gray-headed, yet gracefully aging, handsome man in a black pin-striped suit walked through the door. He strolled across the dressing room, briefly glancing around at the various Broadway posters adorning the bare, red brick walls and the dozen campaign staff members bustling around on cellular phones. "You did great!" he stepped toward Cindy's chair, handing her a bouquet of yellow roses and kissing her sweetly on the cheek.

"To what do I owe the pleasure?" she smiled wildly shifting her gaze from the bouquet to her husband and back. "What did you do wrong?"

"I didn't meet you sooner in life, my dear," he flirted back. "You did a great job tonight, and since we're on Broadway, I thought you should be treated like a star!"

"Well, thank you. They're beautiful," she handed them to Sandra. "You really think I did okay, Donny?" she looked a little worried.

"Sure," he sat in a chair next to her and placed his hand on her shoulder. "I think you made a great and lasting impression on the voters for your last debate. He's tough, but I think you showed that you're not intimidated by him and fired back at everything he said."

"God, I hope so," Cindy shook her head and lowered her eyes. "Now we just coast. The hard part is over and we just wait for the polls. A few more rallies, and I'm good. At least there, everyone agrees with me," she smiled. "At least all the challenges are over."

"Well…" he winced slightly.

"What?" her eyes widened. "What's going on," worry filled her voice.

"It's Julie."

"Julie? Our daughter, Julie? What, is she in trouble?" she nearly became frantic.

"No, no. She's not in trouble, but this could be trouble for *you*," he seemed a little troubled. "Some pictures just surfaced. Dana, your press guru, called me just a little while ago when you and Davenport were on, um, healthcare, I believe."

"Oh, no!" she slumped. "What kind of pictures? The Bourbon Street kind? We should have never allowed her to go to college in New Orleans!"

"No, not that bad," he laughed. "But there's a picture some frat boy took on his cell phone of Julie drunk off her ass, dancing on a pool table half naked with a bottle of Jack Daniel's in her hand. And there's another of her triple-kissing her girlfriends at the same party. No nudity, but enough to get the family values people salivating."

"Shit!" she exclaimed in a whisper. "Damn that girl! I know she's having fun in her freshman year, but she's got to be more responsible. This is Mommy's friggin year!"

"I called her, and she's really sorry," Donny assured her. "She feels awful. She says she was at a frat party and she just got drunk really quickly. Before she knew it, she was having a little too much fun."

"Damn it," Cindy whispered and shook her head in frustration. "Okay, Sandra. Call Dana and tell her to spin this thing as best she can. If Bush's daughters could do this crap and him still get elected and reelected, then we can survive this. Tell those blood suckers in the press something about her being an adult and making her own decisions, regardless of the way we raised her."

"Yes, ma'am," Sandra sped off scrolling through her smartphone, searching for Dana's number.

"Come on, Donny," she switched back to a cheery, yet tired disposition. "You ready for a little play time?" she stood up taking her husband's hand in hers.

"You bet, sweetheart," he grinned coyly. "Champagne's already chilling in the hotel room."

"Sandra," she called to her advisor across the room. "Have the car come around back and take us to the Waldorf."

Chapter 7

The halls were jammed with teenagers from all walks of life and all ethnicities as they made their way from class to class, most trying frantically to make it to the next period before the chiming of the tardy bell. Amongst the sea of backpacks, the mainly middle-class students donned a wide range of fashion statements. Goths and emos with 1980s retro hairstyles, all in eccentric black, trudged aimlessly in groups of no more than three, alone, but together. Their skin-tight black pants, death-metal-band t-shirts, and facial piercings contrasted sharply with the majority teen mall fashions throughout the hallway. Partially hidden by a staircase, the blonde school slut locked lips with the boyfriend of the week, allowing him to place his hands below the waist, and trying not to get caught by on-duty staff members. Kids actually trying to get to class on time found themselves dodging the stragglers who had met friends along the way, ever risking the tardy slip and detention.

As the time grew near, the high school students began slipping into the classrooms lining the hallway, briskly thinning the crowd within that last minute. With no clocks in the halls, it was as if their internal clocks had become set, and alerted them subconsciously to the fact that the doors were all about to close. By the time the tardy bell had echoed from wall to wall, only a few people were locked out of their classrooms, and began trudging toward the attendance office for a tardy pass.

Twenty-eight students began settling into their hard-plastic desks held together by bright stainless steel. Backpacks fell to the cobalt blue carpets, most leaning against the legs or the under baskets of the desks as the teenagers rummaged through them to retract spiral notebooks, binders, and pens. The class was filled with mainly grade-conscious, well-behaved students, who were particularly good about entering the classroom calmly and getting settled with minimal noise or disruption.

The gray walls were covered with social-studies-oriented posters and paraphernalia, without the cliché motivational quotes and sappy teacher humor. There were no fat cartoon pencils or apples, no childish borders around the bulletin boards, and no bright, optically painful color schemes. There were posters depicting and explaining world religions, old World War II propaganda, explanations of communism, capitalism, and socialism, and various maps of world regions with either historical or geographical perspectives. One poster in the corner showed the design plans of Leonardo da Vinci's greatest inventions. On another wall hung a replica of a 1628 world map. It was a bit heavy with a wooden body and two replica gold hemispheres crudely traced with the outlines of the continents in exaggerated inaccuracy. The bulletin board was covered with 4"x6" snapshots of the young teacher's extensive world and domestic travels.

Mr. Devereaux sat upon his rolling swivel chair behind his black metal desk, staring into the monitor of his computer while he moved the mouse, clicked, and typed in a sporadic pattern, setting up all of his programs for the coming lessons. He was relatively young; old enough to play the role of the adult, yet young enough to relate to the young people in his classes. It was casual Friday, so he was of course wearing jeans, rather than the ever-present dress slacks. His silver and black pin-striped button down was stiffly-starched and pressed, but untucked, hanging down over the loosely fitting blue jeans. His name badge hung from his belt loop on the right side, mostly covered by his shirt tail, as the lanyard for his classroom keys dangled from the back left pocket.

Though young, he was beginning to show the signs of aging. His young-looking messily spiked hair was starting to turn silver along the sides as the short brown locks were thinning at the crown. There were even traces of gray in his full, yet short and stubbly beard.

With a deep voice that carried like thunder, names began to leave his mouth and resonate through the room. Each student called from the alphabetically oriented roll list responded with a varying form of "here," or "present."

"Ashley Dykes," Mr. Devereaux called, looking up.

"Here," a soft, but firm voice returned from the opposite end of the room.

She smiled in a natural way that usually sent anyone around her the message that she was a genuinely happy and congenial person. She pulled her silky, dark brown hair back as if to put it in a ponytail, but simply stroked at it over the front of her left shoulder, allowing the shampoo-commercial-perfect locks to cascade over her orange ladies polo.

Kyle could not help himself. He sat two rows over, admiring her tan complexion and the way her dark eyebrows sat perfectly above her deep brown eyes. She, however, never returned his gaze, nor did she ever reciprocate his inevitable smile. She simply never noticed him. Suddenly there was a dull laughter generated from a few kids in the room. He shook his head as if to come out of a trance, looking around spastically to find that everyone was staring at him.

"Kyle Perkins!" Mr. Devereaux said in an elevated tone, clearly having already called his name a few times.

"Yes. Yes sir. Here," he said, hanging his head in embarrassment for a moment before lifting his eyes again to Ashley, who finally glanced at him from the corner of her eye and giggled warmly.

"Okay," the young teacher stood from behind his desk and pointed to the dry erase board, "your quote of the day is from Voltaire, a writer of the Enlightenment. 'Anything too stupid to be said is sung.' Don't believe it? Try actually paying attention to the words of the songs you listen to."

The students giggled and smiled lightly as some of them named inaudibly some of their favorite songs that fell into that category.

"This day in history. In 1803, Congress ratifies the Louisiana Purchase. In 1882, Bela Lugosi, the quintessential Dracula was born. In 1944, General MacArthur makes good on his vow to return to the Philippines and his men. He made it as dramatic as possible when he jumped out of the boat into the shallow water and waded ashore. The problem was that not very many people saw it, and he recreated it for the film crews that were there. In 1947, the Red Scare hits Hollywood when many writers and actors are accused of being communists. In 1973, the Sydney Opera House opens. And in 1990, the rap group 2 Live Crew is acquitted of obscenity charges brought about by their raunchy song lyrics. This was a time when people weren't accustomed to every song being about sex. In the news, the biggest story of the day, of course, is last night's debate. Who watched the fireworks?" he scanned the room in vain for at least a few hands lifted into the air. "Nobody, huh? I guess who runs your country doesn't hold a candle to who Kim is hooking up with on that stupid reality show you guys are all watching."

He continued to scan hopelessly around the room for someone that might actually care. He did not understand why issues that so frequently affected these kids usually did not even merit the slightest bit of concern or attention. The most important things to them were their phones, their TV, their video games, and their parties. He began to worry about what type of adults or parents these kids would be. Perhaps they would become the same ill-informed, oblivious adults as their parents. But then he saw a hand raised amongst the sea of the apathetic, and that hand seemed to reluctantly be stretched upward by Kyle Perkins.

"You watched the debate?" Mr. Devereaux's eyebrows arched as he grinned.

"Not by choice," Kyle tried to seem uninterested.

"Oh, okay. But you watched it."

"Yeah, my dad makes me watch stuff like that with him."

"And you had no interest in it?"

"There were just other things I'd rather be doing," Kyle shrugged.

"Fair enough," the young teacher began to move about the room, still focused on young Kyle. "That's the child in you that still lingers. And did the adult side of you that should be taking interest in politics and issues make a debut last night?"

"Um," Kyle looked around as if perplexed. "I don't know."

"Come on, you're not brain dead. In fact, I think you're quite intelligent. You can't sit through a three-hour debate and *not* form some sort of opinion or react in some way."

Kyle just stared back at his teacher blankly. He tried to organize his thoughts and remember what he had seen on the television the night before, and perhaps he could have in a different setting. All eyes were on him, including Ashley's, and he was being put on the spot.

"Okay, I'll give you some direction," Mr. Devereaux kept on him. "Who won the debate in your opinion? Who convinced you more than the other one?"

"Um," Kyle concentrated, trying harder to coax an intelligent answer from his lips. "It's hard to say, not because I'm indifferent or anything. I just thought there were issues that Davenport made a better point on, and some that Chandler did better in."

"Well, pundits are saying this is going to be a close race. Neither candidate is really supposed to hit this thing out of the park. But if you were keeping a score card, who made better, more valid points than the other. Really, I'm asking you who you would vote for if the election were tomorrow."

"But I can't vote. I won't be eighteen in time," he tried to dodge the question.

"Doesn't matter. You can still have an opinion."

"That's what my dad says, too," Kyle rolled his eyes.

"Good man. Now who won?" Devereaux pressed on.

"I guess Chandler," he spouted.

"Really?" he was surprised. "In a red state? Well, I guess it makes sense. Senator Chandler is appealing to the young voters, according to polls. Here's another specific question. Most of the focus of this race has been this brutal recession, and a lot of analysts say the race may come down to that. This is an economics class, so I have a vested interest in who you think will do a better job in trying to pull us out of this thing. So?"

"Well, my dad says…"

"Whoa, whoa, whoa! Let me stop you right there. I want to know what *you* think. If I wanted to know what your dad thinks, I'd call him up and ask him. Tell me what you think."

Kyle sat in his blue and gray desk, thinking deeply for quite a few moments. He stared down at his desk top and nibbled the inside lining of his bottom lip in pondering the question from his own perspective and knowledge.

"See, this was one of the ones I was torn about. On one hand, Davenport's 'trickle-down' approach makes sense in the long run, that is, if the corporations actually use the money for staffing and not on bonuses and vacations. But I don't know if the Republican take on economics is very sound. They give too much power to these corporations, and I don't know that these greedy CEOs can be trusted with the well-being of the economy. Especially with the well-being of those of us in the middle and lower classes."

"Wow," Mr. Devereaux was stunned. "That was a very good, well-thought answer. Republicans don't like to spend a lot of taxpayer dollars, but they also don't want to overtax the corporate sector. They would give tax breaks to the corporations, freeing up money to use in staffing."

"But you see, I don't think they would use the money for that. Chandler's plan focuses more on the common man. Tax breaks for the middle and lower classes and stimulus money for improving infrastructure and education," Kyle spouted with an increased excitement.

"And that's the alternative?" another boy chimed in from the back of the classroom. "Instead of putting money in the hands of businessmen that know something about the economy, we put money in the hands of the common man, who is basically stupid and even greedier than the CEO? Everyone who gets stimulus money or tax breaks is going to spend it on something ridiculous that they don't really need. And at the taxpayer's expense."

"Dude, if you had paid any attention at all in this class, you'd know that people buying ridiculous crap is just what we need right now," Kyle turned slightly in the kid's direction. The rest of the class uttered "oohs" over the ruthless rebuttal. "We'd be approaching this from the bottom up. People spending money creates revenue and business for the stores, who will need more staffing to keep the shelves stocked and deal with customer traffic. That creates jobs and puts the unemployed back to work. It also creates tax revenue for local, state, and federal governments that will help with the burden of the money going to infrastructure and education, which also creates jobs. At least this way, the taxpayer's dollar is at least *buying* something, rather than gambling by putting it in the hands of the CEOs."

"Excellent debate!" Mr. Devereaux beamed with excitement. "Looks like you guys did learn something in here after all. And it looks like Mr. Perkins has formed his opinion in all this and found a candidate to back. Now, in other news…"

The teacher's voice faded from Kyle's attention as he sat in his seat smiling and feeling good about what had just happened. He had never really cared enough to form this distinct of an opinion. It was as if he had grown from a boy into a man in an instant, and he felt proud that he had stored away enough knowledge now to apply it to real world issues, and that he had found a voice to help him express it. He looked around at the class, all students focused on the teacher and laughing at his quips and anecdotes—all but one. Ashley gazed at Kyle through the corner of her eye, attempting to maintain the illusion of indifference about him, but her smile told yet another story, and he finally picked up on it, smiling sweetly back at her.

Chapter 8

Late October

It seemed as though the road was getting bumpier as the trip verged on hour number two. Derek's journey from the discomfort of home and work at the auto repair shop to the United States Marine Corps had already been a grueling one, and he had not even arrived at the training facility. He kissed his teary-eyed mother goodbye, and his friend Jake drove him to the airport at six in the morning. Rain most of the morning delayed his flight by three hours, followed by another three hours in the air to get to South Carolina. Then there was this long bus ride out to the training depot. He prayed that this trip would soon be over, even if that meant getting reamed by some old gunny at boot camp.

What made matters worse was the discomfort of the bus itself. He did not exactly expect a tour bus with reclining seats, personal air conditioning vents, and television screens displaying some sappy romantic comedy. But the bus that he was sitting in was borderline unfit to ride on. It was a converted school bus that must have rolled through the assembly line in the late 1970s, and since painted a light gray color on the exterior. The interior was hot and poorly ventilated, even with the windows dropped down. The gray metallic walls and thinly cushioned, dark blue vinyl seats added a level of anxiety that made Derek even more nervous about the hell he was about to enter.

No one on the nearly full bus really spoke to one another, whether they were antisocial or deep in thought and contemplation over what basic training would be like. Perhaps they did not want to get to know one another just yet. The heat was beginning to melt away the last remnants of antiperspirant that the men wore in their underarms, and the potency of body odor was beginning to course through the bus. They were getting anxious and restless, almost to the point that they would randomly leap from their seat and begin pummeling one another without a word or warning.

One could nearly see the humidity in the air outside the bus. Even in October, the air was warm, and the moisture held on that warmth making it unseasonably muggy and sticky. The marshy, mosquito-infested land beyond the elevated paved highway surely contributed to that. Finally, in the near distance ahead, a small cluster of buildings grew ever closer. As the structures neared, Derek became somewhat disappointed. Nestled among a small grove of oak and palm trees were a set of nicely-constructed gate houses that resembled a bus stop and visitor center. He expected, and even hoped for, run-down cinder block shacks dating to the 1950s. He expected concrete, gray paint, and asbestos. What he got was fresh green metal roofs, fine red brick, and high-and-tight jarheads standing guard at the main gate. And there was the sign.

The giant red sign evoked a different emotion from Derek, somewhere between pride and fear. The sign was painted red and bordered by more red brick, and emblazoned in big white letters, it read, "Marine Corps Training Depot." It was a nice sign, but most of the emotion emerged from the sight of that classic emblem of a globe and anchor, crested with a majestic eagle. Derek could not understand why he was getting goose bumps covering his body. No one in his family had ever been in the Marines. He had not waited his entire life to join the corps. Previous to a month ago, it would never have occurred to him to join the military at all.

The clunker of a bus squealed to stop and the driver shifted into park. Derek could not help but smile at the thought of the break job and the tune-up the bus needed as he listened to the engine sputter, idling low. He felt himself eager to jump off that bus and take a look under the hood. Apparently, old habits die hard.

He could see across the aisle and through the windows on the left side of the bus that there was a tall, hulking man heading toward them, striding twice the distance of a normal man, and moving briskly with mission and purpose. The lines in his aging face were like ravines, deep enough to create their own shadows in the interior. Beneath his round, wide-brimmed hat, his brow was dropped low with a nasty corresponding scowl that could very well have conveyed that he had a very bad day, though Derek firmly believed that this expression was almost permanent. He circled the front of the bus and made his way up the four steps into the vehicle. For a moment, he just stood there, silently looking over the now petrified recruits, many of them not long out of high school. His sour face did not change as he scanned the young men. He simply beamed malice from his eyes, sizing up his new recruits and taking stock of what the next three and a half months was going to be like. Then he spoke.

"What the hell are you ladies looking at? Grab your shit and get the hell off this bus!" his deep voice resonated, almost literally filling the space. No one moved. They just stared, unsure what to do. "What? Are you faggots waiting for an invitation? Get off the goddamned bus, on the fucking double!"

In unison, every warm body jerked into life, frantically gathering their duffel bags and backpacks, filled with a few reminders of home. Some brought pictures of family and girlfriends. Others only brought toiletries and a change of clothes, especially those who had traveled a long way. Some had even foolishly brought with them their phones, which they would soon pay for dearly, despite that they only wanted to let their loved ones know that they had safely made it to camp.

The young men scrambled into the narrow aisle, falling over one another, each of them somehow eager to be the first off the bus and into the mouth of hell. They packed into an awkward line stumbling backward and forward, everyone pushing and shoving the way that they did when they rode the bus to school in their youth. One by one, they each exited down, some of them skipping steps to the point of even leaping from the top level to the ground. The gravel crunched and grinded beneath their tennis shoes and boots as they pivoted to the left, and then rushed toward the main building without really knowing exactly where to go.

Three enlisted men stationed at the training depot directed the fresh meat to the parade grounds in front of the building, and tried their best to line them up into formation. They were disorganized, rough, and unpolished; a ragtag bunch of civilians in t-shirts and blue jeans. They were used to disconnecting from the world in front of a video game. They were used to lattes and cell phones. They were used to Mommy and Daddy taking care of room and board. Now they would become men.

The menacing drill instructor began moving in the direction of the new recruits in the same fast-paced way and with the same long strides as before. He seemed to become even meaner, with an even more dreadful expression as he grew closer. He stopped short of the men and stood before a corporal, who promptly saluted, which the instructor reciprocated.

"All recruits are checked in and in formation," the square-jawed corporal seemed to look beyond his superior officer as they both swiftly brought their right hands from the salute position back to their sides.

"Thank you corporal. You are dismissed," he responded, sending him away.

The drill instructor said not a word at first, moving slowly and purposely amongst the men, who were all trying to stand at attention without really knowing the correct way of doing so. His dark eyes scanned every inch of every recruit, sizing them up with immeasurable scrutiny and impunity. One young man could not help glancing at him through his periphery, and unfortunately, the instructor noticed. He bolted into position before the young African American boy, and stood tall, though significantly shorter than him.

"What the hell are you looking at? You eyeballing me? Eyes front at all times, asshole!" he screamed as the young man's eyes, quickly darted into a frontward direction, yet twitched nervously.

He continued to move about the men, checking every detail of his group of green soldiers. Then something else caught his eye—that being another young man who looked about as tense as any human could possibly be. He was obviously nervous as each trembling muscle in his body was tight and rigid, to the point that he did not even appear natural, or even human. The gunny darted in front of that kid, glaring into his eyes with scorn that he had never seen before.

"Jesus Christ! Do you need an Ex-Lax? You look like you've got to take a shit! You're supposed to be standing at attention, not rigid! You've got your ass cheeks tightened up like you're expecting Uncle Dave to sneak into your room and drill you tonight. None of that shit here—loosen up private," his voice carried across the grounds, echoing off the buildings.

The boy next to him was standing about two feet too far forward, and the gunny noticed it immediately, bolting into position before him, and grabbing him by the shoulders. He shook the recruit hard as he moved him back and forward several times in an exaggerated way before positioning him where he should be—flush with all the rest of the young men in the line.

"What's wrong with you pukes? Can't even lineup right? You are going to have a hell of a time over the next few months!" he began moving about the recruits again, his arms crossed behind his back. "I am Sergeant Phillips, and I am your senior drill instructor. Many of you can now see that I am an asshole. I do not care where you come from or what your religion is. I do not care about the pampered lifestyles or hardships. My job is to build Marines. It is time to grow up, ladies. Time to become men. Time to wipe off that acne and separate your lips from Momma's titty! Your days of lollipops and Saturday morning cartoons are over! Your days of jerking off to a yearbook picture of the prom queen are over! You no longer have Mommy and Daddy to hold your hands and wipe your little asses! You will shed nearly two decades of boyhood in a mere fourteen weeks, and I will guide you through it. I will teach you. I will run you! I will drill you! You will puke. You will ache. You will have your ass chewed every day, and no—you can't ever do anything right, and you will never please me. Not until you become a well-disciplined Marine—a weapon of the highest caliber at my fingertips for the using. Do you understand?"

"Sir, yes sir!" they all chimed in unison.

"Outstanding! Now report to barracks two-two-one, and stow your shit, which *will* be searched for contraband. Then report to the main building and to the barber. You dickheads are going to get a little haircut. Don't worry, we'll keep it stylish. Dismissed!" he shouted as enlisted men guided them off in a disorganized fashion.

Chapter 9

Election Day, Nineteen months before the bomb

Sherry Putnam struggled to rise to her feet from her chair in the family room. She held her smoldering cigarette butt between her index finger and thumb, and repeatedly snuffed it out amongst the mounting pile of older butts. She gripped the front of the armrests and pulled with all her strength, pushing up with her legs and slowly erecting herself.

There were somehow more wrinkles in her paling face, and her hair was wiry and ill-kept, as if she had not groomed it in months. She was wearing the same blue and white-striped nightgown that she had been wearing for two days. She limped like an elderly woman as the blood began to course more naturally into her lower extremities, giving her that irritating "pins and needles" sensation in her feet and toes. It was as if the lack of use of her legs was causing her muscles to atrophy. The circles beneath her eyes were growing darker and puffier, and she was developing a yellow tint to her right middle and index fingers and to the center of her lips.

She continued to limp through to the kitchen, cursing the tingling sensation in her feet the whole way and bracing herself using chair backs and the countertops. As the tingling faded, her gait turned more to a shuffle, the thin plastic soles of her light blue cotton slippers grinding the grit and dirt on the linoleum floors.

She reached the front door, turning the corroded old doorknob, and opened it, letting in the cool, November air. She paused for a moment, actually basking in the rush of fresh, fall breeze, something that she did not experience every day. She then stepped out onto the creaking porch boards, and across to the front steps and down before strolling out to the mailbox near the street to fetch the day's mail. She opened the black aluminum door and reached inside the mailbox, extracting a stack of envelopes, advertisements, and church flyers. As she turned around to head back toward the house, her eyes transfixed upon the mail in her hand, she flipped through several bills and bank statements until she found a hand-written envelope that caused her to cover her mouth and generate tears of joy.

For the first time in weeks, she perked up and added some gusto to her step, quickly shuffling up the walkway and up the stairs to the porch. She burst through the door and headed straight for the easy chair where she spent most of her waking moments. Turning into position, she plopped her posterior onto the cushion, which had by that point molded to her back side like a pair of custom-fit dentures. She briefly glanced upward at the droning of a news station on the television while frantically ripping and tearing at the adhesive fold of the envelope, yet still careful not to rip the return address on the outside. Finally, she was able to extract the tri-folded papers within, and extended them to reveal a hand-written correspondence from her youngest child.

"Dear Mom," she shed a single tear, almost able to hear Derek's voice speaking the written words. "Sorry it's been several weeks before I could write you. I've been slightly busy here at Paris Island. I finally found some time to sit down and give you a shout, so here I am. I knew I needed to send you something soon or I would never be able to give you a chance to write back. That's something I think I need. All the other guys are constantly getting mail from girlfriends, family, and friends, and it seems to make the time away a little easier to deal with. Otherwise, it's lonely, even though I'm constantly around others. The fact is, the platoon does everything together; even shower and use the head. One guy got the whole platoon in trouble because he couldn't use the bathroom with the other men. So he got caught using Sergeant Phillips' personal head. We all had to do up-downs until a few guys actually puked."

"That's mainly what we've been doing these first weeks. It's been conditioning, obstacles, running, marching, learning how to stand at attention with a rifle, running some more. All the basics. They even taught us how to correctly make our beds—the Marine way. But we only get 45 seconds, and I got tired of not meeting the mark. I was doing 30 pushups every morning, so I just started tying the corners of the sheets to my boot laces to keep it tight, and sleeping on top of the covers."

"The basics are almost over though, and the cool stuff begins. Next week we'll start live-fire exercises and get to shoot stuff. Pretty soon, we get to learn some hand-to-hand combat. I'll get to learn how to kill a man with my pinkie. All in all, I'm pretty happy with being in the military, and pretty soon, I'll be able to send back lots more money. Of course, I'll be happy as long as Senator Chandler doesn't send me to war somewhere. I'm convinced she's going to win—I hope she does."

"Anyway, I hope you can write back soon. Give the address to Jake. I'd like to hear from him and the guys at the garage. I miss you all, and I'll be home before you know it—at least for a little while. Then I guess I'll get stationed somewhere. But write back soon. I love you. Love, Derek."

Sherry pressed the letter to her chest, nearly closing her eyes in a teary squint as a smile of both joy and pain graced her aging face. She was happy to hear from her boy and happy that he was growing into a man. He had never really had a man around the house as an example of masculinity. She did her best as a single mother. She was able to work to provide a shelter and food for her son. That was easy, at least in the sense that it did not require much finesse. It came as second nature. But when it came to guiding Derek through puberty and adolescence, she was unable to provide a man's point of view on what was happening to his body. She answered questions where she could, but one of the best things she could do was to get him a book on male puberty and leave it on his bed for when he came home from school one day. It was discrete and it helped.

But her tears of joy were also tainted with the poison of regret. She had always regretted that her marital and occupational situation did not allow her to provide as many extras for her son. But moreover, lately, she realized, she had been disconnected and absent from not only her son's life, but from life in general. Getting laid-off from a job that she had held for so long made her feel expendable and unwanted, something that is detrimental to a woman. As a result, she retreated from life, cutting all ties with the world, and even her son. All she knew how to do was sit in front of the TV and chain smoke herself into oblivion. Inside, she kicked herself for not appearing more supportive when Derek tried to talk to her about the military. It was not until he was riding away in Jake's clunker of a car that she realized the error of her actions.

She held the letter to her breast a few more moments as she squeezed a few tears from her eyes down her cheek and chin. She then fought back the torrent, wiping her eyes before folding the letter neatly back into its original tri-fold and laid it on the end table beside her ashtray and cigarettes. With that, she picked up the half empty pack, opened the flip top, and fingered around for a smoke, finally pulling it from its sheath. She placed it between her lips, and then reached for her lighter. As she lifted it up to the end of the cigarette, she tried to roll her thumb over the metal wheel, but noticed a slight twitch in her hand. She shook it off with a perplexed look and tried again, only to have the twitch repeat itself. She also noticed that her thumb did not quite work correctly, as if her hand muscles were cramping and locking. Finally, she rolled the wheel, producing a bright spark and a flame. The end of the cigarette glowed bright orange as she inhaled the first drag, and then blew a plume of smoke toward the television.

"It's election day," the anchorman crooned with enthusiasm. "It's the day we've all been waiting for and fighting about for nearly a year. It's been projected that this election will have the highest voter turnout in history, and so far, voters have been living up to that prediction. Katie Janssen caught up with some of the voters lining up in the polling stations."

The screen cut to a scene showing hundreds of voters lining up in a school cafeteria in Pennsylvania. People of all ages packed the space nearly chaotically as they made their way up the long line to the check-in table and then to the voting booths lining the back wall.

"How has it been?" the reporter asked a slightly overweight woman leaving the polling station.

"It took forever," her eyes squinted in the sun. "I was supposed to do this on my lunch break, and so far I'm almost half an hour late back to work."

"Who did you vote for?"

"Chandler! It's about time we had a female president!"

"Who did you vote for, sir?" she asked a gray-haired, elderly man with a black cap bearing the name of some ship that he served on in the navy.

"Oh, Davenport," he smiled.

"What do you like about him?"

"Well, he served his country, and I think he'll do a good job protecting it as president."

"Who did you vote for?" she asked the same question to a young man with ear gauges and a black-metal-band t-shirt.

"Chandler," he seemed high. "Davenport would ruin this country. We can't have four more years of the same president we've had."

"As you can see, people are definitely practicing their civil duty," the reporter spoke to the camera. "People of every age group and every party affiliation came out today. I want you to see something. Pan the camera and try to get these people across the street," she instructed the cameraman.

The camera zoomed and auto-focused on an intersection, where across the street, at opposing corners, two separate groups rallied in one last attempt of persuasion, to convince incoming voters to vote the way they want them to. On one corner, a group of Republicans held red, white, and blue signs bearing the Davenport name, chanting some inaudible slogan of the campaign; hoisting and lowering their signs in rhythmic unison. There were various signs with various slogans and images, as was the same for the Cindy Chandler supporters on the other corner, bearing similar patriotically-themed signs.

"As you can tell, the chanting and yelling has remained heated. I've even seen these two groups get into debates and arguments today over policy and platforms. If you look at the Davenport supporters to the left, you can even see signs with images of Cindy Chandler with a red background and Soviet hammer and scythe symbol, claiming that she's a communist. On the other side, they keep ranting about Davenport's infidelities that just came out, also questions about the campaign finance corruption allegations. It looks like this race is going to be every bit as controversial as predicted. Tom…"

"It certainly appears so," he grinned. "We're here with two panelists. John Fitzsimmons is one of our contributing Democratic analysts and Dan Albright, one of our conservative analysts. Dan, how do you see the day turning out?"

The panelists sat slouching behind the modern, contoured desk, as stark contrast to the dignified suits they adorned. They were each in their forties or fifties, both wearing crows' feet in the corner of their eyes and receding hair lines. They sat patiently awaiting their first line of questioning, each perched behind an open and waiting laptop computer, doubtlessly loaded with figures, statistics, and projections.

"I think it's going to be a close one, Tom," he grinned beneath his 1970s style moustache. "Davenport has been strong in his home state of Wyoming, of course, but that's not going to really help him as there aren't very many delegates to be had there. I think he's going to carry the south and some of the more rural counties of the blue states, but Chandler is going to get these big-number urban counties. I think it's all going to be a solid blue state/red state thing. It's going to be close," he nodded his head gravely.

"Alright, what about you, John?"

"I agree with Dan," he motioned to his counterpart. "It's going to be, and has been, a long, hard battle. And it IS going to largely come down to red states or blue states. There are a few wild cards, though. Statistically, the elderly and the middle classes seem to be aligning themselves with Davenport, but the real story is the record number of newly-registered voters—particularly the young ones. According to the polls, the caucuses, and primaries, Chandler has been getting about seventy-three percent of the voters between ages eighteen and twenty-five. She's also going to get the female vote. Sixty-three percent of women, regardless of party affiliation, have been aligning themselves with Chandler. So I think that's going to give her the edge that she needs."

"There has been a lot of discussion, as our reporter in the field just mentioned, about the e-mails leaked from Infodrive. There are questions about corruption and there are obviously questions about his integrity. Originally, Davenport denied the validity of the e-mails, but Infodrive spokesmen are confirming they are true. And now with the actual mistress that the e-mails were allegedly addressed to has come forward—I don't know. What do you guys make of all this?" Tom spurred the discussion.

"It's horrible that someone tampered with this private information," the conservative analyst said. "It's dirty, and I think people are going to look past this."

"Like they looked past Chandler's daughter's party pictures?" the liberal analyst fired back. "No, Republicans took that one and ran with it, though it had nothing to do with Chandler herself. I think the public is going to pay attention to this. We saw the video earlier of Gloria Davenport still by her husband's side. She's doing what should be done for the party, but I think the damage is already done."

"Alright. Thank you, gentlemen. We have to take a break, but stay with us. We're covering the election all day and all night as the results come in, so don't miss any of the action. We'll be right back. Don't go away," he smiled as the screen cut to a commercial.

Chapter 10

Cindy Chandler's hand was trembling ferociously, causing the ice cubes in her small, empty glass of vodka and tonic to jingle like it was Christmas time. She promptly set the glass neatly within the condensation ring on the coffee table before her, and motioned one of the waiters on the catering staff to bring her another one. She tried to brush out some forming wrinkles in her fine, black skirt suit, straightening her back while in a sitting position. She did not want to appear ill-kept as she stepped onto a stage later in the evening. She then lifted her right hand to the top of her head to check the tightly secured light brown bun that her hair was pulled into. Satisfied with her appearance, she again motioned the waiter to bring her another drink. She knew that she had to calm her nerves somehow, so the best way was to self-medicate.

She peered around the spacious hotel suite, taking in all of her surroundings. There were about twenty people mingling about the room, mostly friends and staff members sipping martinis and champagne. They were all chatting quietly about the past year's campaign and high hopes that their Cindy would take up residence in the presidential mansion. If they had doubts, no one expressed them, at least not that night, in that room. A few waiters carrying small beverage trays caddied libations about the small crowd as staff members seemed almost permanently attached to their smartphones.

The centerpiece of the hotel room, strangely, was not the clearly nervous Democratic candidate, but the forty-two-inch flat-screen television permanently tuned to national network news. Though there were several to choose from, the obvious choice was one of the more liberally-biased channels who would, even in the event of a Republican election, lean more in the direction of support for Cindy Chandler. The program that night was continuous coverage of the presidential election, and even when advertisements offered a reprieve from the endless pundit commentaries, the screen was framed and flashed with a ticker of which states' polls were in, and what percentage at the bottom of the screen. It was early in the evening, so only a few states that lined the eastern seaboard reported that enough of the results were in to show that little green check mark next to the name of the candidate that would carry that state. Not surprisingly, Virginia and the Carolinas showed a Davenport victory, but Chandler had already carried Pennsylvania, Rhode Island, Connecticut, and Massachusetts. So far, the race was a bit of a draw.

The senator looked away from the screen to thank the waiter as she received the drink she ordered. She reached into the glass, fishing out the wedge of lime, and holding the ends with her finger and thumb, she squeezed as much of the juice as she could into the vodka before returning the rind to the liquid, and took the first savory sip.

She glanced down at the two separate sets of paper placed neatly on the table, yet wrinkled and crumpled from heavy use. Her eyes darted from one set to another in deep contemplation as she wondered how the night would end. She was hoping to read from the stack on the left, ending in glorious uproar of cheer and support, yet she gulped her vodka in quiet acceptance and preparation that she may in fact have to deliver the concession speech to her sea of supporters.

She looked to her right, gazing at her wonderfully supportive husband, who was watching the television attentively, his hands clasped behind his head in relaxed tension. Her daughter Julie, who had flown in from New Orleans that morning, sat glued to her mobile phone, feverishly text messaging her friends at school or elsewhere. She curled her dark brown hair, which her mother loved, but got to see only so often, and wore a very classy and very expensive black cocktail dress. Though she exuded beauty and class, it was marred by the typical college party girl mainstay—a cold domestic longneck bottle of beer; her fourth by Cindy's count.

"Having a good time, Julie?" Cindy asked her daughter with a fake smile, as if to prod a small confrontation.

"Sure, Mom," she only looked up from the phone long enough to motion the waiter with her bottle that it was time for another one.

"You better slow down a bit. Pace yourself. I don't need you dancing on the podium after my speech or passed out backstage," she became more direct.

"Mom, honestly!" she rolled her eyes, looking up from the small screen.

"What? I don't want you to treat this like a frat party," she shrugged in faux innocence. "I can't have you French kissing my campaign manager Sandra by the end of the night or puking on a Secret Service man."

"When are you going to let that whole thing die? It was months ago. I've been really careful and good lately."

"I'll let it die when the media does. When I stop seeing an up-skirt shot of you on a pool table flashing across the TV screen on the nightly news or at least I know it's not going to stop me from getting elected, I'll stop hounding you."

"Daddy," she looked to Donny Chandler for support, flashing those big brown eyes that her father had always had such a hard time resisting.

"Hey, leave me out of this," he threw his hands into the air in neutrality. "This is a mother-daughter thing. There's no place for Daddy's word here."

"Hey, we just took Vermont, New Hampshire, and New York!" Sandra shouted as the Chandler family snapped out of their little domestic quarrel and a slightly elevated enthusiasm came over the room.

The family all smiled at one another, looking back and forth from each other's faces to the screen. They put the petty things aside for a moment to relish in the small victory. They were optimistic. They were hopeful. But they were also nervous, and they all knew that the further west and south the results began to pour in from, the tougher this was going to get. It would be a long night.

Chapter 11

The door of the Perkins home swung open quietly as Kyle slipped in still wearing the backpack and clothing he wore to school that day, though the world was dark beyond the front porch. The floor popped and crackled as he crossed the threshold and made his way down the hardwood walkway between the office and the formal living area, emerging into the back area of the house where the kitchen and the family room were. The kitchen had been cleaned. The table had been cleared, and his mother and father were sitting on the couch watching the television.

"How did the study session at Ryan's go?" Angela said without turning her head.

"Fine," he set his backpack down, leaning it against the base of the kitchen bar. "He's starting to get it. He'd fail Spanish if it weren't for me," he chuckled a bit as he rounded the side of the couch. He did not dare reveal the truth that they had only worked on Spanish for about an hour, and spent the rest of the time hanging out, listening to music, and playing video games that involved fighting zombies with shotguns and phosphorus grenades.

"Well it took you long enough," she responded. "It's 9:30. Did you eat at Ryan's?"

"Nope."

"Well, there's a plate in the microwave. All you've got to do is heat it up for two minutes."

"What is it?" he moved toward the kitchen.

"Pot roast, mashed potatoes and gravy, and lima beans."

"Sounds good," he dialed in the numbers and pressed the start button.

He spun around, awaiting the reheating of his dinner and leaning against the counter as he watched his parents intently glued to the flat-screen television. The coverage from the conservative network news was just as it was from the liberal news. There was a barrage of commentary from analysts and even celebrities while polling results flashed across the bottom of the screen along with a running count of how many delegates each candidate had won.

"Chandler's ahead, huh?" Kyle gathered from the information on the screen.

"Yeah," his father turned his head toward him. "You haven't been keeping up with it?"

"Nope, all conjugation and the past tense tonight."

"Yeah, well she's ahead now, and I know she'll probably pick up California, but I'm hoping the working class in Washington and Oregon will put Davenport over the edge," he nodded, turning his head back toward the TV. "I'm just worried about the young vote."

"Mr. Devereaux, my economics teacher, has been saying the same thing—the young vote will be a big factor. And then there's the corruptions stuff and cheating on his wife… "

"Mr. Devereaux?" he turned to his son. "Sounds like you have some interesting conversations in there. I just hope he's not pushing his own personal agenda or trying to influence his students."

"No, he purposely stays away from giving his personal opinion. He says it's irresponsible for someone with as much influence as him to give strong opinions in the presence of the impressionable. He hates that about even celebrities. Anyway, he said he'd rather hear *our* opinions. He wants us to form our own opinions and learn to debate them."

"Good man. That sounds good. The sooner the better."

"Yeah, I've really become more interested in current events since he always goes through it at the beginning of class."

"Good," Drew nodded in approval as he continued to watch the poll results.

The microwave chimed three times to alert the young man that his dinner was ready. Kyle pushed the button releasing the door and reached inside, retrieving the steaming plate. He then opened a drawer and reached in for a fork, pulling one out, and almost slamming it shut before carrying his food into the family room and sitting across from his parents on the loveseat.

"So who won in the mock election? Davenport?" Drew asked his son.

"Actually," Kyle took another bite of his mashed potatoes and continued speaking with his mouth full, "Chandler won."

"No shit? Are you kidding?" he leaned forward.

"No, she won pretty big," he continued eating and watching the TV. "Mom, this is really good," he looked at his smiling mother.

"That's the young vote," Drew shook his head. "Completely dazzled by the rhetoric and empty promise of hope and cleaning up the corruption. No one can clean up the corruption in Washington, especially not this…" he paused short of what he really wanted to call her.

"This what, Drew?" Angela cocked her head. "Bitch?"

"Well you voted for Davenport, right?" he shook off his wife's comment.

"No, actually I voted for Chandler," he fired back, almost provoking his father.

Drew said nothing for a long moment, trying to collect his thoughts and wrap his mind around what his son had just said. He hunched over with his elbows on his knees and grimaced as if in pain, while staring at Kyle with no understanding of any of this.

"What do you mean? After all the conversations we've had about this? I told you she would be bad for this country," Drew snapped.

"Whoa, whatever happened to you approving of my beginning to learn to form my own opinions?" he threw up his hands in shock.

"Yeah, well," he tried to remove his foot from his mouth, "I at least thought you would learn to make the right decisions."

"Right according to who? You?"

"This is that Devereaux talking, huh?" he began to get agitated. "He's been pumping your head full of liberal bullshit, hasn't he?"

"Actually, no. I told you Mr. Devereaux doesn't like giving his own opinions. This was *my* decision. I like Chandler. I think Davenport is a bully. He'll go around the world picking fights in the name of 'making the world safe for democracy.' Chandler will at least *try* to use diplomacy. And don't even get me started on the economy. He's going to protect his buddies on Wall Street while the common man suffers. I like that Chandler wants to create jobs by fixing the infrastructure and lowering taxes on the middle and lower classes."

Drew was speechless. Once again, he could not quite find words to express what he was thinking. Actually, he did not know what to think. He surely did not agree with his son, but simultaneously, he was proud that Kyle had taken a stand—a well-thought, intelligent stand.

"She'll bankrupt this country," Drew struggled for the words. "She's..." he paused as his smartphone rang to alert him to a new text message.

He picked up the device, pressing a few buttons to bring up the screen where he could read his message. His lips moved ever so slightly as his eyes traced every line of the message, and then burst into a fit of uncontrolled laughter.

"My buddy Steve..." he laughed some more and then began to read. "The Joint Chiefs of Staff, the CIA, and the Department of Homeland Security have all met and agreed that the red nuclear button should be removed from the oval office for one week out of the month!" he began laughing as hard as before.

Angela just stared at the crudity of her husband's chauvinistic taste in humor, crossing her arms and displaying the kind of expression that was reserved for the most vile and sarcastic of men.

"What?" he threw up his hands. "It's funny."

Angela then turned her gaze to Kyle, who was having a hard time keeping a straight face. His mother gave him an even dirtier look than his father. But that did not stop Kyle. He could not hold on any longer. Laughter erupted from his mouth like a geyser as he joined in with his father, shrugging in the wake of Angela's look of disbelief at the sophomoric humor.

The television screen changed, and from the corner of his eye, Drew noticed, so he turned his head in accordance to see what was happening. The anchor hosting this segment of the election coverage strolled across a stage on the set of the newsroom in front of an enormous LCD screen that seemed to stretch from the floor to the ceiling. Across the screen, there were charts and statistics of the close presidential contest, but as the well-dressed, aging man came to a halt in his position before the cameras, the screen changed to a new set of stats.

"We're ready to project that Cindy Chandler will carry the states of Washington and Oregon," he pointed to the numbers beside each state's name. "And with that, our analysts, I'm being told, also project that, despite the results not completely in from California, Cindy Chandler will be the next president of the United States of America. The U.S. has elected the first ever female president."

The television screen at the Perkins household flashed to scenes being filmed at various Republican and Democrat watch parties across the country, each scene showing the reactions of partisan supporters as the news had been broken to them. Republicans reacted as if their favorite football team had just lost a play-off game, grumbling and hanging their heads in disappointment, and even anger. Of course, at the other parties, there were shouts of joy, cheering, and hugging—a celebration of their victory. The screen then cut to a scene in Philadelphia, where at the domed multi-purposed arena, throngs of Chandler supporters cheered in deafening victory. Under any other circumstances, one would have taken this scene as one from a major rock concert or sporting event. Thousands of people from all walks of life shouted for joy with their hands in the air. Close-up shots showed gray-haired old women with tears rolling from their eyes down their cheeks—a silent, anonymous story telling of a life-long struggle to become equal in a man's world. Other shots were of young people who were ecstatic that their vote had actually made the difference that they had always been told it would.

"This is the scene at the Philadelphia rally where President-elect Cindy Chandler will make her victory speech within the hour," the anchor commented, invisible on the screen.

"God damn it!" Drew shouted as if he had dropped a sledge hammer on his foot. Startled, Kyle and Angela's heads jerked toward the upset man as she punched him in the arm for the obscenity.

Chapter 12

The motorcade came to a halt in the rear of the arena, splashing through the puddles left by a short rainstorm just half an hour before. The blackness of night was pierced by a rhythmic pattern of blue police strobes emanating from the tops of the four Philadelphia police cruisers that escorted the black limousine from the luxury downtown hotel to the awaiting fans inside. Already, staff members were exiting the black SUV in front of the limo, all carrying clipboards, checking their messages on their smartphones, and beaming with the excitement that their candidate would soon be the next president of the United States.

The doors of the limo had not yet opened, and behind the extremely dark tinting of the windows was a melting pot of mixed emotions. Senator Chandler reclined in the rear leather seat, engulfed by the upholstery as if it were form-fitted to her body. She did not move. She could not move. She sat motionless, glaring out the window to her right, her elbow propped up on the ledge below it while she gnawed softly on the long nail of her index finger. Her expression was one of concern and contemplation. One could only imagine the flurry of thoughts and questions that swirled through her mind. She seemed almost apprehensive at the thought that she would lead the free world, beginning with an address to thousands of adoring fans and supporters.

"Try not to look too excited, darling," Donny smiled jokingly at his wife, flush with happiness over her historic victory.

"What?" she snapped out of her trance, gazing back at her family and her manager Sandra, almost dazed.

"You look like you've got a lot on your mind, Mom," Julie added, also visibly excited for her mother. "Either that or you had one too many vodkas back at the hotel."

"All the vodka in Poland couldn't calm my nerves," she shook her head, and looked back out the window.

"You were just elected president," Donny spoke again. "You should be gleaming with happiness!"

"I don't know if I can do this, Donny," she shook her head at him, looking back out the window. "It's too big. It's too much responsibility. What was I thinking? What if I screw up? I've made all these promises. What if I can't deliver? What if I get dealt another 9/11 like Bush did back in 2001? I don't know if I can handle it. What if I don't fix the recession? What if it becomes a depression? If I screw up, what if it's another two hundred plus years before another woman has a shot at being elected president?"

"Hey, hey, hey," Donny grasped his wife's left hand and spoke in a calming and understanding voice. "Stop right there. You're going to be great. Look, all you can do, is do what you think is right and what you think is in the best interest of the country. That's all any president has ever done. If everything were easy, there would be no need for the courageous," he smiled warmly.

"You're right," she erupted in a smile, thankful for such a loving and supportive husband and daughter.

"Alright then, Mrs. Pres..." he paused, arching his eyebrows in contemplation. "What do we even call you? Mrs. President? Lady President?"

"Someone once suggested to me that I be addressed as Madam President," she smiled and shrugged, as if unsure of whether or not that would be the appropriate title.

"Okay," Julie nodded. "I could see that working."

"Yeah," Sandra spoke up. "But it kind of sounds like you'd be running a presidential whorehouse out of the Lincoln bedroom."

"High rollers only," Cindy laughed along with everyone else. "Maybe we could help balance the budget for once," she added as she opened the door, and stepped out of the car, followed by her family and trusted advisor.

The entourage of staff members and newly assigned Secret Servicemen joined and surrounded the Chandler family as they walked through a large, trailer-sized loading dock and up the slightly inclined ramp. The fluorescent lighting rudely contracted their pupils as they switched from dark to extremely bright. As they approached the hallway leading to the dressing rooms and backstage areas, a dull roar of the masses progressively grew louder in anticipation of the arrival of their hero.

"We're not going to the dressing room at all," Sandra looked at her boss. "Your fans await, so there's no time. Are you okay with that?"

"Absolutely," she responded. "As long as I look okay. Do I?" Cindy stood before her aide, brushing out any wrinkles left from the sitting position she had been in.

"Perfect," Sandra smiled. "Presidential."

"Alright," she glared nervously as they reached the backstage area. "Here goes. Thank you for everything."

"My pleasure, Madam President."

"Knock 'em dead, tiger," Donny kissed his wife as Julie smiled on.

Cindy marched up the black metal steps leading up to the platform, the crowds of people cheering and yearning for her to step out and greet her destiny. She moved nervously through the backstage shadows, yet confident in herself finally. As she approached the opening to the stage, just hidden from public view, the stage manager gave her a nod, signaling that he was ready if she was. To that, she nodded back, blowing a stream of breath through her puckered lips, and swaying back and forth. The man pushed a button or two on his small control console, and then picked up a microphone.

"Ladies and gentlemen," he crooned as the lights in the arena dimmed and the crowds raised the volume. "Without further adieu, I am proud to present to you your next president of the United States, Cindy Chandler!"

He cued the music that had become the official campaign song for more than a year, and as Journey's "Don't Stop Believing" echoed through the auditorium, the president-elect strolled across the black stage, a blindingly concentrated spotlight beam trained on her movement as she approached the podium. The sea of supporters roared louder than ever as she came to a halt behind her podium and absorbed the scene, the moment, and the energy. Pride took over as she gazed across at the countless faces to see people of all races, religions, and ages. She had not just won over a few concentrated demographics. She had won over America. There were old men and women, college students, blue-collar workers, and even toddlers hoisted upon the shoulders of their fathers; brought there to witness such an historic event.

As the stage manager slowly lowered the volume of the theme song, the noise remained high. Chandler stood smiling proudly, looking from right to left and from the ground level to the cheap seats before she tried to start her speech. She wondered how long this crowd would remain cheering before she said a word. With that, she began.

"Thank you," she said, almost drowned by the cheering and chanting. "Thank you very much," she repeated, yet the crowd was relentless.

Without another word, she simply raised her right hand like Moses calling to God. And magically, as she slowly lowered her hand, the volume of the cheering lowered accordingly. She felt like Christ standing on a boat filled with disciples, adrift in turbulent seas. With a word and a raising of her hand, she calmed the waters.

"There are those who said," her voice echoed across the auditorium and the quieted supporters, "that this day would never come. They said America wasn't ready for this. Tell them what you think of that now!" she opened the floodgates for the loudest and most joyful screams of the evening. She let it go for a few moments before raising her hand again to quiet them.

"But this is not a victory for women. This is not a victory for the Democratic Party. This is a victory for all who are tired of the corruption in Washington and tired of their elected officials not working in their best interests, as they were chosen to do. It's for the overtaxed single mother working two or three jobs to make ends meet and feed her too often hungry children. This victory is for the college-educated middle class family man, laid off and unable to provide for his family. It's for those of you who are tired of decadence on Wall Street and in the halls of the U.S. Congress."

Solemn and nodding faces across the nation watched on intently.

"It's for the common family," the Perkins family sat transfixed to the TV.

"It's for those without health insurance," Sherry Putnam's concerned face turned from the screen to the spasming right hand that she clutched and rubbed.

"It's for the American servicemen and women who are tired of being used as global bullies. It's for the world citizens who are longing to respect us once more. This victory is for the tired and poor. It's for the hungry and sick. It's for the rich and famous. It's for the unsung heroes of everyday American life. This victory is for you, and with your help, if we all work together, we can pick up the pieces and lift this country back to greatness. We can live up to our own belief that we are the shining example of freedom in the world. So do not cheer for me. Do not cheer for this historic moment. Cheer for you and the American people. Good night!" she stepped back from the podium, smiling and waving as the overcrowded stadium erupted with jubilation.

In contrast, the Republicans of the country who had not already turned off their televisions were staring into the screens with expressions of doubt, disappointment, frustration, and even malice. For some of them, this was not over.

Chapter 13

January, Seventeen months before the bomb

A stampede of people, all carrying some sort of bag over their shoulders, flooded forth from the opening to gate C-17 at the Cleveland airport. Most were backpacks or purses. A few people rolled behind them small upright suitcases, allowing the owners to skip overpriced bag-checking rates. But emerging amid, and almost hidden by, the crowd of airline passengers was a young man carrying an olive drab military duffel bag. The nylon cord was pulled tightly, bunching the opening together and cutting into the owner's shoulder as the bag hung behind his back. Upon the sickly green fabric, there was a black stenciled name that read, "Putnam, D."

He strolled confidently past the check-in counter at the gate, crossing the bluish gray carpet that seemed present in every airport in the United States until reaching the tiled main concourse walkway where the leather soles of his military-issued black dress shoes clapped loudly. He made his way to the glass revolving door leading to the baggage claim area, dodging passers-by nimbly as he went.

As he exited the merry-go-round of a door, the passageway opened up into a wide expanse of a room, complete with several big, steel rotating luggage carousels, which were mobbed by former passengers all fighting to get to their bags. Luckily, he did not have to deal with that. Between fourteen weeks of perpetual brotherhood, bus rides, and all too intimate plane rides with various people, he wished not to be around crowds. He just wanted quiet and simplicity for a while, until he was to report to his base assignment.

Bypassing the multitudes of travelers, he could see the light of day through the windows and doors that lay across the room. He briskly paced his movement in that direction, his eyes trained on the exit as he approached with purpose. Placing his right hand on the door's lever, he applied enough force to swing it open, immediately raising his hand to his face to shield his eyes from the bright late-afternoon sun. He began scanning the curbside for Jake and his beat-up old sedan. He looked over about a half dozen cars, all with their owners standing in front, waiting for their loved ones. A young woman jogged by him from behind, ending with an abrupt, close embrace with what looked like her sister. His eyes drifted from the warm, loving homecoming, still searching for his own.

Damn it!, he thought to himself and looked down at his left wrist to check his watch. He knows what time my flight got in. Where the hell could he be? Did he get stuck in traffic?

As his frustration mounted, something caught his eye to his right, and his head stopped moving to the left. He thought he had seen the old station wagon his mother used to take to work. But that could not be possible as it had not run in almost a year. As he was about to disregard, he spotted the woman near that car. She was slowly moving toward him, smiling lovingly with her fingers interlocked affront her thighs.

"Mom?" he dropped his bag and started toward her. His mouth dropped open as a smile slowly graced his face.

Sherry beamed with joy and pride as her handsome son approached her for a hug. She almost did not recognize him. It was amazing how the military transformed young men. Her Derek was no longer the shaggy, unshaven, oil-stained kid that left a few months ago. He had straightened his slouch, towering high with an obviously thicker and leaner physique. His custom-tailored dress khakis were virtually flawless, pressed with heavy starch and wrinkle-free. A few small, colorful decorations adorned the left side of his chest and a single pointed private's stripe was sewn onto each arm. His closely shaven face was crowned by the classic high-and-tight Marine haircut, topped by his garrison cap. Sherry always hated those caps. They looked like the old paper caps worn by soda jerks and teenage fast food hamburger flippers. But somehow it looked nice on Derek. It was fitting. He was handsome.

They locked together in a loving mother-son embrace, ecstatic to see one another. They had always been such a large part of one another's lives. Derek's father and sisters were long gone, with no sign of ever coming back. They were all each other had, and being apart for this long was a first. Neither of them ever expected that the distance for such a long period of time would be so hard on them. Soon, Derek would have to leave again, reporting for duty at some distant base.

"Mom?" he stepped back a bit to look her over. She was wearing some blue dress he was sure may have looked nice ten years ago, but at least she was trying. She had done her hair up in a curly pony tail and put on makeup that she hadn't worn in years. He couldn't believe she had left the house. Yet, she still looked bad beyond the superficial. It was like a brand new paint job and racing stripes on a 1973 Gremlin. Even more, the scene was almost surreal, as if it were prom night, and the two of them were going on a date.

"What, I can't pick up my boy from the airport?" she smiled, then took his face in her hands and stretched up to kiss his cheek.

"Well, yeah. I just didn't expect you. I thought Jake was coming to get me. I knew you didn't have a …car. Mom, the car is running? How…?" he looked at the old vehicle with amazement and shock.

"Yeah," she briefly peered over her shoulder at it, and then faced her son again, "Jake and the boys fixed it a couple of weeks ago. They were all so proud of you that they all got together and fixed it free of charge. Even Dickie helped out. I think he's more proud of you than the rest of them."

"That's awesome!" he smiled. "So what now?"

"We should go home and maybe we can order out for Chinese," she replied, glowing with joy. She couldn't get over how he had changed. Even his voice was different. It was commanding and full of volume. He sounded like a man, yet it was subtly gentle still, with a remaining bit of that boyishness of his youth.

"I've got a better idea. You're already dressed up, so let me take you out for a nice steak dinner. There's that place down on the waterfront we could go to. What do you say?"

"Um," she was at a loss for words, but still not at a loss of smiles. "Can we afford it?"

"Doesn't matter. I'm about to start making better money. Besides, this is a celebration of new beginnings."

"Um, okay. Sure!" she nodded happily.

"Outstanding!" he walked her to the car, and even opened the passenger side for her before jogging around to the other door.

They drove off, navigating the ever complicated roadways to exit the airport, and merged onto the interstate headed downtown. Through most of the drive, as Derek kept his eyes focused on the road, Sherry could not keep her eyes off of her son, still astounded at his appearance, demeanor, and his overall transformation from boyhood. But it was not an uncomfortable silence with staring; there were plenty of things to talk about. There was nothing new going on with Sherry. Regretfully, she sat in that same chair smoking those same cigarettes for the entire length of time that her son was at boot camp. So naturally, being the star of the homecoming show, the focus of conversation was on Derek's adventures in national defense.

"Yeah, Mom," he told her, "it was rough, and even though you seemed like you were in danger all the time, you really weren't."

"Really?" she was shocked. "It wasn't dangerous at all?"

"Well, there were live fire exercises like when we had to crawl on our bellies through the mud with rounds whizzing over our heads. There was weapons training, which always holds the risk of some idiot not pointing his muzzle in the right direction. We got to use live grenades. There were a few instances where someone got a rib or a wrist broken in hand-to-hand combat tactics. A few guys had to deal with sprains on the obstacle courses. Other than that, it wasn't too bad," he explained nonchalantly, to his mother's horror.

"That sounds pretty dangerous to me," she gaped.

"Not to a Marine, Mom," he grinned with pride and testosterone.

"Was it hard? I bet it was."

"Honestly, the hardest part was getting yelled at and the physical demands. We were always running, doing PT, climbing—stuff like that. After a while you get used to it. It no longer hurt to exercise. Getting yelled at became a fact of life. You just learn to do what you're told, and do it right. Some guys couldn't hack it."

"Oh yeah? Do they get to quit?"

"Nope. They sign a contract. Unless they get injured too seriously or they get a section eight..." he was interrupted.

"Section eight?"

"You can be discharged for losing it. We had a few guys that couldn't hack all the yelling and punishment. They just went bat shit."

"And what happens?" she was curious.

"You get booted, unless..."

"Unless what?"

"We had a couple of guys try to punch their own ticket. One guy succeeded."

"You mean he..." she was horrified.

"Yeah Mom. Suicide. He hanged himself from the rafters of the barracks with a belt. It didn't break his neck, so he didn't go unconscious. He likely just slowly strangulated. I'm sure it was painful."

"Okay, okay. Enough. I don't want to know any more," she was beginning to feel sick at the thought of all the things her only son had been exposed to.

Derek just grinned. The truth was, he wore every experience of boot camp, from the PT and physical abuse to the suicides and getting screamed at like a badge of honor. As a Marine, the more he's exposed to, the harder he becomes. He will become a better soldier and a better leader. He felt for the guys who had a section eight, and even the guy who killed himself, but perhaps it was for the best. They were weak, and there is no room for weakness in the United States Marine Corps.

Finally, the station wagon pulled into the concrete parking lot of the ritzy steak house. It was built in the style of a French Alps lodge, complete with brick and thick, wooden beams. The backdrop of Lake Erie glimmering in the setting sun made it much more special as Derek and his mother approached the front door.

They entered the restaurant, the warm air rushing out as a welcome from the bitter January air on the outside. Some light jazz song played softly through the speakers strategically hidden from plain view. The lights were dim and small votive candles flickered on every table amid wine glasses and fresh flowers. Waiters and waitresses gracefully moved about the seating areas performing various tasks—carrying martinis to the patrons, taking orders, and bringing out masterfully prepared dishes to hungry diners. The young woman behind the hostess stand reacted to Derek's appearance as any girl would toward a handsome young man in uniform. She smiled and looked him over as she picked up two menus and began to lead them to their booth in the far corner of the room.

"Your waiter will be with you shortly. Enjoy your meal," she left the table, but not before again grinning coyly at Derek.

"Wow," Sherry smiled at him. "Amazing what fourteen weeks at basic training will do for you."

"Yeah, why didn't I do this years ago?" he joked.

A waiter very quickly appeared at their table. He was in his thirties—a bit older than the college students most people were used to at the large chains and theme restaurants. He seemed to be a professional. He had tan, leathery skin with greased-back jet black hair. His white tuxedo shirt displayed no sign of staining, despite likely working around food every single day.

"Hi, I'm Rob. I'll take care of your every need this evening. Can I start you out with a bottle of wine from the wine list, perhaps?" he began with the up-sell.

"Um, Mom?" Derek offered the opportunity to his mother, questioning as much with his eyes as with his words.

"Not for me, thanks," she waved the waiter off with a grin. "I'll just have water."

"Someone is already having water and bread brought to the table. And for you, sir?" he turned to Derek.

"I'll just have a draft beer," he nodded.

"I'll certainly have that out to you soon. In the meantime, enjoy the bread coming…whoa, there it is," he was slightly surprised by a young woman strolling up to his side with two waters and a big loaf of fresh bread, complete with butter and a knife. With that, he ran off to enter Derek's drink order.

"Mmm …" Sherry quivered at the sight on the table before her. "I love fresh bread."

She reached for the knife and prepared to slice into the bread, which was still warm from the oven. She positioned the handle of the steak knife in her right hand, yet could not seem to get a firm grip. She tried to hide her struggle, looking up and smiling at her suspicious son, and then back to her hand, concentrating on cutting her own bread. Her fingers seemed that they had lost essence and strength. They had less life. They lacked functionality.

"Mom," Derek peered at his mother. "Are you alright?" he was beginning to get concerned.

"Yeah, I'm fine, dear," she became more frustrated, ever struggling with her grip on the knife and trying frantically to cut the bread. Finally, she half threw the knife down with a startling clang, and gripped at her right hand, massaging it with the other as shame and worry crossed her face.

"Mom, what's wrong?" he was fully concerned now.

"I," she tried to regain her composure, calmly telling Derek about the last couple of months. "I noticed this back in November. My right hand has been acting up. It's hard to do even simple things with it. Lighting a cigarette. Opening a jar. It's like my hand has no strength anymore. I can't grip as well, and sometimes it seems to just dangle lifelessly."

"Have you gone to the doctor?"

"I went a couple of times last month—used my Medicare. Both times I went, the doctor was baffled. He took an X-ray to see if I had fractured my hand somehow—nope, totally normal. They did an MRI and couldn't see anything wrong. Next month, I have an appointment with a specialist. I think it's a neurologist or something. But they don't know what's going on."

"Shit, Mom," Derek gazed at his mother. "That's strange. Ah, it will be fine. I'm sure it's nothing. Maybe carpal tunnel from all those years in the factory. Don't worry. We're on Uncle Sam's health insurance soon. We'll take care of it."

"I know," she faked a smile, and again clutched her right hand. She dared not tell her son that her left hand was beginning to do the same thing. This was to be a happy day. She did not want Derek worrying about her.

Chapter 14

The old station wagon screeched to a halt before a run-down, slightly decaying house in Cleveland. Everything about the place was broken, from the cracks in the concrete sidewalks to the chipping brown paint on the exterior. The wooden rails alongside the concrete front steps were beginning to split and sway. There probably had not been a working light bulb on the front porch in years. What did function quite properly was the neon blue and red beer sign cutting the blackness of night with its sharp luminescence.

Derek lifted the gear shift upward to put the car into park, leering off to his right at the house. As he pulled at the door handle, and stepped out into the cold, he could hear the bump of the stereo system inside amid sporadic bursts of laughter. He stepped around the front of the car, his hands in the pockets of his relaxed-fit blue jeans, attempting to warm his hands. For a moment, he just stood there before the curb, freezing and staring up at the aged and decaying house. He was not smiling excitedly at the thought of seeing his friends. Actually, he sighed in apprehension, literally able to see his regret materialize and condense in the cold before his face.

This was his first day home from boot camp. He had been traveling all day, first by bus, and then spending hours in airports and on airliners. Added to the jet lag and travel fatigue was the burden of a loaded baked potato and a twelve-ounce rib eye in his gut. At this point, all he wanted to do was to curl up in his own bed and actually sleep *beneath* the sheets for the first time in months.

Reluctantly, he moved forward, stepping up onto the sidewalk from the street, and lifting the metal latch of the gate with an irritating metal-on-metal screech. He continued up the walkway, able to feel the difference in elevation of the clumps of weeds between the concrete sections through the soles of his shoes. As he stepped up onto the first of four concrete steps before the front door, he could already smell beer, whether it was seeping through the cracks around the door frame, or an old smell permanently soaked into the front yard from keggers past.

He reached up to the screen door, taking the small, rusted handle in his fingers, and flung it open. Before the spring linking the screen to the house could contract, he knocked loudly on the main door. He looked down at his knuckles and saw that they were covered in brown paint chips. He brushed them off on the leg of his jeans as he waited for someone to answer the door.

After a few moments, the front door opened, releasing a rush of dense, stuffy air and the pungent odor of beer, liquor, and cigarette smoke. It poured out into the cold night air in a cloud, almost overwhelming Derek and physically knocking him over. There in the doorway stood his best friend, Jake, holding a plastic cup of keg beer, and already slightly inebriated. He looked bad. He looked worse than Derek had remembered, as if he had aged and declined severely in health in just the couple of months that they had been apart. Jake had not shaven in days, and appeared to have not showered. His hair was oily-looking and shaggy. The plaid shirt he wore was wrinkled and dirty. But that old familiar smile shined brighter than ever. It cut through the darkness of his appearance, beaconing his friend for a long-awaited hug and welcome home.

"You son of a bitch!" Jake shouted. "Ha ha! You know better, boy! You don't have to knock on the door at this house. This is home, brother. You're family! Come here and give me a hug!"

Derek stepped up into the doorway and over the threshold, embracing his friend in a tight, warm, and yet masculine hug. Derek said nothing as they released one another. He just looked into Jake's face with a smile—a behavior that he reciprocated in a moment of happiness and understanding. They simply enjoyed the moment.

"Well, hey," Jake shook off the silence, ushering Derek into the smoky room, "come in and get a beer—HEY DAVE! GET THIS

MAN A BEER! HE'S A NATIONAL HERO! DEREK'S BACK, EVERYBODY!"

Derek looked about the room littered with beer bottles, empty cups that people had forgotten the location of before just getting another, and various mismatched sofas and chairs, all stained with alcohol, vomit, and probably semen. The dozen or so guys standing about the space began cheering for him as if he had just single-handedly won a foreign war against the greatest of adversaries, and come home after receiving the Congressional Medal of Honor. He knew most of them. He either worked with them at the shop or knew them through coworkers. But he couldn't tell who was cheering him out of true pride in him or just drunkenly doing so because they were told to. Nevertheless, he grinned a bit bashfully, lowering his head with a level of humility, and raising his right hand as if to hail a cab.

"Hey, hey," Jake stumbled a bit from side to side. "Give me a salute, ya bastard!" he tried to stand at attention, lifting his hand to his brow, then jetting his hand out before his face like one would see in a movie.

"No, you asshole. You're not doing it right," Derek smiled. "You have to sharply click your heels together like this," he demonstrated. "And the hand snaps up, you hold, and snap it back to your side."

"Holy shit, that's so weird to see you do that," Jake laughed as someone walked up and handed Derek a beer. "Look at you. You're a changed man! Look at that haircut." He rubbed the top of Derek's head. "And you slimmed down. I bet you're ripped up like a son-of-a-bitch!"

"That's what running ten miles a day and doing smurf jacks for an hour will do to you."

"Smurf what?" he looked confused. "Never mind, I don't even want to know. So we got poker going on tonight. Yeah? What do ya say? Hang out with the guys? Catch up and tell us war stories?"

"Yeah, that's fine, but where's all the trim?" Derek looked around the room confusedly.

"Trim?" Jake shrugged. "We don't need trim. Guys' night! Manly men doing manly things like poker and pissing out in the back yard!"

"And what then? Circle jerks? Licking each others' assholes?" he laughed. "Dude, I've been around nothing but guys for fourteen weeks, and you welcome me home with a sausage fest? I'm tired of jerking off. I need to get laid!" he shouted to the laughter of those within earshot.

"Shit, didn't think about that, bro," Jake thought deeply. "Well, Joselyn is coming over later, and I think she's bringing her cousin with her, but I think she's kind of a whore."

"And this is a problem why?" he laughed. "Outstanding," he slapped his leg. "Let's party. I've got some catching up to do!"

He began pounding beer after beer, going back to the keg for more and more of the flat, cheap brew. A few more females trickled into the party over the course of the night, scantily clad and naturally drawn to Derek's military demeanor and clearness of voice. He told countless tales of physical punishments for wrongdoing and mastering hand-to-hand combat. He even demonstrated some by taking Jake gently to the floor and putting him into some strange Brazilian jiu-jitsu hold. He told of weapons training and the tragedies of fellow recruits committing suicide. They laughed, joked, rough-housed, spoke nastily, and even spoke seriously about politics and the state of their country.

This type of night goes quickly. The old adage is that time flies when you are having fun, and that night was no exception. The night and the fun pass quickly, followed by a slowly-passing day of headache and agonizing nausea.

Derek was awoken by the wet tongue of a nasty English bulldog named Jake, Jr. The dog breath entered Derek's nostrils, and the saliva went into his mouth and nose as he grimaced and shook his head. His eyes slowly opened with much labor as he struggled to sit up on the itchy couch. His brain was functioning slowly with a head full of cheap keg beer. Slowly, short scenes of the night's events returned to him. He could tell that beneath the blanket someone had brought him he had no shirt on, exposing his lean, muscular Marine physique. But under further investigation, he found that he was completely naked beneath the dingy blanket, and so was the young woman sleeping next to him, to his surprise.

She groaned and grumbled, but did not awaken as he tried to slowly slide off of the light blue sofa. He did not dare wake her up and have to face the awkwardness of the post-one-night-stand. If he left undetected, each of them could regret the event in their own way. If she opened her eyes, they would have to uncomfortably make small talk and feel obligated to exchange phone numbers. Actually, he did not know that he regretted having sex with this young lady. She was dark-haired with soft, olive skin. Her breasts were exquisite—just big enough to complement her slender frame. If she weren't so whorish-seeming in this setting, she might have appealed to him even more. She looked like an excellent lay. He just wished he could remember more about how it was. He began to worry about whether or not he "protected" himself. He looked around, finding the condom wrapper on the floor, open and empty, but where was the actual condom? *Whatever*, he thought.

Nevertheless, he slipped on his green t-shirt and jeans, quietly put on his brown leather shoes, and searched for his jacket. He found it draped over the back of one of the loveseats in the sofa graveyard. He picked up the thick, blue coat, slipped it on, and smelled it to find it soaked with the odor of smoke and alcohol. He sneered in disgust, but shrugged, and made his way through the door to make his escape.

Chapter 15

Inauguration Day

Kyle pushed hard on the metal bar release of the large, heavy door leading from the relative quiet of the deserted school hallway into the sudden blast of noise and commotion of the bustling lunchroom. All around was laughter, teenage boys and girls sending text messages to other kids on the other side of the room, various cliques from goths to jocks eating either at the round tables or beneath the stairwells, and overall glee to be temporarily free from boring lectures and math problems.

He pushed into the organized chaos with mission and purpose, his eyes trained on something specific near the entrance to the auditorium. Ashley's long, brown hair cascaded over her white hoodie, and the designer jeans were made for her body, following every contour of her lower half. His entire walk in the direction of her and her friends was spent staring at her ass, not because he was a pig. His animal instincts had ignited and he was on the prowl.

He had rehearsed what he would say to his crush a thousand times in his head, and unrealistically, each scenario ended with Ashley becoming completely enamored with his charm. He would finally ask her out, nearly four years after the first time he laid eyes on her. His pace picked up as he could almost detect the scent of his prey. He became the focus of his own National Geographic special; a wild cat stalking, and then bolting for his prey on the open savannah. Yet, one thing that never happened in those nature shows was a last-minute instance of apprehension and doubt before aborting the mission. Kyle's anxiety built as he neared his beloved, and just as he was about to pounce, she turned incidentally toward him, sending him into a panic. He diverted himself to the side, and as she caught sight of the predator, he tried to seem as though he did not see her, throwing his gaze about the room almost in confusion.

"Hey, Kyle," she turned and smiled.

"Oh, hey, Ashley," he faced her, trying not to make eye contact. "I didn't…I didn't see you there."

"Ah," she grinned and nodded, as if not to believe him. "So what have you been up to?" she nudged him. "Arguing with teachers in their classrooms?"

"Oh," he chuckled, loosening up a little, "did you like that?"

"Actually," she laughed, then became a bit more serious, enchanting Kyle with a deep, sweet gaze from her sparkling brown eyes, "I thought it was pretty amazing."

"Really? You like that kind of thing? Debates and such, I mean," he said uncomfortably.

"Well yeah," she nodded. "Intelligence is attractive," she looked down at her feet, suddenly embarrassed about what she was implying.

"I thought popular and…well, beautiful girls just liked the jocks and the bad boys."

"Come on, I'm not that shallow, Kyle," she smiled, almost offended.

"No, I didn't mean…" he back pedaled.

"Let me tell you—little girls like the jocks and bad boys. But women like intelligent, nice guys."

For a few moments, they stood in uncomfortable silence, swaying and smiling. Kyle couldn't believe Ashley had just said that, and neither could she. Was she implying what he thought she was? Was she really making this that easy for him?

"So…" she tried to break the silence. "So that was pretty crazy that they wouldn't let us watch the inauguration today."

"Yeah," he followed right along, "I couldn't believe that. And it was a stupid reason. The school district said that it wasn't part of the curriculum, so we couldn't take time out of instruction time."

"That's so messed up! This was history in the making—something we would look back on in fifty years, and we didn't even get to see it."

But the conversation didn't last. It was a valiant attempt to free themselves of the awkwardness, but it failed in the end. Neither of them could take their minds off the first part of the conversation. The question was simply which of them would address it further. With that, Kyle decided to execute the previous plan and do what he had come to do.

"So Ashley," he broke the silence, "I was wondering...I mean, I didn't know if you'd want to. Um... Would you want to go see a movie or something sometime? I mean, you don't have to...obviously..." he stumbled over his words in an attempt to ask his question, but end it quickly.

"I'd love to," she smiled. "Saturday night?"

"Um, yeah," he couldn't stop smiling in amazement. He would have said more. He tried to say more, but the bell chimed the end of lunch and the beginning of third period.

"Got to go," she smiled. "I'll see you Saturday night," she extended her arm and grabbed his hand. It was only a momentary touch, but a strange energy or electricity flowed from her soft fingers into his trembling hand. It was all over for him as he grinned, and watched Ashley bounce away, her long hair swaying behind her. He couldn't wait until Saturday.

Chapter 16

Inauguration Day, plus one

Cindy Chandler's palms grew sweaty as she tried inconspicuously to wipe them on her gray suit, hoping the large, darkly stained podium would hide this act of nervousness. She knew that these ravenous wolves could smell fear, and that if she did not exude confidence, she would fall prey to a feeding frenzy that may leave her wounded and bleeding as a lame duck. She could not allow herself to fall into that dark place; not with so much on the line in this country. She would have to be firm and strong. She would have to use her gift of rhetoric and ability to easily explain to drive her point home.

She took a deep breath, adjusted her glasses resting on the bridge of her nose, and straightened her posture, once again allowing the roar of discontent fill her ears. A few minutes before, Speaker of the House James DeWitt whispered to her that he had never seen this kind of blatant disregard for parliamentary procedure in all his years in Congress. Normally, this place was dull and quiet. Congress members gave speeches from time to time, and the rest of the members who were actually present for a change just slumped in their chairs or fiddled with their smartphones. It was normally like a bad zombie movie, only the walking dead in this case did not feast on human brains, they sucked the money from the pockets of the taxpayer.

"Well maybe that's a good thing," she had replied with a smile. "Wake these bastards up. Energize them. Make them do their job for a change."

The babble of both support and discontent intermixed on the floor of the House of Representatives as Republican naysayers vocally objected to the new president's previous words on the economy. Any Democrats in close proximity to them rebutted their comments, and open debate ensued, while some shouted directly across the expansive room at the president herself.

For a few moments, Chandler allowed this to go on. She watched on as her fellow office-holders, Congressmen and Senators, stood behind the deeply and beautifully stained desks, and finally discussed this issue as it should be. The commotion echoed from one end of the chamber to the other; from the wooden panels all around to the black marble columns behind the podium that seemed to dwarf the president, the vice president, and the speaker of the house. It jumbled together in a mess of hot tempers and big egos, and rose high above the royal blue carpet to the upper level seating.

"Ladies and Gentlemen," Chandler motioned for everyone to quiet down, but it did not happen immediately. "Hey!" she raised her voice, but within the bounds of respect. The speaker began to arise from his seat behind her in order to gain control of this mob, but the president shook her head, motioning for him to refrain. "Hey, listen to me for a moment so we can discuss this like adults," she turned back to the floor, and watched as every mouth ceased to move. Many were in disbelief that she had used semi-motherly discipline to quiet the United States Congress.

"Look," she began, "I know this is my first real day on the job, and I know that some of you felt I was too soft or too inexperienced to hold this office. But make no mistake that I am here, and I am ready to get to work. Our country is in bad shape, economically. We all need to calm down and start talking about this recession rather than fight over it. Harsh words and hot tempers aren't going to fix this mess, and I promise you that I will do my part to work with each and every one of you so that we can meet somewhere in the middle."

It was a good start. Many of the faces of the more conservative legislators were still red and pessimistic, but at least she had their attention. Since her earlier scripted speech had already been given, she was now firing from the hip. She thought long and hard about what she would say next, but knew that if she waited too long, she would lose her momentum, sending the chamber back into anarchy as it had been before.

"Let me reiterate what this bill entails. There would be a tax restructuring to increase income tax by five percent for households making $500,000 per year or more, and a tax cut for all middle and lower class families. Plus, there would be a $1,000 increased child credit for those households. This is designed to give the majority of Americans a little more security without further increasing the deficit. It also puts money into people's pockets so that consumer spending goes up and businesses start making money again," she maintained sharp eye contact with the audience, ensuring that she still had their attention. "It is not the time to worry about the deficit. It is the time to worry about the soundness of the economy as a whole. After that, we'll worry about the deficit."

"The second part of this bill," she continued, "is basically a stimulus package. It provides funding to every state for the repair of infrastructure, education and technology in the schools, raises for teachers, grants to small businesses and other companies to keep their employees working and keep their doors open, and a plan to help smaller banks to offload some of the bad mortgage properties they can't get rid of. By the way, in time, the government will actually make money on those properties in the long run."

"And how much is this going to cost the taxpayers, Madam President?" a congressman from Oklahoma stood up, adjusted his belt, and questioned the commander-in-chief with a thick country drawl.

"As far as we can estimate," she paused a moment, afraid to continue, "about $500 billion."

The commotion began again as grumbles and head shaking commenced. She knew that the overall good of what could come out of this bill would ultimately be overshadowed by the issue of price tag.

"Are you going to let the cost deter you from doing what's right?" she asked.

"But we're already at over a trillion dollar deficit. China could repo Texas if they wanted to," the Oklahoma congressman resounded. "We can't afford another half trillion."

"This money is for very important improvements that must be done, not to mention the millions of people that need this break," she argued. "You can't put a price tag on that."

"Oh yeah we can," he fired back.

"Congressman," she narrowed her eyelids, "I drove through your state on the campaign trail. I've seen what some of your highways look like. They look like they got hit by a meteor shower. And I guarantee most of the country has roads that are just as bad. Without working highways, bridges, communication, and other forms of infrastructure, commerce does not happen, and our situation gets worse. Is that what you want?"

"But this education money and this small business bail-out," a senator from West Virginia chimed in before the congressman could answer. "What happens when the money runs out, and the burden is left to the states? What happens when we give teachers raises and once the federal money is gone, we've got to keep it up? And what about the maintenance of these technology systems?"

"And taking money from the hard-working upper class to give to the lazy folks who won't look for a job?" another legislator followed. "I'm whole-heartedly against supporting the people who have chosen to live off the government with the taxes of the hard-working."

"Socialist!" someone shouted from the upper level, sending the audience into an uncontrollable wildfire of shouting and arguing.

"I see we're not going to resolve this today," President Chandler shook her head. "But let's talk about it over the next couple of weeks. Keep in mind that there's a level of urgency to this matter. We can't table this forever—our people need us."

With that, she pushed away from the podium as the speaker and the vice president arose from their seats to accompany Chandler from the chamber. The president looked pessimistic and disappointed, but the speaker did not.

"I don't get it. I..." she shook her head.

"Cindy," he interrupted her, "it will be okay. We've got control of the House. We can get this done. The Senate is majority Democrat, too, but it will be a little trickier. Don't worry. We'll make this happen," he reassured her as they trudged up the main aisle toward the exit door, past dirty looks and unfounded grumblings about socialism.

Chapter 17

Inauguration Day, plus three

The old station wagon roared down the lane at much too fast a pace for the airport departures gate. Sherry Putnam gripped the armrest of the door to her right, thinking if she clutched tight enough any impact with another vehicle might be softened. She briefly glanced at Derek in the back seat with concern for his friend's driving skills, yet he seemed surprisingly undaunted by the break-neck speeds. She then turned her head back to Jake, who continued to speed along with a careless grin, unaware of her anxiety.

"Jake," she spouted, "for God's sake, slow down!"

"Oh," he snapped out of his trance. "Sorry. We're almost to Derek's gate," he shrugged.

He changed over to the unloading lane without warning or turn signal, and slammed his right foot down on the brake pedal, leaving a short skid mark on the concrete beneath them, grinding them to a halt. Everyone in the car was flung forward, their seat belts engaging and catching them abruptly. When they had finally pulled together their wits, they looked around to find the curbside check-in staff staring at them in disbelief.

"Thanks for driving, Jake," Derek opened the door and reached for his duffel bag. "You didn't have to come all the way out here."

"Oh, but I wanted to," he opened his door, as did Sherry. "I wanted to see you off. God only knows when you'll have leave again."

"Yeah, Jake," Sherry stepped out onto the curb with the two young men. "I would have driven him myself, but my damned hands have been acting so funny lately. I don't know what to make of it. Arthritis?"

"Promise me you'll go have that checked out, Mom," Derek took her hands in his with a look of concern on his semi-smiling face.

"Oh, I will. I made an appointment the other day," she explained. "I've already seen my regular doctor about it, and he says he can't diagnose anything like that, so he referred me to a neurologist."

"Neurologist? How do your hands have anything to do with your brain?"

"I don't know," she shook her head. "But I'm going anyway. I'll let you know how it goes."

"Take care of her," Derek looked at his friend.

"Don't worry, buddy," he assured him. "I'll check in with her every few days and help her with grocery shopping and stuff."

"Alright," Derek nodded.

"Hey, you know Carly has been asking about you," Jake almost forgot to mention. "Maybe you could give her a call sometime or see her next time you're up here."

"Carly?" Derek was not sure who that was.

"You know. From my party," Jake widened his eyes to implicate that Derek knew this girl quite well, and even on a carnal level.

"Oh, Carly," he nodded. "Yeah, sweet girl."

"Jesus," Sherry shook her head, fed up with all of the cryptic language and gestures. "I hope you used a condom."

Both of the young men first displayed shock, and then hung their heads in a semi-embarrassed giggle. They tried to be courteous and respectful, but apparently, they overdid it.

"Mom," Derek sought relief from her imploring gaze.

"What?" she defended herself. "You're a grown man. I'd be a fool to think you weren't getting some here and there. I just hope you're protecting yourself."

"Okay, okay, Mom," he laughed. "Yes, I used protection. And can we please change the subject," he shot Jake a look that indicated for him to find a new topic."

"So North Carolina, eh?" Jake answered his friend's request.

"Yeah," Derek gladly replied. "Camp Lejune. I was kind of hoping for San Diego, but I got the dirty south, instead."

"What's wrong with North Carolina?" Sherry inquired. "I hear they have nice beaches there."

"And fine-ass southern belles," Jake chimed in with the usual immaturity.

"Oh yeah," Derek replied. "And toothless rednecks, mosquitoes the size of this 737 I'm about to get on, and a climate in the summer like the inside of somebody's mouth!"

"What do they have you doing there?" Jake asked.

"Well really, my training's not done," he explained. "I've got drills and general training exercises, but I've also got some specialty training stuff to do."

"Specialty? In what?"

"To be a…specialist. You know. Like in demolitions or something."

"That would be cool. Get to blow shit up for a living!"

"Hey," a voice came from far off to the side. "You're going to have to move that car! You've goodbyed for long enough."

They looked over to see a balding TSA employee sticking his chest out through his white button-down uniform shirt with authority. He was clearly the type of man who had always wanted to be a cop, but could not make the cut. He likely had a controlling wife at home, and the airport was the only place that he could exert control.

"Hey," Jake shot back at him. "Can't you see that my boy here is about to go off to defend this great country? Who knows how long before we see him again? His mother is going to miss him dearly!" Jake motioned to Derek's camouflage fatigues, combat boots, matching cover, and his duffel bag. "Cut us a break, dude."

"Alright," the TSA man said reluctantly. "Finish up your goodbyes and get that car out of here. There are others trying to get in and drop off their departures, too."

The three of them did not say anything to one another for several seconds. Their rapport had been broken, and the conversation was dead. Perhaps there was nothing more to say. This was it. Derek was about to leave for his first assignment of duty, and all were apprehensive about it. Finally, Derek stretched his hand out to embrace Jake's, and they pulled one another into an ultra-masculine hug, complete with firm back slapping.

"Love you, man," Jake smiled. "Take care of yourself."

"I will," he nodded as they both stepped back.

"I'm so proud of you," Sherry moved in for her turn, touching his cheek, smiling, and finally embracing him like only a mother could. "Be careful."

"I will, Mom," he hugged her back, and then kissed her cheek.

"I love you, son. Keep in touch."

"I will," he stepped back. He picked up his duffel bag, threw it over his shoulder, and smiled at his friend and teary-eyed mother. He then turned, and walked across to the automatic doors. They slid open, allowing him access, and he disappeared into the dimness of the airport.

Chapter 18

Inauguration Day, plus four

The silvery aluminum and glass doors opened into the cool January night air as throngs of patrons clad in sweatshirts and coats poured out of the theater, bringing with them the distinct aroma of popcorn and butter. Amongst those in the crowd, Kyle and Ashley strutted out beneath the bright lights illuminating them from the awning above. They said nothing at first, but each of them smiled. They did not even really look at each other, perhaps in awkwardness. They had not the need to make conversation during the movie. All they needed was body language, and that conversation was a good one. Her legs remained crossed with her foot touching his blue jean-clad leg much of the time. A few times, their hands touched with a spark of attraction before each of them retracted.

They stood outside the theater for several moments before they turned to each other. Ashley pulled her long brown hair out from inside her dark gray overcoat, and let it drape down over her shoulders. Kyle looked out across the full parking lot and across at the cars zooming down the interstate highway as he brushed embarrassing bits of badly-aimed popcorn from the front of his black leather jacket.

"So did you like it?" Kyle suddenly turned to his date.

"Hmm?" she quickly turned her attention to him.

"The movie," he clarified. "Did you like it?"

"Um," she thought, "it was pretty entertaining. It was a little predictable."

"Yeah, I see that," he agreed as they began moving slowly out into the lot. "And I thought the part of the fiancée was miscast. She was too one-dimensional."

"Yeah, she almost had no purpose," she nodded. "I think a lot of that is writing. She needed to be a bigger part of the plot and the action, and they needed someone with a bigger name. She was a no-name."

"It was entertaining, though," he added.

"Right. Not an Oscar winner, but it was entertaining."

Kyle began laughing as they neared his father's car. She grinned, turning toward him, back straight, and back again. She could not figure out what he was chuckling about, and finally she asked.

"What's so funny?" she giggled.

"Oh," he began, choosing his words wisely. "I don't know if you can tell, but I haven't had many girlfriends—not that I'm jumping the gun with you. I just haven't had many. And I haven't really been on that many dates."

"I don't know why," she interrupted. "You're a cute guy."

"Well," he smiled and blushed. "Thank you. I guess I'm just not very assertive, and when I am, it's with the girls that aren't interested in the nice guy."

"Nice guys definitely don't finish last," she grabbed his arm.

"Well, what I was going to say was that any time I've been to the movies with a girl, I've never been able to have a conversation with her about it," he explained.

"You mean analyze the movie?"

"Yeah. It's usually, 'did you like it?', and a 'yes' or 'no'. I guess I wasn't expecting to be able to do that with you."

"I'm not like most high school girls. I have a brain, and I like to use it."

"I didn't mean…" he back-pedaled.

"I know," she reassured him. "Sometimes I like the mindless action flick, but I prefer a movie I have to think about."

"Me too," he smiled.

"And regardless of whether or not it's that kind of movie, I like to analyze everything from the writing to the screen shots and casting."

"I'm the same exact way," he agreed. "Usually, the only person I can do that with is Ryan."

"You two spend a lot of time together," she commented.

"Well yeah," he shrugged. "He's been my best friend since second grade. We were thinking about going to the same college, and rooming together, but it doesn't look like his grades are going to be good enough."

"Well you've got plenty of time, still, to figure that out."

"Where are you going to school?" he asked her.

"I'm going to stick close to home and go to TCU," she nodded.

"I got accepted there, too, but I haven't made up my mind. I got accepted to UT and A & M, too. I don't know. I don't know if Ryan will be able to get into any of those schools."

"You can't look after him forever, you know," she told him. "I mean, at some point, you have to do what's right for you."

They arrived at the silver Infinity, finally, and as they did, they stopped, and faced one another. They did not move to get into the car, and Kyle could not figure out what the next move was. Did they continue the conversation? She had to be getting cold. But he did not want to end what seemed to be a good chain of events. If he rushed her into the car, it would be as if he were ushering in a premature ending to what could become a more exciting night. They looked into each other's eyes for a long moment, while he tried to formulate the next move or conversation piece.

Suddenly, Ashley made up his mind for him. She leaned in, and pressed her soft, pink lips against his. It startled him at first, sending a wave of anxiety and excitement through him. His heart beat rapidly but finally calmed, and he wrapped his arms around her waist to pull her closer. He turned his head slightly to the side as their tongues met at the tips, and they enjoyed the soft, but passionate kiss for quite a few moments. They mutually retracted their lips, and gazed into one another's eyes, smiling sweetly.

"Wow," she softly uttered. "Are you sure you haven't had a lot of girlfriends."

"I guess I'm just a natural," his little boy face turned slightly more pink.

"What are we doing next?"

"Um," he thought for a moment, "ice cream?" he opened her door.

"To start with…"she grinned and slipped into the passenger seat.

Chapter 19

February, Sixteen months before the bomb

"Controversy today on Capitol Hill as congress passed the president's 'Hope for America' stimulus bill," the anchorwoman broke the news, her well-painted face taking up a great deal of the television screen. "Democrats are calling this bill, which calls for hundreds of billions of dollars worth of government spending, a 'necessary evil,' while many Republicans are livid that such a bill was allowed to pass in such an economically tight time."

"It's irresponsible," the screen cut to a Republican congressman from Idaho, who gave a press conference after the vote. "With all due respect to the president, she has no clue how the economy works, and her Democratic cronies in the Senate and the House are obviously following her blindly into the oblivion that she is leading us into."

"Now Republicans may be upset at this time," the anchor continued, "but Democrats are celebrating this vote as a victory for the American public. Here's what President Chandler had to say earlier today."

"I know times are tight," the screen displayed the president's outdoor press conference in the rose garden. Her hair and beautiful skin were bathed in the pure February sunlight on this unusually warm day. "Many Americans are wondering why the government has decided to spend more money when there's less of it to go around. It's an investment in the future of the United States. It will bring our country into the educational system of the future. It will insure that our roads and bridges will still be around for generations to come. And in a time when unemployment is the highest that it's been in more than three decades, this stimulus will provide jobs to millions of Americans over the next two years."

The screen suddenly went black with an audible electronic click. Sullen expressions were plastered across the faces of the four men sitting in the plush, brown leather couches and chairs of the well-furnished office. The rather large space was lined with book-filled shelves and paintings, providing an academic atmosphere. Colorful rugs sprawled across the hardwood floors beneath the heavy oak desk, the couches, and the antique coffee table.

The men seemed to quiver in their expensive suits and Italian leather shoes as they hung their heads and sipped their scotch, each in an awful mood. They each looked as though they had just seen the final seconds of a football game pass to zero, and their favorite team came up short of the win.

"Well, that's where it's at," Ronald Cowart, a senator from Florida stood up, and tossed the remote control onto the chair where he had been sitting. He ambled over to his small wet bar, and removed the crystal stopper from the top of his decanter full of scotch. "Nothing we can do about it now. If only Davenport had kept his pecker in his pants," he sulked as he poured himself another drink.

"That woman is not going to be happy until she bankrupts this country," one of the men shifted on the leather couch to turn toward Cowart. In the process, he slid atop the leather, producing the mock sound of flatulence, to which the other men in the room had to restrain themselves from laughing. "If she knew anything about economics, she'd know that all we had to do is ride this whole recession thing out, and it would even itself out. I mean, it's a market economy. By nature, everything evens out. Supply and demand set prices, wages, and even insurance rates. Eventually, spending would go up, businesses would make money, and unemployment would go down."

"Yeah, but the Democrats cater to that younger crowd," another man spoke. "They, and Americans in general, can't wait that long. They have to have everything now. Instant gratification. That's why we're the most medicated country in the world. That's why we have such high teen suicide rates. It's got to feel better NOW. It's got to get better NOW," his temper began to rise.

"Well what do you expect?" Cowart interjected. "It's the information age. If you want to know something, you can find the answer on the internet in a matter of seconds. The world is at your fingertips. You don't even have to leave your house to go shopping anymore. You can order diapers, hemorrhoid cream, and condoms online and have them shipped to your door. Hell, I remember a time when if you wanted to watch a porno, you had to get off your ass and go to an adult movie theater. Now you can find whatever kind of porn you want in a matter of seconds! The American public is an agoraphobic crackhead that's got to feel better now, and that's the way the Democrats want it."

The room was still and silent for a long moment. No one moved on the leather upholstery. No one coughed. No one even sipped their scotch. It was pure silence, contemplation, and thought.

"So what do we do?" one of the men broke the silence as he adjusted his glasses.

"Nothing," Cowart spoke into a sip of his drink. "There's nothing we can do except pray that she doesn't screw this country up too bad within the next four years, and try to get one of our guys elected at that time."

A strange noise pierced the air within the luxury office. It was foreign, unlike the constant chatter and rhetoric of GOP conversation. It was cold, electronic, and irritating. It was enough to break the men from their alcohol and defeat-induced trance, and cast their gaze upon the man in the chair at the far end of the room.

He hastily rummaged through his pockets to find the source of the distraction. He was embarrassed, although all of these men had smartphones, and at any time, any of them could have begun ringing. He finally reached into the inside pocket of his gray wool winter suit, and extracted his phone, pressing the "ok" button to reveal an e-mail. For a moment, he read, and his face changed from embarrassment to shock.

"What?" one of the men noticed his expression.

"It appears the party isn't going to just sit around and do nothing," he looked up and faced the men in the room.

"What, impeachment?" Cowart blurted.

"I just got an e-mail from Governor Spencer back home in Austin," he continued with his typical Texas hill country drawl. "Apparently he copied me on an e-mail to all of the Republican governors in all of the red states."

"Well, what does it say?" one of the men sat forward in his seat, anxious to hear what the message read.

"Let me read it. 'As a faithful member of the great Republican party, I am contacting you all in an urgent plea to stop this madness in Washington. No longer can Cindy Chandler and the Democrats at the federal level be trusted with the well-being of the nation and its people. I am hereby inviting you all to join me at my ranch near Mason, Texas, to discuss the means by which we will deal with the mismanagement of our government and our taxpayers' money. We must separate ourselves from this wasteful spending and look after our own people in any way we can. I look forward to seeing you all this Friday, and I hope you can fit it into your busy schedules. Sincerely, Jack Spencer.'"

"Oh Shit," Cowart placed his right hand over his eyes, and rubbed his temples as if he were developing a headache.

"What?" one of the other men perked up. "What does that mean?"

"I don't know," Cowart lifted his eyes. He was playing dumb. He knew exactly what that message sounded like, but he did not reveal his anxiety. "But it doesn't sound good. This situation is going to get a hell of a lot worse before it ever gets better."

Chapter 20

The bell chimed down each hallway and within each classroom of the high school, signaling the end of the school day. Teenagers poured into the halls in droves, their weariness converting to relief, and even playfulness, as they interacted with friends. Up and down the hallway, teachers and administrators ushered students out into the commons of the school, urging and prodding them to leave the building. Most faculty members could not understand the student mentality of doing their best to get out of class, ditch school, sleep during lectures, and all of the signs of a lack of interest in school, yet when the final bell of the day rang, they never seemed to want to leave. They had to be forced by teachers moving them along like riot control officers, and by administrators with bull horns.

Kyle stopped and talked to no one on his way out, which was relatively normal for him. He was never very popular, nor was he ridiculed. He also wasn't invisible. He was somewhat of a coffee table in the school. He was not super important, nor was he useless. Often, he was simply there. Though he never loitered after school, he would in the past at least wait for Ryan, and walk out with him. Not lately. He traversed the crowded commons of the school, headed for the front entrance, his book bag thrown over his shoulder.

"Hey Kyle," he heard from behind him as he exited the building. "Wait up!!"

Kyle stopped between the two sets of doors, looking around behind him for who could be calling his name. As he suspected, Ryan was jogging toward him, almost thrown off-balance by the heavy book bag swinging over his shoulder. He had to slow every few steps to adjust and pull up his loosely fitting pants. Kyle waited, but did slowly begin to impatiently push through the last set of doors in reverse, as if in a hurry.

"What do you have goin' on today, dude? Wanna hang out? Play some video games or something?" Ryan smiled. It was awkward, as if the two had not spoken in a while. Neither of them knew quite how to act around the other.

"Sorry, man," Kyle gave an expression of genuine regret, "I'm already going over to Ashley's this afternoon. We're going to study for that Econ. test next week."

"Is that what we're calling it? Studying?" Ryan laughed.

"What the hell are you talking about?" Kyle smiled.

"Dude, don't try to bullshit me. I remember you telling me about you and her on the Ferris wheel or whatever a few years ago. She's giving you some, right?"

"Ryan, that's my girlfriend. I'm not going to talk about that stuff to you. It's disrespectful to her," he shook his head, lacking the heart to admit to him that the Ferris wheel thing was an immature lie to make him appear more experienced.

"What happened to you?" Ryan lost his smile. "What happened to the Kyle that used to come over and watch porn, and goof off? I never see you anymore, man. We've been best friends forever, and all of a sudden a girl comes along..." he shook his head.

"Ryan, we're still friends. Just because Shelley broke up with you doesn't mean I'm dating you. Ryan, wait," he tried to reach out to him, but Ryan was already walking away. A lump of guilt welled up from the pit of his stomach, and almost up to the top of his throat. He began to go after his friend, but was stopped by the honking of a car horn behind him.

Kyle turned around, already knowing the source of the horn. He locked eyes with his exceedingly beautiful girlfriend, who had dropped the ragtop in celebration of the first sixty-degree weather in weeks. Though preppy, her look, combined with the bright red sports car, was fitting for her. To add to her high school rock-star look, she had her luxuriously shiny, dark hair pulled back into a tight ponytail and wore a huge pair of designer sunglasses. A month after their first date, he still could not believe that this girl had chosen him. It was his dream come true. For years, he had chosen her as his dream girl. Most guys did not get to have their dream girls. He was lucky. And for that reason, his mind drifted from the betrayal that his best friend felt, and he ran over to his ride with a smile.

He hopped into the candy-apple red convertible with enthusiasm, smiling like a child as he leaned in for a brief kiss from his lady. As was usually the case, they just looked into one another's eyes for a few moments. The relationship was still heavily coated in newness. They were usually each still on their best behavior with one another, though they were beginning to grow comfortable enough to let their true selves shine through. A few days before, Kyle accidentally farted in front of Ashley, and rather than become appalled, she just giggled. The day before that, he caught her picking her nose when she thought he wasn't looking.

"What was that all about?" she glanced over his shoulder at Ryan sulking away.

"Nothing," he briefly peered back over his left shoulder. "He's pissed off that we don't hang out much anymore. He's just jealous that I have such a wonderful girlfriend," he went sappy as he leaned in for a kiss.

"Well go hang out with him," she awkwardly kissed him. "We're not married. You don't have to spend EVERY afternoon with me."

"I'm not smothering you am I?" he became suddenly paranoid, his eyes ablaze with worry.

"No, no, no," she shook her head. "I just don't want you to neglect your friendships on my account."

"No, it's fine. He'll be fine. I'll hang out with him later. We've been friends forever. We'll get through this. Besides, you're a better kisser than him," he smiled.

She smiled back, and all in one motion, she shifted into gear, and peeled out of the parking lot like a racecar driver. Kyle looked around at all of the other students, either loitering in the parking lot with friends, getting into their cars, or walking home. He began to feel unavoidably like a loser, riding with his girlfriend every day. The American standard was the macho guy picking up the hottest girl in school in his hot rod, and sweeping her away. But roles were reversed. Everyone knows that he walks to school every day with is buddy. Many knew that he had a broken down old muscle car rusting in the driveway, begging to be restored. So in that, he felt like he was the loser charity case—like Ashley had taken pity on him. Did her friends talk about him behind his back? Did they question why she was with this reject?

Yet, looking over at her melted those insecurities away in an instant. It was not anything that she said, necessarily. It was not anything physical. It was the way she looked at him; something in her eyes. She had the radio all the way up, and was singing loudly and smiling while she drove way too fast down the residential streets. Her musical tastes differed drastically from his own. He really got into classic rock favorites, blues, and rock, while she stuck to the electronic pop songs of the week. But from time to time, during her bubbly serenade, she sent him a glance of genuine affection, and it put him at ease.

After several left and right turns, screeching and squealing past naked winter trees and large uppermiddle-class homes, the red sports car roared into the inclined driveway of probably the largest and most luxurious house in the neighborhood. Though there were no leaves on the trees, no color to the grass, and the flowers did not bloom, one could tell that the lawn and gardens were professionally maintained. The chateau-style home featured lots of steep roof angles, exposed wood beams, and light natural stone.

She put the vehicle in park, as both exited and began moving toward the front door. Ashley skipped giddily and happily as she fumbled with her rather large bundle of keys that seemed to be mostly made up of brightly-colored girly key chains. She finally found the correct key as Kyle kept his distance in apprehension. She inserted the key with the typical clicking of the pins in the tumbler, and turned, opening the door into the cavernous foyer of the house.

Kyle was slow to move forward. He wasn't sure why he was so apprehensive. It was not the first time he had been to her house. He kept waiting for Ashley's father to pop his head through the door, someone he had never met. He wondered how the man would like him. Would he approve or be protective of his little girl?

"You coming?" she backed out of the doorway.

"Um, yeah," he moved forward. "Your parents home?"

"Oh no. Never. They're not here that much," she chuckled and shook her head.

He looked around at his surroundings; always in awe of the beautiful space. White marble covered the floors of the foyer, which led into near-white carpeting in the formal living area to the left. There were plenty of tall windows that allowed natural light to wash over the interior of the home, brightening it in an appealing way to the eye.

"What do they do?" he followed her up the spiral staircase to the bedrooms above.

"My dad is a VP at a medical software company in Las Colinas, and Mom is a lawyer in Dallas, so they pretty much live at work," she loudly stomped up the carpeted stairs.

"Hmm," he did not know what to stay. "Wow, so you guys never really see each other? Not even on weekends?"

"In theory, we would see each other on weekends, but Mom is usually at some kind of women's club event, like a bridge game or something. Dad's either hunting or playing golf and drinking beer at the nineteenth hole."

"So you kind of fend for yourself? Even for dinner? You never have dinner as a family?"

"No, not really. Rarely," she hung her head a bit. "But I have my car, and they let me go shopping for clothes, and now I have my wonderful boyfriend to keep me company," she took his hand and smiled as she led him into her bedroom.

The comment sent up a red flag in his overactive, insecure mind. She was an only child, and seemed to have no one around to keep her company. He could not help but think that this was the only reason she kept him around. Was he something to keep her busy? Nevermind. She was beautiful and he did not care.

Walking into Ashley's room was always refreshing for Kyle. In any social setting, she almost seemed to have stepped off of a cover of *Vogue* magazine. She had impeccable fashion sense and was always chic and well-groomed. But her style and demeanor sharply contrasted with the atmosphere of her bedroom. It appeared as though it had not been redecorated since she was six years old.

The bright white walls were covered with multiple-sized pink polka dots; in fact, everything in the room seemed white with pink trim, from the window treatments to the frilly comforter on the bed. The four-post bed was covered with stuffed animals and teddy bears accumulated over the years. There was a white vanity crowned by a framed heart-shaped mirror.

Despite being the bedroom of a little girl, there were, of course, the trappings of a modern teenage female. The costume beads and plastic bracelets that once filled the heart-shaped jewelry box on the vanity were now replaced by fine white gold and diamond pendants and earrings. Stacked haphazardly beside it were a few recent issues of *Cosmopolitan* magazine picked up at the last minute in the checkout aisle. Atop the desk in the corner was an open laptop computer surrounded by the textbooks Ashley did not need that day, pens and highlighters strewn about, and an MP3 player still docked to the laptop.

Kyle stood about without purpose as his girlfriend moved about the room as if he were not even there. She set her pink backpack down, leaning it up against the wall, and set down her designer handbag. She then began kicking off her brown leather boots on her way to the dresser. She opened the second drawer from the top, and rummaged around before deciding on a little plain white tank top. She closed that drawer, and opened the one below it, immediately extracting a pair of thin, pink sweat pants.

She walked right past Kyle, barely even glancing in his direction as she crossed the room to his left, and immediately dropped her form-fitting jeans to reveal her pink bikini-style panties. She removed her red long-sleeve blouse, and unfastened her bra with one hand. She did not face him completely, but enough that most could be seen. Kyle was still a little surprised that she did that. Though he had seen her nude before, it was still new and uncomfortable enough for him that he felt the impulse of respect kicking in. He averted his head to the other direction, but his eyes followed the protocol of animal instinct. He watched from the corner of his eye as she stepped into her sweats and pulled the tank top down over the curves of her torso.

"You can sit down on the bed," she began moving about the room again, smiling at him with affection. "You're so cute. Still so rigid and uncomfortable. Relax."

He smiled as he took her advice and admitted without a word that she was exactly right. As he sat on her frilly sheets, his back was stiff and upright. His hands were clenched together into one giant fist, which rested in his lap. He was still on his best behavior, a throwback to how he was raised. He was in the bedroom of a girl that he had sex with, and still could not be at ease or comfortable.

"I'm just going to check my e-mail," she walked over to her desk, jiggling the mouse, and clicking to log in. She pulled up her web-based mail provider, and briefly glanced over the latest headlines on her way to the *check mail* button.

"Oh my God," she uttered with astonishment and wide eyes.

"What?" Kyle was surprised with the sudden words of shock.

"Turn on the TV," she stumbled over her words as he frantically searched for and found the remote control on the bed. "Find a news network—any network."

Kyle was trembling as he pointed the remote control at the flat screen on her dresser. He had no idea what he was to find or what had caused such a stir with Ashley. Anxiety mounted in anticipation of what he would find. Images of terrorist attacks and terrible natural disasters in U.S. cities filled his head as he brought up the channel guide, and scrolled down through the channels in search of a news network.

"There it is," Ashley pointed out that there was a news channel on the guide. "That one will do."

Kyle pressed the down key until the news channel was highlighted, and then he pressed *ok*. He felt his heart drop into the pit of his stomach as the guide disappeared and the screen switched to the programming at hand. Luckily, it was just returning from some fast food commercial that was ruining one of his favorite classic rock tunes for the sake of advertising recognition and conditioning. The images on the screen switched to that of a handsome young man in a nicely tailored suit, sitting behind a news desk. *Breaking News* emblazoned the top of the screen.

"If you're just joining us, we are covering a breaking story," the young man began with a stern kind of look. "It seems that between yesterday and this morning, twenty-nine states have held emergency special sessions of their legislatures, each calling together successful votes to secede from the United States of America. We don't know much about the situation, like whether or not these states will be forming their own central government, but what we do know is that this seems to be an organized move, as all have done this within a twenty-four hour period. All states are predominantly Republican states. There are also reports that Texas Governor Jack Spencer may have been a major player in organizing a unified secession of states. Remember that this sort of thing has not been experienced in this country since 1861, and certainly the White House and Capitol Hill are reeling in shock from these actions. We're going to show you a map with the twenty-nine states claiming that they are no longer members of our union."

The shot switched to a large sound stage backed by a huge video screen featuring a map of the United States. It featured the states that had not seceded colored in blue, and red states that had split from the union. The news anchor had stood up from behind his desk and walked out in front of the screen, pointing up at the map as he spoke.

"Okay, here is a map that will show you which states have seceded," he began. "And I imagine that many average citizens in each of these states are just receiving news of this secession. Let's start in the west. As you can see, California, Oregon, and Washington, notoriously liberal states are isolated away from the rest of the blue states, while most of the western half of the U.S. has in fact seceded. Idaho, Wyoming, Montana, Utah, Nevada, Arizona, New Mexico, and Colorado are all secessionists. And then there's this central plains corridor. Every state from here in Minnesota and North Dakota, down through Texas, which is thought to possibly be the instigator of this act, are all secessionists as well. In the eastern half of the country, it almost looks as if this has followed the same pattern of secession that was followed just before the Civil War. All of these states here in the Deep South have seceded, with the exception of Kentucky, and unlike the secessions of 1861, West Virginia has broken from the Union, and so has Maryland. Hawaii and Alaska seem not to have seceded. So that's all we really know right now," he folded his hands and squared up with the camera. "But we have word that some spokesmen for these red states will be holding a press conference soon, and we anticipate a statement from President Chandler later this evening."

Kyle and Ashley both sat upon her bed, hunched forward with mouths wide open and expressions of shock. They briefly glanced at each other in silence, but immediately returned their attention to the story unfolding on television. Neither of them had fully allowed this news to sink in. It was inconceivable to think of what this meant, exactly, and neither of them really knew how they felt about it. In a way, perhaps, both of them kept thinking that maybe someone in the news room had gotten faulty information, and a quite mild situation was blown well out of proportion. But deep down they knew this was not so. They were now experiencing history in the making, and only time would tell how their lives would be affected.

Chapter 21

"This is a decision that pains us all," Governor Spencer spoke from behind a podium on the front steps of the Texas State Capitol in Austin. "All of us who are involved in this act are ardently patriotic Americans. We believe in the Constitution. We believe in the Bill of Rights. And it is precisely for this reason that we have taken this action. Like our ancestors in 1861, we believe that we should remain loyal to our Federal government only as long as they are true to the original concept of our nation. This great experiment in government that we know as the United States of America can only work if states are allowed to remain free of the tyranny of the central legislature in Washington. We are a band of individual states, or even countries if you will, complete with our own governments and systems of law, and we are only to submit to our federal overseers when the greater good of the country and the American people are involved. But we feel that Washington has overstepped a line. They have become too powerful, greedy, and hungry for control. They have impressed upon us their will and their irresponsible decisions for the last time. So many of our founding fathers that even members of the Democratic Party hold upon a pedestal felt this way, as well. Men like Thomas Jefferson, in penning the Declaration of Independence, used the wisdom of Enlighteners such as John Locke, Rousseau, and Montesquieu, to demonstrate the point that when the government of the people has wronged them or misused their power, we should throw off the shackles of despotism, and seek perfection in legislature elsewhere. It is for this reason that twenty-nine states have successfully given notice to the U.S. government that they are no longer our lords. We intend to band together to form a more perfect union, and with that, I announce that delegates from each of the twenty-nine shall meet here in Austin in one week to embark upon the task of forming a new union of states—one in which we can practice our own views of government. Thank you," he stepped away from the podium, despite the insistence of the press to answer questions.

"And that's where we are, Madam President," the Chief of Staff, Michael Darrin muted the television at the far end of the long, wooden table within the dimly-lit White House Situation Room. "You know as much about this as the rest of the American people. We haven't had much communication with these red states, and Intelligence wasn't really expecting this. Unfortunately, also, the CIA is headquartered in Langley, Virginia, which is a secessionist state."

Chandler sat there for a long moment, unable to speak, and unable to even move. She stared deeply into the muted television screen, deep in thought. She had never anticipated anything like this would happen during her administration. Who would? Certainly, Lincoln never saw anything like this coming. Bush never foresaw the attacks of September 11th. She thought she would be faced with the task of repairing the U.S. economy, and that she was prepared for. She was not prepared for this.

"Madam President?" Darrin pressed.

"What do we do?" Chandler looked around, weary and tired. "Military action? I mean, this isn't some country halfway around the world invading their neighbors and committing mass genocide. These are Americans. How do we attack our own citizens?"

"Well, according to Spencer and all these other lunatics, they are no longer citizens of our country," General Harlan Bates of the Army said smugly, cross-armed in his heavily-starched dress uniform.

"We can't go immediately to warfare, General," she shook her head at him. "We have to think diplomacy, first, or else risk living up to Governor Spencer's accusations of despotism. What else do we know?" she propped her head up on her up-stretched fingers, and massaged her forehead.

"Um, not that much," Darrin shuffled through some papers on the table before him. "We're pretty sure most of the House and Senate delegates from these states are on board for this, and I'm sure some knew about it before it happened. They are all clearing out their offices and preparing to head back to their home states. And then there are some

Republican sympathizers in Congress from blue states that are resigning their posts and doing the same."

"Jesus Christ," she hung her head. "I'm going to be remembered as the president that let the whole damned country fall apart during her administration. And no female president will ever get elected again."

"Cindy," Vice President Coffman said with a gentle and reassuring tone, "don't let yourself go to the dark side. You can do this. We're all behind you," he said as she nodded.

"General Bates," she tried to regain her composure, "do you know what's going on at the military installations? If this thing escalates, somehow, into war, we need to know where we stand."

"How do you mean?" he replied with a raised brow.

"Well most of our military personnel have their own personal political views, General. How do we handle soldiers, sailors, and airmen of the Republican persuasion? Will they not be seen by their comrades as traitors? Will there not be tension?"

"Um," everyone could tell that he had not really thought about that. "Arrest them for dissent? I don't know."

"That's a tough one," Coffman interjected. "General Bates is right. You could arrest them, and that way, if there is a military conflict, the red states will be short on personnel."

"But on the other hand, they are Americans with the freedom of speech and choice of political affiliation," she thought aloud. "Once again, we can't risk appearing to be tyrants. During the Civil War, Lincoln suspended the writ of habeas corpus, and had people arrested without charging them for a crime, and he was largely unpopular for it. You see where that got him, huh? No, I think we have to preserve the freedom of choice in those men and women on our bases. For now, allow anyone who wishes to leave to do so. And if they want to stay, allow them to, but remind them that they have to follow orders. If there is a military conflict, they have to go. We can't have the other soldiers feeling like there is a traitor or spy in their midst."

"Done, Madam President," Bates nodded his head. "And what about our bases in the red states?"

"Oh, shit," she shook her head. "That's going to be trickier. Hopefully our red counterparts will allow the same to happen, but if they start taking Democrats on base as prisoners, we may have to strike."

Everyone became very quiet at the mention of a military strike on another American state. Their heads filled with endless scenarios and possibilities of things that could go wrong. No one had fully been about to wrap their minds around the complexity of this situation. There was so much to address militarily, economically, and politically. No one knew what was going to happen, and this was a frightening thought.

"Look," she pushed away from the head of the table and stood erect. "We've got some time to hash out some of the finer details, and a lot of the things we've got to deal with as they come up. Right now, I've got to address the nation, and reassure them that we are giving this thing our undivided attention. Be on alert," she said as she exited the room. "I'm sure we're going to have many more of these little chats."

Chapter 22

Derek's thick-soled boots clapped against the concrete floor of the mess hall as he moved down the chow line carrying his tray. There was never much to choose from in the mess hall of a military installation. The Marine Corps was not very concerned with flavor or spice. They were more concerned with quantity. They had thousands of base staff and infantry grunts to feed each day. He knew that as he accepted the plate of mystery meat, mashed potatoes and gravy, and peas. He then grabbed a little chocolate milk carton, and headed off to find a table.

The mess hall was quite large; big enough for almost a whole battalion, but not everyone on the base had lunch at the same time. It was done in shifts to help alleviate the pressure on the food staff, therefore it was pretty empty. There were a few small groups of friends that sat in clumps throughout the room, and then there were those like himself who usually ate alone. It was not that he had no friends, or that he was antisocial. He had made several friends in his bunkhouse, but none of them ate lunch at the same time as he did. So he took his tray of mediocre food, and found an empty spot at one of the long folding tables.

The plastic tray made that familiar plastic-on-plastic sound as he set it down. He removed his cover, and placed it on his knee as he sat. Immediately, he put a fork in his hand, and began hoisting food into his mouth.

"This is crazy," another Marine walked up to the other side of the narrow table. "What's going to happen, now?"

"I don't know, dude," his friend followed behind, both sitting right across from Derek.

The two high-and-tight jarheads continued their banter of disbelief, without really disclosing what the issue was. It was quite mindless, yet intriguing enough for Derek to perk his ears. He hesitated; unsure of what to say to these two men he had never met.

"What's..." he paused, and even stumbled over his words. "What's going on?"

"Seriously? You didn't hear?" one of the guys looked astonished.

"Um, no."

"Dude," the Marine leaned over the table, "a bunch of states broke off from the country yesterday."

"Like," Derek paused, "seceded? Like during the Civil War?"

"Yeah, a whole bunch of them. Like thirty, or something," he laughed in astonishment himself.

"You're joking, right?" he smiled. He peered at the two men across the table, waiting for a punch line. His eyes darted back and forth, still smiling. The notion was ridiculous. If they were going to play a joke, could they not choose something that was slightly more believable?

"No, man, I heard it from some Corporal this morning. I've heard other guys talking about it, too. And have you noticed," he leaned forward again, and pointed at Derek, "there have been no top brass around all morning?"

Derek sat there for a long moment. By now, he had completely disregarded his lunch, not that it was very appetizing to begin with. There were too many things filling his head for him to handle. He could not quite wrap his mind around this idea. It felt almost unthinkable. Was this true?

"Why?" was the only thing he could manage to utter.

"All I know is that it's some kind of red state/blue state thing. All the states that split are Republican states," he tried to remember what he had been hearing. "Probably something to do with the economy and the stimulus bill."

"Well, which states seceded?"

"From what I understand, they're out west and in the south," he shrugged.

"So not Ohio..." Derek hoped

"Is that where you're from?" the Marine on the right asked.

"Oh, yeah," Derek shook his head at the absence of his manners, and smiled as he extended his hand. "Sorry man. Derek Putnam. And yeah, I'm from Ohio. Cleveland."

"Alex Jasper," the guy who told him of the secession shook Derek's hand.

"Jackson James," the other introduced himself.

"Jesus," Derek giggled, "you sound like a college star quarterback. You do realize that that you have a last name as a first name, and a first name as a last name, don't you?"

"Yeah," he sneered at the laughter of the other two. "I'm aware."

"Where are you guys from?"

"Oh, Connecticut," Alex spoke up. "Both of us. We went through basic together. Grew up together."

A sudden burst of commotion erupted across the mess hall, interrupting the friendly banter between the new acquaintances. Shouting of indiscernible words, accented by obscenities echoed through the spacious room as the small group in that area drew a slightly larger crowd. With the word "traitor" shouted by one of the men, the verbal assault turned violent. Fists flew between two angry men, as strikes to the jaws and eyes turned to the clutching of each other's fatigues. They fell to the table, and then rolled off onto the floor. As other men tried to help, others grabbed, punched, and kicked one another, quickly escalating things to the level of a typical bar brawl. A couple of soldiers ran out the door.

The brawl carried on for several minutes as Derek and his new friends watched on from a distance. They could see blood flowing from noses and lacerations around the eyes. They were pummeling each other. This was no ordinary drunken fist fight. These were Marines trained to kill with their bare hands. Perhaps it was this understanding that brought in the Military Police so quickly. A dozen flowed into the mess hall, and began pulling apart the involved, carrying them out of the building, some with ease, and some with a lot of hardship and struggle.

"Jesus Christ…" Jackson turned back to his friends.

"Yeah, I have a feeling this is going to get worse," Derek commented, but was suddenly interrupted by the feedback in the intercom speakers.

"Attention," the sound pierced everyone's ears. "All Marines and staff are to report to the parade grounds at thirteen hundred. That's half an hour. Do not be late. That is all."

"Oh shit," Alex rolled his eyes upward at the speakers in the ceiling. "Here goes."

The temperature was peaking in the low 70s by one o'clock. The sunshine blanketed the parade grounds as Marines and staff marched in by the platoon, and orderly formed into companies, and finally a battalion. Men and women stood at attention, perfectly aligned in every direction on the grass of the grounds. Silently, they faced the long stage and short rise of bleachers behind it, unsure of what this may be about. Sergeants and Corporals stood out in front of the men, facing the stage, sure that they had successfully assembled their Marines. Fully-armed MPs flanked each side of the formation of soldiers, but many looked from the corners of their eyes, and they noticed that their numbers were short. There were far more MPs on such a major Marine Corps installation than were present at the moment.

After several minutes of waiting, finally, the brass marched up to the stage, ascending the metal stairs with rattling and clanking of its joints. Derek counted thirty-six high-ranking officers upon that stage, all clad in their normal green dress uniforms, and all displaying a stern expression almost of pessimism. There were certainly more ranking officers on this base than stood before those Marines.

From amongst the ranks stepped the ranking officer of the entire base, General Nathan Hutchison. Four polished brass stars glimmered upon his shoulders and a gold cord hung about his left shoulder. The left side of his chest was a checkerboard of colorful decorations, cresting above five medals of distinction. He was a shining example of an experienced and respectable Marine. Through wartime and peacetime, he had distinguished himself as a man of honor and capability.

"Marines and staff," he spoke into the microphone aloft above the podium, sending his southern drawl echoing from the outdated loudspeakers and across the parade grounds. "I'm gonna keep this short and to the point. No doubt, many of you have heard rumors. I'm here, unfortunately, to confirm those rumors. We have confirmation that yesterday, no less than twenty-nine states have chosen to cut ties with the United States government, and venture out on their own. These are all states that are majority Republican, mostly in the south, and west of the Mississippi River. This is a Democrat/Republican issue, and I'm sad to say we will all have to make a tough choice. I have received word from the President as to what is to be done. Unfortunately, I have also gotten an order from the governor of North Carolina claiming this base as state territory," he paused for a long moment, as Derek and other Marines subtly reeled from the news, and hung onto every one of the general's words.

"I'm a native of the great state of Tennessee. I am also a Republican. I love my state. I love my country. I love my Corps. This decision was tough for me at best. I've spent nearly forty years in the Marines, and I've served my country loyally. But do I sell out my political views for the sake of my career? Or do I piss it all away, shifting loyalty to my political party and the power of a state government?" he paused once more.

"It is with regret that I have decided to stay on in command of this base, but under the authority of the independent state of North Carolina," he spoke clearly as gasps erupted from the staff below him. "Effective immediately, there will be a restructuring on this base. I have already relieved ranking officers whose loyalties lie with the U.S. government. Now it is your turn. If you are from a blue state, and you aren't a card-carrying, registered-to-vote Republican, by state order, you are relieved of duty and will return home. If you are from a red state, and you are registered Democrat, you will also ship out to a blue state. For the rest of you, it is a choice. No matter where you are from, or whether you leave by choice or by mandate, if you remain loyal to the United States, you will be shipped out to the nearest U.S. military installation still within the union. That would be Wright-Patterson Air Force Base in Dayton, Ohio. A bus will leave at zero-nine-hundred tomorrow morning. So it's time for you to decide where your loyalties lie. For those of you on your way out, I won't allow any aggression toward you. I won't have it. Good luck to you. Now go and get your shit together. Dismissed."

He and the other brass walked off the stage as confusion set in amongst the men. Normally, platoons reformed and marched back to their respective areas of the base in an orderly fashion. But it was as if the chain of command had no more meaning. Those who knew that they were shipping out in the morning wandered aimlessly about, no longer feeling that the rules applied to them. They were now unwelcome amongst their own, though they were the ones who were still U.S. Marines, not these rebels. They wandered about and muttered in disbelief creating a unified incomprehensible mess of sound.

"Derek," Jackson shouted as he and Alex ran up to a visibly stunned Private Putnam. "Crazy shit, huh? We're Marines in occupied territory."

"I can't believe it," was all Derek could muster.

"Well believe it, Marine," Alex placed a firm hand on his new friend's shoulder. "We ship out tomorrow morning. I understand it's the closest thing we have, but I hate we're going to end up on a goddamned Air Force base."

"Yeah, well it might work out well for me," Derek replied. "They can't keep us on an air base. They'll probably give us leave until they can sort out all this shit and reassign us. But that's close to home for me."

"Oh yeah. I forgot. You'll be close enough to see your family in just a few days."

"Yeah, well maybe you two guys can come to my house for a few days before you head home. Meet my mom, have a few beers with my buddies. Hey, there are always a few loose broads around you can get to know."

"Sounds good," Jackson shrugged. "It's a date."

"Yeah," Alex nodded. "Now let's go get our gear together before the natives get hostile."

Chapter 23

A light tapping at the tall, white door resonated through the room, jolting Cindy Chandler from her concentration on not just issues with the growing rift amongst the states, but from normal, everyday bills and business that came with running a country. She looked up from the papers that lay before her on the Resolute Desk, and stared at the door leading into the Oval Office. She did not answer the knocking right away. For a moment, she pictured herself in the shoes of the presidents that preceded her. As she rested her chin upon her fists, her elbows firmly planted on the old wooden desktop, she wondered if this was how Lincoln felt when he learned that Fort Sumter had been attacked. She wondered if this was how Kennedy felt, sitting behind this very desk, just one of many to use it since Hayes in 1880, as he learned of the failed attack on the Bay of Pigs. How did Roosevelt feel, sitting at this desk, as he waited for the final reports from Pearl Harbor?

"Yes?" she finally composed herself, and answered the knock.

"Madam President?" the young female aide gently pushed herself into the room, laden with a thickly-loaded clipboard. She seemed like a lost puppy; wowed and disoriented by not only working in the White House, but overwhelmed with the current situation as well. "Um, General Bates is here to see you."

"Well, show him…" President Chandler stopped short, as the tall, aging officer pushed his way past the young aide with the typical forcefulness of a hardened military commander. Chandler smiled as she watched him barge in without being formally admitted, and watched the confusion on the flustered young woman's face. She tried to protest, but had no idea how to reprimand a member of the Joint Chiefs of Staff. All she could do was send astonished, protesting expressions toward the president, darting back and forth from her to the general.

"It's okay," Chandler smiled and reassured the aide. "You can go. Thank you. Shut the door please," she continued to smile warmly as the door shut.

General Bates ambled in, admiring, first, the beauty of this office. He had only been inside the space a handful of times, and he was floored by it each time. Its elegant, executive beauty was captivating, from the royal blue carpet and presidential seal to the gold and white accents of the walls and curtains. The historical portraits of past great presidents like Washington, Lincoln, and Jefferson reminded him of the history that had taken place within those walls, though Jefferson and Washington had never actually entered that particular office.

He made his way to the center of the office, ambling with a head hung in discontent and disappointment. His emotional status transmitted into his trudging gait as he passed the antique coffee table, and turned to face his president.

"You don't have good news for me, do you general?" Chandler shook her head in pessimism.

"I'm afraid not," he grunted in his already gruff voice as he crouched with his old and achy joints in preparation to sit on the beautifully upholstered white and gold sofa. "We sent out orders to every base in every red state on how to handle the changes. Unfortunately, all these red states claim those bases as state territory, and they sent orders of their own."

"Oh, Jesus," Chandler removed her glasses and buried her face in her hands. "How many bases did we lose?" her voice was a bit muffled by her hands.

"All but two," Bates dreaded delivering that piece of information. Chandler's heart sank. "Eglin Air Force Base near Pensacola, Florida, and Fort Polk in Louisiana. It turns out a majority of the bases in the red states are commanded by top officers who happen to be Republicans. And even the ones who had Democrats as top ranking officers had Republican subordinates that relieved them of command. They have rounded up any Democrats or anyone from a blue state, and shipped them out by bus to the nearest U.S. military installation over the borders as of this morning."

"Any fighting?" she hung her head, and then brought it back up to look Bates in the eye.

"From what I know, no combat. Just a few scuffles between individual soldiers," he responded. "The fact of the matter is that these red states have actually been very civil and respectful to our loyal service men and women. No persecution, no ill will."

"Well that's a plus," she commented, and then sat there for a very long moment, staring into space in contemplation over what exactly she wanted to say and do. Bates gazed at her for quite some time, anticipating her next decision. He actually grew impatient as it became obvious that she may not say anything for quite some time.

"Madam President," he broke the silence, "should we consider this open insurrection?" he opened his folded hands, his elbows resting on his knees.

"Are you kidding?" Chandler's head sharply turned as she snapped in frustration. "The whole damned thing's open insurrection! From the moment they decided to secede!" she closed her eyes and shut her mouth, trying to regain her composure. "I'm sorry, general. The stress is getting to me. I'm not getting much sleep."

"I understand, ma'am," he nodded.

"If you're asking if we should retake these bases by force, the answer is still 'no'," she said calmly. "The red states have labeled us as bullies and tyrants. If we go in and invade, what kind of message does that send to the world? The red states will have vindication. We WILL be the bullies they say we are. We don't need that kind of press right now. We need the rest of the world and the United Nations on our side."

"Understood, ma'am," Bates nodded.

"What's the situation on these bases that are getting the men and women from the red state bases?"

"Disorganization," he put it simply. "You've got Marines on air bases, army troops on navy bases—it's havoc. The people arriving on these bases often have no loyalty to that branch of the military, and don't feel that they have to take orders from the commanders there. They're just kind of wandering around aimlessly, and others have already hitched a ride home. They're short on sleeping space. They're short on food. It's a big damned mess."

"Okay," she thought for a moment. "Put these men and women on leave. Send them home for now. They've been through a lot. Let's let them be with family. If they're from red states, let them go back home, but give them the option to come back. In the meantime, have your staff work out the logistics of reassigning them to other bases."

"Done," he stood up, nodded, and exited the room. "It's going to work out, Madam President," he smiled as he walked out the door.

Passing the general at the entrance of the doorway, Donny Chandler smiled and nodded to him with respect, but uttered not a word. The general simply grinned lightly, slumping out of the office. Donny turned his head forward and smiled at his wife as he entered and shut the door behind him. She was still behind the presidential desk, hunched forward and resting her head in the palms of her hands. He noted that she looked tired. He had never seen her so exhausted and stressed in their twenty-year marriage.

"How are you doing, sweetie?" he tried to give her a sympathetic, yet cheery smile as he worked his way across the room, crouched, and sat upon the same place General Bates had just occupied.

She just lifted her head to display her weary eyes and expression of delirium and fatigue. Her mouth gaped open and her brow hung low as her forehead muscles wrinkled her skin in an attempt to hold her eyes open.

"That bad, huh?" he winced. "What did Bates have to say?"

"We lost all of our red state bases but two," she shook her head in disappointment. "This is not the presidency I wanted!"

"I know," he nodded in sympathy.

"I mean," she continued her rant, "I was supposed to come in and fix the economy and work on national security! Instead, I've lost most of our domestic military bases, I've got blue state bases with more than double the occupancy they were intended for, and over half of Congress is gone—they've already cleared out their offices and gone back to their red states. That includes Democrats from red states! They're no longer a part of the Union, so they have no state to represent! And now all these states are about to form another Confederacy! And big surprise—Bates wants to use military force! This is not the presidency I was supposed to have!"

"And I'm sure Lincoln said the same thing when he took office," he pointed out. "FDR sat right there at that desk thinking he was just going to fix the economy, too. I'm sure he said the same things you are when he got the news about Pearl Harbor."

"Oh please," she scoffed. "He knew that was going to happen. He was dying for a chance to enter World War II, and he let that happen so he didn't have to just settle for Lend-Lease anymore."

"Either way, things don't always turn out the way we plan. We have to adapt accordingly. Lincoln, FDR, Madison, and Truman all had to adapt, and they rose to the occasion. They did fine, and you're every bit as capable of a president as those guys. You'll do fine."

She hung her head, and then stood up, moving around the desk and across the room to the sofa that her husband was perched upon. She pouted her lips a little as she turned and plopped down beside him, nuzzling up to him. He wrapped one arm around her shoulder and pulled her tight, to which she responded by laying her head on his shoulder.

"I don't know what to do," she looked down at the presidential seal on the carpet. "Tell me what to do."

"I'll tell you exactly what you need to do," he looked down at her. She lifted her head a little, still resting on his shoulder. She was surprised at his response to her rhetorical question, so she waited eagerly for what he would say.

"You should get some R and R," he continued as his wife lifted one eyebrow in perplexity.

"What, like a vacation?" she pushed slightly away from him. "In the middle of the worst crisis since the 1860s? I can't just take off to the lake house in a time like this. I'll be Louis XVI heading to the Netherlands while people are suffering during the revolution!"

"You don't have to take a vacation, Cindy," he shook his head with a smile. "Just go to the driving range for an hour. Or come play a round of golf with me."

"To alleviate stress?" she laughed. "I might be better off and less tense dealing with insurrection!"

"Okay," he added another suggestion, "how about a bubble bath… with me."

"Ah," she grinned coyly. "But I thought I was supposed to relax, not get more excited," she rubbed his knee.

They smiled for a moment, and then it faded. Donny could tell that her mind was drifting back to her troubles. Now she just looked sad and worried. The situation was taking its toll; making her age beyond her years.

"Hey," he shook her shoulder. "You're going to be fine. We'll get through this."

"I hope so," she nodded and grinned. "I hope so. Now how about that bubble bath, Mr. First Gentleman," she looked up at him with a sinful grin.

Chapter 24

Restless feet shifted along the narrow back-seat floorboard of the compact car. For over three hours, they had desperately searched for an adequately comfortable place to rest, but with such little space between the front and back seats, and being attached to relatively long legs, the cause was lost. They just moved position every ten minutes or so, pushing aside trash like empty soft drink bottles and beef jerky wrappers.

Private Jackson James sat uncomfortably in the back seat. His legs ached from the calf to his buttocks. He had tried almost every position imaginable in order to get the blood flowing a little better. His back was stiff and his eyes were tired. The pungent, vinegar aroma of ketchup arose from the paper fast food bags on the seat to his left, filling the car. He looked past Derek in the driver's seat and out through the windshield at the interstate moving swiftly beneath the rental car. He turned his head to the right, peering out the window at a city veiled in overcast gloom.

"Are we there yet?" he whined in the manner of a child on a long family vacation.

"Don't make me stop this car, young man!" Derek turned his head slightly behind him as all three men began to giggle. "Actually, we are almost to my house," he added as he exited the interstate.

The car slowed on the way down the off-ramp, and stopped briefly at a traffic light. It changed to green, and Derek turned the wheel to the left, rolling into his neighborhood. His two new friends took in the sights of the dim little suburb with its crumbling homes badly in need of paint jobs and maintenance. The streets were lined with older cars that were in bad shape, some up on cinderblocks, and all dotted with traces of melting snow. The sidewalks were cracked and littered with random trash and clutter. The trees were naked and the grass was dead and yellow. Alex thought that somehow this neighborhood might actually look better during the spring or summer, but winter made an already decaying neighborhood look even worse.

"Guys," Derek said as he could tell that his friends were silently critiquing his hometown. "I have to warn you. I don't come from much. I probably should have told you this before I invited you to come and stay with me. As you can tell, this is a less affluent neighborhood. My dad split when I was young, and my mom worked in a textile mill for years until she got laid off. I was working as a mechanic to support me and my mother before I joined the Corps."

"Hey, man," Alex reassured him. "No worries. You don't have to be self-conscious. Besides, we're Marines. We're trained to adapt. We're trained to sleep in third-world jungles halfway around the world."

"Well, you don't have to rough it quite that bad," Derek smiled and chuckled in relief. "You'll at least have a couple of clean, soft beds—much softer than the concrete slabs at Lejune. You'll be in the room my two older sisters used to be in."

"Used to be in?" Jackson chimed in from the back. "You mean your sisters won't be in those beds waiting for us when we get there?"

"No, they're gone, too," he laughed. "They probably would have screwed you, too. No, they left a long time ago. They're a couple of junkie strippers living somewhere off in the northeast. And I'm pretty sure they've done some low-budget porn, too."

"Ah, internet stuff, huh?" Alex nodded.

The silver compact car hummed down the streets of the neighborhood at a moderate speed, rolling roughly over uneven patches of asphalt intended to repair potholes. They made a few lefts and rights, snaking through the declining subdivision until finally coming to a rest along the curb of Derek's house. To him, his family home looked worse every time he saw it. Not much had changed over the previous months, but it somehow looked worse. Perhaps it was psychological. He knew that his mother did not do much. In fact, lately, she was incapable of doing much.

The men in front opened the doors, and stepped out of the vehicle. Alex pulled a lever behind his seat, allowing it to lean and slide forward with enough space for Jackson to climb awkwardly from the back. Derek walked to the back of the car, inserted the key into the trunk's key hole, and popped it open so that they could all retrieve their military-issued olive drab duffel bags. Hoisting them over their shoulders, they began to move through the chain link gate, up the front walkway, and up onto the creaking porch.

"Mom," Derek opened and cracked the door, peering in cautiously. He had informed her that they would be arriving that day, so she was expecting them, but he did not want to risk walking in on her naked after a shower. "Mom, we're here!" he reaffirmed their presence.

"Come on in, sweetie!" a happy voice yelled from across the house.

He pushed the door fully open, leading his two comrades in across the threshold. Their boots pounded on the linoleum of the kitchen and resonated through the hollow, raised floor as they entered the run-down old house. It sounded like an invasion. Alex and Jackson looked around at the dated interior, yet not judgingly while Derek caught sight of his mother, trying her best to push up on the armrests of her easy chair. She scooted forward in the chair, and used both arm and leg muscles, struggling to stand erect so that she could hug and kiss her boy.

"Mom, are you alright?" Derek rushed to her with a look and tone of concern. She seemed exponentially worse; even deteriorating.

"Yeah," she grunted as she straightened her back and stood with his assistance. "I'm fine, dear. I just have a little trouble getting up these days," she smiled.

"Are you having trouble with your legs? I thought it was just your hands," he hugged her briefly, and then pushed away to examine her in worry.

"Yeah, my legs are starting to do what my hands are. They just don't work as well as they used to. Maybe I'm just getting old."

"Mom, you're forty-five, not sixty! Did you go to the doctor?"

"Yeah, I went to a neurologist last week, and they did all kinds of tests. They called me back the other day and said everything came back normal. They don't know what to make of it," she shrugged and threw her hands up, all out of explanations. "I'm supposed to go back in tomorrow morning."

"I'll take you," he nodded.

Her look of concern turned to that of affection in an instant as she looked into his face. A big smile spread across her aging face. Her right hand was placed upon his cheek. She laughed in happiness as she finally just threw her arms around her son, and embraced him.

"I'm so happy you're home!" she squeezed him. "It's so great to see you!"

"You too, Mom," he smiled and ended the embrace. "These are my friends, Alex Jasper and Jackson James. They're going to stay with us for a few days before they go on back to Connecticut. Guys, this is my mother, Sherry."

"Hi, Mom," they chanted in unison.

"How do you do?" she nodded and smiled. "Jackson James, huh? Are you aware that you have a last name for a first name, and a first name for a last name?" Everyone erupted in laughter as Jackson nodded and smiled, almost embarrassed.

"Gentlemen, you can take your bags down this hall and to the right. That will be the bedroom you will be staying in," she motioned to the hallway door. "Make yourselves at home. And for dinner, we'll order out for Chinese. Sound good?"

"Yes ma'am," they smiled, and started down the hall.

"Nice boys," she said to her son as they disappeared from sight.

Right about that time, the door swung open with great force, and Jake entered the house without knocking. It was his bull-in-a-china-closet style to begin with, but this had become even more common of an occurrence in the Putnam household over the last few months. Jake had been helping Sherry quite a bit in Derek's absence, and would often swing by the house after work to check on her. He even had his own key.

"Where's my brother?" he shouted and smiled, flinging the door open.

He rushed over to his friend, wrapping his arms around Derek in a very masculine, caveman fashion. He tightened his bear hug almost to the point of vicious attack, and picked the much smaller Derek up.

"God, it's great to see you, brother!" he slammed Derek back to the floor with a heavy thud, and then kissed Sherry's cheek. "I still can't get over this uniform," he tugged at the fatigues his friend wore.

"Good to see you, too, buddy," Derek smiled and shook Jake's hand once more.

Alex and Jackson appeared in the doorway of the darkened hall, both with a look of disorientation and confusion. They heard the commotion, and crept out into the common areas of the house hesitantly. Their "fight or flight" instinct enacted somewhat, not sure whether the commotion was friendly or malevolent.

"Hey! More Marines!" Jake shouted as he caught sight of the two men.

"Yeah, these are my buddies Alex and Jackson from down at Lejune," Derek introduced his fellow servicemen.

"Hell, yeah. Jake. Nice to meet you guys," he reached out and shook their hands. "The few, the proud, the LOYAL," he added. "What do you think about this crazy shit?"

"I don't even know," Alex shook his head. "One minute, it's business as usual, and the next, we're getting kicked off our base."

"Yeah, I don't know about the political side of things, but it's got all the bases and the entire military system screwed up," Jackson added. "The few established bases in the blue states are carrying the brunt of all loyal personnel. We got to Wright-Patterson, which isn't even a major, active base anymore, and we didn't have a place to sleep. They had to order catering from restaurants in Dayton to provide enough food for everyone."

"Damn," Jake shook his head. "Well this crap has been all over the news. I've never watched so much news in my life. They're saying now that the red states are forming their own country pretty soon."

"Messed up, man," Derek shook his head. "Who do those bastards think they are? Things aren't going their way, so they just get to give up? Drop out? They're like a bunch of angry kids on the playground at recess. The other kids don't want to play the same freeze tag rules that they do, so they throw a fit and start their own game."

"Heard that," Jake nodded. "So to celebrate you fine, loyal, U.S. servicemen, we're gonna have a little shindig at my place tonight," he smiled, and looked directly at Derek's new friends. "You guys ready to party?"

"Hell yeah," Alex smiled.

"After dinner," Sherry interrupted. "These boys need a decent take-out meal."

"Hey, Derek," Jake put his arm around his buddy's neck with near head-lock strength, and began walking him toward the door. "Come out on the porch with me. I need to talk to you."

Derek was a bit confused, and perhaps even a little more worried. He couldn't remember a single conversation with Jake that began this way. It seemed like a serious conversation from a man that rarely took anything seriously. They crossed through the threshold and into the chilly February air, closing the door behind them. Jake swayed back and forth as the boards beneath his feet creaked and squealed.

"You remember Carly?" Jake peered into his friend's eyes.

"Carly?" one eyebrow raised in thought.

"Dude, you do this every time I mention this girl. Is it that hard to remember a girl you screwed?"

"Oh, yeah. Your party last time I was here," he nodded his head. "Dude, you've got to cut me some slack. I was so drunk. I woke up next to her on the couch. I barely remember what happened."

"Yeah, well she wants you to call her," he said.

"Yeah, I might call her," he nodded.

"Yeah, that's what you said last time I talked to you about her."

"Why are you suddenly playing match maker?" Derek seemed annoyed.

"Man, just call her," Jake pulled out his cell phone, and scrolled through his contact list, and pushed the *ok* button to dial her number. He handed it to Derek, and walked inside, leaving his friend puzzled and listening to the ring tone.

"Hi, Jake," a sweet voice answered on the other end. That was something Derek surely did not remember. In fact, he did not remember a single conversational word that the two of them had ever exchanged. He just recalled snippets of her face throughout that night, her sitting in his lap, and a few memories of her naked body on the couch. He just could not get over the honey in her voice.

"Um, it's not Jake," he squeaked nervously. "It's Derek. You know, from the party?"

"Oh yeah," she smiled. "Good to finally talk to you again. I take it you've talked to Jake, then."

"Um, not about anything specific," he said. "What's going on?"

"Well," she started, and then hesitated. "I'm pregnant, and I'm pretty sure it's yours."

There was no response at first. Derek stood dumbfounded, his mouth hanging ajar as his eyes darted from one side to the other in thought. Images and worries filled his head. *How am I going to be able to take care of a child? I'm active duty. Am I supposed to marry this girl? What's my mother going to think?*

"You're sure?" he finally spoke up.

"Well, when we were together, I hadn't been with anyone in a couple of months, and I definitely haven't had sex since," she solidified the claim. "Actually, I haven't wanted to. I was hoping to see you again next time you're in town. You know, get to know each other a little better when we're both sober. You're going to Jake's tonight, right?"

"Yeah," he smiled. "Are you asking me out?"

"Yeah, I guess I am," she giggled back. "I guess you won't be totally sober, but at least we can start off that way this time."

"Yeah," he grinned. "I'd like that."

"Okay, well, I guess I will see you tonight at Jake's," she said. "Bye."

"Bye," he pushed the *end* key, and stood there for a long moment, trying to fully take in the implications of what he had just learned. He was surprised. He was worried, of course. But he was strangely at ease with this. He did not know why. Perhaps he felt positivity in Carly's vibe and demeanor. She comforted him without even trying to. Perhaps this would not be so bad. With that, he turned and opened the door, creeping inside slowly. All eyes were on him, especially Jake's.

"Mom," he smiled at his mother. "It looks like you might be a grandma soon."

"Uh oh," Alex whispered.

Sherry could not wipe the surprise, or perhaps even terror, off of her face. She could only seem to muster two words. "Oh shit."

Chapter 25

"Wow," Sherry looked around, speaking silently. "This is the nicest doctors' office I've ever been in."

"Haven't you been here before, Mom?" Derek raised his eyebrow.

"Once," she nodded. "It's still nice. Now I just have someone here that I can tell that to, instead of keeping it to myself."

"Neurologists," he commented as he took in the environment. "I'm sure they make all the money."

The truth was that it was a very nice office. The counter and sliding glass window where patients check in was a bit generic, but how does one spice that up? Other than that, the paint was a combination of earth tones, accented by beautiful white molding. There was even a chair rail that enclosed the perimeter of the waiting room. The window treatments were busy, yet they were not bright, and they went well with the rustic 19th century safari décor. Framed prints of old African maps and sketches of lions and giraffes hung strategically placed upon the walls. A large globe sat in the corner, where a young boy played with and examined it in exploration. Even the end tables and coffee tables almost seemed to be authentic antiques, yet something told Derek that they were very expensive replicas.

But it still had that smell—that sick smell. He hated being anywhere that medical care was given, from clinics to hospitals. It did not matter whether the clinic was a family practice with the smell of flu-infested children vomiting the entire contents of their stomachs or a neurologist's office that usually did not receive patients who were ill from germ exposure. The smell was always the same—sick; sterile.

"I still can't believe you got that girl pregnant," Sherry shook her head.

Derek felt blind-sided by that comment. He was left wondering where it came from as he leered up and smiled uncomfortably at the people walking past. Surely they had heard every word of what his mother had just said.

"You're not even married," she paused and thought. "I mean, how are you going to take care of a child?"

"I think it's going to work out, Mom," he reassured her, trying not to continue this conversation loudly.

"I guess I'm not one to talk," she shook her head. "Your father and I were properly married before kids, and you see how well that turned out."

"That's why we're not getting married," he peered into Sherry's eyes.

"You're not?"

"No," he continued. "We both agree it's a retarded idea to get married just because we have a kid together. For what? To keep up the appearance of morality and Godliness? What happens if we find out after marriage that we don't like each other? Won't the kid pick up on that? So he'll be unhappy aside from us being unhappy."

"Wow, you feel strongly about this," she said. "Good. I sometimes forget that you're an adult. You can make your own decisions. You're a grown man—old enough to vote, drink, and die for your county. Good for you," she grabbed his arm. "It sounds like you've talked to her quite a bit about this."

"We talked a lot last night," he nodded. "I enjoyed it. This isn't going to be a chore. You know, we agreed we wouldn't get married just because a kid is on the way. But that doesn't mean we're not taking steps toward a relationship," he smiled wide, as did his mother, still clinging to his arm.

"Putnam," a nurse in pastel blue and magenta scrubs appeared through the door leading into the back.

Sherry and Derek looked at one another as they stood. His arms were still locked together with his mother's, gently pulling up to help her. It was strange to him that she was having such trouble physically, when just a short time ago, she had no major ailments. He had never seen his mom so weak. She had always been a strong person, both physically and emotionally. She worked very hard in the mill for a long time. She showed amazing poise and composure when her husband left, and dealing with two trouble-seeking daughters was no task for the squeamish. Yet now, she had degenerated into a broken and worn version of herself.

He helped her slowly past coffee tables stacked with volumes of magazines from months past.

"How are you, Mrs. Putnam?" the kind young nurse gleamed as the two shuffled past her and her clipboard.

"I guess we'll see in a little bit, won't we?" Sherry responded with a forced grin.

The young nurse, probably fresh out of nursing school, had no response but her uneasy smile. Sherry noticed this. The girl behaved almost as if she had been attacked or something. Sherry was dissatisfied with the social skills of the younger generations. Someone her own age would have replied to her cynicism and nervousness with something encouraging or witty. This girl was a product of a generation of antisocial zombies. They have spent enough time texting, watching television, and surfing the internet to ruin them socially and emotionally. Of course, Sherry had become no better, spending most of her time since losing her job chain smoking in front of the television.

"This way, please," the nurse shut the door behind them, and then moved out in front, leading them to an examination room.

The scene was typical of a doctor's office. They walked past a nurse at her desk, advising a patient on an issue at home. Artwork randomly dotted the taupe walls of the hallway as they passed. There were scales and blood pressure evaluation stations. Staff members scurried around carrying open laptops displaying files and charts, while no doctors seemed to be anywhere around.

"Right here," the young nurse motioned to an open exam room. "Doctor Jenkins will be with you shortly.

Sherry and her son silently entered the room and lowered themselves slowly into the two dark gray, plastic chairs to the side of the paper-covered examination table. The door shut behind them as the air seemed to thicken around them immediately. Soon would be the moment of truth, and their surroundings did nothing but promote the mounting anxiety and dread. There were all manner of tools to poke and prod hapless victims in this office. Jars of cotton balls, swabs, and tongue depressors lined the gray countertops. They couldn't imagine why. There was a little hand-washing sink with paper towels, complete with a hole cut into the counter with a waiting trash can below. Aside from the posters and diagrams of all things nervous system on the wall, there was the over-present bin of used hypodermic syringes displaying the bright orange "biohazard" sticker on the front.

In most cases one would wait for quite some time in an exam room for a doctor to actually enter the room. That goes for any clinic. Both Sherry and Derek were fully prepared for this to happen. Not today. Barely two minutes passed before the door once again swung open, and in walked Doctor Jenkins in his thick, black eyeglass frames, a stethoscope hanging around his neck. Thick, dark hair plumed from beneath the sleeve of his white lab coat like an eighteenth century ruffle cuff. The animal-like paw gripped the doorknob as he pushed the door shut with finesse. It appeared that most of the hair atop his shiny head had migrated to the rest of his body, save the bit that circled just above his ears like Friar Tuck.

"Hi, Sherry," he sat into his low rolling stool, and crept toward them. "How are we doing today?"

"You tell me, Doc," she grinned painfully as she motioned toward the file in his hand.

"Fair enough," he returned her grin and nodded. "We've poked and prodded you enough, and as I kind of expected, every test we've run has come back negative. On paper, there's nothing wrong with you."

"On paper…" she nodded.

"But you see her hands and legs," Derek chimed in. "What do you mean you expected it?"

"Since you first came in with these very specific symptoms with the muscles in your hands, and now in your feet and legs, I've had a diagnosis in the back of my mind. But there's no real test for it. We have to rule everything else out, which we have. I've consulted with my colleagues and we all agree," his tone became somewhat soft and somber as they both hung on to every word. "We're diagnosing you with amyotrophic lateral sclerosis, or ALS for short."

"I've never even heard of that," Derek shook his head.

"It's not common enough for most people to have heard about it. It's not like cancer. And you probably *have* heard of it, but not by that name. It's commonly called Lou Gehrig's Disease."

"I have heard of that," Sherry nodded. "It's what Stephen Hawking had."

"Yes, but his was an extremely rare case where it just stopped progressing," the doctor said.

"You mean that smart guy that talks like a robot?" Derek chuckled.

"He talks like that," Jenkins lowered his brow, stern and almost reprimanding, "because he can't use his tongue or jaw muscles to speak. He speaks through a computer."

"Oh," Derek felt like a heel.

"This is what happens," the doctor continued to speak to Sherry. "It's in the same family as Parkinson's and multiple sclerosis. But this is a neuromuscular degenerative disease. The reason you are losing your mobility in your extremities is that your muscles have atrophy. This is caused by the nerves dying in those areas. Nerves don't just allow you to feel. They allow you to move. If the nerves die, the muscles don't move. If they don't move, they atrophy."

"So what? I'll be in a wheelchair for the rest of my life?" she threw up her hands.

"Yes," he nodded.

"I guess that's not so bad," she said.

"I haven't told you the rest," his eyes became softer. "It doesn't stop there. Your nerves are all connected. It's like a chain reaction; a fuse that's already lit. It works its way up your nervous system from your extremities into your body. It will eventually affect every muscle in your body. You will lose your ability to speak and chew food. You will be on a feeding tube. The last step is your lungs. We will have to check your breathing capacity frequently to make sure you're getting enough oxygen. In the end, we can keep you on a ventilator for as long as you want, but…"

"But eventually you'll have to pull the plug," she nodded in final understanding. "This is going to kill me."

"I'm sorry," he nodded regrettably. "If it makes you feel better, there was no *catching* of this disease. You can't get it from a germ or get it like lung cancer from smoking. We're really not sure what causes it."

"So what's the cure?" Derek asked. "What's the treatment?"

He paused for a long moment, perhaps to find a gentle way of putting it. Really, he did not know what else to say, so he put it bluntly.

"There isn't one," he folded his hands.

"What do you mean? Can't you do chemotherapy or something?" he began to get angry.

"It doesn't work that way. It's not cancer," he explained. "There has been some research to show that stem cell therapy may be the key to curing it."

"Stem cells?" Derek puzzled.

"It's what they get out of aborted fetuses," Sherry told her son with a touch of contempt for the subject.

"Originally, yes. They discovered embryonic stem cells through abortion, but since then, they've found that they can harvest stem cells from other places like bone marrow. Stem cells are basically cells that haven't decided what they want to be when they grow up. In Europe and Asia, they've successfully manipulated them to become whatever type of cells they want. They've even begun to build organs and some body parts for transplant patients. Theoretically, your own stem cells could be turned to nerve cells and repair your nervous system."

"Well let's do that," Derek nearly jumped from his seat.

"Can't," Jenkins put it bluntly. "There hasn't been enough research here in the US, and it certainly hasn't been FDA approved."

"Well why the hell not?" Derek fired back. "I bet if it were a cure for cancer or AIDS, they'd sure as shit approve it."

"Yeah, but those don't involve stem cells. You see, in the mind of the average American, stem cells equal abortion, no matter what. These are people that thought Reagan was the antichrist because his first, middle, and last name each had six letters. There's no changing their mind. Republican lobbies have manipulated lawmakers into voting down federal funding for stem cell research for years. That's beginning to change, but it's slowly progressing at best."

"God damn it!" Derek exclaimed under his breath. "These selfish bastards can't do for anyone but themselves. They don't like the president, so they form their own country. They don't like stem cells, so my mother has to die!"

"It's going to be okay," she rubbed his arm. "You're supposed to be comforting me, not the other way around."

"My suggestion to you is to get your insurance to buy you a motorized power chair. The less strenuously you move, the slower the progression will be. Plus, you're going to need it," Jenkins offered. "Hopefully, they will cover a helper or a nurse to come in and assist you periodically while Derek is at work."

"I'm in the Marines," he said. "Active duty. I was at Camp Lejune in North Carolina, and I got kicked out for being from a blue state. I'm just home until I'm reassigned," he explained, and then paused in thought. "Hey, you could come live with me on whatever base I go to. It might be San Diego."

"The VA hospital or sick bay on the base could probably be very helpful to you," the doctor commented.

A long silence fell over them. No one had anything else to say. It had been said, and all were in thought. Sherry was beginning her process of acceptance, surprisingly. Doctor Jenkins searched for a kind and comforting word, yet fell short. Derek, however, developed redness around the eyes as the anger and sorrow welled up from within him. Tears flowed down his face as he turned to his mother. He would now lose the only family he had left.

Chapter 26

March, Fifteen months before the bomb

The western sky was a Monet; a blurred combination of pastel pink and blue with fluffy lavender clouds crowning a brilliant orange horizon. It was as beautiful as Texas sunsets get, and sharply contrasted with the veil of black that draped over every tree and home in the neighborhood. It seemed appropriate that the last fleeting rays of the sun be accompanied by some background score of soft woodwinds and harps, but the closest it got to any tribute at all was a cuttingly obnoxious neo-punk anthem blaring from the red convertible scorching down the residential street.

Ashley's car barely even slowed before cutting to the left and into the driveway of the Perkins home. It came almost immediately to a stop, and then inched up the inclined driveway, resting parallel to Kyle's project car, covered with a pollen-coated tarp. Ashley shifted into park, and then set the emergency brake because somewhere along the way, someone told her that she should do that when parking on an incline to keep stress off of the transmission. She did not know if that was true, but she had been doing it ever since.

They both hopped out of the sports car, but each on different levels of enthusiasm. Kyle was quite excited for his family to finally meet his girlfriend. He was also fairly stoked that he could even call her that now. But she, conversely, stopped short of rushing up to the house and into the Perkins family. She stood in the driveway, her feet and hands together and her head hung slightly. If she could have crawled inside of herself, she would have. She transformed from a bubbly and outgoing young woman into a shy and introverted new kid in school with not a friend in the world.

"Are you okay?" Kyle approached with caution, gently touching her arm.

"Yeah, I'm okay," she glared up at the home, which stood like a castle on a hill, brightly lit by the garden floods.

"You don't seem okay," he smiled. "You seem kind of nervous, actually."

"I am," she nodded admittedly. "I don't think I've ever met the parents of anyone I've ever dated. I mean, I guess they never thought that was important."

"It's important to me," he smiled as he caressed her arm. "I care about you, and I want my family to care about you."

"That's what I love about you," she grinned. "You're so genuinely kind. But that still doesn't make me feel any less anxious. I mean, what if they don't like me?"

"Are you kidding?" he laughed. "My brother will think you're hot, and won't stop staring at your boobs. My dad will think you're hot, but not in a creepy way—just in a 'way to go, son' kind of way. And my mom will run up and hug you right away, and just go on and on about how beautiful you are. They will be mesmerized by your beauty, and then captivated by your personality. They'll love you for the same reasons I do," he said, realizing afterwards that he had just basically told her he loved her. Maybe she would not pick up on it.

She gave no indication either way. She just smiled, and her face lost the anxious tension. She nodded, and then took Kyle's hand as they strolled up to the front door. He gripped the doorknob, and turned it slowly, trying his best to push the door open with a minimal amount of noise. Ashley puzzled over why he was entering his own home like a cat burglar, but as the door became ajar, she realized why. A big, gray Weimaraner tore through the house toward them, her claws clicking on the floor as she slid around almost out of control. She began with erratic nose-nudging against Ashley's leg, and then maneuvered her whole body against her. Her nub of a tail wagged quickly and uncontrollably as her hind end tried to keep up, swaying back and forth. As they moved forward into the foyer, the dog backed off, and then resumed the assault, now threatening to jump up to greet the new guest eye-to-eye.

"Heidi!" Kyle swatted at the dog, trying his best to disallow her to be rude, though that's just what dogs do.

"It's okay," Ashley petted the dog, but not with exuberant emotion. "I like dogs."

"Yeah, but this is a Weim. She's absolutely nuts. And she thinks that everyone new that enters the house is here to see *her*."

The jittery dog finally calmed and retreated into the depths of the home as the two of them proceeded onward. The front foyer and formal areas were dark, but all lights were on beyond into the family room and kitchen. A combination of aromas filled the air and pots could be heard banging lightly. The bright lights of the television flashed against all surfaces, accompanied by sounds and voices it produced.

"Hey there," Angela perked up, diverting her attention away from all things culinary.

"What's for dinner, Mom?" Kyle looked around the kitchen.

"Um," she looked around at the evening's work. "Chicken cordon bleu, potatoes au gratin, and French-cut green beans. We're just all kinds of French tonight," she giggled ecstatically. "You must be Ashley!" she ran over and hugged the startled young woman, and then held her away by the shoulders, while looking her up and down. "You are absolutely radiant! So beautiful!" she looked at her son in approval.

"Thanks," Ashley blushed.

"I can't believe you've waited this long to bring her around, Kyle," she scolded light-heartedly. "How did you two meet?"

"We've known each other since the beginning of high school, but we have Mr. Devereaux's economics class together, and we started talking," Ashley summed it up bashfully.

"And you finally asked her out?" Angela beamed at her son.

"I almost did, but I chickened out. She actually asked *me* out. She couldn't resist," he laughed as Ashley gently punched his arm.

The moment that followed was one of awkwardness. It was the silence of all introductory small talk being depleted too quickly. All anyone could do was nod and smile uncomfortably, silently begging for someone to break it.

"Well, I've got to finish up on my beans," Angela took the initiative. "Make yourself at home. The TV's on over there. Dinner will be ready shortly."

They both ambled over to the family room, directly across from the kitchen where Kyle's father, Drew, sat transfixed upon the television set and the national network news. He said nothing, nor did his gaze ever break from the flashes of light emanating from the TV. He did not acknowledge their presence. He just stared. So they took a position on the brown leather couch, and watched along with him.

"Well tomorrow's the day," the gray-haired anchor said. "Tomorrow, government begins for the newly-created North American country that the twenty-nine call The Republic of America. And Byron Davenport, former U.S. presidential hopeful will be its president. Only last week did statesmen and women originally elected to the United States legislature, along with various other delegates, come to a consensus, and even draft their new constitution. According to sources in Austin, Texas, where the capitol of the new republic will be located, not much was changed from the original 1789 U.S. Constitution. The same basic rights and provisions apply, but with major tweaks in the area of states' rights. According to the new constitution, the federal government will control major undertakings like defense, education, some overall economic issues, and other regulations. But for all other legislation, the individual twenty-nine states of the Republic will have the final say. So far, the Republic and the United States have been pretty cooperative with one another, but there are obviously going to be bumps in the road. One such bump comes in the form of taxes. For that, we'll go to our chief economic correspondent, Alan Stone. Alan?"

"Yes," the shot cut to a fairly young man with impeccably groomed brown hair with a part on the left side. "Business begins for the Republic tomorrow, and one of the things that it includes is tax collection. Businesses in the red states have already received orders from their respective governors to cease and desist the collection of income taxes to be sent to Washington, but tomorrow, they will officially be funneling that money to the national government in Austin. But one thing we have to remember is that this is not 1861. Businesses in those days were local. There weren't the national and multinational corporations that exist today. Now you may have a corporate headquarters in the Los Angeles area with branch offices in Atlanta, Dallas, and Philadelphia. You may have a grocery store headquarters in Arizona, but have stores in almost every state. So the tax issue is a little more dicey than it was in Lincoln's day. So far, most companies have been pretty cooperative about this issue, especially with companies headed up by known Republicans on both sides of the border. But there have been a few instances where corporations headquartered in blue states have refused to send tax withholdings to what they call a government of traitors. The problem is, they might not have a choice. If the company refuses to send income tax to Austin, and instead sends it to Washington, there will be chaos. People will refuse to work in those offices and stores if their money is not going to their own government. The red state that the office or store is located in may shut down the operation completely. Or the company may just cut ties with that office entirely. Either way, that's bad for the company's efficiency, quality of product, and overall, their bottom line. I see these more stubborn corporations folding under the pressure, and paying income tax to the Republic. Back to you," he folded his hands and smiled.

"Thanks, Alan. Over the last few weeks, the social backlash over the secessions has taken several forms. Democrats protested outside the capitol buildings of most of the twenty-nine states at some point or another. There have been brawls and fights in various towns everywhere over loyalty issues. Democrats have even protested against their own choice for president, demonstrating on Pennsylvania Avenue, claiming that Chandler hasn't been tough enough with the separatists or even attempting to preserve the Union. But just in the last week, something a bit more unexpected has been happening. We have been seeing massive migrations of people moving across the US-Republic borders. No one is sure how many have made the exodus, but some reports total migrants well into the thousands."

The television screen was a montage of scenes and footage that showed much heavier traffic than normal on various interstate highways that now took travelers across international lines. There were other scenes of chaotic jams of vehicles awaiting their turn to buy gasoline at filling stations.

"So far, though there have been some Republicans living in the blue states who have made the trek, most of the movement has been of Democrats and U.S. loyalists crossing the border into the United States. Why? Experts say that most of the Republicans in the blue states live in rural areas where they are surrounded by others who align with their own political views. They don't feel the pressure to hold their conservative opinions or to move to the Republic. It's also important to remember that not every Republican is pro-secession. Conversely, Democrats mostly located in the larger cities and college towns of the twenty-nine, do not populate those areas exclusively. A liberal living in the suburbs of Houston may very well live next door to an extremely right-wing separatist."

"We're just loyal U.S. citizens, and we want to bring our children up that way," a woman wearing faux designer sunglasses, and standing in front of her SUV at the filling station said as she brushed wind-blown strands of red hair to the side of her face. "Florida shouldn't—and none of these states should—have the right to break away from the U.S. just because they don't like the president. So we're moving out."

"Do you know where you're going?" the journalist asked.

"Yeah, I've got a sister in the Philadelphia area. She's going to let us stay with her for a while until we can find something."

"What about jobs? What about your house?"

"That's going to be tricky. We have two little boys to raise and provide for. I've been doing freelance technical writing, so I can keep doing that, but my husband had a corporate office job, and with the economy the way it is, we're not sure what the job market is going to offer. We put the house on the market, but our realtor told us to not get our hopes up for a quick sale. No one's buying right now. Banks don't have the capitol to make loans, so we might just end up not paying the mortgage, and foreclosing. Hopefully credit agencies and banks will be willing to overlook it, considering the circumstances," she shrugged.

"There were a hundred stories we heard just like this one, but another one we heard quite a bit was of threats, fear, and harassment," the anchor commented as the screen cut to an older African American man wearing a Denver Broncos ball cap.

"All we did was fly an American flag on the little pole by our front door," he shook his head as if he still could not believe it. "We didn't want to really leave our home, secession or not. We've been in the same house thirty years. We kept getting threatening phone calls—anonymous ones. Then one morning, my windshield was smashed in, and somebody spray painted 'get the hell out, blue nigger' on our garage door. That's when I said I'd had enough. So we're headed to Chicago."

"In fact, many of the people we were able to talk to had some family in a city still located in the United States, but scores more are headed east and north with no prospect of a job or a place to even live. It's also worth mentioning that almost all of the people moving from the red states to the blue were from more affluent backgrounds—middle class and up. Experts say there won't be many minorities from inner-cities making this trip, though they make up a large portion of Democratic loyalists in red states, because of the sheer cost of it all."

"Crap," Kyle's father uttered as his trance was finally broken, and he looked to the right to see his son sitting in the room. "Oh, hey Kyle. And this must be Ashley," he smiled as he stood and walked over to embrace the young woman's hand. "Very nice to meet you," he grinned like a high-schooler, shooting a look of almost devious approval at Kyle.

Kyle nearly began laughing out loud, silently confirming to Ashley with a grin that his prediction of his family's first impression of her had indeed so far been accurate.

"Okay, dinner's ready," Angela announced in typically loud Texas fashion, smile in her voice. "Dylan!" she called up the stairs, where her youngest son was doubtless listening to the music of his MP3 player at way too loud of a volume, and playing video games. "Dylan! Dinner!"

They could hear the shuffles and heavy feet trudging down the stairs as they all descended upon the prepared meal on the table. All of the warm food steamed from the casserole dishes they were prepared in, resting upon country-style pot holders and kitchen towels. Before each wooden chair, a fancy, decorative green place mat was laden with shimmering, polished silverware and a matching napkin with sterling silver rings slid over them.

They all sat as the Weimaraner trotted up to the table to beg for scraps, and just like most nights, Drew shooed her off to lay down in the family room. By the time each of them had found their place at the table, Dylan had finally made his way into the room as well. He lazily plopped his posterior into the chair, shifting the songs on his music player.

"Hey, take those damned things off," Drew scolded him. "You know better. No ear buds at the table. Family time. Besides, we have company," Drew continued.

"Hey," he smiled like a stoner as he lifted his gaze to greet his brother's girlfriend. And just as Kyle had foreseen, his eyes darted from her radiant face to her chest, nearly unapologetically. Kyle shook his head in shame as Ashley grinned with an uncomfortable blush.

"So how long have you two been dating?" Angela asked politely as the family passed around the various dishes, scooping hearty helpings onto their plates.

"Um," Kyle began, somewhat distracted by the task of serving himself some potatoes au gratin. "A couple of months."

"A couple of months?" Angela was appalled. "And you just brought her to meet us? Christ, you might as well be married already! Why has it taken so long, Kyle?"

He looked up from his plate, taken aback by a question he was totally unprepared to answer. He looked into his mother's waiting eyes, a devious grin upon her face. Looking around the table, the males seemed uninterested in the question, or perhaps they, having a Y chromosome, silently felt for him in this situation. His eyes returned to his mother, and then to his girlfriend, who had quite the same expression on her face as Angela.

"Yeah, Kyle," she tapped her fingernails on the table top. "Why haven't you brought me over yet?"

"Um," he uttered in a frantic attempt to at least appear that he had a rational explanation.

"Did you just meet this year?" Drew rescued his son, a twinkle in his eye. He knew what he was doing, but he never even looked up from his food.

"Actually, we've known each other since freshman year, but we just started dating," Ashley smiled at him, and then grinned at Kyle, still frazzled by the estrogen assault.

"Oh, do you have a class together or something?" Drew politely covered his mouth as he spoke and chewed.

"Yeah, we have economics together," Kyle added.

"Oh," Drew nodded with a touch of disdain. "Devereaux's class. He's somebody I wouldn't mind seeing migrate to a blue state."

"But why?" Ashley boldly challenged the patriarch she had all too recently met.

"He's filling your heads with his liberal bullshit every day, and I think politics have no place in a high school classroom," he shook his head.

"Politics have every bit a place in classrooms," Kyle challenged his father, something he had never done before. Perhaps he was doing it because he wanted to impress his girlfriend. But perhaps it was also time that he gained a level of independence and stood up for his beliefs. Nevertheless, he was petrified, and shook with timidity as he spoke.

"Oh?" Drew urged clarification.

"Yeah. If not in a classroom, then where else are we supposed to learn about politics? Where else are we supposed to learn to form and voice our opinions? I'm going to be old enough to vote soon, and I need to know these things. Mr. Devereaux doesn't teach us by injecting his opinions into the lesson. He plays the Devil's Advocate to get us to discuss the issues."

Drew did not respond. He did not even lift his head or raise his eyes. The air was uncomfortable and silent to the point that one could easily hear the sounds of chicken and potatoes being gnashed between molars. Kyle was nervous. Was his father poised for a delayed counter-offensive? Did he really have nothing to say in argument? Or was it that the uncomfortable silence was retaliation enough for the bold statement his son had just made.

"Speaking of the migrations," Angela tried to break the silence and change the subject without being too obvious. "Have you kids lost any classmates? One school in downtown Fort Worth lost almost three-hundred."

"Not really," Ashley responded. It seemed that they possessed the same traits of a matriarch, always keeping the peace. "I lost two in my physics class."

"I lost one in math," Kyle chimed in. "Oh, and that girl, Shaye, in economics."

"Oh yeah," Ashley's eyebrows raised. "I just thought she'd been skipping. She moved?"

"That's what I heard. Of course, I don't think anybody's going to miss her," Kyle laughed lightly.

"Kyle," his mother reprimanded. "That's not a very nice thing to say."

"I'm not trying to be mean, but it's the truth," he explained. "She's got this horrible chip on her shoulder all the time. She's rude, she's inconsiderate, and she's genuinely ignorant."

"But that doesn't stop her from opening her mouth," Ashley added and nodded. "It's true. She's got a bad attitude, and is even disrespectful to Mr. Devereaux."

"Hmm," Angela nodded, chewing her food. "I guess she brings it upon herself, then."

There was once again silence at the table. Forks and knives dinged and scraped the china as everyone chewed, painfully uncomfortable. Kyle almost wished the exchange between he and his father had happened later in the evening, after Ashley had left. Discomfort would have been more tolerable if she were not there to experience it.

"Ashley," Drew spoke up, finally lifting his eyes to her. "What do you think about this whole forming of a new country?"

The question was blunt, and caught her quite off-guard. Kyle winced in silence and disbelief that his father, who had only met his girlfriend a few minutes ago, was already putting her to this type of a test. It was a question reserved for perhaps a fifth meeting, once they had become more comfortable around each other. But he said not a word, and Ashley chewed her food for an extended period of time, giving her an opportunity to solidify the perfect response. It had to be intelligent and truthful, while maintaining a level of diplomacy. She had to be careful to speak her mind without being a bitch, yet she could not seem intimidated. It was do or die.

"Well," she began. "It depends on your political views. Do you maintain that states are only bound by federal law as long as they agree with it? Or do you believe that the constitution is the law of the land, no matter what? Personally, I think that the founding fathers provided for a government that could be flexible and also accommodate differing opinions in legislation. I don't think that even Jefferson, the author of the Declaration of Independence would have agreed with this. They put together a system that could change with the times, yet keep a core ideology that everyone can abide by, and as long as all states can follow and agree on those core rights, the country should stay together. They're causing a rift based on some off-to-the-side details. It's like Catholics and Baptists fighting over who's right and who's wrong, when aside from a few minor details, they believe in the same exact thing. The truth of the matter is that the red states are being petty and whiny. Something doesn't go their way, and they act like a little kid—throw a tantrum. It defeats the purpose of democracy. There are supposed to be differing perspectives. But they're supposed to work together to find a solution, not list 'irreconcilable differences,' split up, and call it a day."

She was nervous. She did not know if she overdid it, but judging from Angela's smile, she had the mother's vote, and in many cases, that's all that mattered. Still, she waited in anticipation of Drew's response. She worried over an all-out debate over dinner. She watched him chew, his eyes pointed down as he nodded, processing all that she had just said.

"I don't agree with you totally," he said to her horror. "But you make a damn good case." He looked up at her and smiled. "You're going to fit in just fine around here."

Chapter 27

"He'll see you now," the young assistant said in her sweet, southern accent.

President Chandler smiled and nodded at her as she motioned toward the door. She giggled at the thought. It was strangely humorous in its negativity that at this point, the President of the United States had to make an appointment to have an audience with a state governor. She started to head for the doorway, but stopped short in hesitation, turning instead to her husband, who had accompanied her. She looked into his light blue eyes, begging encouragement and sympathy.

"You're gonna do fine," he consoled her in a whisper, clutching her shoulders. "We need this. Stand up to him. Let bitch Cindy come out to play, and show him who's boss."

She nodded, and turned to the door and the forced smile of the governor's assistant. She brushed her light pink skirt suit, and straightened her posture before heading confidently into the office. The expansive office was comparable to her own in size; just not as iconic. It was carpeted in a rich burgundy, dotted by darkly stained furniture. Bookcases lined the walls, an entire section filled with law books accumulated during the governor's days as an attorney. On one wall was an antique map of the state of Maryland. It appeared frail and worn behind its protective glass and frame. The wall behind the desk was like a shrine to Reagan, decorated with numerous framed photos of Governor Ericson's multitude of meetings with the former president.

Jesse Ericson stood from behind his large desk, which was neatly accented with ornate paperweights, expensive metallic pens, and a knock-off Tiffany lamp. He was a thick, tall man, built like an offensive lineman. Cindy was pretty sure that she had seen another picture on the far wall of him in a college football uniform. Yet, his suit was tailored perfectly to fit his figure. She appreciated that. Bigger men often did not bother to have alterations in their suits, thus making them appear bigger, and even fatter than they were. Combined with his nicely combed black and gray hair, he appeared quite astute.

He rounded the oak desk to the left, nearly tripping over the small wastebasket that he surely often forgot was there. He walked briskly in her direction, meeting her before a finely upholstered red and gold paisley sofa. Cindy wondered how much it cost Maryland taxpayers, but smiled and responded to the firm grip he placed on her hand.

"Please, sit down, Madam President," he motioned to the expensive couch.

"Thank you," she sat. "You have a beautiful office."

"Thank you," he said warmly. "It's not bad. I had my sights set on your office in a few more years, but I might have to settle for Austin now."

"Who knows?" she shrugged suggestively about what she was about to discuss with him. "You could still make it into mine eventually. I assume you know why I'm here."

"I think I have an idea," he sensed the small talk was being dispensed with. "Let me take a crack at this," he reclined a bit. "Washington, DC, is now completely surrounded by a state that is no longer in the United States. And I'm assuming you are here to try and talk me into returning to the fold, so to speak."

"Couldn't have said it better myself, governor," she grinned.

"And what makes you think I would do that?" he continued to seem light-hearted.

"I sense you are, at heart, a reasonable and patriotic man who loves his country."

"You would be right," he agreed. "But now my country is the Republic of America—a much closer vision to what the founding fathers saw the United States as in the 1780s."

"The United States cannot be divided," the smile quickly fell from her face. "Look, governor, our capitol is now essentially in another country. It might as well be in Canada or Cameroon. We can't run an effective government that way."

"So move it," he put bluntly. "Move it back to New York or Philadelphia, or somewhere."

"Seriously?" she replied. "Those are established cities. There's nowhere to put it. We're talking about thousands of administrative buildings aside from the Capitol building and the White House. And then there are the monuments, the landmarks, and the museums. It's impossible. And we can't build a new capitol in the middle of nowhere—the way they built DC."

"We're doing it," he commented. "They're building the new administrative buildings and Republic Capitol building in Austin as we speak."

"On oil money," she dropped her brow. "The Republic has authorized the expansion of offshore gulf drilling, and that's going to fund the construction. That's the whole reason Europe hasn't had much to say about this whole thing. They need the refined oil products and fuel. We don't have that. All we have is rusted, abandoned factories and a Wall Street that has screwed up the entire economy."

"I don't know what you want me to say," he threw up his hands. "Hell, I shouldn't even be talking to you about this. You're going behind President Davenport's back. I'm just an individual state governor."

"I thought individual states' rights were what you guys were all about," she jabbed.

"I'm an executive," he side-stepped the comment. "You know as well as I do that a governor, or a president, in your case, can't just snap his fingers and change legislation or make a decision for the whole of the people and the government. I've got Senators and Representatives I have to pass this through. And how am I supposed to work that out?"

"Charm, charisma, reasoning," she fired back. "Get in there and reason with them."

"And what negotiation point am I supposed to use?" he leaned forward to her. "You know damned well that these lawmakers don't do anything without reciprocity. They're gonna want something from you. What's your bargaining chip?"

"What are you insinuating? Go back on the stimulus bill? Wipe out all the progress we've made? Waffle on everything I stand for?"

"For starters…" he put it bluntly.

"I can't do that," she shook her head. "You said yourself that you can't just snap your fingers and get that done. I've got Congress that won't budge and I've got average Americans that make this country run counting on me to get this right. Our legislatures and yours, too, have pretty much become one-party-systems. I can't convince them to go back on this and watch me become a lame duck, bowing to the will of the Republican party every time you people decide to throw a hissy fit over not getting your way. I can't convince them of that."

"Use a little charm, charisma, and reasoning," he grinned deviously.

"Thank you for your time, governor," she leapt to her feet in rage.

"Thanks for the visit," he said with a smile. "You sure you won't stay for coffee or something?"

"Good day, governor," she even neglected to shake his hand as she stormed out of the room.

She was furious over his audacity and pomp. The worst of it was how calmly and expertly he had caused her to lose her cool. He did it all with genuine politeness and smiles. He was reasonable, and now she appeared the opposite. She appeared hot-headed and bitchy, but it mattered not. The fuse was lit, and he had gotten the best of her. Now she would have to play hardball.

"Call General Bates," she stormed past her husband on her way out. "Tell him to meet me with the Joint Chiefs in the Situation Room in three hours."

Three hours was overkill, but it was enough time to give the president, as well as the Joint Chiefs of Staff to prepare for what was to come. Mainly, she just wanted to regain composure. She was furious and fuming. She wanted to cool down before entering the Situation Room, plus she needed time to freshen up. She hated traveling by helicopter. It was easier in the sense that she could land right there on the White House lawn, and did not have to deal with Dulles International, but her hair blew grossly out of place when she stepped in and out. Unfortunately, Dulles was in Virginia, and under Republic control, as was any other airport remotely close enough to board Air Force One.

It was only about a thirty-five mile trip, so she would not have had that option anyway.

Unable to cool down as much as she would have liked during the three hours between her meeting with the pompous governor and entering the Situation Room, she stormed in, throwing the door open and then slamming it shut. All men and women were assembled, from the Joint Chiefs to Vice President Coffman and Secretary of State Jessica Delaune. They all bore the look of seriousness. They were grave. They hunched over papers and files, filled with statistics and data. They all watched Cindy blaze into the room like a gunfighter, and all waited for her to give the order.

"Bates," she sat down and folded her hands. "What do you have for me?"

"I've got several scenarios for you," he opened a file. "It just depends on what you want. We've been kicking these around since the secession happened, just in case things went bad, and I guess they have."

"Oh yeah. They have," she nodded with great exaggeration. "The fact is that we can't exist as a capitol in a rebel country. We're surrounded by enemy territory, as far as I'm concerned. We need Maryland, and we at least need everything in Virginia from here to Mount Vernon. Otherwise, we can't function as a government. They are unwilling to concede, so I am now willing to take drastic measures."

"Okay," Bates pulled some papers from a file. He then picked up a small remote control from the wooden table top, pointed it toward the projector, and powered up the digital display.

"The scenario we've mapped out, as the first strike, will be largely unexpected. I don't think the Reds are expecting a Democrat to call for a military strike," Bates began.

"Is this going to require a lot of personnel?" Coffman asked, interrupting the General.

"No," he replied. "There are no major standing military forces in this area yet. I don't think Austin has gotten that far. They just drafted a constitution, so war mobilization is not on their list of priorities."

"I don't like to think of it like that," Cindy stopped him. "War mobilization. I'd like to think of this as a police action. I don't want us to jump the gun and consider this war. I really don't want it to come to that."

"Madam President," the Air Force Chief responded politely. "If we do this, I think it would be wise to at least prepare yourself for the possibility that they may retaliate." She nodded acceptingly.

"Anyway," Bates continued his thought process. "It shouldn't require much personnel. Seven thousand, tops—just to be sure. The majority of the troops," he brought up a map of the Maryland, DC, and Virginia areas on the screen, and then used a laser pointer to indicate the places he was referring to, "will be needed closer to DC. We will need to secure the borders of the capitol, and we will need a relatively large force to take control of major governmental installations in Virginia."

"Langley, the Pentagon, etc.," Cindy clarified.

"Yes. I think that's doable," he seemed optimistic. "The Republic has, so far, been very hesitant to move on such high-profile U.S. government complexes, so those should be easy—they're just big. The tricky part is Annapolis. That's going to be what pisses off the rest of the Republic. That's what is going to be seen as an act of aggression."

"So how do we do it?" she asked.

"We have to act now," he stressed, peering deeply into the president's eyes. "We have to launch from Pennsylvania, where there are really no bases to speak of. We've been stocking a makeshift base of operations about twenty miles north of the Maryland border. We've stockpiled weapons, gear, vehicles—everything we'll need for this operation."

"Wait," she interrupted. "Stop there. Why have you been setting this up?"

"Just in case, ma'am," he replied apologetically. "Chance favors the prepared mind, to quote the famous line. We figured this might have to happen eventually."

"Okay, okay. Continue," she snapped, clearly annoyed.

"We've got troops on standby, ready to move them to the staging point right now, so we have to get on the horn, and mobilize them now if we're going to get this done in two days' time," he continued.

"Two days?" the Vice President was shocked. "Why so soon?"

"We need the element of surprise if this is going to work with minimal casualties," he explained. "No doubt, the governor of Maryland is getting in touch with that asshole Davenport as we speak, and telling him all about the little chit-chat he and the President had this morning. All those folks in Austin are going to raise an eyebrow, and you can bet this will be much harder if we wait a week. Plus, if we mobilize now, there will be less time for the families of the troops we send in to run their mouth and let the cat out of the bag."

"Can we get it done that fast?" the Secretary of State inquired.

"We're not going to run the operation until about two o'clock that morning. If we act now, we can just barely pull it together," he nodded.

There was a pause. No one said anything; rather everyone simply took a moment to think and fully take in the concept of what was about to happen. There was not a single joyful or optimistic expression in the room. This was something that no one wanted, except, perhaps, General Bates.

"Okay, what's the best scenario?" Chandler folded her hands in front of her face, as if in prayer.

"First and foremost," Bates picked up his laser pointer, and leaned over to indicate the DC border, "we have to secure the capitol. A small force will take critical positions around the city, especially along major highways and bridges across the Potomac. They will also carefully monitor the Metro stations. We have to keep a close watch on the commuters coming into DC for work in the morning."

"Okay," she nodded. "Good. Can't have the whole city shut down for business over this. Continue."

"A force of two thousand will cross the Potomac into Virginia, and take control of the CIA complex, as well as the Pentagon and other various administrative buildings. We have loyalists on the inside of both, so those objectives won't be hard. We'll have to infiltrate every room in both of those installations to make sure there is no internal sabotage. The rest of the troops will occupy the most highly populated areas of Alexandria and Fairfax Counties. Hopefully, any resistors like rednecks and cops will not have the guts or grit to try and fight back. So our occupying force is really there for intimidation purposes. They will fortify the area and enact martial law. A curfew is necessary. Questions?"

No one answered. They hung on to every word, but sort of spaced out during the dialogue. It was dream-like; almost surreal. Who would have guessed that this event would happen within their lifetime, if ever?

"Good," he continued. "Phase three. Baltimore. This is a more urban area with a CBD and a higher concentration of population. We will need to fortify the city, and seal it off. By the time people start waking up for work in the morning, martial law will already be in place. The highest concentration of troops will be in the inner-city, and we will run patrols of the suburbs to make our presence known. Similar to Fairfax. Two thousand troops."

He paused to catch his breath and take a drink of water before continuing.

"And the tricky one," he began. "Annapolis. It's the capitol, so on top of the same scenario as Baltimore, we have to secure all state governmental buildings. That's not really a big deal. We just have to take possession of all of them—make sure no one gets to their office and makes a call to Austin. All other administrative buildings are a piece of cake. We also have to take possession of the naval academy and base. This is a huge objective, considering we've lost most of our bases in red states."

"And the governor?" Chandler sneered.

"Before anyone wakes up, a special forces team will force their way into the homes of the governor and lieutenant governor. No one will be harmed, obviously. It might scare the shit out of them, but they won't be harmed. They will remain under house arrest until further notice. The remainder of our troops will occupy smaller towns dotting the Maryland map—mainly county seats. We don't anticipate any resistance here. It's all for show. Any questions?"

"I, um..." Cindy shrugged and looked around the room for feedback, but did not get much. Everyone was in agreement that this had to be done, but as far as the nuts and bolts of the military planning, no one else in the room other than the Joint Chiefs had ever been in the military, so the plan sounded as sure as any. Cindy stopped, looked down for a long moment, and thought about what was to happen and what the consequences could be.

"Madam President?" Bates tried to regain her attention. "What are your orders?"

She took a deep breath, closed her eyes, and finally released her inhibitions.

"Do it," she uttered. "Green light."

Chapter 28

The interstates and highways pulsed with uncommonly high traffic for such an early hour. Normally, the darkened roads bore only a few signs of life with occasional truck stops and big rigs moving down through the sleepy countryside. But tonight, they bustled with life. Personnel trucks, olive drab in the daytime but black in the moonless veil of night, roared down the asphalt. Humvees cruised alongside and between them, all traveling at speeds that were a blatant disregard for the traffic laws. They had to cover a lot of miles in one night.

Soldiers in the Humvees had the luxury of a windshield to peer through, while those who sat in the backs of the personnel carriers did not. The Humvee troops could see how close they were getting. The country was beginning to give way to the suburbs, and the low glow of the city ahead sent shivers through them. Most of the men and women were too young to have taken part in the overseas wars on terror. They were greenhorns, so the closer they got to their objectives, the more nervous they became. They were told that this would be a piece of cake, but that did not stop their hearts from fluttering, their hands from shaking, or adrenaline from coursing through their vessels.

Trucks and Humvees began splitting from the rest of the convoy, and exiting the main highways for smaller ones, and even residential streets. Hundreds of vehicles skirted the borders of the District of Columbia. Some veered off to the sides of the main highways leading in, and began to unload soldiers and supplies, while others coursed through the residential streets of middle class neighborhoods like Mt. Rainier, Chillum, and Silver Spring. Others headed south to less affluent areas like Barnaby Terrace.

Once in place, each group did the same. They parked the vehicles along the side of streets where the parked cars of residents left space, and began unloading troops and supplies. There were, of course, loads of weaponry and boxes of ammunition. Threats and intimidation are nothing unless one can back them up. They also began construction of makeshift bunkers out of hundreds of sandbags. As the sun began to rise in a few hours, commuters would find checkpoints dotting the quiet streets leading into the city.

To many of the soldiers, this felt more like a training exercise. They knew that they were on a serious guard detail, but the surroundings made it feel otherwise. They were looking at the homes of Americans, not Afghanis. Someone's Yorkshire Terrier was annoyingly yapping in a backyard somewhere, obviously rousted by the breaking of the stillness of night. Wind chimes could be heard on a front porch in the distance. A pink tricycle was mistakenly left in the front yard the evening before. This was suburbia, not a hotbed of fanaticism and militancy.

While the perimeter was being set and the checkpoints were being constructed, yet another branch of the convoy continued into DC, taking Highway 50 on to Washington. The city was sleeping, and the streets were mostly empty, lit dimly by street lamps along the way. Occasionally, the men and women aboard the trucks would see a convenience store. Its brilliant light pierced the dimness as if it were a religious shrine; a place holy in the late hours to hungry insomniacs looking for a snack.

"Can we stop for a Slim Jim and a Pepsi, Cap?" one corporal asked his commanding officer within the Humvee. The men erupted into laughter as they passed the store. They needed that. The mood was tense, and they were all on edge.

The convoy traveled New York Avenue into the heart of the nation's capitol, finally linking up with Interstate 395. There was an ambiance to the long, sprawling National Mall, lined with endless museums of the Smithsonian, all filled with priceless treasures of the country's past. It glowed with dim street lamps, drowned out by the blinding lights shining on the giant obelisk-shaped Washington Monument. To the left, the capitol building gleamed in the flood lights. It was imposing, and not one soldier in the military transports failed to think of the fact that the arguing and partisanship within those halls had led to the operation at hand.

Cindy Chandler, just a few blocks away in her bed, could hear the thundering of the convoy roaring through the city. Most people wouldn't hear through their REM cycles. It was subtle, but Cindy noticed—she anticipated it. She rested there in her light blue nightgown, her husband snoring gently beside her. She had stared at the ceiling all night, with not a wink of sleep, though she could have used it. The night was filled with prayers that this would all go smoothly and without incident, but now she heard the angry rumble of the gods of war. She was filled with fright, and possibly remorse.

The vehicles continued south through downtown Washington, then curved west in the direction of the Potomac River. They began on the Francis Case Memorial Bridge, first crossing the Washington Channel, providing an excellent, yet distant view of the Jefferson Memorial before they traversed the wide and lazy Potomac. This meant that their objectives were close, for just opposite on the Virginia bank lay the massive, iconic Pentagon building.

Much of the convoy fanned out into the suburbs filling the county, stopping at key intersections and setting up checkpoints and sand bag bunkers along the way. Armed soldiers filled the lifeless streets in preparation for the rush hour to come in a few hours. Men and women took guard at the Metro subway stations and at major bridges like the Francis Case and Theodore Roosevelt.

The head of the convoy continued northwest through Arlington and Cherrydale, all the way to Langley, Virginia. They rolled down the increasingly lifeless highway as one could see the white and gray modern building complex in the near distance. They approached a chain link security gate, guarded by two night watchmen. Not one vehicle even feigned an attempt to slow down. They had no intention of asking for clearance. The first of several dozen transports sped toward the gate, nearing it at ramming speed, and crashed through with ease, sending sparks and bits of metal airborne as the gates flew open. The watchmen, taken aback by the display, stared in awe-stricken reverence as they watched the trucks file through the gateway.

Soon, they entered the huge, expansive parking lots, which contained a few private vehicles, but were largely empty. Intelligence was a full-time task—terrorists are awake in the Middle East while Americans sleep. The CIA was remote, and had kept it that way for a reason. It was a complex comparable to that of a corporate headquarters, nestled within acres of forested land next to the river. It was an anomaly, and it was intimidating. This was the CIA, and the nervous troops were about to enter and conquer it.

As the trucks halted in the parking lots, they gushed personnel, all jumping from the backs as if they were storming the beaches of Normandy generations ago. The difference was that there were no armed enemies waiting for them, ready to kill. They simply overwhelmed the front entrance in force, completely taking the watchman inside the lobby by surprise. The aging and balding man just stood in shock, elevating both hands at the sight of dozens of hoisted assault rifles. The troops began filtering through every hallway in the complex, regardless of security clearance levels. They kicked in every door in sight, clearing every empty office and interrogation room. Occasionally, an analyst could be found sitting before a set of computer screens, watching surveillance of God knows what, while also browsing internet social networking sites.

"Step away from the desk," they were each told. The stern words seemed to roll down the gun barrels, and each of the tech geeks silently stood from their computers, taken into custody.

Meanwhile, a similar force exited Interstate 395, and looped down the ramp. To the right, the Pentagon was imposing. It almost emanated light; taking on a life of its own. All of the troops took their orders from the Pentagon, yet most of them had never seen it. It was huge, though only four stories high in every segment. It sprawled for acres within its flanks of hardwood trees overlooking the capitol and the river.

Then, to the left was yet another capitol area icon. The men and women of the convoy uttered not a word as they stared in reverence at the darkened rows of white headstones in the near distance. Most of them had never been there, yet they knew exactly what it was. Arlington National Cemetery was the most famous burial ground in America. It was once the home estate of Confederate General Robert E. Lee. While he was away at war, a Union officer began burying fallen American soldiers in the shadow of his house so that he would be reminded for the rest of his life of the innocent young men whose death he had caused. But he never regained the estate, and the land was designated a national burial ground. The soldiers who were part of the military convoy were about to forcibly seize the headquarters of the United States Armed Forces a stone's throw away from a cemetery that began the last time the country fell apart at the seams.

This convoy actually stopped at the security gate house. This was a military installation, not an agency. It was respect. Two young army corporals walked out to meet the head vehicle, stunned and confused as to what was going on. A Major General stepped out of the lead Humvee to meet the two young men, each saluting and at attention.

"At ease, boys," he said in a gruff, aging voice as the two men loosened a bit. "I need you to open that gate."

"Sir, the Pentagon isn't even open," one of the corporals said. "And I don't have any clearance for you."

"Young man," the general seemed annoyed. "I'm not gonna be on that list. Now open the gate."

"With all due respect, sir, I can't do that. I don't have authorization," he shook his head, fearful of retribution.

"Come here, son," the general motioned the young man over, and put his arm around his shoulders gently. "You see this line of transports?" he motioned to the seemingly endless convoy. "This ain't no social call, and my authorization comes from the Commander in Chief. I don't need your permission, but I'm trying to be polite because I'm in a good mood. So I'm gonna ask you again. Please…open the fuckin' gate."

"Yes," the corporal trembled. "Yes, sir," he stumbled as he approached the gate booth, and pressed the button to lift the heavy steel gate arm.

"Colonel," the general motioned over another high-ranking officer. "Replace these young men with twenty armed guards, and take these two into custody until they can be cleared. Seal off the entire perimeter. Take the rest of the detachment and enter the building. Leave no office unchecked. Until we get word from the White House, no one enters the premises. The Pentagon is closed for business."

Under the cover of night, another detachment entered downtown Baltimore. Designated trucks and Humvees branched off the main interstates, and onto other major highways. They began lining streets in the suburbs, and setting up their checkpoints and bunkers, while the main bulk of the vehicles headed straight for the CBD.

Baltimore was an interesting city. It was an eighteenth century town that had grown into a decent-sized metropolis. The streets now bustling with military transports and personnel featured similar sights that one might see in Boston, New York, Philadelphia, or New Orleans. They are all colonial cities that have a bizarre mixture of old and new. Graveyards with badly-weathered centuries-old headstones hid in the shadows of ultra-modern high-rise apartment buildings. Restored nineteenth century tenements that once housed dozens of poverty-stricken immigrant workers apiece, now shared the same block with skyscraper office buildings. Even the old harbor buildings were overshadowed by modern, all-glass maritime and naval history museums.

Now the entire city was under martial law. Police cars would be stopped before they could radio military presence, and precinct buildings would be commandeered, as they were across the state. It was the first time since Reconstruction that martial law had been seen in this city. In April of 1861, though Maryland never joined the Confederacy, Baltimore was the site of a major riot. As Union troops marched through the city en route to Washington, angry Confederate sympathizers attacked them with whatever they could find. With that in mind, no one could be sure what would happen in the morning. It could be said that the troops securing the capitol, the Pentagon, the

CIA, and the DC suburbs would have it much easier. Many Republicans in those areas would no longer be making a commute into the city. They would find little trouble in the morning. No one could say exactly what the first rays of the sun would bring in Baltimore. As the people of that city began to fuel up on lattes and bagels on their way to their corporate office jobs, they would certainly have a surprise waiting.

Meanwhile, a cool March breeze was sweeping gently across Chesapeake Bay and its lightly restless waters. It coursed across the open sports fields of the Naval Academy and rustled the new spring leaves in the trees of St. John's College. It was quiet and peaceful. Nothing stirred but the breeze in the tranquility of the early hours of the morning. Yet, the hum of big diesel engines in the distance subtly began to fill the vacuum of serenity, getting louder every minute.

A team of transports and other military vehicles rolled in via Spa Road from the west, leading them closer to the heart of the city as the road became West Street. Another detachment came in from the northwest, traveling Highway 70 across Weems Creek, and then College Creek as the highway became Bladen Street.

Entering Annapolis, Maryland, was like taking a journey through time and space. After crossing the bridges from a world of newer homes in the suburbs, it was like entering a different historical era. Many houses downtown were built in the eighteenth century—some had become museums, but some still served as private residences. The combination of Georgian and newer nineteenth-century buildings, plus the absence of the corporate and modern provided the feel of a small town, rather than a state capitol. In fact, it *was* small. The peninsula occupied by the town was only about a mile and a half long and just over three quarters of a mile wide, making Annapolis an easy military objective.

The trucks and Humvees fanned out across the area, thundering down the picturesque streets, and taking their positions. Troops donning traditional green camouflage fatigues, Kevlar helmets, and various articles of gear crossed athletic areas like Worden Field and Ingram

Field, their boots crunching the tiny bits of red clay of the track as they closed in on the heart of the United States Naval Academy. The men and women given this objective, as well as the top army brass, hoped that this would be an easy success. Though it was a military installation, it was really more of a college than a base. No one marched the grounds carrying rifles. No one was trained to kill hand-to-hand. The vessels in the marina between Dewey Field and Farragut Field were little skiffs, not warships. These men and women were being trained to command ships, give orders, and develop naval strategies.

The Academy had, however, become a strictly red state installation. The property, less than a mile from the capitol building, was one of the first federal properties claimed by the secessionist state of Maryland. Therefore, it was run solely by officers loyal to the Republic, and all Democrats and U.S. loyalists had either dropped from the rolls or had been expelled. Thus, some degree of force was to be exercised, and the brass on campus would have to be arrested.

Soldiers began taking positions across the campus, surrounding empty administrative buildings and classroom halls in preparation for the coming of first light. The primary objectives were, however, people. A large force created a perimeter around Bancroft Hall as troops began moving into the building. The concern was not an armed enemy, but the sheer number of people who lived there. Though many of the men and women enrolled in "Canoe U" were no longer there, this was still the world's largest college dormitory. The apprehension was that too small of a force could be overpowered by an angry mob of three thousand young students.

One thousand armed personnel entered Memorial Hall, their boots clapping the marble floors. The sound of invasion echoed from wall to wall beneath the rotunda dome and from column to column. They trotted up the beautiful and timeless white marble staircase and coursed the veins of the building, ready to commence evacuation. Once every hallway was filled with troops, they waited for the order.

"Commence," the order squawked from radios carried by squad leaders in each hall.

"Alright!" boisterous voices yelled in each hall. "Everybody out of your rooms! Every room! Now!"

A moment or two passed before the first dorm rooms slowly opened. A few sleepy cadets emerged, rubbing their eyes sluggishly, and still clad in white undershirts and boxer shorts.

"Why are we doing PT at three in the morning?" one young man uttered in a raspy voice before his eyes adjusted.

Each cadet began to see that this was no training exercise. The first things they could see were Kevlar helmets and automatic rifles carried by dozens of camouflage-clad soldiers. Their eyes widened and they became alert almost instantly as adrenaline filled their arteries and their pulses increased.

"Move! Move! Out of the building and into the T-Court!" soldiers yelled, waving the frightened young cadets along down the halls.

In the female-occupied hallways, the procedure was quite different. Men in the building were ushered out in their skivvies, but the troops in the building did not plan for female cadets emerging from their rooms in t-shirts and panties. They wore no bras beneath, and the all-male strike force could tell that the cadets were not supported beneath their night shirts. Mortified and frightened, the young ladies darted back into their rooms. The first instinct of the strike force was to treat this as resistance, but they quickly understood what was happening.

"Ladies!" a commanding officer yelled down the hall. "Dress yourselves quickly, and then evacuate the building!" he exclaimed with a slightly amused smile.

A few moments later, the women reemerged from their dorm rooms wearing sweat pants or whatever they could find. They had put on their bras beneath their t-shirts, and covered their feet with slippers or tennis shoes. They hurriedly filed down the hallways and down into the Memorial Hall area, joining the throngs of other cadets herded into the courtyard outside.

The colonel in charge of the detachment stood inspecting the group all surrounded by armed troops. They were slightly chilly, largely frightened, and totally surprised by the actions they were just confronted with.

"Is the building clear?" he spoke into his radio.

"Clear of all cadets who came out willingly," was the response. "There are a few doors still closed."

"They may be vacant," the colonel responded. "Attendance is down due to secession. Kick them in, and check anyway—just in case we have a few cadets holding out on us."

"Yes, sir," a voice crackled back over the radio.

Inside, troops in the hallways began kicking in the doors to unopened bedrooms. Wood splintered and doorknob assemblies broke apart completely as the doors swung open violently. Up and down the hallway, soldiers yelled, "Clear," as they checked for occupation. One African American soldier forced his way into a dorm room to find a seemingly empty room until a young man leapt from within the small closet to the left, attacking him with a small desk chair. The soldier reeled at first, taking a blow to his left shoulder before using his rifle to block further swings, and then to crack the cadet across the jaw, rendering him unconscious.

"Ahh," he rubbed his shoulder in pain. "Son of a bitch."

"You okay?" another man yelled from one room down.

"Yeah," he responded. "Can you help me carry this asshole outside?"

Thousands of cadets and guarding troops filled the courtyard outside, overlooking the trees, monuments, and old cannons in the commons. The area was almost a park, surrounded by the splendor of old administrative buildings, including the towering dome of the campus chapel. Next door to that was the last major objective on the academy grounds—the Superintendant's Quarters. A much smaller force surrounded the two-story Victorian home as a few troops forced their way in to take custody of the aging superintendant and his wife.

Across town, a similar force was mustering in the heart of Annapolis, particularly focusing around State Circle and Church Circle. The State House's red brick and white rotunda gleamed in the flood lights as it towered over the rest of the city upon its hill. It was not what one would expect in a state capitol building. Many states had built modern twentieth century replacements, and converted their old state houses into museums. A building like that, however, would be extremely out of place in Annapolis. There were no high-rises. Everything still appeared quite colonial. The late-eighteenth century Maryland State House was the oldest continually-used legislative building in the country, and it was complemented by Georgian colonial buildings that lined State Circle and the streets leading up to it.

As the perimeter was secured and the rest of the downtown area was being occupied, a force surrounded the wrought iron fences of the Government House; residence of Governor Ericson. Police officers on guard and patrolling the vicinity were subdued, and the Special Forces unit was preparing to enter the property. The three-story, red brick, late nineteenth century home was a knock-off colonial Georgian example of Annapolis architecture. It was a successful attempt to remain with the continuity of the authentic eighteenth-century structures that surrounded it—particularly the adjacent state house and St. Anne's Church.

Night vision goggles pressured the Delta men's neck muscles as they compensated for the extra weight on their black-painted faces. They wore black and dark green combat uniforms, allowing them to move amongst the trees, gardens, and hedges of the mansion property largely unnoticed. The house itself was well-lit, so infiltration had to be quick. The team of eight approached the gate to the front entrance. All men crouched low, clutching their HK MP-5s as another team member swiftly negotiated the picking of the simple lock to the gate. As the hinges squealed with the opening of the black iron gate, the eight men forced their way into the governor's mansion.

The beautiful interior of the mansion featured expertly crafted plaster and stone fireplaces and antique hand-made rugs and furniture. Chandeliers hung in the major parlors, offices, and dining rooms. The Delta team members were sure this would be a beautiful home to tour in a normal situation, but the bright green of the night vision washed out any detail or color of their surroundings. It was not a time for marvel; it was a time for business.

Two men stayed downstairs, standing guard, while the other six proceeded upstairs, carefully navigating the private areas of the home.

They passed several closed doors before approaching the one that intelligence claimed was the governor's bedroom. This was the one of primary concern, as Governor Ericson had two children but both were away at college.

One of the Delta team members quietly and carefully grasped the handle as the other men poised for entry. He slowly turned the knob, thankful that it was unlocked, and swung the door open. Silence irrelevant now, all team members swept into the room, initially failing to wake the governor and his wife. Within seconds, however, Ericson stirred and turned before opening his eyes. Recognizing that something was amiss, and catching the silhouette of a strange person in the bedroom, he quickly sat up, his eyes wide and heart pounding. The start that he was given awoke his wife, who also sat up, and shuffled backward into the headboard in terror. Soon, they came to the realization that these were soldiers, and the governor's face relaxed, fully aware of what was happening.

"Governor Ericson," the team leader lowered his weapon. "By order of the President of the United States and the Joint Chiefs of Staff, Annapolis and the state of Maryland in general is hereby under U.S. jurisdiction. Martial law is declared, Maryland is no longer autonomous, and you and your lovely wife are to be placed under house arrest until further orders from the Commander in Chief."

"Perfect," Ericson sneered.

Chapter 29

"Breaking news: Thousands of people this morning were shocked when they walked outside to pick up their morning paper or leave for work, only to find soldiers occupying their cities and neighborhoods," the anchorwoman announced on television. President Chandler bit her nails while watching with the Vice President, her husband, General Bates, and the rest of her executive staff.

"In Fairfax County, Virginia, and in the suburbs surrounding Washington, commuters were slowed down for hours even on residential streets, waiting to pass security checkpoints before entering the District of Columbia," she continued as scenes of checkpoints, traffic, military trucks, soldiers, and lots of confused civilians flashed across the screen. "And this is the scenario that can be seen all over Maryland, including Baltimore and Annapolis."

"It's crazy," one woman said, being interviewed roadside while waiting to cross the Theodore Roosevelt Bridge. "I don't know what to think. There were soldiers on my street when I woke up this morning. It's scary. I mean, are we under attack or something? Terrorist watch alert?"

"President Chandler is set to address the nation from the White House any minute now," the anchor picked up again. "But for now, all we know is that there are United States Army personnel enacting martial law in the Virginia suburbs of DC, in various larger towns in Maryland, Baltimore, and even the capitol in Annapolis. Apparently, government functions of the state capitol have been completely shut down, leading us to only guess what is going on in Maryland. One such person who is making guesses is President Davenport of the Republic of America, who is calling this tyranny."

"All I know," Davenport's voice rang out through a PA system atop the steps of the state capitol in Austin in a tape that was recorded earlier in the morning, "is that I received a phone call from Governor Jesse Ericson from Annapolis a couple of days ago, and he told me that Cindy Chandler had paid a secret visit to him that morning. He said she tried to coerce him into breaking ties with the Republic so that Washington, DC, would not be surrounded by Republic lands. There the Democrats go again, putting Washington ahead of the rights of the people!" the crowd erupted into laughter.

"This is an abomination," he continued. "We are a sovereign country. Every one of the twenty-nine states of our union made the decision to put the people before big government and mismanagement of the country. And here they are bullying us again. This is an act of war!"

"None of the claims are confirmed," the anchorwoman returned. "But as we said, the President will address the country soon. President Davenport isn't the only one upset about these occurrences. While the DC, Baltimore, and Annapolis areas are mainly shocked and confused, the small towns, full of working class Republicans, have amassed in anger of the military occupation. Crystal Dane is on the scene in the small town of Stonebridge, Maryland. Crystal, what are you seeing there?"

"We're here outside the courthouse, where crowds have amassed in protest," the young journalist reported from the scene. "It's hard to tell just what anyone is shouting, but as you can hear, it's getting pretty loud and heated. We spoke to a few citizens earlier who felt pretty strongly about the U.S. government not having the right to occupy a town or state like this. They felt it is unconstitutional, akin to locking people away in a jail somewhere without charging them with a crime."

The camera shot panned across the main intersection of the pristine southern town, capturing the image of scores of angry citizens increasing pressure on the occupying force standing guard before the courthouse. From across the street, four men in their thirties and forties, wearing button-down work shirts and jeans approached the crowd gathering and chanting at the steps of the courthouse. At first, they were a minor image part of the whole panorama. Then, the camera operator noticed something about them, and zoomed in on them exclusively.

"What are we seeing, Crystal?" the anchorwoman asked curiously about the change in camera shot, but there was no response. "Is that a gun?"

All four walked with conviction and purpose, leaning into their strides, and intent on completing some sort of mission. One man was holding a hunting rifle of some sort, grasping its trigger area and the underside of the barrel with a readiness to fire. The other three men brandished semi-automatic handguns, carrying them muzzle-down, as they followed their leader across the street. He stopped suddenly, yelling something inaudible against the shouts of the angry mob, and then raised his rifle to his shoulder, took aim, and fired.

One of the soldiers atop the steps of the courthouse fell to the ground as the other three men raised their pistols, and began firing round after round. One more of the guarding troops fell before the rest were able to take cover behind the columns of the Greek Revival façade of the building. Shrieks of terror filled the air as the crowd dispersed in all directions, preventing the soldiers from gaining a clear shot of the four men. Finally, as the street became empty, the troops opened fire with their assault rifles, and the four men fell to the pavement, lifeless in the morning sun.

Cindy Chandler, watching the scene from the Oval Office, gasped in shock, her hand covering her mouth out of reflex. Her staff reacted in a very similar fashion, except for General Bates. He simply hung his head, shaking it back in forth in disappointment. It was not disappointment in his soldiers. They did exactly as they were trained to do. He was simply disappointed that the operation had gone so smoothly, without a shot fired up until that point. He now feared that since violence had erupted, the situation would soon deteriorate.

"Well," Cindy stood up and brushed the wrinkles from her suit. "With that, it's time to go and face the wolves."

She strolled confidently, but wearily toward the Oval Office exit, her team of assistants behind her. The General, her husband, the Vice President, and the Secretary of State all followed. The entourage made a left down the interior corridor of the White House, the deep crimson carpet beneath their feet. It seemed to go on forever as they passed wood and glass display cases filled with memorabilia. This was the presidential residence and business office, but it was just as much a museum, open to the public by appointment. The corridor was empty except for the Secret Service agents at seemingly random places along the wall. The crystal chandeliers hanging from between the molding on the ceiling provided just enough ambiance to unnerve the President. She felt as though she were being escorted to her own execution.

Chandler finally stopped short of the entrance to the east room, which typically, being the White House's most expansive room, hosted press conferences when they were needed. A small military band was present, perhaps to provide the drum roll to her death by press. A staff aide held a microphone, ready to announce her, but waiting until the final tests were made to the teleprompters on either side of the podium.

"Don't," Cindy choked on her words, but took a breath and cleared her throat. "Don't play 'Hail to the Chief,'" she shook her head at the band leader.

"What should I play, Madam President?" he implored.

"Nothing," she replied with grave seriousness. "Don't play anything. It's not a state dinner. In fact, you're all dismissed."

"Yes, ma'am," he nodded, and led the small band back down the corridor past the president's entourage.

"And you," she reached out to the man that would be announcing her. "You won't be needing that microphone."

"Yes, ma'am," he exited as well.

Now she simply awaited the go-ahead from the podium test crew. She was like a professional football player, standing in the entranceway leading from the tunnel to the stadium. It was game time. Her heart pounded as she tried to take deep breaths. She swayed heavily from one foot to the other, psyching herself up, yet trying to remain calm before finally getting the signal from the men checking the stage.

The dull rumble of reporters' voices filled her ears as she entered the room, but came to an eerie halt when she came into their view. Hundreds of eyes were upon her, analyzing her in silence. They sat, some crossing their legs, in the rows of gray metal folding chairs, clutching digital recorders and note pads, ready for her first words. Photographers began snapping the first images of her on their expensive Japanese-made cameras, and live-feed cameras rolled in the back of the room as she began to speak.

"I'm sure you all have plenty of questions," she began, "but as you are well aware, I have recently acquired a very busy schedule. So there will be no questions at the end of this conference, but I assure you that I will explain everything you could ever hope to know."

The room remained hushed; hanging on to her every word and following her every move. She would have to be conscious of even her body language, as the entire world would eventually see this statement. She tried to shake her excited nerves and take deep breaths before continuing.

"No one in this country could ever have imagined that a crisis like this would happen again. In the 1850s and 1860s, our country was going through its adolescence. We were coming of age and learning to deal with new and unique challenges. We were rebellious and hot-tempered. We threw a fit when we didn't get what we wanted. But we matured, and learned eventually what was more important in life. It was a speed bump in the ongoing experiment in democracy that is our United States of America. But now, it appears, we have entered a mid-life crisis of sorts. We are turning away from what's important; rebelling once again against the greater good in favor of our own selfishness."

She paused for a brief moment, scanning the room and the faces of the journalists, many of whom she knew quite well. She was fishing for reactions and gauging the effectiveness of her analogy before continuing. The expressions varied, usually depending on the political views of each reporter and the network or newspaper they worked for.

"As you are well aware, Washington, DC, is surrounded on three sides by the state of Maryland, and on the fourth by Virginia across the Potomac River. These are secessionist states. So effectively, the capitol of the United States was in exile. This is no way to run a government. It makes no logical or geographical sense. It has also been my fear and the fear of my staff and cabinet that should the Republic become aggressive or hostile, Washington may become a sitting duck. It had been my hope since the beginning of this ordeal to resolve the crisis with diplomacy and compromise. It never seemed feasible for me to send a military force against my own people. Two days ago, I met with Maryland's Governor Ericson at his office in Annapolis. My goal was to perhaps convince him to compromise with our government. I attempted to negotiate for the return of the state of Maryland back into the fold. Unfortunately, these negotiations did not end well, and I was left with no choice."

"I followed the precedence of a former great president in that the Union should be preserved at all costs, and it became my decision to begin this process. In the early morning hours, a large military force began an operation to secure the capitol of Washington, DC, for our country. As a security force secured the perimeter of the District of Columbia, another force crossed the Potomac into Virginia, occupying most of Fairfax County—particularly the important government installations at the Pentagon and the CIA. Another group secured Baltimore and most of the county seats of Maryland. Lastly, to ensure that the state remains in U.S. hands, Annapolis, the state capitol, has been occupied, and its governor has been detained."

Gasps filled the empty air. No one could believe this was happening.

"It was our hope that this would be a surprise operation, and that no one would have the chance to react. Militarily, this is accurate. It is unfortunate, however, that in one of the county seats, a handful of understandably angry citizens took it upon themselves to attack the troops sent to occupy their town. For this, I send my deepest condolences to the families of these four men. I also offer my condolences and gratitude to the families of the U.S. soldier who was killed and the one who was seriously wounded in the operation in that town."

"It is with that that I close in saying that this crisis of sectionalism and partisanship is no easy fix. This will take time, and it will be a difficult road. I pray, and ask all of America to pray, for a peaceful solution.

Let cool heads prevail, and let us find a way to negotiate peacefully, lest we see any more bloodshed in the coming months. Thank you."

She then exhaled greatly, and closed her eyes, allowing herself to calm, all to the rising rumble of voices throughout the room. She then turned gracefully, stepped down from the stage, and disappeared into the corridor of the White House's interior.

Chapter 30

"I can't believe this shit!" Kyle heard his father spout in elevated volume as he opened the front door.

His eyes widened, turning his head to the rear to see what Ryan's reaction was to the sudden outburst. Ryan was startled, but grinned a bit in discomfort, unsure that this was a good time to be visiting the Perkins household. A little embarrassed, Kyle simply shrugged it off as a fairly common occurrence lately.

"I mean, who the hell does she think she is?" Drew continued his rant. His tone was angered, but not directed at anyone in particular.

"She's the president of the United States, Drew," Angela fired back in a less boisterous manner. "And it's her job to keep this country together."

"Well she screwed that up, didn't she? Just couldn't budge or compromise, and now look what's happened!"

"You mean she didn't give in to the Republican Party," she pointed out. "If the American people wanted Republican leadership, they would have elected that dipshit Davenport. She implemented her views, her party's views, and the people's views. Davenport would have done the same, and would we have been any better off?"

Kyle and Ryan slowly inched closer to the kitchen and family room, where this heated debate was taking place. They were like a Special Forces team creeping up on the enemy. Eventually, they would have to make their presence known, but timing, they felt, was everything.

"Well I think this bitch…" Drew stopped short as he spied the two young men entering the room.

"Hi, Dad," Kyle greeted his father nervously and embarrassed, revealing that he had brought home a friend.

"Hey, son," Drew tried to calm down and feign normalcy. "Didn't hear you boys come in."

"Hi Ryan!" Angela erupted into her usual cheery, high-pitched host mode. "Haven't seen you in a while. How have you been?"

"Fine," Ryan said awkwardly.

The silence that followed only lasted a few moments, but it was about as awkward and intense as it could be. No one could think of what to say next, nor could either of them deny or shroud the perfectly normal, yet usually private argument. It became obvious that no one else would attempt to change the mood, so Kyle took it upon himself to remove the tension.

"Well we're going to go upstairs," he motioned to the staircase.

"Sure, sure," Angela nodded with exaggerated interest. "Are you staying for dinner, Ryan?"

"Um, yes ma'am, if you'll have me," he replied. "I just have to text my mom."

"Okay, see you in about an hour," she retreated into the kitchen.

The two turned and began up the carpeted staircase into the upper floor. The boards squeaked lightly with each step, something that Kyle found almost irritating. They reached the apex where the media and game room was situated, passing the sectional couch and the entertainment center, which was complete with a television, movies, and a gaming console.

As Kyle shuffled past his brother's room, he peered in from the corner of his eyes to see Dylan just lying on his bed which had not been made in months. This was what he did with most of his free time. While Kyle read books or watched educational programming, Dylan lounged around nearly comatose, listening to his MP3 player. The ear buds never seemed to be detached from his ears. And when they were, they were looped up through the inside of his shirt, and were left hanging from the outside of his collar.

"Hey, douchebag," Kyle slapped Dylan's open door frame twice, but his brother did not really hear. All he knew was that Kyle had likely called him something demeaning.

The two young men entered Kyle's well-organized bedroom, and set down their backpacks. The walls were covered with posters of popular rock bands with an accentuating electric guitar and amplifier collecting dust in the corner. He was quite good at it, but with a girlfriend, his hands were rarely idle enough to play. He had played once for Ashley, and she showed how impressed she was in a physical nature.

The rest of the room contrasted greatly with the rock and roll theme. There were history, philosophy, and fictional books placed neatly on his shelves. His desk was dust-free, and the pens and pencils were well-organized into little wire baskets. His large flat-screen computer monitor scrolled a Voltaire quote in a banner-mode screen saver. The bed was made, and there were no dirty underwear on the floor. This was not an attempt to appear tasteful and mature to his girlfriend. This was just the way he was.

"I'm sorry it's been so long since we've hung out," Kyle sat down at his computer, moving the mouse to remove the screen saver.

"I know. It's the girlfriend thing. I'd probably be the same way," Ryan plopped down on the bed. "Where is she, by the way?"

"Oh, she's off visiting her grandmother in Tyler for a few days."

"So, this whole reunion is temporary?" Ryan sneered a bit.

"No, dude. She understands. We don't have to be together all the time. She'd like to hang out with her friends, too. And she'd like the three of us to hang out," Kyle said.

"Are any of these friends hot?" Ryan perked up.

"Of course," Kyle smiled.

"Get me laid?" Ryan smiled.

"I can lead you to the promised land, Gideon," Kyle replied in his best God voice, "but it is you who must slay the Canaanites."

They each burst into laughter at the jest, but it died down rather quickly as their expressions became uncomfortably serious. It was clear that they had been apart too long to have that natural rapport one would find in two life-long friends.

"Man, I can't believe we're actually going to graduate soon!" Ryan broke the silence.

"Yeah, I can't wait," Kyle nodded. "What are you going to do after graduation? Have you figured that out?"

"Um…" he hesitated. "I've been looking at the military."

"The military?" Kyle was shocked. "For the Republic? Do they even have a standing military?"

"Yeah, you know all those bases that were confiscated? Some of the troops stuck around, loyal to the state. You haven't seen the military guys at school, trying to recruit seniors?"

"Haven't really paid attention."

"Of course not. You have an ultra-hot girlfriend," Ryan smiled. "They offer basically the same deal as the GI Bill—money for school, so I have that option after I put in my time."

"What if there's a war or something?" Kyle asked in a concerned voice as he surfed the internet. "Holy shit," he stared at the latest news headlines. "That might already be happening," he blurted, finally understanding what his father had been raving about downstairs.

Chapter 31

Early April, Fourteen months before the bomb

It was humid. The spring had brought back warmth, and gulf moisture was swirling up through Louisiana, clashing at least twice a week with cold fronts, creating violent spring storms. At least the rain had relinquished for the day, but now the night was cool and damp. Each soldier was covered with leftover rain droplets that had dampened their fatigues as they grazed the light underbrush of the forest. Pine needles and leaves beneath their feet were water-logged, so they did not crackle. They also provided a barrier against the potential mud beneath.

The men were tired, and the worst was ahead. They had been on foot for miles carrying lots of gear, entering the pine forest surrounding Fort Polk from the nearest highways. The trucks and transports dropped them off and left so not to alarm any enemy personnel in the area. There would be no tank support or Humvees. There would be no air support from the nearby Air Force base. This operation was exclusively infantry.

It was a large force—it had to be. Fort Polk was a giant installation and training center. The woods were used for field training and survival instruction. Before the secession, it was home to about eight thousand personnel at any given time. The bright side was that the majority of the troops on this base were Republican sympathizers who left after the secession. Many were on this assault team.

Each and every man advancing toward the mostly sleeping Army base, at some point, thought back to two days before, and the briefing given to them by General Daly.

"Gentlemen," he faced the men in the auditorium, microphone in hand. "We have been ordered to take control of Fort Polk, which is near Leesville, Louisiana," his voice boomed in its light southern drawl.

"If Cindy Chandler thinks it's okay to invade two sovereign states of the Republic, then by God, we're gonna take back the bases that are rightfully ours."

The men cheered, and the general paused with pride growing across his face.

"Eglin Air Force Base in Pensacola is gonna be a cake-walk. Those boys have got it easy. There's no standing infantry there and no way to get any there. They'll be sunning on the beach with little umbrella drinks, and whistlin' at all the spring break tail by that afternoon," he smiled as the men erupted into laughter, cheers, and whistles.

"But you ain't gonna have it so easy. You've got an ordeal on your hands, and I'm afraid that most of you are gonna have to fire your rifles. I trained at Fort Polk, as did many of you. The good news is we know the terrain. We know the facilities. But those blue boys do too. And they're gung-ho. And they're well-armed. And they're well-trained. There are currently just under three thousand troops on that base, and they're doubtless startin' to run low on supplies. They're isolated, so once we take control of this installation, that's it. It ain't gonna be easy. We're gonna hit 'em with a force of four thousand, so we'll be able to overpower them, hopefully."

"Fort Polk is nestled real snug in the middle of a pine forest. It's pine forest for miles in every direction, except in the direction of Leesville to the north. We'll have to hump it on foot from the nearest highways. We're gonna do this under the cover of night, so we need the element of surprise. No choppers, no tanks, no vehicles. Just blood and guts. We can get this done, men. Start prepping and we'll see you in a couple of days!"

The men crept between the towering pines without a sound. Not even the wind stirred. No one spoke and no sound could be heard anywhere, except for the crickets and bullfrogs. They could tell that they were drawing dangerously near to the base. Orange fluorescent night-sensor bulbs dully illuminated the rising mist and turned the pines into silhouettes. Now they would lose the cover of darkness.

Republican troops began to emerge from the shadows of the woods into the inside of the base complex. They fully expected that they had the element of surprise, but they remained cautious anyway. They could not have known what they were literally stepping into. Beneath their feet, throughout the forest they so carefully traversed, pressure sensors lay buried beneath several inches of soil. Leaves and pine needles where then scattered over the disturbed ground, giving the illusion that nothing was there. With each foot that stepped unknowingly down upon one of these sensors, the signal was transmitted back to central command as a blip on a satellite image of the base and its surroundings.

"Sergeant," a private monitoring the satellite screen spoke with concern in his voice, "we have movement in the woods."

"It might just be a deer," the sergeant did not lift his eyes from his magazine.

"That's a lot of goddamned deer, sir!"

The commanding officer finally looked up to see dozens of sensors flashing on the private's computer screen. A look of terror flashed across his face as he dropped his magazine on the floor. He stood up, and crept slowly closer to the computer console, crouching and peering at it in disbelief. He finally bolted back to his radio, picked it up, and then began to speak frantically.

"Code Red, Code Red," he spouted. "We've got company!"

The call went out to a number of people across the base. Troops stationed in sand-bagged fox holes across the interior of the base began quietly loading their M-240, M-249, and Browning M2 automatic rifles. MPs entered the homes of the top Army brass, alerting them to the coming assault. Gunnies within enlisted barracks began waking soldiers, ordering them to quickly dress and retrieve weapons and munitions from small arsenals installed within the housing.

Republican troops slowly crept into the base grounds, their weapons raised and their eyes carefully scanning for resistance. From the shadows within the barracks, eyes watched to see the enemy moving toward the interior, which was exactly what they wanted—surround and crush them. Men crouched behind the sandbags of the randomly-placed machine gun nests, waiting for their prey to come to them.

The Republican troops began fanning out in the direction of their objectives. Some headed for the main administrative building, while others made their way toward the arsenal. Once enough of them were showered with the dull orange luminescence pouring from the fluorescent lights above, the U.S. soldiers manning the machine guns opened fire.

The guns thundered from behind their bunkers, piercing the night and echoing from tree to building. The sound was as terrifying as it was deafening. It was all of Hell's fury, swirling around the grounds of the base. The muzzles flashed with fire as every fifth round was accompanied by a tracer. The Republican soldiers' hearts immediately began beating at three times the normal rate, pumping adrenaline throughout their bodies with rage. The excessive heart rates caused dense, crimson blood to spray violently from their chests and abdomens with each bullet that pierced them.

Panic ensued amongst the Republicans as they had no artillery or mortar support to destroy the machine gun nests. It was open field, so there was no place to take cover. It was a turkey shoot. One soldier no older than twenty removed a grenade from his utility vest, and pulled the pin, intent on lobbing it into one of the bunkers. He was cut down by a hail of gun fire as the grenade dropped from his hand causing the safety lever to separate. The grenade exploded, sending shrapnel into a deadly fifteen-meter blast radius. Several other Republican troops dropped to the ground bleeding and dying, peppered with chunks of steel.

To add to the confusion, dozens of men began pouring from within the barracks in an attempt to surround the Republicans and prevent any retreat. But one of the objectives of the assault was to secure those very barracks. As the soldiers began moving out of the bunk houses and toward the Republicans to the interior, they experienced fire from behind them. At other barracks, men were pierced with bullets just as they exited the door.

As Republicans piled up around the bunkers, U.S. bodies began heaping near the bunk houses. The men began breaking windows from inside the barracks, and firing from within. The thin walls were not enough to stop the Republican bullets fired at them, and they fell lifeless on the beds, soaking them with blood. Other Republican soldiers threw grenades in through doors and broken windows, clearing the long buildings of remaining personnel.

US troops who did manage to teem from within their bunkhouses moved around to the opposite sides from their enemy, attempting to gain cover, while sporadically peeking around to fire back. They drew fire, however, from enemy troops to the interior, and were surrounded.

"What the hell do we do, sir?" one private yelled to his sergeant.

He looked around at his men pointing their rifles in both directions in futility, several of them dropping in a spray of blood. It all seemed to move in slow motion, and the roar of gun fire overwhelmed his senses and his judgment.

"Move to the interior!" he finally yelled back.

"Sir?" the private could not believe what he was hearing. "You want us to charge them?"

"Neither side will fire! They won't risk hitting their own men! We'll have to take our chances hand-to-hand!" he screamed over the gunfire and bullets ricocheting around them. "Now move!"

As the men around that bunk house stood erect and ran into the interior, the other pockets of U.S. soldiers caught on, replicating the move. Several bursts of fire cut down a few of the charging men, but then ceased. Knives and bayonets were unsheathed, and side arms unholstered as men clashed in hand-to-hand combat rarely seen in the modern era. It was as a medieval blood bath of infantry with blades slashing at throats and men wrestling to the ground in a struggle for survival.

One blue soldier clutched the throat of his opponent pinned to the ground, and then successfully drove his utility knife through the man's chest with a crackle of bone, cartilage, and tissue. He then grabbed the pistol to his side, and sprang to his feet, spinning around to shoot the man behind him, dropping him to the ground.

"What the hell are you doing?" his comrade grabbed his arm. "That's Mitchell—he's in your own bunk!"

He lowered the pistol to see the familiar, but lifeless face of one of his own men. A shutter of remorse and sickness to the stomach overtook him. He had just murdered one of his own, but his eyes began scanning the deadly scene around him, horrified at what he saw.

"I can't tell who's who!" he answered. "Everyone is wearing the same goddamned thing!"

The massacre continued at the interior of the base. The machine guns had since stopped firing for fear that they would hit their own men. All they could do was watch the carnage before them in horror. American pummeled American with fists and rifle stocks. Jaws broke and foreheads were smashed in. Blades sliced and cut at human flesh as blood spilled to the dirt, forming a brownish-red mud. Pistols fired, finishing off men subdued on the ground, and young soldiers choked the life from one another's bodies with their bare hands.

A storm of red troops engulfed the inactive machine gun nests as a few bullets were fired into one or two resisting operators. The rest threw up their hands in defeat, and were pulled from the bunkers. As the prisoners were forced to the ground under threat of being shot, Republican troops took hold of the machine guns, pointed them at the sky, and squeezed the triggers, creating a sudden thunder of fire that echoed across the field of battle. It was a signal. Resistance was now futile. Reds surrounded the hand-to-hand scene, their rifles pointed into the melee. The fighting slowed, and the battle was over.

The remaining U.S. troops were taken prisoner, and were marched toward the least damaged barracks. Some were hoarded into the mess hall as the base teemed with the second wave of the invasion. Soon would follow trucks filled with more men, supplies, and munitions.

The general in command of the base was marched onto the open battle grounds, his hands and the hands of his subordinates clutching the backs of their heads. The general was met with General Daly of the Republican Guard. They squared off with one another. Daly's pleased expression contrasted greatly with his opponent's sad, sour dismay.

"General," Daly grinned, "you and your men are now prisoners of the Republic of America. You will be held here indefinitely. You will not be harmed. Polk is now rightfully Republic territory. Enjoy your stay," he antagonized, and then walked away with a smile.

Chapter 32

"Sit down, Mom," Derek looked up from the skillet of sizzling scrambled eggs he was stirring.

Sherry hobbled across the living room on her weak and wavering legs, hunched over as if she had osteoporosis. Her legs shook and threatened to give out as her increasingly limp hands clutched the remote control. She approached her motorized wheelchair, reaching for it with her free hand, and slowly turned her body, positioning her rear end above the cushioned seat. She released a sigh of relief and near exhaustion as she plopped down into the seat, winded from her excursion.

"Mom, you have to stay in that seat. I could have gotten that remote for you," he lightly scolded her as a father to a child.

"I can still do it," she continued to breathe heavily. "I'm losing the ability to do normal things. I have to hold on to what I still have."

"I know, Mom," he hung his head. "I just don't want you to fall and break a bone. Hey, let me know when you need to go to the bathroom, and I'll help you onto the seat."

"You see, that's exactly what I'm talking about," she shook her head in shame. "Normal stuff like going to the bathroom I've done by myself for decades, and now I have to get my son to put me on the toilet and change my diaper. It's humiliating."

"It's humiliating for me, too, Mom," he reminded her. "Just hang in there. We'll make due."

Sherry held the silver remote control in her left hand, limply grasping it from the underside. She had to balance it on her palm now that her hand muscles were growing so weak. With her right index finger, she aimed and pressed the power button at the top of the remote, struggling to apply enough pressure without upsetting its balance in her other hand.

"You want me to get that?" Derek glanced over at her fighting to turn on the television.

"No, I've got it," she insisted, finally hearing the click of the TV springing to life. "Let's see. What have we here? News? Works for me."

Derek grinned as he turned off the burner, and began scooping eggs onto two blue paper plates. The eggs completed the meal already present on the plates—toast, hash browns, and sausage. He grinned because he knew that it wasn't news that his mother particularly wanted to watch. She just did not want to fight to change the channel. She knew that he would see her struggling and ask to help her. That would never happen.

He placed her plate on a bed tray, along with a cup of orange juice with a straw, and grabbed from the drawer a special thick-handled fork that would be easier for her to grip. The reporter's voice on the television was just babble to him until he carried his mother's tray into the living room, and set it upon her lap.

"Thank you, sweetie," she smiled.

But Derek's eyes were now fixed upon the screen, paying no attention to his mother. His eyes widened, and his mouth slowly became ajar in disbelief over what he was hearing and seeing on TV.

"What is it?" Sherry's gaze darted from her son to the TV and back.

"Shh. Look," he nodded toward the screen.

"If you're just joining us this morning, we're covering some breaking news," the brunette anchor spouted sternly. "Last night and early this morning, a Republican force of thousands launched an attack on the last two remaining United States bases in Republic territory."

"Oh my God," Sherry uttered silently.

"We have no images or footage, as we are unable to make it into the areas, but we do know that Eglin Air Force Base fell easily. The worst fighting was at Fort Polk in rural Louisiana. Over a thousand are reportedly dead in total. All, according to General Daly of the Republican Guard, dead U.S. servicemen will be sent back to their families for proper burial. In response to this, President Cindy Chandler has asked the remaining membership in Congress to declare war on the Republic—something that was promptly done. Take a look."

"I had hoped that it would never come to this," Chandler spoke from behind her podium in the White House rose garden. "The prospect of American-versus-American warfare has been unthinkable until now. Most Americans thought that these political growing pains of sectionalism and partisanship were far behind us. But last night, surprise attacks were launched by the Republic against our bases at Eglin and Fort Polk, killing countless scores of men. Now it is inevitable that we must respond to this aggression in a sacred mission to prevent any further hostility from this renegade government and to once again preserve the Union in our great country."

"Oh my God," Derek searched for words to express how he felt.

The phone rang, startling him from his trance, and he rushed over to pick up the receiver of the aging thing. The ringing stopped as he pushed it to his ear.

"Hello," he said with hesitation. "This is he. Yes sir. Yes sir. Thank you," he replaced the phone on the hook, and hung his head low.

"What is it?" concern stretched across Sherry's thinning face.

"Active duty," he replied with sorrow. "I leave in the morning."

"San Diego?" she asked excitedly.

"Rhode Island," he shook his head. "I don't think I'll be staying there, either," he motioned toward the TV.

"Oh God," she placed her withering hand over her widening mouth. Horror swept over her, and tears developed in the corners of her eyes. "Oh God," she began to weep.

Derek rushed over to his mother, and cradled her head into his chest, trying his best to console her, when the truth was that he could use some consoling himself. His expression was one of concern and contemplation. His blue t-shirt was becoming soaked with his mother's tears.

"It's okay, Mom," he whispered.

"What's going to happen to you?" she sobbed. "Who's going to take care of me?"

"I'll call Jake. He can help you out for now, and cook small meals you can put into the microwave when he's not here. Shit! I've got to call Carly. She might be able to help until she's further along with the baby. Shit! I probably won't even be here when my kid is born!" his sullen mood was turning to that of anger. "I've got to call her," he jumped up. "I've got to pack!"

Chapter 33

The faces surrounding the long, rectangular wooden table were sullen and stern. It was a buildup of potential emotion, ready to become kinetic. The President and her cabinet all stared back at one another and at the Joint Chiefs of Staff, each anticipating that someone else was going to say the first word. Ultimately, it came to President Chandler to get the ball rolling.

"Okay," she parted her folded hands, "where do we stand?"

"Well, Madam President," Secretary of State Delaune spoke after a long moment, "it looks like the rest of the world is really staying out of this one. No allies. No enemies."

"No one's going to help us out?" Chandler asked in disappointment.

"We still aren't on the best of terms with much of the world since our war on terror. England looks like they are afraid to back the loser, so they're staying out of it. Europe and Asia will continue to trade with both us and the Republic, as if this isn't even happening."

"Can we threaten embargo with those who trade with the Republic?" Vice President Coffman chimed in.

"Not without a reciprocal embargo," Delaune put it bluntly. "We can't afford to go without international trade. We'd be shooting ourselves in the foot. We need funding. Wall Street can't carry this burden alone, and that's all we have. But even then, thousands of homeowners with mortgages through US-based banks are refusing to pay their loans back, so they're losing money, and so are investors that underwrite the loans. And there's not a damned thing we can do about it. There's a little industry here in the blue states, but finance and international trade is our heartbeat."

"While the Reds have something tangible—oil," the president interrupted.

"And lots of it," Delaune continued. "They've ramped up off-shore drilling three hundred percent in the last two months, and that's not counting the fact that most of the huge natural gas reserves on this continent are in red states. Then there are the financial and corporate centers in Dallas, Houston, Miami, Tampa, and Atlanta. The Reds are well-funded."

"And we're borrowing from Peter to pay Paul," Coffman added.

"I get it," Chandler broke up the banter. "That's out. Is there anyone backing the Republic?"

"One, Madam President," Delaune stated. "Mexico. We don't know what the relationship is at this time, but it appears that Mexico has chosen their side."

"Does it look like Canada is going to have our backs?" the Vice President asked.

"They're divided," Delaune replied. "The industrial, financial, and governmental end of Canada in the east is all about it, but they're getting resistance from the western provinces bordering the Republic in the west. It's more rural out there, like the states they border. The exception is the Vancouver area, and that's west coast like California and Oregon."

"Okay, okay!" Cindy touted in frustration. "First things first. This occurred to me during the press conference. Stop all communications to red states. Newspapers, magazines, news channels—cut it off. We don't want to broadcast our plans to Austin on CNN."

"A gag order?" the Vice President raised his eyebrows.

"No, not a gag order. We don't want to screw with the first amendment. Just stop all broadcasts to the twenty-nine. No more publication delivery to the Republic. Refusal of service."

"And the internet?" Delaune inquired.

"Find a way to block users from having online access to that information."

A long pause of silence ensued for several moments. They had broken the ice in a way, but there was still an eight-hundred-pound gorilla in the Situation Room that no one quite wanted to tackle. This was the issue of further loss of human life. Logistics and economic issues could be discussed all day long. Military action and the planning of death was a bit more sensitive of an issue.

"Madam President," General Bates cleared his throat. "Would you like to know the Pentagon's plan of attack?" he asked with hesitation.

Chandler sighed, and closed her eyes. She removed her thin, wire-rimmed glasses for a moment and clenched the bridge of her nose as if she were feeling the onset of a headache. She replaced the glasses onto her face, and then opened her eyes, now more focused.

"Yes, please, General," she cocked her head to the side, giving him her full attention.

"First," he began, "we have to blockade the coasts just as Lincoln did. I'm assuming that could be the appeal to an alliance with Mexico. We'll have to keep an eye on smuggling and shipping activity between them and the Republic. But we have to take things a step further than Lincoln. We have to shut down the gulf ports and try to keep all that off-shore oil from getting to market, just like Lincoln cut off cotton export from the Confederacy. It's their financial lifeline."

"What are the key objectives?" Chandler was thoroughly engaged.

"I don't think we have much to worry about on the southern eastern seaboard—not even Miami or anywhere in Florida, for that matter. The main area of focus should be from Alabama to Texas. We'll send the Marines to take Mobile, New Orleans, Baton Rouge, and the Galveston/Houston area. Those are the biggest shipping and oil ports. The lower Mississippi River valley is particularly important because of all the refineries. There are also some refinery objectives to hit in eastern and southern Texas."

"Okay, that takes care of the southern coast. What about the rest?" Chandler spurred him on.

"Most of these western states don't really have any importance to us militarily," he began again.

"What about all the missile silos and such in those states?" Cindy cut him off.

"I don't think they're going to be using them. I don't think they want American cities that they too love, to be decimated. I don't think they want to inflict that much death and destruction on us. They will be on the defensive. They just want to be left alone. Besides, if the major red states fall, they have no support, so they will follow suit," he explained casually.

"Okay, so what *are* the objectives?"

"Atlanta and the southeastern states up and down the Atlantic is a start. We'll hit hard-line red state capitols in Alabama and Mississippi. We'll take territory and ports all along the Mississippi River. And then, of course, there's Dallas/Fort Worth and Austin. We'll push through these areas, and deal with any skirmishes on the way, but once we hold these positions, they'll fall apart at the seams."

"No bombings of American cities. Maybe bases," Chandler said firmly.

"No, ma'am. Understood. This isn't Fallujah. We actually care about preserving the cities and infrastructure when we can," Bates smirked.

"My Air Force guys," the Air Force Chief spoke up, "will aid in paratrooper transportation and delivery, as well as fighter support."

"This whole thing is going to depend on the Navy blockade, infantry, and artillery," Bates concluded.

Everyone paused once again. This was a big decision. This was the planning of a total war on home soil. It would cause the loss of potentially thousands of military and civilian lives. One could never make that choice lightly and casually. Chandler pondered the strategy in her head, using what she knew of economics and geography—subjects she had not actively studied in over twenty years. It was all she could add to the planning. She was never in the military, so she was lost on the topic of tactics.

"Okay, general," she said. "Do what you know best. Begin organizing troops and ramp up weapons, vehicle, and supply production."

"Um, Madam President?" Secretary of Defense Jay Shields was awkwardly silent during the discussion until that moment. "That's another problem."

"Great," she shook her head. "Another problem. That's what I need. What is it?"

"Well, ma'am, there are some logistical problems that didn't exist in Lincoln's day. One problem is that most gasoline production is done in the south, and they're surely going to cut us off, so we'll be limited in our ability to move troops and transports. Most food production is done in the red states. Our civilians are already going to have to deal with inflation and higher costs of food and gas, much less our troops."

"Shit," she buried her head in her hands. "Okay, I'll give an executive order to temporarily lift tariffs on imported foods from Canada and Europe. Let's also start rationing gasoline while we work out something with the Saudis. In the meantime, put the auto companies to work on ethanol and electric conversion solutions."

"We can retro-fit the vehicles," Bates spoke up, "but most ethanol is produced from corn, and most of that is grown in red states."

"Actually," Delaune corrected, "we can make ethanol from anything that is or was plant life. Scientists have synthesized an enzyme produced by bacteria that breaks plant life into ethanol. We could recycle your morning paper into fuel if we wanted."

"Perfect," Chandler cheered. "Get on it for the military, and I'll work on getting Congress to pass a tax incentive for the average family to convert."

"And then there's weapons," Shields added. "Most of our guns and ammunition are made here in the States, or they're imported from Europe, but many of our plants producing planes, choppers, and tanks are located in red states. I'm sure they'll be getting to work producing for the Republic."

Cindy thought for a moment, tapping her pen on the table. It was almost deafening in the silence of the room, as everyone became slightly annoyed by its repetition. She nibbled on the inside lining of her lips, and stared down at the table until the grain lines in the wood blurred.

"We'll just have to make due with what we have," she lifted her eyes, and then glared at the Joint Chiefs. "Make every plane, tank, and truck count."

"Yes, ma'am," Bates nodded.

"Let's do it," she stood up and exited the room to go to another engagement.

Chapter 34

President Byron Davenport sat behind his massive wooden desk in the temporary presidential office in the Texas State Capitol building. He peered out the window into the gardens below, watching as the Hispanic gardeners manicured the capitol grounds. He felt for them. It was hotter than normal for April. There had been not a drop of rain in Austin, or much of the state, in a couple of weeks. The deadly rays of the sun super-heated the surface with little resistance from cloud cover. Temperatures had been climbing into the nineties, when they should have been topping out at eighty this time of year. He was glad that he had an indoor job.

He was, however, beginning to regret getting this particular indoor job. This was the first break he had all day. He enjoyed and also loathed this chance to be alone. The problem was, being alone with his thoughts was dangerous at this point. His thoughts were tainted with regret and stress. There were too many things to think about—the construction of the new capitol of the Republic, protecting his new country, recruitment of military personnel, and everything that went along with a declaration of war.

He was shaven and his silver hair was all in place, yet he did not look good. He looked old and tired. Dark circles and puffiness sat below his eyes. The lines on his forehead were deepening. The coat to his suit was draped over the back of his chair, and the top collar of his white shirt was unbuttoned. The gray, black, and white tie hung loosened and sloppy. If he were at a red carpet Hollywood event, this would be stylish, but he was a statesman.

He opened the bottom left drawer of his desk, and hunched to reach inside. He grunted, feeling his muscles ache and his bones creak before grasping what he was looking for. As he straightened his back and sat up straight, he revealed in his hand a bottle of fine single-malt scotch. He refilled his small glass, and placed the bottle carefully back into its drawer.

He sighed as he brought the glass almost to his face, and then stopped to stare at it for a moment, almost in hesitation. His nostrils detected the distinct scent of the libation, causing his mouth to water with craving. With that, he had no choice but to drink it down, and he did so with one gulp. The liquid burned his mouth, and then his esophagus and stomach on the way down, causing him to wince as if in pain.

But it was not pain he was feeling. It was relief. It made him feel better. It seemed to obliterate his worries and concerns, if but for a moment. And it was only a moment's relief. Soon the torrent of stress and toxic thoughts filled his head again, combining with the alcohol to actually make things worse. And the stress was, indeed, about to become greater.

"Mr. President?" the door opened and Davenport's secretary peeked her head in.

"Yes?" he lifted his head, almost startled from his trance.

"Your military advisors are here," she smiled. "Should I show them in?"

"Um," he began buttoning his collar, "give me a minute, and then show them in."

He seemed to struggle with the button, fumbling with his fingers until he finally got it right. He then tightened his Windsor knot and straightened it before standing and snatching his coat from the back of the chair, and putting it on.

The door opened again. In stepped former U.S. Army General Dale Weaver and former Navy Rear Admiral Denton Haskell. They each wore their traditional military dress, complete with all the decorations earned during their service to the United States. The difference was the newly adopted twenty-nine star red flag of the Republic upon each of their shoulders.

"Sir," Weaver waltzed in astutely, "we're not bothering you, are we?"

"No, no," Davenport sat behind his desk and frantically grabbed at his scotch glass to hide it in one of the drawers. "Please, sit down," he motioned to the two chairs before his desk.

The two men approached the desk with posture that could only be taught in the military. They each pulled a chair back toward them slightly, and rounded the side to sit and face their new commander in chief.

"Where are we, gentlemen?" Davenport asked them.

"In…" Haskell began hesitantly, looking around. "In your office, sir."

Davenport giggled a bit with a big, toothy smile. It would have been one thing if the admiral were joking, but his serious and confused expression told the president otherwise. Davenport should have been worried for the mental capacity of one of his top advisors, but instead, he appreciated the much needed laugh.

"No, admiral," Davenport clarified. "I mean, where are we with defenses?"

"Sir," Weaver interjected before his counterpart could embarrass himself more, "we're sending all the troops and ships we have where they need to be."

"And what's the plan? Remember, we're not going on the offensive. We don't want to invade and take over the United States. We just want our autonomy."

"Of course, sir," Weaver nodded. "We're sending troops to fortify and protect our biggest cities—Atlanta, New Orleans, Nashville, Dallas, Houston. But we're still limited on personnel. We're getting a lot of volunteers from rural areas of the country—rifle-packin' shit-kickers. But we're gonna need more."

"Alright," Davenport nodded. "Step up recruitment in the high schools. Our version of the GI Bill should be enticing enough."

"Done, sir," Weaver said. "Other than protecting our big cities and our capitols, we have to fortify the gulf coast. They're gonna want to hit our oil lines."

"Okay, are we good on weapons?"

"We have plenty of jets, planes, tanks, and transports on the bases we hold. We should be alright on that. We'll be a little short on guns and ammo if we get the recruitment we want, but we can always import that from Germany or Austria," he shrugged. "Looks like we're good to go."

"Alright, gentlemen," the president stood, as did his advisors. "Make it happen."

"Yes sir," they each said, shaking his hand.

They turned with one more nod to their leader, and strolled casually out of the office, shutting the door behind them. Davenport changed dramatically from the firm, charismatic leader he showed his advisors to a slumping, weary mess with the shutting of the door. He placed his elbows on the desktop, and buried his face in his hands, sighing with dismay. He dreaded what could happen in the coming weeks. Another drink.

Chapter 35

Late April

"I got the mail," Carly chimed sweetly, entering the Putnam household.

She smiled, feeling the cooler air inside the home, and walked over the creaky floor in the kitchen. She was beginning to show maturity, a transition from her wild party days. Her clothing had become more conservative. Her first maternity blouse draped over her, allowing for her slight protruding belly to have some room. It was not too baggy, however. The blouse was cut in a way that accentuated her otherwise normal form, and neither hid, nor hugged her pregnant shape.

Her light brown ponytail shifted and swung behind her head, as she approached her future mother-in-law, sitting and smiling in her power chair. The television was blaring and the living room was clouded with smoke. Beside Sherry was an end table covered with everything she needed: a remote control, a pack of cigarettes, a push-button torch lighter, a drink with a straw, half-eaten lunch, and a pair of adjustable pliers that allowed her to grip certain things that her hands could no longer grasp.

"Hi, sweetie," Sherry smiled upward at her. She had grown to love her son's girlfriend, and truly appreciated her helping.

"I see Jake made it by today," Carly motioned toward the food.

"Yeah, he came by to fix my lunch and mow the lawn," she sighed.

"You want me to refill your drink?" Carly reached for the empty plastic cup and handed Sherry a stack of mail that she had not even bothered to look through.

"Sure. There's a bottle of Dr. Pepper on the counter," she began flipping through the mail as the young woman reached into the freezer for a few more cubes of ice.

The ice clanked against the cup's plastic as she dropped them in, yet it was barely audible over the blaring TV. Sherry had been watching the news for hours, listening for updates on the war. So far, all she could gather was that U.S. forces had pushed southward through most of Virginia, West Virginia, and Kentucky, and with little resistance. All the newscasters seemed endlessly astonished that the combat had been so light. The casualties reportedly only numbered in the dozens in the past couple of weeks.

However, none of this was any concern of Sherry's. Her son was a Marine, and the forces invading the northeastern Republic were mainly Army. She had heard nothing of the Marines in any operation thus far. Then, as she flipped through the stack of seemingly endless bills, she came across a hand-addressed envelope. Her son's name was at the top, above the return address.

"Ha ha!" she would have leapt from her chair if her legs had the strength. "It's a letter from Derek!" her mouth gaped with an enormous smile.

Carly spilled a bit of cola on the counter, startled by the sudden outburst. She, smiling wildly now as well, slammed the plastic bottle onto the counter, sending a spurt of cola into the air, and back to the surface. She left Sherry's cup fizzing in the kitchen, and bolted for the living room where the deteriorating woman sat frantically struggling to open the letter with her increasingly limp fingers.

"Let me help," Carly grabbed at the envelope, meeting resistance.

Sherry would not relinquish the letter, partly because she was attempting to retain some autonomy, and partly because she still felt that Derek was still her son above being Carly's baby's daddy. She finally worked her right index finger beneath the adhesive flap, moving it long-ways along the envelope's back and tearing it open. She finally grasped the letter within, and began to read.

"Dear Mom, Carly, and Jake," she read aloud. "Sorry it's taken so long to get a letter out to you guys. I've been here about a week, training non-stop. It's been hard. At least it's cooler here than it was in Ohio. It's kind of a good thing North Carolina and South Carolina are in the Republic because I don't think I could have handled Camp Lejune or Paris Island and all the humidity. There have been some positives. Alex and Jackson are here, and they're even in the same bunkhouse. So I have some people here that I know."

"I don't know what's happening next. They won't tell us anything. They just keep drilling and training us. I can't tell you everything we're doing for security reasons. In fact, I'm sure they're going to read this letter before I send it to you. All I can say is they've introduced some new equipment I haven't worked with before. I hate not knowing what's in store or where we're going. They won't tell us until we're under way. I guess they don't want some blabber-mouth jarhead sounding off to his girlfriend about top secret missions."

Carly smiled, as she knew he must have been smiling at the thought of her in writing that sentence.

"Either way, I'm doing fine so far. Don't worry about me. I'm a good Marine. We're invincible. I love you all. Please take care of my mother, and Carly, sing my baby a lullaby for me every night. Tell her, or better yet, him, I love him! Hugs and kisses. Love, Derek."

"Ah," Sherry sighed and smiled as she folded the paper back as it had been done before.

"I'm relieved," Carly said, feeling satisfaction that her man was safe.

At that very moment, some 850 miles to the south-southwest, Derek's ears rang with every blast that he heard and felt through the hull of the ship. It made the final briefing nearly impossible to hear in that steel-encased room deep within the ship. His commanding officers had to yell at times to be heard at the level of a whisper.

"Okay," the commander yelled, pointing to the islands at the south end of the bay, "once we get these batteries out of the way, you'll move in aboard your landing craft—forty men per boat. First and Second Brigades will land at Point Clear on the eastern side of the bay, and push north to take control of I-10 and the bridge. Third, Fourth, and Fifth Brigades will land at the Mobile Downtown Airport further north, and push up into downtown. These sites were chosen for optimal navigability, landing, and control over the most populated areas. The water is pretty deep until you get right up to the shore. You shouldn't experience much resistance initially. Now remember, you have a long way to go from this ship to your landing zones. We're about four miles out from the entrance of the bay. First and Second Brigades have about another eighteen miles until they get to Point Clear. The rest of you have about twenty-five. Can't do anything about that. We can't risk bringing the warships into the bay and becoming surrounded. They'll tear us to pieces, but the landing craft does move pretty fast."

The commander was interrupted by a shell exploding in the water uncomfortably close to the ship. The room shook with shock to the hull, sending the map of Mobile Bay crashing to the floor. The commander appeared coolly startled, while the greenhorn Marines shook and crouched with terror.

"Remember your training, and you'll be fine, Marines!" the commander touted. "Semper Fi!"

"Hooah!" the men yelled back in unison.

"Johnson, did you piss yourself?" a man laughed in the back as the others joined in ridiculing a fellow private.

Blasts continued to rock the ship back and forth as the men and women made their way up the stair cases toward the top deck. They stumbled and stretched out their arms in an attempt to balance themselves. A young man lost his footing, and tumbled backward against Derek, who, struggling on his own, pushed at his back to hoist him again to his feet.

As the soldiers neared the deck, shelling ceased. There were no more canon blasts, nor were there any exploding shells threatening the U.S. ships. It was eerily quiet as they all began meeting the open air up top. Derek walked to the rails, his eyes squinting from the blinding sunlight. The humidity was sweltering. He placed his hands on the metal railing, only to retract them immediately in pain. Toward land, he could see two separate plumes of smoke rising upward to the few small clouds in the sky. To the left and right, a line of hundreds of ships formed the blockade and the invasion force. He could see men a few ships over struggling to extinguish flames aboard the USS Dayton. A destroyer beyond that one was already half-way submerged below the surface.

"Get your gear and get on the landing craft!" his sergeant yelled.

Derek and the rest of the men and women filed past the gun racks and equipment distribution section of the deck. Each soldier adorned flak jackets hanging with grenades and loaded with extra magazines of ammunition. They were handed assault rifles, machine guns, and mortar equipment, depending on what their role was in the ground force.

"Alright, over the side!" commanding officers and NCOs yelled as men began climbing down the World War II-style netting covering the side of the ship. Derek followed dozens of comrades, his rifle slung over his shoulder as he fought to keep his grip on the water-logged nylon. Seas were choppy, and the ship tossed to and fro, making it difficult to hang on, much less climb down. One Marine lost his footing, and fell dozens of feet into the rough gulf waters.

"Man overboard!" someone yelled, but Derek focused instead on his own boarding the craft below.

He finally reached the landing craft, his nerves a little more frayed over being one more step toward actual combat and shots fired in anger. As more troops loaded into the craft, space became more cramped. The sun's brutal rays baked each Marine, cooking them within their layers of clothing and gear. Smells of sweat and body odor hung low around the men and women, filling Derek's nostrils and strangely reminding him of high school gym class—a course that he actually earned A's in.

The landing craft were nearing their maximum capacity. There were scores of them, filled with thousands of scared, young soldiers. Reality was beginning to set in for Derek. He may not come back. The boats were strikingly similar to the World War II invasion craft used in the Pacific, Italy, and Normandy, only faster and lighter. Still, they were some distance from the landing zone. It would take over an hour to get there.

Derek's convoy of transports experienced no shelling as they approached the opening of Mobile Bay, and he could see why. To the west, he could see the smoldering remains of Fort Gaines on the eastern point of Dauphin Island. The Island was a major colonial outpost dating back to the seventeenth century. Fort Gaines was a Civil War era fortress, constructed in the classic five-pointed configuration of the day. It was a museum for decades, but now it had been retro-fitted with modern long-range cannons and new barracks. Now nothing remained of it. A few cannon barrels protruded from the rubble that doubtlessly crushed many men below.

To the east was a similar sight. Fort Morgan was a slightly older battery upon the Edith Hammock peninsula, yet similar in construction and with modern updates. The two forts staged a valiant attempt to guard the bay, but did not stand a chance against the massive firepower floating in the gulf.

Derek had a lot of time to think while struggling to keep his balance in a boat moving at high speeds over choppy seas. He began to understand what his great-grandfather's generation felt during their combat days. Aside from the more sophisticated weaponry and gear, Derek felt as though he were about to hit Omaha or Utah beach, going head to head with the Nazis. But he was not in some distant foreign waterway. They were Americans, and Derek would have to kill them.

The ride north through the bay was tiresome and nerve-racking. Short bursts of adrenaline shot through his body and increased his heart rate with a flutter each time he thought of what was to come. He sporadically felt the urge to urinate, and then each time, it passed. There was no cover to the landing craft, so for the duration of the ride, the relentless sun ruthlessly cooked the men with all the fury of ultraviolet radiation.

"Almost there, men," the driver suddenly yelled over the whoosh of wind and tide.

"Alright," their sergeant turned and looked at all his men, "once we land, you'll have to move quickly! We'll take the airfield first, which is where they will establish a command center! We'll begin pushing north into the suburbs from there! They know we're coming, but the fighting at the airport should not be heavy! The heavy stuff comes later! Good luck, Marines!"

Derek's heart sank deep into the pit of his stomach, first hearing the words of his sergeant, and then being unable to think of anything but that front ramp opening to the enemy. They always said to remember your training, but there was no amount of training that could prepare a man for this.

He could finally see the end of the runway as it ended at the bay itself. The boat passed some sort of giant pipeline that stretched out to the depths of the water and disappeared below the waves. His boat passed the point, intending to land further north of the runway, but he could see to the left that other landing craft were landing along the shore from the south end of the runway, all the way up.

His boat slowed from its wide-open throttle in preparation for landing. He could see no passenger planes or jets taking off. In fact, he could see no planes on the ground at all. He watched from afar as the first boats opened the front ramps, flowing with Marines storming toward the runway area. Small, twinkling flashes began further up the runway, and at first, Derek could not tell what it was. But then, looking back at the shoreline, he could see men falling to the ground, the sand, and in the shallow water.

Loud blasts of cannon fire echoed across the bay and shells exploded in the ground and the water all around. Giant craters and falling sand replaced the ground upon which his comrades were standing. Men and weapons disappeared in a geyser of earth and then rained back to the ground, never to rise again. To his right, shells sent bursts of sea water into the air between the attack boats. He watched in helpless horror as a traveling landing craft was ripped apart, obliterating every living being within it.

His boat finally struck beach, and simultaneously, the ramp opened before him. Immediately, bullets began whizzing around and ricocheting off of the metal sides of the boat. A young man to his right caught a bullet through his head, sending a spray of blood spattering across Derek's face. He could do nothing but drop his jaw in shock, and then do his best to exit the boat without being hit himself.

The gunfire they were taking north of the runway did not seem as heavy as he had seen further down. Perhaps the trees and brush behind this line of beach was stopping some of the bullets, or the gunners did not have a clear line of fire. There was a bit of a ridge that had to be climbed—a natural embankment that kept Derek's squad somewhat shielded, but not entirely. And they still had to push forward into the line of fire.

Troops filed off of the landing craft in droves, as some became pierced with bullets, and fell dead in the sand. The living fell to the ground as well, taking some cover beneath the lip of the ridge. Bullets cut through the grass and brush above their heads. A dozen dead bodies lay gushing blood all around Derek. He was petrified. He could not move. He could barely think. The cannon fire continued, taking chunks out of the beach and ridge around him.

"We've got to push forward!" a lieutenant yelled over the barrage. "We've got to make way for the next wave! Get up that ridge!" he ordered, and reluctantly they followed.

The men and women surged upward through the brush and small trees, arriving at a paved street. On the other side, surprisingly, was a neighborhood, isolated by runway to the south and west, and by airport administrative buildings to the north. Even in the midst of battle, Derek could not help thinking that the owners of the houses had made a horrible real estate investment.

Like flies to a slab of rancid meat, the Marines swarmed to the homes for cover. They began lining the back sides of the houses, and the more men that huddled behind them, the less fire they took. The gunners obviously did not want to risk killing any civilians still within the homes.

"Okay, we've found their weakness," the lieutenant peeked around the side. "Mortar squads, start putting some shells on those gunners up there," he ordered, pointing to a line of bunkers about half-way up the runway. "Gunners, set up your M240s and put some fire on them. Move it!"

The gunners began assembling their bipods. The two-man teams placed the medium machine guns onto the bipods. One fed the ammunition in through the side of the chamber, as the other pulled, and held down the trigger, sending a wall of gunfire toward the bunkers from between the houses. Rounds began piercing the sandbag bunkers, sending the filler pouring out the front. No one could tell at that distance whether or not any enemy personnel were being eliminated.

The mortar squads began setting up the long M120 tubes and adjusting the trajectory from behind the homes. Once they were set, which only took a few minutes, they began dropping 120mm live mortar shells down the barrel. The rest of the troops watched to see where the explosives were hitting in the distance.

"You overshot," Derek shouted back at them. "Adjust the arc. Sixty degrees should do it."

The mortar squad adjusted the tube's trajectory, and dropped yet another bomb down the tube. The pin at the bottom pierced the bottom of the round, and sent it zooming into an upward arc. It fell squarely into one of the bunkers, sending weapons, debris, sand, and bodily limbs flying into the air. Cheers resounded amongst the troops as the mortar squad began dismantling the Republican first line of defense.

Relief came over the men and women hunkered behind the homes at the north side of the runway, and a level of relief was given to those troops landing further to the south. The machine gun nests had taken a heavy toll on them. There was no cover to speak of for them. Yet, the cannons were still pumping shells into their landing position. Derek and his comrades could see the muzzle flashes of the large cannons on the tarmac over a mile from the landing site.

"We've got to get those cannons out of the way!" the lieutenant saw the urgency of the situation. He picked up the radio, and dialed up the command center located on the flagship.

"Command, this is Echo Company, First Brigade. Do you read?" he called, somewhat winded from the excess adrenaline.

"This is command. What is your status?" someone replied on the other end.

"Machine gun nests are cleared. The cannons are still in place. We do not hold the airport. Requesting air support. Over," he spouted back.

"Air support a go. Have one of your men paint the target. ETA, ten minutes."

"Roger," he said, and then dropped the radio. He looked around at the soldiers immediately surrounding him. "Putnam, get up on that house in the front, and paint the target."

"Yes sir," Derek responded reluctantly.

Another soldier handed Derek an olive drab nylon bag. He took the weighty satchel, and hoisted the strap over his shoulder, simultaneously laying down his assault rifle. He was hesitant for a number of reasons. First, he had only worked with this device once before, and though it was easy enough to operate, he was still nervous that he would not operate it correctly, causing a mistake in targeting. Otherwise, he was still a little nervous about putting himself into the open. Even though all the known enemy machine gunners were eliminated, other nests accompanied the cannons further back, still somewhat pelting the invading forces.

"Ross, go with him," the lieutenant ordered another man.

The two trotted forward between the houses in a crouched position, looking for a fence or something that could be stepped on in order to reach the eves of the roof. They frantically scanned houses in the immediate vicinity, but were coming up short on options until Ross spotted something.

"Right there," he said, pointing to a house to the left.

Derek saw what he was referring to. Next to a small, red brick house to the left was an aluminum ladder, laid long-ways against the side of the house. They both ran over, and began picking the light, metallic ladder up. Derek and Ross's hands burned as the ladder had been heated by the vicious sun all day long. They erected it, propping it against the eve of the roof, and Derek began to climb up with Ross holding the bottom.

The dark gray shingles were blazing hot. The air above them distorted in the usual wavy manner, seeming to fry Derek's hands as he pulled himself up to the rooftop. The nylon bag weighted him down, making it somewhat difficult to balance. He always hated being on roof tops. He had never been afraid of heights, but there was something about the slant and the lack of safety railings that made him quite nervous.

Nevertheless, he scrambled to the top, his lieutenant yelling for him to hurry.

He could hear the distant thunder of jet engines to the south. The aircraft carriers were positioned only about ten miles to the south of the bay opening, so it wouldn't take the jets long to get there. He quickly pulled at the zipper and opened the bag, extracting the laser target designator. It was basically a scope with a built-in transmitter and a laser beam that marked the spot that the jets were to fire on. Derek pulled out the tripod stand, attempting to set it up on the rooftop, but unfortunately there was not a level place to set it up. He threw the stand to the side in frustration, and just set the designator upon the peak of the roof, laying behind it on the slant. Using the viewfinder, he put the cannon positions in the distance in the cross point of the scope, the laser coinciding.

He had an excellent view of the airport from the roof of the house. He could see the cannons and the abandoned airport in the distance, but he could also see the southward landing zone to his left. Shells still exploded all around amid sporadic machine gun fire, and all the troops could do was to move forward, hoping to not be hit. His muscles weakened and he felt sick in the pit of his stomach as he watched fellow Marines blown to bits. They lay, missing limbs, bleeding in the sand and sun. Those who were not quite dead screamed and writhed in pain. Sickness turned to anger. These were Americans, and they were being killed by Americans. How could they do that?

Derek was becoming a bit shaky. He returned his attention to the scope, peering through to paint the target for the inbound jets. He peered through with rage. It was as if his eyes were the lasers. His gaze could burn the canons and their operators into heaps of rubble, leaving no need for the coming jets.

But the roar of the six jets from behind him indicated that would not be necessary. The guidance system homed in on the canon positions, loosing cruise missiles rocketing from above. They flew in with trails of exhaust, aimed at the cannon positions. The impact was a spectacle of fire power. Plumes of fire rose upward with Hell's fury. The entire tarmac was ablaze, and the shelling ceased immediately, sending scores of Marines into joyous uproar.

As he climbed down the ladder, Derek was swarmed by troops moving past and forward into the open airfield. Their weapons were shouldered as if they were currently being opposed. More landing craft hit the shores unanswered by fire of any kind; thousands pouring into the objective, ready for action.

"Good job, Marine," the lieutenant handed Derek his rifle, but did not take the bagged up laser targeting device. He would likely have to lug it around for the rest of the day.

It was eerily quiet in the interior of the airfield. The grass was yellow and dead from heat and lack of rain. Crickets and cicadas squealed in the baking sun—the classic sound of warm weather in the south. The cannons had stopped, and the popped sandbags smoldered in the mortar craters, littered with enemy bodies.

It was a long mile and a half to the northwestern side of the airfield. The airport itself was lifeless, neither bustling with people, crew, or planes. It was desolate, shut down, anticipating this point may be an invasion zone. Further to the north of the airport stood hangars, warehouses, and administrative buildings, all equally lifeless. Interstate 10, just beyond, seemed deserted, as not one vehicle traveled it, not even military ones.

But the silence was suddenly broken by the familiar pop of an M-16. Like a slowly-starting afternoon shower, it began with a few, and slowly became more frequent, sending a deadly shower of projectiles in the direction of the Marines. Then came explosions all around, bursting concrete into the air as they moved upon the main airport terminal. The mortars were being launched from safe points behind the buildings and gunfire rang out from the corners and roofs all around. In essence, they had the high ground, while the invading Marines had little shelter.

There was no choice for Derek and his fellow troops, but to push forward and try to overwhelm the enemy with sheer numbers—now counting in the thousands. Derek and a group of soldiers ran through a hail of gunfire, straight up to one of the metal buildings. The Republican troops aloft hung their rifles over the sides of the roof, firing downward in massacre. A soldier frantically pulled a grenade from his vest, and lugged it upward as men were shot all to his left and right. The grenade bounced off the metal wall of the building, almost to the top, and came falling back toward them.

"Grenade!" men yelled as they dove all around, some rounding the sides of the building, where they were shot by waiting riflemen.

Derek rose from his cover angry and tired. He ignored the bullets whizzing around him and hitting the dirt at his feet. He jerked a grenade from his vest, and lobbed it up onto the roof, waiting for it to explode. A light boom ensued, and smoke rose to the air, silencing the rifles above them.

He spied a set of thin steel doors in the front of the building where he stood, and shouldered his rifle. He fired two short, three-burst sets of rounds into the doorknobs and deadbolts, and then ran at the doors with all of the force he could muster. He dropped his shoulder in a football fashion, and crashed through the doors.

As he lay face-down on the concrete floor, his shoulder aching somewhat, a score of Marines rushed in for cover, one stopping to help him to his feet. The one-room building was dark, smelling of grease and rusted metal. Skylights above provided the only light, which illuminated old engines, equipment, and tools. Steel shelving was packed with boxes of spare parts and hoses. Large machinery lay draped with canvas.

One Marine saw a set of metal stairs in the far right corner, and once he moved in that direction, Derek and the others followed. They proceeded cautiously, in case there were any enemies hiding in the shadows. The stairs clanked beneath their feet, even as they stepped lightly, moving up to the roof.

They reached the top of the stairs, a landing with a door that opened onto the roof of the building. Slowly, the door was pushed open, and to the welcome of several bullets piercing and killing the men inside the doorway. Blood spattered all over the walls as one Marine removed a grenade from his vest, and tossed it out the door, allowing it to explode and terminate the defenders on the roof.

The door remained open, and the rest of the troops waiting on and at the bottom of the stairs listened for more shots, but they never came. Slowly the Marines peeked into the doorway, scanning for more enemies. They emerged into the sun, weapons drawn in preparation for more resistance. Bloody, shrapnel-filled bodies lay on the hot, metal roof, cooking in the sun. Derek passed one of the bodies, and looked down to see the lifeless face of a young man no older than himself. He looked like the average American kid. He was dead, possibly killed by Derek's grenade. He felt remorse, and then anger.

Each soldier on the roof ran to the side opposite the airfield, taking cover behind a three-foot-ledge wall, and sporadically popped up to answer the enemy's fire from other rooftops. It was largely futile for both sides. Sometimes, a lucky shot would strike the enemy, as would happen to the Marines with Derek on the roof.

For several minutes, the firefight continued. Mortars among the Marine swarm continued to explode. Mortars flew through the air into the enemy position as well, blowing holes in rooftops where Republican troops once stood. Then it seemed that the tables would turn. Derek looked back toward the airfield to see Abrams tanks rolling near the terminal, surrounded by attached infantrymen.

The tanks stopped, adjusted their trajectory, and began firing into the Republican position. One tank took aim at Derek's rooftop until it was seen that the men on top fired into the enemy position. Giant holes were ripped into the warehouses and administrative buildings. A barrage of tank fire decimated the airport complex into a pile of twisted steel and burning rubble. The tanks rolled into the complex, followed by thousands of infantry troops, sending the Republicans fleeing across the railroad tracks and I-10 that ran parallel. The airport was now secured, and the enemy was on the run.

Chapter 36

"I just don't think it's a good idea for you to go out tonight, Julie," Cindy Chandler battled her daughter over her cell phone, walking briskly down the staff-crowded White House corridor. "It's just not safe right now."

Jabbering filled her ear as she rolled her eyes at the aides that tried to keep up with her. A few of them were around her age, and also had adolescent young of their own. She was sure that they understood.

"I know you're bored. You've been cooped up in this house for a month," she spoke with her other hand, as if Julie were standing right in front of her. "I know you miss Tulane. God knows you miss the bars! You'll be starting at Penn in the fall. Then you'll be out of here."

Cindy saw General Bates and the Navy Chief standing casually at the entrance to her office. They had amazing poker faces. She observed and analyzed their expressions for any kind of indication on how the Mobile invasion was going, but to no avail. They were stone and stern, showing nothing but neutral business appearance.

"Julie, I don't have time to argue about this right now. Did you ask your father?" she paused, listening to Julie's response. "Of course he told you to ask me," she rolled her eyes. "It's not as if I have a country to run and the preservation of the union to deal with or anything! We'll talk about this later over dinner," she pressed the *end* button, and entered the office.

The two men followed her in. She moved with haste and impatience. She was frazzled—clearly fatigued and stretched thin with not only war, but other governmental issues as well. She stormed across the Oval Office, rounded her desk, and plopped down behind it.

"What's the word, gentlemen?" she did not even look up at them from the documents on her desk.

"There's a situation in Pakistan," Bates began. "Militants are growing in numbers and threatening to make a run on Islamabad."

"Not interested," she did not look up. "That's over there. I'm more interested in Americans dying in our own backyard."

"Well then," Bates began slowly, "things are going okay so far. Both landing forces have successfully made it ashore. First and Second Brigades have done really well. They landed at Point Clear with little resistance, and within a day have pushed just to the north of Daphne."

"That's on the east bank of the bay, correct?" she finally looked up to give her undivided attention.

"Yes, ma'am. They are approximately three miles from their objective—I-10. It doesn't seem like the Reds have concentrated as much personnel on that east side of the bay, although there is expected to be heavier resistance as they get closer to the interstate. They obviously have concentrated the majority of their forces on Mobile proper and the port."

"So how is the other group doing?" she grew concerned.

"Much heavier resistance, Madam President," he winced and hesitated. "The landing at the airport was tough. There was a lot of open space, so little cover for our Marines. They were met with a lot of machine gun and cannon fire."

"Oh God, it wasn't successful?" her eyes widened even more.

"Oh, it was successful, and we hold the airport. But it was hard-fought. And the Reds are fighting tooth and nail. They've been pushed north of the interstate into the Arlington suburbs. From there, we just have to push them up further, take downtown, and as long as the Reds fall back north of Prichard, the city and the port is ours."

"Good," she seemed relieved. "And what are the casualties?"

"You're not going to be happy," he grimaced.

"Yes?" she looked back up at him, anxious about what she was about to hear.

"Seven hundred fifty-three dead, and about nine hundred wounded in some way," he stated.

"Oh, Jesus," she hung her head and closed her eyes.

"We knew it wasn't going to be easy, Madam President, but this objective has to be taken," he tried to reassure her. "It's absolutely necessary."

"Okay," she raised her gaze and met with his eyes, shaking her head. "Anything else?"

"Um, Madam President," the Navy Chief spoke up, "we are encountering naval skirmishes off the coast of North Carolina and southern Virginia. Nothing real big, but I thought you'd want to know."

"Thank you, Admiral," she nodded. "Anything else?"

"Yes," he replied. "We have confirmation that Mexico's role in allying with the Republic is for shipping and smuggling. Our Naval Intelligence sources have confirmed a shipment of weapons ordered from Germany has landed at Veracruz, and will likely be shipped northward across the Texas border."

"Shit!" she exclaimed. "They've got enough oil funds to buy as many weapons as they want, for as long as they want!" she paused for a moment to think. "Blockade the Mexican coast."

"I don't think we can do that," the Admiral said. "We're spread thin as it is. So many of our ships were in southern coastal harbors that we had to steam most of the Pacific fleet from Pearl and San Diego through the Panama Canal. We can't afford to take ships off the southern blockade."

She simply hung and shook her head. She was frustrated. Her military was suffering, while the Republic enjoyed the security of being a full-fledged superpower a couple of months into their existence.

"Do what you can, Admiral," she continued to hang her head. "Report back to me tomorrow," she said as they left. She flattened her arms on the desk before her, and laid down her head.

Chapter 37

The sun was setting west of Mobile, and it should have been getting cooler. Derek knew that back home, it would be. Actually, it normally wouldn't be this hot back home at all. There in southern Alabama, with the gateway to the gulf in plain sight, the humidity simply would not relinquish the heat.

He still donned his Kevlar helmet in case of a surprise attack, but had stripped his torso down to a t-shirt, and he could still feel the sweat seeping from pores all over his body. He sat behind the sandbag bunker that he and a couple of other Marines had constructed on the blazing hot concrete beside the airport terminal. He reached down beside him, picking up a half-empty canteen, unscrewed the cap, and took yet another conservative sip in an attempt to keep his body somewhat hydrated.

He placed the canteen back on the ground beside his propped-up rifle and looked around with his fatigued eyes. He had never been this exhausted in his life—not even at basic training. He leaned backward against the semicircle bunker, facing the runway and the scores of tanks, trucks, equipment, and the command center tents that were being erected far away from any immediate potential action. Just a few hours before, he had been running across that open space, where his next step could have been his last. Now the top brass were setting up shop—clean, shaven, and rested.

The place bustled with vehicles and personnel. In the distance, he could see rows of green blankets laid out individually like some kind of morbid military quilt. He had never seen anyone die before. Deaths and suicides in basic training were things he heard about. Now he had seen hundreds of deaths, and in the most violent and despicable ways imaginable for the average person. He knew that behind him, closer to the interstate, it was likely that the rubble of the old warehouses and hangars was still riddled with bodies of Republican Guardsmen. Still staring at the rows of dead Marines, he wondered if he should care. Enemy or not, they were still people. Who knew what their personal feelings were about the secession? Maybe they were just doing their duty. They still shot at him. That was something he could not shake. There really was no reason that thousands of men and women should have died that day.

One of the men who helped Derek construct, and would share with him, the bunker within which he sat, suddenly appeared from behind. It startled Derek, first hearing the grit grinding between his boots and the concrete, and then having him plop down next to him. He had never met Jay, or "Queens" as other guys called him, before this day. In fact, everyone he knew within the Marines was either not assigned to this invasion, or they were in the other landing force far across the bay. But Jay seemed like a nice guy. They had chatted lightly, but nothing too serious or deep.

Queens and dozens of other men were re-entering their bunkers, preparing for some sort of rest after having fought all day in the southern heat and helping to set up base for the rest of the operation. He propped up his weapon beside Derek's, and slid his back down the sandbags, finally bringing himself to a sitting position. He removed an MRE bag from his pack, and began opening it with his field knife.

"I wonder if these Red assholes realize that 'The Republican Guard' is what Saddam's army was called. What do you have there?" Derek leaned over, eyeing Queens' meal.

"Beef teriyaki," he said in his thick New York dialect, removing the contents. "What do you have?" he looked over to see Derek opening his own MRE.

"Um, cheese tortellini," he said, struggling with the packaging somewhat. "Trade?"

"No way, man," he began adding water to the flameless ration heater in his hand. "This is the good shit."

They each added water to the flameless ration heater and inserted their MRE pouches, which contained the food they would consume for dinner. They brought the pouches level for a few moments, allowing the heater to soak in water, and then stuffed the whole thing into a paper carton. They then each propped the cartons up on an incline against their gear packs, allowing the food to heat.

"Yeah, all these MREs are pretty good," Derek replied.

"They beat the hell out of the old canned rations the World War II GIs got. Ever seen any of that crap?" Queens smiled.

"In the movies," Derek smiled back. "My only problem is how long this thing takes to heat up. I mean, in the fifteen minutes it takes, we might start taking fire, and there goes dinner."

"Shit," Queens fired back in a friendly tone, "you can eat it cold if you want. This ain't a five-star restaurant. It's a battlefield. Be glad you have a way to heat it up at all."

"Yeah, I guess you're right," Derek smiled.

Initially, it seemed as though they were going to run out of things to talk about, and not only did they have about ten or fifteen minutes to go before their food was ready, but they would likely have a lot more of these types of encounters while in the Mobile area. Queens stared at his MRE, willing it to heat more quickly somehow. Derek stared off at the runway, nibbling on the lining of his lip and playing carelessly with his field knife.

"Where did you say you were from, again?" Derek struck up more conversation.

"What, my accent wasn't a reminder? Queens, New York. You?"

"Cleveland."

"Damn, I see why you joined the Marines," he joked.

"Yeah, not the most cosmopolitan city in the world," he laughed. "But I'd much rather be back there right now. Not just because I might get shot today or tomorrow, but because I've got a pregnant girlfriend there and my mother needs somebody to take care of her."

"Why? What's wrong with her?"

"She's sick. She has Lou Gehrig's Disease," he hung his head. "Her muscles are dying. Eventually, she won't be able to walk, move, speak, or even breathe. And that will kill her."

"So how do you cure it?"

"There isn't one," Derek replied. "Stem cell therapy has always looked promising, according to the doctor. But the damned Republicans have always blocked any federal funding for research."

"Why?"

"They still think you have to kill babies to get stem cells," he nodded, his face beginning to display anger as tears began to show briefly. "Even if they started now, we'd be years behind other countries, and my mother will still be dead."

Queens stared at the rows of bodies, their visibility fading increasingly into the dusk. He became somber, and even morbid in thought.

"Looks like we're all going to have to get used to the people around us dying," he hung his head as Derek stared off into oblivion, unable to stop thinking about his friends Alex and Jackson on the other side of the bay.

Chapter 38

The clubhouse at the Lake Forest Country Club in Daphne, Alabama was cleared. All tables, from the large rounders to the small, square four-tops, were haphazardly laid and stacked in the far back corner. The sun had not risen, nor would it for nearly two hours, so the house lights were on full blast, illuminating every yawning officer in the room with energy-saving bulbs.

The tables had been removed, but all of the green and blue upholstered chairs remained. They were banquet-style chairs—easy to set and remove. The frames were thin, faux gold metal, and provided nothing to rest one's arms on, so they were quite uncomfortable. Perhaps that would keep the sleepy officers awake during the briefing.

General Gibson stood at the head of the room affront the rows of uncomfortable chairs and their occupants. Behind him hung an eight foot by eight foot projector screen. From the back of the room, a projector hummed as it emitted the streaming image onto the white screen. It was a zoom satellite image of their position and all that surrounded, from the tufts of trees around the fairways of the golf course, to the northern interstate.

"Here we are, gentlemen," his raspy voice scratched at everyone's ears. "Um, and ladies…" he corrected as he spotted several contemptuous female NCOs from the corner of his left eye. "Right in the middle of a country club to the east of Daphne. We've had it easy so far, but things are about to get exponentially tougher. You see this interchange?" he pointed to the area where main street Daphne met Interstate 10. "This is the very mouth of Hell."

"Gentlemen," he paused for a short moment, "and ladies, we MUST control this causeway that crosses the bay. If we don't, the Reds will run reinforcements in against our troops on the west side all day long. The Reds know this. They've got multiple machine gun nests here at the interchange. They have tanks, mortars, and about fifteen hundred troops, so this won't be a walk in the park. Most of the personnel are concentrated in this shopping center right by the interchange. It's a Stein Mart and fast food joints—stuff like that, which are non-operational, needless to say. But they've turned this whole parking lot into a command center. Make no mistake—they control this interstate and this bridge completely," he spoke as the audience remained silent.

"So the plan of action," he continued, "is to take control of the highway, and we can't do that without taking that command center. You'll have about two thousand troops to do this with—two battalions to the west up Main Street to take the interchange, and two to the east to hit that shopping center. But there is going to be a logistics problem. You're not going to be able to just hit them all at once and waltz right in."

"To the south of the shopping center, between us and them, is a big pond or lake, or something," he pointed. "We don't know how deep this is, so we're not going to chance trying to wade across it. So the first two battalions are going to have to move up Main Street, here. We'll drop you and your men—ehem—and women several blocks back. We'll kill the power temporarily at the substation and let you move under the cover of darkness. There will be plenty of shops, stores, and restaurants to use for cover. We can't pull the plug for too long because it will start getting hot here in the command center and all these houses. Here's the problem. Once you get up here to the west side of the shopping center, it's water—this stupid pond thing—on one side, and swamp on the other. You've got to cross this bridge right before the interchange."

"Can't my men," one captain raised his hand, "um, and women, just wade across the swamp? I mean, it can't be that deep."

"Where are you from, son?" the general inquired.

"Oregon, sir," he replied.

"Well I know they don't have these where you come from, but you're not going to want to come face to face with an alligator, water moccasin, or any of the other nasty shit they have in there."

"Well," the captain smiled and spoke to the man next to him under his breath, "at least alligators don't shoot at you."

"No, people," the general continued, "you've got to cross this bridge. And to make things a little more difficult—so you don't get too comfortable—you won't have any tank support," he said to a low grumbling in the room. "Yep, no tanks; no mortars—nothing that threatens to blow this bridge before we even cross it. But on the bright side, they won't chance it either. They're going to want the chance to come after us if things go their way. Cross the bridge, take out those guns, and take control of the causeway. Any questions?"

The room was relatively silent, aside from the occasional cough or sniffle. It was allergy season, and many people had their annual springtime colds. There were a lot of itchy, red eyes and small packs of tissue being passed about.

"No? Okay, the other two battalions will move up Bay View Drive which is a stone's throw right over here to our east. The bad news is you still have no artillery support and you have to deal with another bridge. The good news is this bridge here crosses a little creek that feeds into the swamp. It should be shallow enough to wade across, and I don't think there are any gators or anything there. Just keep your eyes peeled, though. Either way, you won't have the bottleneck issue that the other two battalions will face. You move across and hit the command center from the east. Any questions?"

"Yes sir," a female lieutenant raised her hand. "What about the rest of us?"

"The rest of you?"

"Yes sir," she continued. "We have about five thousand troops here, and we're only hitting their fifteen hundred with two thousand. Why not overpower them with everything we've got?" she asked as the room fell dead silent.

"Yeah, that was the next thing I was getting to," he sighed and winced like someone delivering bad news. "Satellite reconnaissance has detected enemy movement just behind the Florida/Alabama border. Reinforcements headed for Mobile. And it's a big convoy, too. We don't know just how many troops, but judging by the number of vehicles, we're estimating between twenty-five hundred and three thousand."

The officers within the room unleashed a low fog of whispers, groans, gasps, and sighs. Their barely audible whispers to one another accompanied expressions of fear and shock. The general let it go for a moment, perhaps to let it sink in. He knew this was a bombshell. It was unexpected even to him until just earlier.

"Okay," he raised his hand to shush the crowd and present the plan of action. "You see this stretch of woods along the south side of I-10? We're going to spread the rest of our three thousand, or so, troops all along the whole two-and-a-half-mile length of it. The woods and the darkness should give you plenty of cover. You will wait until the convoy gets about half a mile from the enemy command center, and hit the whole force all at once. This is an ambush. We're going to hit them fast and hit them hard. We cannot let them get to the command center, or we'll never take it. And we certainly can't let them get across that bridge to Mobile. Questions?"

"Alright, brief your troops, load up, and get the hell out of here," he said when no one spoke. "And make it quick. We have to get into place before sun-up. That is all."

The room began clearing amidst louder talking, leaving the general with a look of concern. He never liked giving orders that would likely cost even a few soldiers their lives. He knew more than a few would die today. He remembered his service in Afghanistan, sending young men and women to die in the interest of the greater good. At least the enemy was culturally different in Afghanistan. Somehow the killing of anonymous extremists was easier. Now, not only did he risk the lives of the troops under his command, his men and women surviving required the deaths of other red-blooded Americans.

He wondered if George Meade or Ulysses Grant ever felt this way, sending Americans to kill Americans. History books never stressed the brother against brother aspect of that war as much as the biased perspective of putting down a rebellion and ending slavery. He considered himself a military historian, and it always irritated him that the story was told from a winner's point of view. United States citizens grew up learning that the Civil War was fought over the immorality of slavery, and that Abraham Lincoln was the sole moral compass to bring it to an end. This simply was not so. It was a war over sectionalism, states' rights, and way of life—the social gap between north and south.

Now he watched his officers finish clearing out of the dining room and exit down the center hallway. As the rumble of their chatter faded and silenced, he stood alone in front of that satellite image, staring at it in silent prayer for all of his Marines entering the slaughter.

A young captain exited the clubhouse into the warm, humid night air as his pores immediately began pumping oil onto the surface of his face. He strolled briskly, his eyes trained on a group of men sitting upon the distant seventh green of the golf course. He thought it a shame to see all of the trucks and Humvees tearing up such a pristine course. He wondered how many of these troops appreciated how much work went into the upkeep of the greens and fairways. Once they had gone, it may take years to get this place back into shape. Perhaps this was the cost of rebellion against the indivisible nation.

"Captain Andrews," a young corporal stopped him, jogging up.

"Yes, corporal?" the captain stopped.

"I was told to inform you that you will be short a man," he spouted. "A Private Shoemaker?"

"Yeah, what happened? The brig?"

"No, dead," the corporal corrected. "He must have thought all these houses were abandoned, and not all of them are. He broke into one of these ritzy homes, and the owner greeted him with a twelve gauge."

"Shit," Andrews reacted. "Dumbass. What did you do with the owner of the house?"

"Detained," he answered. "On the general's orders, he's in light captivity—don't want him going off on a rampage, picking off our guys. The weapon was confiscated, and the general ordered all these houses searched for more weapons."

"I hope he can spare the personnel for that. Alright. Thanks for letting me know. I'm sure the Department of Defense will write a nice, flowery letter to his family telling them about how heroic he was on today's operation."

The captain continued on his course down the fairway to the seventh green where his men and women awaited. He walked with purpose, his Kevlar helmet tucked under his right arm. His troops did not seem to notice his approach, so he could begin hearing their conversation.

"Everybody does it," one private said with a smile.

"That's disgusting," another said.

"It's sterile," Alex Jasper laughed. "You can't tell me you've never done it! Everybody does it at least once. It's early, you haven't woken up, and you get a little lazy when you're in the shower…" he raised his hands in a shrug while Jackson and the other men laughed.

"I've even done it," a female private revealed.

"What about you, captain?" Alex asked their ranking officer as he approached.

"What exactly are we talking about here, Jasper?" Captain Andrews grinned.

"Pissing in the shower, sir," he smiled back.

"These disgusting people here," the other private pointed around at everyone, "all piss on their feet in the shower."

"Well," the captain paused, still grinning, "if you're going to piss on yourself, the shower is the place to do it. Hell, sometimes I piss on my wife's feet just to keep the spice in our relationship."

The Marines all erupted into laughter, which was slightly drowned in the droning rumble of truck and Humvee engines. They needed that. The previous day was long, and it was early. The sun still had not risen. And this day would prove to be much harder than the previous.

"Where we going, captain?" Jackson asked as the laughter died down.

"Right up Main Street, private," he pointed off into the distance. "We're gonna off-load about half a mile south of the interstate, and head that way. We have to take the intersection of I-10 and Highway 98 and take control of the entrance to the Mobile Bay causeway."

"Sounds easy enough," the female private said.

"Yeah, if you take away the fifteen-hundred troops, the dozen or so machine gun nests, and the fact that we're going to have to bottleneck into a bridge to get to the objective."

The troops fell silent as reality set in. They had heard that the Marines that hit the airport the previous day took heavy losses, but on the east side of the bay, action was relatively light. Perhaps they had been spoiled with that easy day. It was now sinking in that today would be much more dangerous.

"Alright, gear up and load up," he clapped his hands together as the men and women joined the ranks of troops all over the golf course strapping on their helmets and utility vests, and began loading up onto the transport trucks.

The wheels began turning, their weight leaving deep ruts in the fairways and greens of the golf course. They passed over the roughs and through breaks in the trees, finally rolling up onto the narrow residential streets. Alex, sitting near the open back of the transport truck, could see the street lights suddenly go lifeless with the cutting of power to the neighborhood. Silhouettes of trees and houses became invisible and everything went black. Drivers began pulling night vision goggles over their eyes in lieu of turning on their headlights.

Main Street seemed abandoned in the dark. There was no light and no traffic. There were no cars in the parking lots of the strip malls, boutiques, and fast food restaurants. The engines on the trucks and Humvees provided the only sound, echoing off the shops, through the trees, and across the bay. It was eerie. It was dead. No one had ever seen such a lifeless street, and that seemed to foreshadow a horrible near future.

Suddenly, the trucks halted. No one did anything for many moments. The Marines, laden with gear, clutched their weapons in anticipation, but no one stood up, nor did they even move.

Young Captain Andrews appeared at the back of Alex's transport. He said nothing, and hesitated in even giving the order to dismount the truck. Finally, he motioned his hand toward himself, a silent order to unload, and begin the operation.

Alex hopped down out of the back of the truck, followed by Jackson, their boots clapping against the pavement. The other troops followed them. Jackson looked around at their surroundings. Trucks were unloading as far as they could see. They could begin to see a very dim glow on the eastern horizon, yet the highway was still black. Fast food signs were dead. The neons were dull and almost opaque. The Marines were ready for action.

As trucks began turning around in the medians and headed back to the golf course, the troops, accompanied by dozens of Humvees to the rear, moved almost aimlessly up the highway. They spread out across the roadway—some on the pavement, some in the median, and some even in the parking lots of the stores and shops. No one said a word, not for fear of losing their element of surprise. It was just silent and dark. No one dared break that. It was as if the night itself had ordered silence in the ranks. The only sounds were crickets playing their love songs and bullfrogs croaking in the bogs and ditches.

It took quite some time for the thousands of men to hike the half-mile stretch of highway toward the bridge. They moved somewhat slowly and cautiously. They kept alert, watching every inch of their surroundings for signs of an enemy ambush. Finally, an NCO in the front of the pack could see the approaching bridge. He stopped, signaling everyone else to do the same. His signal reverberated back through the ranks as thousands of men and women stopped. It was like a stone cast into a still pond, rippling the water outward from the epicenter. They began spreading out. Some hit the deck right there in the middle of the road. Others chose the lip where the road descended into the ditch-like median. Troops took position at the corners of restaurants and small office buildings, all awaiting further orders.

"What have we got?" the captain crouched next to a lieutenant near the front.

"Three gun emplacements," he pointed ahead. "One in front of each of these two bridges servicing Main Street, and another at this third bridge to the east that's part of the access road."

Andrews looked around for a moment as he strategized the next move. He visualized the attack in his head, trying to determine the plot that would cost as few lives as possible.

"Okay," he began, his eyes narrowed in thought. "We've got to break silence at some point, and we can't do anything without taking out these first nests. See that patch of trees between Main and the access road? First put some men in there. It will provide them cover enough to take out that gun. Send four Humvees in a frontal assault against the other nests. That should do the trick."

"Yes sir," he ran in a crouched position, gathering up some of his own men.

A dozen soldiers ran across the north-bound lanes of the highway and into the section of trees separating Main from the access road. They quietly crept through the patch of trees until they could see the easternmost gun emplacement. There, they waited with racing hearts and blood full of adrenaline as they watched the slight movement of men within the machine gun nest.

Within a few minutes, their signal became obvious. Four Humvees raced up the highway amid Marines crouched and ready. Their fifty-caliber rifles began blazing against the unaware defenders. Punctured sandbags spewed as two defenders were immediately hit. The survivors opened fire, sending bullets through the windshield of one of the Humvees. The driver and the front seat passenger slumped over lifelessly as the vehicle veered right ahead of the bridge, and plunged into the swamp below.

The soldiers in the woods began their barrage as soon as they heard the fifty caliber rounds fired into the night. All of them opened fully automatic fire on the emplacement as the defenders returned volley. Two Marines were hit instantly, but the assault overwhelmed the machine gun nest, and the guns fell silent in a flurry of gunfire and bunker sand.

Another Humvee roared at full speed toward the last remaining sandbag bunker. The gunner unleashed a fury of gunfire, hitting one of the men behind the bags. Bullet holes filled the windshield, sending blood spraying across the cab before the vehicle crashed into the bunker, crushing the lone gunner. It flipped over, grinding down the bridge with a brilliant shower of sparks until it came to a halt.

The first line of machine gun emplacements was silenced. A third Humvee flew past the wrecked bunker and vehicle up the southbound bridge, while the fourth halted in the middle of the northbound bridge. Their fifty-caliber rifles raged against a now alerted enemy infantry. Some rushed the bridges, while others crouched and fired. A rocket-propelled grenade shot suddenly across the bridge, slamming against the front end of the moving Humvee. The explosion pierced the darkness of the twilight hour, sending the vehicle hurdling into the air and over the side of the bridge into the swamp below.

The one remaining Humvee, stationary on the bridge, was pelted with endless gunfire until its gun fell silent. Muzzles flashed like violent fireflies on both sides of the bridge as men fell to the earth by the dozens. It was a slaughter unlike most of the young soldiers had ever seen. Only a few of the older officers had seen action like it in Afghanistan or Iraq.

"You see those tracers?" the captain pointed out to a sergeant, both of them crouched behind the corner of a burger restaurant. "Two more nests in the medians just beyond the bridges. Get some men in those woods overlooking the swamp to the west of the highway. And get a sniper up on the roof of this little office building in front of us. He'll take out those gunners and make our lives a little easier. Move it!"

The first rays of the sun were beginning to peek over the eastern horizon as the glass door to the office building was shattered by a rifle stock. A very young rifleman finished breaking out the glass, and crouched in under the metal bar handle, glass crunching beneath his boots. He could see the darkened outlines of computer monitors and cubicle dividers in the small room. He searched for a staircase, and finally spotted it at the far end of the room. He sprinted past the empty desks and up the staircase to the upper floor, looking around for a way onto the roof. He found a ladder in the same staircase that led upward to a small square hatch in the ceiling. He threw his rifle strap over his right shoulder, and began scaling the ladder. Reaching up, he turned the lever that released the hatch, and pushed up, gaining access to the roof.

He grunted as he hoisted himself onto the tarred roof of the building. The air conditioning units jutting up from the roof were silent. He crouched as he slowly approached the edge of the roof and fell to his stomach. He uncapped the scope atop his rifle, and hung the barrel over the edge. Looking through the eyepiece, he could see enemy soldiers all over, furiously defending their position. Finally, he found one of the two nests. He chambered a 30.06 round from the waiting magazine. He squeezed the trigger slowly, fine-tuning the crosshairs on the gunner, and then the muzzle erupted with a short burst of fire. He watched as the machine gunner slumped over the sandbag.

He chambered another round, watching the other man in the bunker take hold of the machine gun, and then killed him as well. He continued the process, taking out the other bunker before adjusting his sights to take out three more machine gun nests to the north at the I-10 interchange. His own men cheered as the enemy machine guns fell silent. The chaos of the battle made sure no attention was paid to the sniper until the gunners far beyond the gunfight fell. A smile crossed his face, still searching for more targets through his scope.

A different sound faded into earshot. It was low and droning, and it became clear that it was an engine of some sort. He scanned the scene for the source using his scope, and then caught it. An Abrams tank rolled up the access road from the west, and then onto the ramp, stopping in the intersection. At first, it did nothing, and then the young rifleman saw the turret turn, and the 120-millimeter barrel was trained on his position. The muzzle flashed, and the entire area around him—roof and part of the upper wall—was blown into oblivion, taking him with it.

The tank then brought the barrel back to the front, and rolled forward toward the action, stopping intermittently to fire another round into the Marines' position. Alex and Jackson continued to lie next to each other in the median, firing at the enemy.

"Shit! Ahh!" Jackson shouted, slapping at his arms and shoulders.

"What? What?" Alex stopped firing.

"Ants! Fire ants!" he jumped up out of instinct, and began swatting the stinging insects off his clothes.

"Jackson, what the hell are you…" he stopped as he watched his friend take three bullets to his chest and torso, and then fall lifelessly to the side.

And that was it. Over twenty years of life, experiences, emotions, memories, and training were lost in an instant. He was someone's son and brother—people that would never see him again. Someone loved him, and would always love him. They would be told that he fought valiantly, completing an important mission, yet his demise was ultimately fire ants. They would never know.

Alex watched the battle rage as he took up firing his weapon again. Despite heavy losses on his side, it seemed that the enemy was wavering. The bodies were piling upon one another, and they were falling back, in spite of having that Abrams tank on their side.

"RPG!" a sergeant called. "Get some RPGs up here and take out that goddamned tank! Aim for the tracks," he said as a couple of privates ran up to his position with the rockets.

They each knelt down, quickly inserting the projectiles into the tubes, and shouldered them. They took aim at the giant tan dragon spewing fire from its long, slender mouth. After a few seconds, they unleashed their rockets, one after the other. The first missed, sending dirt and body parts flying into the air. But the other hit the underside of the turret, not destroying it, but at least causing the operators to halt their barrage for the moment.

"Hit it again!" the sergeant yelled. "Hit those tracks!"

The third shot found its mark, a burst of flames raining out from its left track. The track fell off the rollers, and onto the ground. It was finally disabled. The Republican soldiers rallying behind the once advancing tank fell for cover, and then began to fall back.

"Move forward," Captain Andrews motioned. "Cross that bridge! Get the rest of the Humvees out in front!"

The Humvees rolled up the highway like a stampede, and across the bridge, leading men in columns behind them. The fifty-calibers and M-16s fired relentlessly and pushed the Republican Guard back toward the interstate and their own command center. From the east, the other battalions pushed into the other side of the shopping center parking lot. Soldiers fell into their own pools of blood on the concrete. The glass of several stores and restaurants shattered with a hail of bullets. It had become a slaughter. Grenades popped and chunks of concrete and brick were blown free of their buildings.

"Cease fire! We surrender!" a voice chimed out over a loudspeaker, repeating the same remark.

For a moment, the Marines were skeptical, and perhaps did not care, even if this were a legitimate surrender. They continued to massacre the Republican Guard for several moments until their own NCOs called a cease-fire. These enemy brass were not their commanders anymore. They would obey only their own officers. They watched as the enemy troops carefully laid their weapons down, and held up their hands. Only then did they stop the killing.

Troops were rounded up and forced to sit on the ground with their hands behind their heads. They were thoroughly searched and relieved of side arms, grenades, and knives. Generals, colonels, and majors were taken into custody while buildings smoldered in the dawn's brilliant rays.

A couple of miles to the east, Marines in jungle camouflage waited patiently, but anxiously for the band of reinforcements from Florida. Through the trees that provided them cover, a light rumble became more audible. Soon, they could see the line of trucks, transports, tanks, and Humvees roaring down the interstate. The force was completely unaware of the trap awaiting. They rolled on for a while longer, spanning the stretch of interstate along the woods where awaited their demise.

In one radio transmission to all troops along the two miles of woods, the attack was launched. Assault rifles blazed, sending bullets through the canvas of the transport trucks. Republican Guardsmen slumped and fell within their transports, wounded and dying. Blood spilled upon the floorboards. The convoy began trying to halt. RPGs shot out from the trees blowing Humvees and trucks clear off the roadway. Republican troops tried to file out of their trucks and fight back, but it was no use. This was an ambush, and there would be no help.

Only a few of the U.S. Marines became casualties—the enemy barely returned fire. The disabled tanks were overrun with Marines climbing up, opening the hatches, and dropping in grenades. Those surviving infantrymen were taken prisoner. It seemed that the Republican army in Mobile would not get their saving grace.

Chapter 39

The afternoon sun was frying the Marines moving up the residential Mobile streets. It was picturesque and perhaps a bit old world. The homes were real—no vinyl or cheap materials. They were Victorian, most built around the turn of the twentieth century. They were made of real timber, brick, and wrought iron. They were nestled between centuries-old oaks and even palm trees, giving a sense of cultural connection to the Caribbean. They had big front porches with swings and rocking chairs. The sidewalks were shaded, but cracked and uneven from the growth of immense tree roots searching for space to expand.

But some were abandoned with the news that war was coming. Some leftover cars were riddled with bullet holes from a recent firefight. The posts of the porches and some of the outer walls were torn up as well. Windows were broken and shot out. One house was completely blown to pieces and engulfed in flames from either a mortar shell or a tank blast. For those who stayed to tough out the battle, Derek prayed that they were okay within. He did not desire for civilians to be killed, but he was beginning to wonder, in their support of the rebel government, if they may deserve it. They supported the secessionists, and thus supported the men who were waging war on their countrymen.

He and the rest of the men were ecstatic to hear the news that earlier in the morning, the Marines across the bay had taken control of the interstate and foiled any attempt for the Republican Guard to send reinforcements to Mobile. The enemy forces in Mobile were on the run. Derek's Marines had been chasing them north through the suburbs all day. The enemy was weak, and judging by the decreasing amount of fire in each skirmish, they were possibly running out of ammunition.

Thousands of Marines were fanning out through the suburbs, descending upon the downtown area. They were accompanied by Abrams tanks and armed Humvees. They had mortar squads and sharpshooters. It seemed lopsided. Perhaps downtown Mobile would prove to be easy.

Derek began to hear gunshots erupting in the distance as he saw downtown through the clearings in the trees. The streets, normally bustling, were dead of any traffic or people. The only sounds he could hear were faint shots and the hum of tanks and Humvees ahead of him. They continued past the convention center, and into the CBD for a few more blocks, growing eerily accustomed to the lack of action.

A sudden few pops erupted nearby. A bullet passed dangerously close to Derek's left ear, whistling as it missed him. He ran, ducking behind a tank moving nearby him. Bullets began ricocheting off the tank as he saw a few other Marines fall dead or wounded. He crept along, using the tank as cover, and frequently jutted out from behind to take a few shots forward. Then he heard the unmistakable sound of an Abrams loosing 120-millimeter rounds, but it was not one of his own. The pavement cratered and rained asphalt down nearby as the tank ahead of him returned fire.

The fifty-caliber machine guns in the Humvees cranked up as infantrymen and tanks fired back at the enemy. Derek could not see ahead of him. He was too interested in retaining cover, so he had no idea the size of the enemy's force. He only prayed that an enemy tank did not shell his cover, taking him with it. Blood vessels bulged in his face and neck. His heart raced as did his mind with emotions of fear and excitement. His head told him to retreat, but his heart told him to fight.

He spotted the entranceway to one of the city's old nineteenth -century buildings. It was recessed, and fearing that his tank was a big moving target, he ran across to the little shop, and took up a position behind the corner of the entranceway. He could almost feel the bullets ricocheting off the asphalt around his feet as he ran full-speed across the street. He reached the doorway, first pinning his back against the wall as bullets took off large chunks of wood from the corner.

As the fire on his position slowed, he felt a little more confidant, and peeked around the corner. He could see enemy soldiers crouched bedside a nearby oyster house. He jutted his assault rifle around the corner, quickly firing several bursts at that position. He saw one of the men fall before regaining his cover, bullets whizzing all around him. He repeated the action several times, taking out a few more defenders before witnessing an RPG shooting down the street in the direction of the enemy. It left a trail of smoke as it soared through the air, finding its mark with the oyster house. Most of the old, historic building exploded in a brilliant display of flame and splintered wood. Surely, the enemy soldiers were vanquished.

The next time he peeked around the corner, Republic soldiers, clad in urban fatigues, were on the run. Dead bodies filled the streets, as did wrecked enemy Humvees filled with fallen troops.

"Run'em down, guys!" his own Marines ran up the streets, sending bullets after the retreating enemy.

He joined the charge, his adrenaline pumping through every vessel in his body. It was a thrill. They had the bastards on the run. Marines, tanks, and vehicles raced up the streets after the enemy for several blocks. Eighteenth- and nineteenth-century jewels of architecture were laid to ruin by gun and tank fire. A trail of fallen Republican Guards led the way, as breadcrumbs to Hansel and Gretel. It was a hunt.

This carried on for several more blocks until Derek could see the charm of downtown Mobile fade into the dirty industrial port. He could hear the gulls calling over sporadic, but dying gunfire. What he found as he closed in upon the port was an enemy surrounded and already laying down their weapons onto the concrete next to the huge cargo boxes. He crossed Interstate 165 and the median, and into the docks, where he could see Marines closing in from the south, west, and north. This small band of Republican Guard was all that was left of the defense of Mobile. The rest could be seen trekking north up I-165, broken, outnumbered, undersupplied, and doomed to retreat without any reinforcements ever arriving.

The Marines cheered in celebration of this first major deciding victory. Enemy troops were being taken into custody, their hands on the backs of their heads.

Cindy Chandler's desk phone rang, startling her from looking over paperwork and proposals. She picked up the phone, and held it to her ear, and without a word, a relieved smile of joy crossed her face.

Chapter 40

Late May, Thirteen months before the bomb

“Say cheese!” Angela Perkins smiled as she snapped a picture of Kyle, Ryan, and Ashley, all with their arms over one another’s shoulders.

They had shed their purple graduation robes. Ashley now donned the black cocktail dress she wore beneath, and the boys still wore their slacks, dress shirts, and ties, loosened and comfortable. All three, however, still wore their flat caps and smiled endlessly in the bliss of being done with high school.

Kyle gazed around the family room and kitchen of his home. It was filled with dozens of family members, immediate and extended, friends, and family friends. Ryan’s parents were standing in the kitchen chatting with Kyle’s uncle, but Ashley was alone. There was no sign of her parents. Kyle still had never met them, nor did he even see them at the graduation ceremony. Yet, he did not let this perplexity ruin the moment, and it did not seem to be ruining Ashley’s. His home was filled with laughter and the people closest to him, all chatting over small plastic cups filled with fruit punch. The granite-topped California Island that separated the kitchen from the family room was covered with cheese and vegetable platters, hors d’oeuvres and a big crystal punch bowl that saw action perhaps twice a year.

“I can’t believe we’re finally done!” Kyle exclaimed, still in disbelief.

“It took forever for high school to be over,” a much older male cousin commented with a chuckle, “but you wait. One day soon, you’ll wake up and realize you’ve been out of high school as long as it took you to finish all twelve years. And it will happen like that!” he snapped his fingers to add drama to the point.

“Not even thinking about that right now,” Kyle responded with a smile.

“Of course. No one ever does,” the cousin replied.

Kyle pulled Ashley close, both grinning inches from each other’s faces. She hung about his neck, shorter than her boyfriend. He smiled into her eyes, dreaming of what would come for them both. They would attend college together, possibly get an apartment together, and in his mind, be together forever. Ryan stood to the side, as always. He usually felt, and even looked, like the third wheel, but he had grown accustomed to it. He had accepted it. He had to. There was no sense in losing his life-long best friend over a girl. But he, too, wondered what would happen in the coming months with Kyle and Ashley going off to college together. He had chosen a different path in the military. He left for basic training in one month.

"Honey, turn that off," Angela called to her husband, Drew, who had briefly turned on the television to check the news.

He had been obsessed with it for the last couple of months. The house had been filled with profanity and outspoken conservative opinion on the secession and then the war. Since the war had started it was on the local and Republic news all day long, informing the public as updates came in. It seemed that the war had spawned yet another smaller war in the Perkins household, too. It was heated, but benevolent. They loved each other, but differed somewhat in political opinion.

"Okay, okay, I'm turning it off," Drew pressed the power button on the remote control. "The news is about the only thing on these days, and I'm getting tired of it."

"And it's all depressing," his sister-in-law added. "Nothing but war. And then there's all that stuff happening in Pakistan with the Taliban trying to take over."

"And who knows how old the information is," joined Angela. "It's mostly local stations. There aren't a whole lot of news programs for the whole Republic."

"That's what happens when you cut ties with your liberal U.S. broadcasting parent companies," Drew commented. "You have to be completely self-funded. No more affiliates."

"And I'm getting tired of old sit-com re-runs," Angela rolled her eyes as others nodded. "I wish they'd start producing some original shows to fill the time gaps. I saw an episode of Days of Our Lives from 1987 yesterday."

"So what do you think about Mobile, huh?" Drew took the opportunity to talk politics. "What a fiasco!"

"Yeah," Ryan's father joined the conversation, his wife at his side. "Amphibious invasion on home turf, and the Republican Guard couldn't even hold down the fort."

"What the hell is Davenport thinking?" Drew shook his head.

"It's not all his fault, Drew," Ryan's father corrected. "It's easy to blame the president, but the fact is, the existing military in this country was split after the secession. A foreign invasion against a unified U.S. military wouldn't have had a prayer. Truth be told, the Republican Guard is undermanned and undersupplied. Another few thousand troops at the east side of Mobile Bay, and things would be different."

Drew was halted for the first time. He had finally engaged into conversation with someone that not only was as opinionated as he was, but also had knowledge to back up his claims. It's easy to shoot off at the mouth. With the right tone and rhetoric, one can force the ignorant into believing they're right, even if they have no idea what they are talking about. Yet, once in a while, someone comes along with brains to match the mouth, and when he or she speaks, it is profound, but no one listens.

"It's an important cause to get young people to join the Army," Ryan's father said. "I was so proud when my boy came to me and let me know he was enlisting," he placed an arm around Ryan, smiling with pride. "It's young men like him that may keep Austin from having to enact a draft."

"That's great, Ryan," Drew nodded and smiled. "I'm proud of you. Thank you for deciding to serve the Republic. We need you. I just wish my son would hear the calling, too."

"Dad, don't start," Kyle walked up with Ashley on his arm. "I'm going to A & M. I got a fifty-percent scholarship."

"And the Republic's version of the GI Bill would take care of the rest," Drew pushed.

"Dad, I'm not going to the military," Kyle reiterated as Ashley winced at where this conversation was going. Kyle was becoming irate, having heard this rant before.

"That's okay," Ryan's father nodded, almost in a condescending manner. "Not everybody is cut out for the service. Though, the Republic needs you."

"You hear that?" Drew pressed on. "You'd be doing your country a great service. Why can't you be more like Ryan?"

The blood boiled in Kyle's head. His fair skin turned bright red as he fumed with anger. His fists clenched. Ashley felt the need to step away. She feared, seeing the course of his body language, that he may turn violent. Yet, she clung to his arm tighter.

"Are you shitting me, Dad?" Kyle erupted, stopping the conversation in the entire room. "I graduated with honors. I studied my ass off all through school! I took AP classes and AP exams. I tested out of ten hours of college classes. I even helped Ryan out when he struggled in History and Spanish! I've got a scholarship to Texas A & M, and Ryan couldn't get into junior college at this point! And I should be more like him? I've done everything you've ever asked me to! Studying, testing, forgoing a social life to get into a good school, and now I should take after a slacker like Ryan? Now it's time for me to do what's best for me! I'm taking control of my own life, and it starts with this decision!"

With his father dumbfounded and shock on the faces of Ryan and his parents, Kyle put his arm around Ashley, turned and walked for the door. He flung it open with rage, and slammed it behind him while the completely silenced room stared. Angela eyed her husband with a disgust she had never felt for him. She had always tolerated and respected his opinions and outspokenness. Now it threatened to alienate their oldest son, and she was enraged.

Chapter 41

June, One year before the bomb

"We're spread thin, Mr. President," General Weaver told Byron Davenport in his office. "We're going to beef up the defenses as much as we can, but enlistment is still lower than we'd like to see."

"The problem is that the younger generations are a lot more liberal than their parents," Davenport responded, his hands folded on his desktop. "We're not far past high school graduations. Boost the ad campaigns and stress the importance of serving. Stress the college money. Do whatever you have to do. We've lost Mobile. The next logical target is New Orleans, and we're not losing that! In the meantime, I'm going to start pressuring the legislature for a draft."

"Yes sir," the general nodded.

"What's the plan in New Orleans?"

"Well, sir," he began. "In Thomas Jefferson's day, they called it the 'Isle of Orleans' because it's surrounded almost completely by water of some sort. There's the lake to the north, the river to the south and west, and swamps to the east and west. So I think we can expect at least some kind of amphibious attack—probably by some of the same Marines that landed at Mobile."

"Go on," Davenport listened.

"So we're setting up cannon emplacements all down the river to thwart U.S. naval ships steaming up the Mississippi," the general unfolded and pushed forward a map of south Louisiana and the New Orleans area. "We're stretched thin, so we're going to have to be as strategic as possible where we put troops. We're going to focus on the south and east mainly, and we're putting the command center in the Superdome. It's big and covered, and let's face it—the NFL season is going to be shot to hell anyway."

"Why just the south and east? What about the lake, here? That's a lot of water and coastline that they can land troops at," the president questioned.

"Sir, as I said, we're stretched thin," the general answered. "See this bridge here?" he pointed to the eastern corner of Lake Ponchartrain. "That's called the Twinspan. It only has one raised area, and it's still not tall enough to get big navy ships through. The Twinspan is I-10. They're going to want to take that bridge intact, and they can't get past it to land men on the south shore of the lake."

"Okay," Davenport nodded. "So where are you putting the bulk of New Orleans' defenses?"

"Remember Hurricane Katrina?" he pointed to a spot on the map. "This is the Industrial Canal. This is the one that flooded the ninth ward when the levee broke. Here's the ninth ward to the east, and the industrial port on the west side of the canal. We're putting a big infantry and artillery force here. This is our first and strongest line of defense. With all these canals that run out to Lake Borgne here to the east, this is a very likely strike point for the Marines. We'll put more cannons here where the Industrial Canal meets the river, and another set of canals on the West Bank, just across from Jackson Square. This will further keep out Navy ships and amphibious attack forces."

"Okay, that takes care of the eastern edge of the city. What about the rest of it?" Davenport inquired.

"Well, we're going to do our best to keep the Yankees out of the historic districts—French Quarter; Garden District. You should have seen what they did to all of the historic homes in Mobile. Those assholes have no clue about respect for southern heritage or history."

"No fighting where the booze and good restaurants are. Got it."

"We don't have to worry much about the Metairie and Kenner areas here to the northwest," General Weaver pointed out. "We're mainly focusing our troops south of I-10 and I-610. We'll be guarding the bridge across the river—the Crescent City Connection. Mid-town will have to be heavily fortified—the seventh ward, Treme; Marigny—and definitely the CBD, where the Superdome is. The rest of the city will be set up and defended in kind of a grid. We'll set up perimeters and fall-back lines at major streets like Claiborne, Canal, Poydras, Bienville, Carrollton, Tulane, etc."

"How many troops are we shooting for?" Davenport nodded.

"Five thousand, we hope," the general responded. "We'll have some tanks and Humvees—the last left over at Fort Polk that had already been manufactured before secession."

"I'm working on that," Davenport looked up at his advisor. "We've got the GM auto plant in Arlington, Texas. Before GM abandoned it right after the secession, it produced SUVs. We still have plans for the civilian Hummers. We just have to implement the military modifications."

"That's great, Mr. President," the general smiled. "God knows we need it. That, and more weapons, armor, and even uniforms."

"Got that coming, too, General," Davenport leaned back in his chair, his navy coat open and exposing his white dress shirt and navy blue tie. "I have shipments coming across the border later this week."

"Thank you, sir," the general nodded, closing his eyes in gratitude.

"Anything else?" Davenport asked. "How are we doing up north?"

"The Blue invasion has stalled in southern Virginia and in Tennessee, north of Nashville. And these hillbilly militias up in the Tennessee and Virginia Appalachians are giving the Blues all kinds of hell. They want that coal mine country, but it looks like they're about to give up there. We've stalled the invasion everywhere in the north, except for the Army pushing into Missouri. The Blues are suffering in the north because they're focusing their resources on hitting the gulf coast."

"War of attrition," Davenport smiled. "The shoe is on the other foot, it seems. Good. Keep working on recruitment and fortifying New Orleans, and keep pressure on those U.S. ships off the coast of Virginia."

Chapter 42

While the temperatures climbed in summertime North Texas, the interior of the Perkins home remained a consistent seventy-four degrees. It was the season of laziness and high electricity bills. Rain was scarce, and lawn-watering regulations took effect. Every school kid in the area longed desperately to run and play outside, but heat advisories and high ozone warnings nearly every day made it almost impossible.

Ashley and Kyle, piled next to one another on the couch in shorts and airy t-shirts, felt as if it would be an endless summer. It was the end of an era. They did not think of college coming in the fall. Really, it was a continuation of classes and lectures they had experienced the vast majority of their lives, but somehow, it felt as though they were out of school forever. It was deceiving.

They were not bothered by Kyle's younger brother. He was upstairs in his filthy, cluttered room; perhaps listening to his MP3 player or sleeping the lazy day away. Maybe it was both. Angela and Drew were at work, the plight of adulthood in the summer. Secretly, most adults long to be school kids during the summertime. They wish they did not have the work and responsibilities they have. They wish for long, hot days at camp, fishing with Grandpa, or playing "Marco Polo" in the swimming pool. It is hard for them to understand why teens wish their adolescence to be over as quickly as possible. They have no idea how easy they have it, as they have nothing to compare it to.

The television was not even on, partially because there was nothing on since the media blackout. They did not need it anyway. They had one another. They sprawled carelessly on the couch in the family room, soaking in the central air and the quiet. Their arms wrapped lovingly around one another, caressing gently, but not in an erotic way. It was pure emotion, free of sexual pressure. It was simply caring that they expressed.

"What do you want to do?" Kyle asked, without so much as moving his head to look at her.

"This," she smiled.

"Fine by me," he briefly pulled her tighter.

They enjoyed a moment of silence, staring at items in the room, often taken for granted with the presence of the television in the room, or with the bustle of everyday existence. Ashley watched the ceiling fan spin at high speed, trying her best to follow the blades with her eyes. Once in a while, it almost appeared as though a blade or two stood perfectly still. Kyle leered at framed prints of old vaudeville and wine advertisements on the wall, trying to figure out why the artists always personified the alcohol bottles and made it seem as if the man or woman in the picture were trying to make love to it.

"How are things going with your parents," Ashley suddenly asked, almost hesitant to bring it up.

"Oh, it's fine," he shrugged. "Dad got over it. Mom jumped his ass, I think, and probably cut him off in the bedroom," he smiled.

"That's gross," she sneered and smiled all at once, while Kyle laughed audibly.

"No," he continued, still giggling, "Dad never apologized. He's sure he's right, but the tension's gone. I'm sure he's sorry he caused a scene in front of everybody."

"Well, at least things are getting better," she smiled. "I can't believe your dad thinks you would ever join the army."

Kyle did not answer or comment. In fact, he became uncomfortably quiet. His body was tense and rigid. His embrace around Ashley grew unnatural. She felt it. She sensed something was amiss, as all women have that uncanny sense.

"I've been meaning to talk to you," he finally said, softly, but with a deepened tone. "I didn't mean for it to be today, but I guess..."

"What?" she sat up, free of his arms.

Kyle paused for a very long moment, contemplating how the next part of this conversation was to go. Perhaps he could not plan this. There was no predicting the course of her reaction, and his reactions to her reactions. Still, he pondered, staring down at where her shaven and beautifully tanned legs met the upholstery of the couch.

"Ashley," he paused for a few seconds, "I'm not going to A & M with you."

"What?" she was shocked. "What, are you going to Tech instead?"

"Republican Guard," he hung his head briefly, and then met her eyes again.

She said nothing at first, her mouth gaping in astonishment, and perhaps a bit of disbelief. She kept waiting for him to smile and admit he was joking, but his expression did not change. His eyes begged her forgiveness as he tried to search her face for understanding.

"Oh my God!" she was horrified. "Did you get drafted?"

"No," he was sullen, "I enlisted."

"The military?" she lowered her brows in nearing anger. "After all that with your dad? No. No! What are you thinking?"

"I enlisted last week. I leave next Thursday," his tone was unchangingly somber in the face of her excitement and anger.

"And when were you planning to tell me?" she yelled.

"I—I don't know," he stumbled. "Not today. I don't know. I guess I had to some time, but I've been dreading it."

"I can't believe this shit!" she stood, leering down at him perched upon the couch. "After all I've heard you say about this secession and this war being bullshit? You hypocrite! Did you reconcile with your dad before or *after* you signed up?"

"Baby," he tried to reach for her hand, but she jerked it back.

"Don't 'baby' me," she looked disgusted. "You're a hypocrite and a sell-out. You drank the Kool-Aid. You bought into all this Republic bullshit propaganda! And what about your scholarship," she raged and ranted.

"They're holding it for up to four years while I serve," he explained. "And then the government is picking up the half of tuition that my scholarship doesn't cover. I didn't know what to do! My dad threatened to lock up access to my college fund!"

"And what if there *is* no Republic in a few years, huh? Did you ever think about that, genius? What if the U.S. Army kicks the Republic's ass and you're shit out of luck with your tuition money? What if everything left in your college fund doesn't cover the bill? What if you lose your citizenship after it all? What if you get killed?"

She snatched her handbag up from the floor, and threw her hair back over her shoulders. She adjusted her shorts and shirt, and turned to storm out. He, through all of this uncertainty and heartache, could not help but note how sexy she always looked when she did those things. It did not matter how angry she was.

"You're not who I thought you were, I guess," she said in a calmed voice, and then turned, walking briskly down the hallway to the front door.

She opened the door with a jerk, and lunged through it, slamming it shut behind her, leaving Kyle dumbfounded. His jaw hung slack as he peered at the front door, listening to the engine of her sports car crank outside. He did not get up to run after her—she was furious, and perhaps she was rightly so. He just turned in his position on the couch, and slumped down to be alone with his thoughts.

Chapter 43

Kyle stood in the parking lot of the mall, the morning heat already beginning to mount. All around him, young men around his age hugged their parents and kissed their girlfriends before loading upon that bus to Fort Hood. The humidity was beginning to cause his gray t-shirt and khaki cargo shorts to stick to his skin. He was sickened by the sight of all these guys and their girlfriends, as his had abandoned him. She had not called, nor had she answered her phone all week. She knew that today was the day. He had hoped that she would have changed her tune by now—that her rage was temporary. He hoped that she would miraculously pull into the parking lot, and run up to him with a big "I'm sorry" and a kiss. Yet, there he stood with his cell phone pressed against his ear, ringing without end. Then the ringing stopped.

"You're not who I thought you were," he detected tears in her voice. "Good luck, Private Perkins," and then she hung up.

He gnashed his teeth and shook his head, half in sorrow, and half in anger. He hung the phone by his side, and then handed it to his grief-stricken mother standing before him. She took it, and stared down at it, empathizing with her son's heartache as only a mother can.

"If she calls, give her the address. I'll send you a letter with it as soon as I can," he told his nodding mother.

Ryan stood beside him, his face displaying sorrow for his friend. He had easily forgiven Kyle's comments at the graduation party. He knew where they came from, although judging by the look on Ryan's father's face, he did not share the sentiment. Ryan slapped his friend's shoulder, and then hugged his own mother and father, both extremely proud.

"See you on the bus," he told Kyle, and then strolled off to board the transport.

Kyle nodded at his friend, and then turned his gaze back to his parents. His mother was becoming increasingly distraught. Tears welled from within the corners of her eyes. She did not know whether to be proud, afraid, or angry. Perhaps it was a combination of them all—difficult to discern between them. She resented her husband for pushing this. She knew there was a war going on out there somewhere, and feared that her son would become one of the countless thousands of killed and wounded on the battlefields. She said not a word. She could not. She simply pulled her boy close, warming his broken heart with her mother's embrace.

"I'm proud of you, son," Drew managed an uneasy smile, and then extended his hand for a firm, warm, fatherly handshake.

Kyle stared down at his dad's outstretched hand. He looked at it for a long moment. He loved his dad. He had never known a moment when he did not grasp that hand, and firmly shake it as only a father and son do. But this time, he just looked at it, and then peered directly into Drew's eyes. He beamed a ray of resentment, anger, and even a touch of hatred into his own father's retinas. He then turned, and walked toward the bus, leaving Drew to hang his hand and his head.

Chapter 44

The sound of tanks and other vehicles made it hard for Derek to even hear the ringing of the platoon cell phone through the earpiece. He paced back and forth across the sidewalk at the north side of the Mobile Civic Center, staring across the street at a few old shops, barely standing in the center of their own rubble, and charred from the inside out. Sadly, much of Mobile looked like that now. Soldiers on duty patrolled the streets in the event that remaining residents decided to band together against the occupying force. The city had lost its charm, trading it now for all the charm of Kabul or post-war Basrah.

Derek was off-duty, still wearing his urban camouflage pants and black combat boots, but stripped to his gray tank top. It was hot, to put it simply. Sweat dotted his forehead and upper lip, and rolled down his chest and back. It dampened the platoon phone, and frequently he had to use his tank top to wipe it and his brow.

"Damn it!" he looked at the phone, pressing the *end* button repeatedly. "Is anyone going to pick up?"

He pressed the *send* button twice to redial, bringing it back up to his ear. Though it was a pain, as well as a loss of individual freedom, it was quite ingenious for the military to provide one cell phone for each platoon. It was kept by the platoon sergeant, and distributed to enlisted men and women on request to call family. They understood the importance of hearing from loved ones in the midst of the conflict, but personal phones could be problematic in terms of operations information leaking out to the public. Therefore, the platoon phones were provided, but could also be monitored by the Department of Defense for any loose lips.

"Hello?" Sherry's voice filled Derek's ear.

"Hi, Mom," he smiled. "How are you?"

"Derek!" she cheered. "Jake, it's Derek! Oh, I'm fine. The question is, how are *you* doing?"

"I'm alright. It's hot," he said. "But seriously, how are you, Mom? You go to the doctor lately?"

"Yeah, Jake took me last week. They checked my breathing. I'm at sixty percent. The doctor's happy with it. I've got a ventilator now, for when I sleep. And he's added some pain killers to my daily cocktail of pills. I've had some back pain with this chair."

"It sounds like you're okay," he spouted, not knowing really what to say about that. It really did not sound okay. It sounded bleak and painful.

"As good as can be expected," she answered.

They did not speak for several moments, each nodding slowly. It was strange that neither of them knew what to say to one another. They were mother and son. They had not spoken in quite some time, and there was plenty that could be spoken about. Sherry, however, did not dare ask about war. She did not know if the Pentagon was listening and if that was okay to talk about. Aside from that, she did not know if she wanted to hear what he would say. Derek surely did not let on what was really going on and what he had seen. He really did not want to share that he had seen men and women younger than he lose their lives and limbs in the most brutal fashions imaginable. He did not let on the kind of danger he faced daily or that he had taken the lives of other men. He simply kept the air that he was doing fine, and the eight-hundred-pound gorilla in the room was left unaddressed.

"Well, you want to say 'hi' to Jake?" Sherry finally asked, breaking the awkward silence.

"Um, yeah. Sure," he answered.

He heard the scratching sounds of the transfer, as he was sure his mother was having trouble handling the phone. This was probably why it took so long for her to finally answer.

"Hey, big boss!" Jake's voice boomed over the phone. "What's going on?"

"Not much at the moment," Derek responded with a smile.

"I just got done building a ramp so your mom can get off the porch with her chair and take a walk, I mean, a roll every once and a while," Jake chuckled.

"I heard that, asshole!" Sherry yelled from the other room, bringing a smile to Derek's face.

"Hey, Derek," Jake opened the front door. "I'm gonna step outside. Your mom's lighting a cigarette. It's gonna be a while."

Jake paused, stepping onto the porch, and closing the door behind him. Derek could hear the porch boards creaking and birds chirping in the background, signifying that he had stepped out.

"How's she really doing?" Derek frowned slightly.

"Dude," he shook his head, "not as good as she says. I've never seen anything like this."

"Neither have I. Hell, most people haven't, and never will."

"Maybe so, but the doctor's concerned, too," Jake rebutted. "Her oxygen dropped from eighty percent to sixty percent in about a month. She's completely confined to the chair. Somebody's got to be here anytime she goes to bed or to the bathroom. So she has to wear adult diapers, and somebody's got to change her. She's got to be picked up to be put on the toilet. She can't help herself anymore. I've done it. Carly's too pregnant to do it. So it's me or the nurse. The doctor seems to think this is moving faster than normal."

"Shit," Derek ran his fingers through his own lengthening hair. "God, I wish I could be there to help."

"No worries, bro. You're doing a great service to the country, and your mom knows it."

"You mentioned Carly," Derek changed the subject, disallowing talk of his mother's condition to further his darkening thoughts of late. "How is she? Tell her I couldn't call her this time because my time was limited."

"Dude," Jake smiled. "She's getting big. Showing big time! And her tits are getting huge!"

Disregarding the lewd, Jake-style comment, Derek could not help smiling at the thought of holding his child for the first time. He could scarcely believe he was going to be a daddy. Nothing prepares one for that. Nothing prepares one for the love that can be felt for another human being when you made them.

"Really," Derek fought back tears of joy. "Five months in. God, once again, I wish so much that I could be there. You know, to take her to the gyno, and stuff. See my kid on the ultrasound. I feel like I'm letting her down. Absent father."

"No, no, no, dude," Jake reassured. "She doesn't feel that way at all. Yeah, she'd rather have you here, but she knows what you're doing. She's proud that her baby's daddy is a war hero. She calls you that, you know? Baby's daddy—and hero. You ought to hear her around everybody. All of us are proud of you."

"Thanks, man. Hey, I'm about to have to go. My shift starts in about fifteen minutes, and I think some broad in my platoon needs to use the phone to call her idiot boyfriend she keeps talking about. Hand me back to my mom for a minute."

"Sure thing. Take it easy, bro."

Jake handed the telephone back to Sherry, who was just finishing her cigarette, snuffing it out in the ashtray on her little table. The smoke billowed up as she released it from the limp grip of her index and middle knuckles, and then took the phone from Jake, pressing it against her head with her entire palm.

"Hey, sweetie. You gotta go?" she smiled.

"Yeah, Mom," he hated to say goodbye. "I just wanted to say 'I love you'."

"I love you, too, Derek," she smiled sweetly.

"I'm not going to be able to call for a while. I'm shipping out in a couple of days. New assignment. I can't tell you where. I just won't be able to call for a while," he said.

"Okay, son. Well you be careful," she closed.

"I will, Mom. Talk to you later," he ended, and then closed the phone to hang it up.

He stood there on the sweltering sidewalk for a few minutes, looking around. He had kind of gotten used to this place. He had settled in. Not all of the guys he was bunking with were shipping out on this next mission. He was nervous. This was going to be a hard one—a city known for outlasting the worst of conditions.

Chapter 45

July, Eleven months before the bomb

Central Texas was not a pleasant place to be in July; definitely not for a soldier in basic training at Fort Hood. The sun scorched the hilly plains relentlessly, with barely a trace of cloud cover in sight. July was notoriously dry and hot in the summer months, and this particular summer was threatening to topple existing drought records. Even the clear skies did not appear completely blue. They were dingy with light brown dust circulating through the air.

Kyle and Ryan were tired, and they appeared tired. The past few weeks were a beating. They were filled with early pre-dawn mornings and days of PT, five-mile runs up rattlesnake-infested trails, and obstacle courses that were designed to break one's body, and rebuild it stronger than that of the average man. The two recent high school graduates were tired and weak, yet they were stronger, somehow, than they had ever been.

In the previous week, the hard work had begun to pay off, however. No longer did their days consist of endless exercise, running, and verbal abuse. They had begun combat training. During peace time, this would not have happened such a short time into their basic training. But training had been shortened from a fourteen week program to a nine week time period. The Republic was desperate for personnel to ship off to the front lines and to beef up the security around the most important metropolitan areas.

The new recruits were beginning to learn the basics of hand-to-hand combat, small arms training, and, of course, the usual marksmanship on the rifle range. But today was going to be extra fun for the young men. They had been herded this afternoon to the range normally reserved for anti-tank and artillery training. Across the range, Kyle could see various targets and small vehicles that he assumed they would be attempting to destroy. The range was littered with various truck and tank parts, blown apart and scattered about through years of explosions and training. The landscape was scarred with craters, small and large. A flutter filled the hearts and stomachs of the young men, as they knew that this day would finally be a lot of fun.

Upon a six-foot-by-six-foot metal platform stood a tall tripod. Perched atop was a rather menacing piece of weaponry. The M2HBA fifty-caliber automatic rifle looked strikingly god-like, as if it were Zeus himself, calling down the lightning to destroy enemies with impunity. It was clean and freshly oiled; ready for action. It was a machine of death.

"Alright, boys," Gunnery Sergeant Williams' voice boomed as he stood towering over the recruits sitting on the ground. "Today you will be operating the M2HBA fifty-caliber automatic rifle. It is a modification of the normally semi-automatic version we've always used since the end of World War I. This one will fire continuously as long as you hold down the trigger. You will most likely see this weapon used as the primary defense on top of a Humvee or on a tripod used by infantry in the field. Normally, this gun can be used by one soldier. It is belt-fed, normally from a case of ammo at your feet. Up in a Humvee, you won't have enough room for a second person to help feed in the ammo like you see in old WWII movies. However, for training purposes, since you have never handled this weapon before, you will operate it in two-man teams. One of you will be firing, while the other helps to feed in the ammo. Then you will switch off. As I said, in the field, you will likely be solo on this gun, but in some situations, you may not have a box with the ammo belt in it, and you can't just let it feed in from the dirt. So you need to learn how to do this in teams."

"Do not forget," he continued, his face stern, "this is not Grandpa's deer rifle. This is a killing machine of the highest order. This is a fifty cal. That means the round you fire is half an inch in diameter. It's a heavy bullet, and a heavy bullet needs a lot of powder. That makes this one of the most powerful small arms on the planet. So use this rifle with precaution. Don't be stupid! Do you get me?"

"Yes, sergeant!" they all yelled in unison.

"Now grab a partner, and let's doe-see-doe!"

Kyle looked around at the men surrounding the platform. All were ecstatic, ready to destroy something. It did not matter whether or not they had enlisted on their own free will or had been drafted into service in the Republican Guard. This was going to be fun.

Kyle's excitement morphed into anxiety. He prayed that he would not go first. He tended to learn by doing, but preferred to learn by example in some cases. He hoped that a few others would go before him, so that he would see what mistakes they made, and avoid the same ones. He was used to being good at whatever he tried. He was not accustomed to struggling, and he did not want the sergeant and the other recruits to find him incompetent.

"Perkins," the gunnery sergeant pointed at Kyle, "grab your girlfriend there, and step up."

Ryan was excited, though Kyle's fears were realized. Ryan was like a child opening a gift on Christmas morning. He had uncovered a new toy that would cause him to neglect all of his other playthings. They stepped up on the platform, Ryan rushing to the trigger without even offering the first shots to his best friend. Kyle, with no other choice, moved to the ammo belt, slightly relieved.

"Okay, boys," the sergeant stepped up. "Everybody put on your ear protection! Listen closely! Ammo man, just feed the belt in straight. Make sure it goes in evenly so it doesn't jam. Just let it glide over your fingers. Don't try to grip it. You might lose a finger, and then you're no use to the Republican Guard. Trigger man, grip the spade handle, point at what you want to kill, and squeeze the trigger. If you happen to see a Red deer out there, go for it, and we'll have a good dinner for a change," he said, sending the men into a fit of laughter. "Alright, fire at will. Anyone named Will?"

Ryan gripped the handle and put his finger on the trigger, aligning the barrel with an old 1980s Ford pickup truck, already full of holes. Kyle braced himself, somewhat wincing in anticipation of the sudden bursts of fire. There was excitement in Ryan's eyes. He was mentally preparing himself. Then he squeezed the trigger, and began unleashing a fury of rounds across the field.

Immediately, bullets began pelting the pickup truck, tearing large holes in the thin steel panels. He turned the barrel, and squeezed the trigger again, obliterating wooden crates and plywood targets. He laughed as he fired, the adrenaline taking over. The muzzle spouted bullets almost at the same rate as his heart beat until the last round fed through the action, and the gun went silent.

"Excellent!" the sergeant yelled. "You're a natural, son! Now switch. Come over here and feed the next belt in. Perkins, you take the trigger."

The two switched positions at the commanding weapon. Ryan began loading it, while Kyle stood behind, his stomach almost turning sour with nervousness. He was an intellectual. He did not count himself a soldier. He was primed for college and academia, not macho destruction and killing. He had been hunting, and he enjoyed it, but this was outside his comfort zone. A 7mm rifle was the biggest gun he had handled. This thing was the wrathful arm of God.

"Fire when ready!" the sergeant yelled loud enough to be heard through the ear protection.

Kyle lined up his target—a crate directly ahead of him—and began applying pressure to the trigger. His eyes squinted and his head shied away in anticipation of the first blast. The muzzle breathed fire as the first few rounds went off, sending the projectiles into the dirt, and across the field, hitting nothing of any importance.

A few of the men sitting on the ground behind him giggled, a humiliating moment for Kyle. He was embarrassed and annoyed to the border of anger. The recoil had startled him, and he lost control of where he was firing.

"Jesus, Christ!" the gunny exclaimed from the ground below. "If that were some kind of bullshit video game, you would have gotten it right. Now hold that gun steady, bear down, and tear some shit up!"

He did just that. He focused, the anxiety somehow destroyed by those first few shots. He pointed the barrel at his chosen crate once more, and began firing, hitting his mark. Wood splintered about, displaying the true destructive power of this weapon. It was as beautiful as it was deadly. But then, the gun fell prematurely silent. Kyle looked down to see if he were already out of ammunition.

"Is that it?" he looked at Ryan.

"No, dude," he jiggled the belt. "And I don't think it's jammed."

"It didn't feel like a jam or a misfeed," Kyle looked perplexed.

The sergeant stood, his arms folded, to the left of the platform. He looked on, unaware at the moment, of what was happening. He began moving slowly forward toward the platform.

"Sir," Ryan stepped forward, passing in front of the end of the barrel for a better view of the sergeant. "We have a problem!"

"Private!" the gunny yelled, rare fear in his eyes. "Get clear of the muzzle, you dumbass!"

"Ryan, what the hell…" Kyle stopped short.

After a slow burn within the bullet cartridge, the main charge finally fired, sending the fifty caliber projectile screaming from the end of the barrel. It tore into Ryan's side, just beneath his left rib cage, and decimated his vital organs inside before exiting the other side. He fell lifelessly off the platform to the front, his left torso with a gaping, bleeding hole, and his right side missing most of its tissue. Blood gushed onto the dirt, forming a deep red mud around Ryan's body. His eyes were open but blank, looking up into the sky as if to project his soul into the afterlife.

"Ryan!" Kyle rushed to the front of the platform, and leapt off to his friend's side. "Ryan! Oh my God!" he looked at the body, afraid to touch it, and clueless as to what he was supposed to do.

"Goddamn it!" the sergeant rushed over. "Go get the medic! Hurry up!" he screamed at the other men, now on their feet. He knew, however, that a medic could do no good. The boy was dead. No one survived a point-blank fifty-caliber blast to the torso.

A couple of hours passed. Kyle sat upon his bed, clad in his PT shorts and shirt. His fingers were interlocked together. He moved them slightly from time to time, staring at them and contemplating the miracle of how the human body works, and how it stays alive. Yet, it was fragile—easily disrupted or damaged. How anyone ever reached old age was a mystery and a miracle. The tissue was so soft. The bones were brittle. Even slight nerve damage could cripple the use of a limb or finger. That said, why would anyone volunteer to go to war?

"Perkins," the gunny sat beside him, a softness in his voice that most recruits had never heard before. "I'm sorry about your friend. I truly am. You're learning a hard lesson long before the rest of these recruits. You have an advantage. I served in Afghanistan. I watched friends die and lose limbs. I watched them blown to pieces. I watched them mangled and sent home to have their diapers and colostomy bags changed for the rest of their lives. Nothing can prepare you for that. All of you here will end up in this war sooner or later. And you will all see these things, too. You can count on that. You will see this again. But keep in mind, he served his country—maybe not in battle, but he gave his life for a greater cause, nonetheless."

He patted Kyle's knee, and looked down. He gave a final expression of sympathy and regret, and then stood, turned, and walked away, leaving Kyle to further stare at his fingers, contemplating the miracle of being alive.

Chapter 46

Naval ships of all sorts—frigates, battleships, destroyers—moved steadily up the mighty, half-mile-wide stretch of the Mississippi River. All around, the flora and fauna of the life-giving river was rich, and seemed unchanged for eons, aside from the towering levee. Wetlands teemed with aquatic life and birds. Oaks and cypress trees stood draped with curly, gray Spanish moss. The swamp was as synonymous with Louisiana as jazz and crawfish. Really, the only things that stood apart from this were the steel warships and the smoke billowing from the 1820s fortress, Fort Jackson, decimated behind them. Retro-fitting the old fortress with modern cannons still stood no chance against the fire power of this U.S. Naval force. But there were more river defenses to go.

Another dozen ships passed unchallenged across the Rigolets waterway at the coastal border between Louisiana and Mississippi. They had opened the railroad trestle that separated the marshlands from Lake Borgne, and moved between large marsh chunks with names like Rabbit Island, Hog Island, and Weems Island.

This place was the bread and butter of the coastal people. It was a place where the fresh water of the Pearl River met the salinity of the gulf, creating a brackish coastal ecosystem that was perfect for the growth of seafood. Shrimp grow to maturity in places like this, before moving out into saltier waters, only to be caught by hard-working fishermen selling to the gourmet seafood restaurants of South Louisiana. The Rigolets were dotted by fishing camps and marinas that sold live bait and tackle to tourist anglers from all over the region. Strangely, there were people in the marinas and boats on the water, just minding their business, and trying to catch a few redfish or speckled trout.

They navigated the wide, deep channel, coming upon the highway 90 bridge, which was already opening thanks to the SEALs who had gone out ahead of the ships, and commandeered the controls. Still unchallenged, the ships steamed another five and a half miles west into Lake Ponchartrain, approaching the Twinspan bridge, which connected the New Orleans area with Slidell on the north shore. The forward guns aimed and blasted from several of the ships, sending geysers of lake water into the air as they exploded near the bridge. Finally, several shells hit their mark, obliterating large sections of the bridge, and sending chunks of steel and concrete to the bottom of the lake.

Neither Derek Putnam, nor his bunkmate Alex Jasper had slept very well the previous few nights, since arriving in Lake Borgne. The ship's guns fired day and night, as did the guns on the ships around them. The naval force was met by considerable resistance in the lake, and before an amphibious attack could be executed, the enemy fleet had to be destroyed. And it had, but at the expense of several U.S. ships and hundreds of would-be invading Marines.

Each night, just as they would be nearing slumber, the cannons would fire again, awakening the entire Marine force on board. Derek and Alex would just lie there all night talking about Mobile. They would talk about Jackson. Derek wondered if his body had made it back home or if his family had even been notified yet. It was difficult to speak of, but had to be done. Talk of blood and watching men die. Talk of taking another's life.

Now they were once again aboard the amphibious landing craft, speeding down the canal, swamp to the left, and the suburban community of Old Gentilly to the right. The area was strangely unguarded, but that could have been a bad sign. Perhaps the enemy was concentrated more heavily to the west. The waiting was the hardest part.

They sped along for miles, drawing ever closer to danger. Derek could now hear the blast of cannons in the distance—a preliminary shelling of the enemy position to make things slightly easier than the landing at the Mobile airport. Though the fear, anxiety, and rush of this moment were no longer foreign to Derek and Alex, there was no getting used to it. Every battle held new challenges and new situations. It was always different and unpredictable.

The cannons ceased to roar as the landing craft passed them in the bend where the canal met the Industrial Canal. The U.S. cannons were surrounded by woods atop a small levee. The men could see boats and barges at dock on the sides of the canal. Tanker crates were blown apart and aflame. The entire industrial port was cratered and destroyed. Concrete chunks littered the area as did Red defenders.

Landing at the port, and the lowering of the ramp generated a mounting feeling of dread amongst the soldiers. They were used to immediate gunfire and bloodshed. But it was more like a building sneeze that never quite manifested. The fruit had not ripened. There were no ricocheting bullets or bodies riddled with mortal wounds. There was relative silence, except for the sound of fires raging in sporadic locales.

Derek and Alex felt shiftless. They felt they should be doing something, rather than standing and waiting for the rest of the troops and equipment to land. But this, they supposed, was the purpose of shelling this spot long before the landing. They waited for quite some time, trying their best not to notice enemy limbs and bodies bleeding and even smoldering on the ground.

Across the canal, Derek could see the Ninth Ward, the famed district that saw more death and destruction during Hurricane Katrina than most areas of the city. In fact, he could see the new levee and concrete wall in the place where the other had broken apart during the storm. At first, he wondered why the Ninth Ward had been attacked before he landed. He thought he was in the first wave. He had gone over the briefings countless times aboard that ship for weeks, and he did not remember anything about an attack of the Ninth Ward. But then he realized that it had not been attacked by the Marines. There were not fires or craters. It had been attacked by Katrina, and much of it still appeared as if it had been invaded and razed to the ground. It reminded Derek that just because the media quit covering it, did not mean that things were normal.

Derek watched as scores of other landing craft moved south of his position, covering the rest of the Industrial Canal. He was glad that he was not in one of those boats. They were about to land in hostile territory. The cannon emplacements only covered the port. They did not shell the much more residential areas to the south. The purpose was to minimalize civilian casualties. It was difficult to do that with large artillery pieces. Besides, they had just landed in the Seventh Ward—old black Creole neighborhoods. They were against the disregard of the Republic's politics toward them. They were seen by many as shiftless people living off the government, when the reality was that most were hard-working, yet uneducated members of society. The people of the Seventh Ward would not give aid to the Republican Guard. In fact, they may even help the Marines.

As Derek and Alex waited for the rest of their force to land, they could hear a few pops of gunfire to the south. It became more frequent. They winced in sympathy for those troops landing closer to the river. There, they listened for quite some time, helpless in their fellow Marines' time of need. After a while, a cannon began firing near the river. It brought a smile to Derek's face. This was a good sound. It meant that the Marines had taken control of the position, and had begun shelling the other cannon emplacement on the West Bank.

It took hours to offload all of the Humvees, tanks, and men required to invade New Orleans. Luckily, there was an actual dock to make this easier. Finally, they began pushing into the city. They crossed overgrown abandoned lots. Humvees accompanied infantrymen up the residential streets, while Abrams tanks moved up every two streets. They crossed neighborhoods where the houses obviously once stood in close quarters with one another, but now were dotted with sections of rectangular outlines where Katrina-torn homes once stood.

Derek and Alex's squad fanned out to the southwest to close a gap in coverage, moving south of Florida Avenue to the north end of the train station. It was quiet. They were sure they would meet resistance by now, but they had seen no evidence of the enemy. The station parking lot was desolate—no person, nor car in sight. They traversed the seemingly endless span of tracks, finally reaching the west side and on, a few blocks toward Almonaster Avenue.

There were homes that appeared abandoned, yet many had old, beat-up vehicles in front. Derek knew there were people inside. Every now and again, he could see a face peek out from inside a window. Some smiled. Mobile was mostly evacuated, but that city did not possess the same kind of poverty class that New Orleans did. These were old families whose ancestors had been in this city since they were sold into slavery from Africa nearly three hundred years ago. These were the oldest families in New Orleans, a contrasting difference between them and the white, European ruling classes that came and went in the earliest days. They were poverty-stricken, but proud. Many of them provided the classic, revered sights and sounds of the street performances and jazz halls of the French Quarter, and had done so for generations.

They had not evacuated for a major hurricane, so what would make anyone think that they would evacuate for an invasion? Most of them had become quite accustomed to sporadic gunfire once in a while, anyway. Few people outside the gulf south had any clue what it took to evacuate a city. They had never had to do so. It was like going on a vacation. Money had to be spent on gas, food, and if one did not have family elsewhere, money had to be spent on lodging. Depending on how long they would be gone, this could amount to thousands of dollars—a price tag ill-afforded by the Crescent City working poor.

The sound of gunfire began to fill the air, echoing across the rooftops and off the chipping, brightly-colored paint of the small homes. They were approaching Franklin Avenue where they could see troops crouched behind the trees in the median and machine guns set up in the intersection. Marines began dropping to the cracking pavement with several bullet wounds each, while Derek, Alex, and others dove behind elevated porches. Bullets whizzed overhead, and took chunks of wood from the sides of the houses and support beams of the porches.

"Mortars!" Derek's lieutenant screamed from behind a car. "Get some mortar fire on those defenses!"

A three-man mortar team ran in a crouched position, toting their gear until reaching a parked car. The back window of the car was blown out as they hastily set up the tube, and opened the case of shells. One soldier peeked from around the black sedan, judging as quickly as possible the distance between them and the avenue where the enemy defended.

With bullets striking the car and the pavement near them, they joined with other mortar squads in adjusting the trajectory of the tubes, and began dropping shells inside. The projectiles rocketed out of the mortar tubes, and began their arcs through the air. They fell from the sky like a rain of death, exploding in the street and the median of Franklin Avenue. Soil and asphalt showered from the sky. Red soldiers fell to the ground burned and wounded as others fell from Marine fire.

The homes and porches provided adequate cover for the men who could find it. The Republican Guard was unshielded, save a few trees in the median. They desperately deployed mortar shells on the invading Marines. Parked cars were obliterated into piles of twisted metal and broken glass. Porches exploded with Hell's fury, sending fiery pieces of wood and man in all directions. Entire homes burst open, leaving their shells ablaze.

The Marines fought on. Derek continued to fire, anger growing inside him. He reached the end of every clip, dropped them, and inserted new ones, running through those as quickly as the others. The fire was becoming less intense from the other side, and suddenly, the unmistakable droning of Abrams tank engines drowned out the sound of gunfire.

Deafening booms filled the environment as large chunks of the Franklin Avenue median and its trees erupted in destruction. The remaining enemy forces began falling back as the rifle shots came to a halt. Derek and Alex peeked over the raised porch to make sure all was clear. They each sighed with relief, their hearts nearly beating out of their chests as they set their guns down. They took a seat to the side of the porch, their backs against the structure, looked at each other, and began laughing—the only emotion they could muster.

Chapter 47

The Italian chicken and pasta salad was starting to disappear, revealing the presidential seal at the center of the fine china White House flatware. With all of the exotic things that the exquisitely trained chefs in the Presidential kitchen could create, this simple meal was one of Cindy Chandler's favorites. It simply consisted of spiral pasta, cubed grilled chicken breast, parmesan, black pepper, and Tuscan House dressing, tossed in a bowl. Her top advisors and cabinet members had come to like it, as well. In these times of turmoil, it was the simple things that kept her sane.

Her husband was joining her for lunch that afternoon, as were Secretary of State DeLaune and the ever-present General Bates. They all had the pasta salad, except for the general, who was more of a cold cuts and wheat bread man.

"Okay, we're lunching," Cindy turned her head to General Bates. "We're here. You said there were reports coming in from New Orleans?"

"With all due respect, Madam President," he said, still chewing a bit of his sandwich, "I meant we could look over it after lunch. Don't you want to finish before you do business?"

"That's like dangling a bag of potato chips over a fat kid's head, and watching him jump for it," her eyes widened as she dabbed the corner of her mouth with a napkin. "You're killing me! Spit it out! I want to know!"

"Yes, ma'am," he shrugged, setting down his sandwich, and dug for the file and map he was carrying in his briefcase. "We lost some ships in Lake Borgne, but the coast is clear now. Ships made it unchallenged into Lake Ponchartrain this morning, and took out the Twinspan here," he pointed to the eastern corner of the lake, "which is also going to keep reinforcements from coming in and flanking us from behind. The Reds expected us to keep it intact. Those ships have blanketed the south shore of the lake. Last I checked, the ships moving up the river are at about Magnolia here. That's about fifty-five miles up the river. They've got a good forty or fifty miles to go before they hit New Orleans."

"They're not there yet?" her eyes widened. "What's the hold-up?"

"First of all, they've already had to deal with about half a dozen cannon emplacements so far," he explained. "They have to deal with that, and they can't just blow by them. They have to be shelled and destroyed. We have to occupy the lower river and delta, and we have to at least make it navigable for future ships to move upriver. We've lost two destroyers on the river. The other thing is they have to move cautiously. The river is unpredictable. It's full of sharp turns, big cypress stumps and logs, sunken barges, and all kinds of tricky stuff. So they have to move slowly."

"Okay, so the navy is pretty much on-target," she nodded. "What about the landing force—the ground troops?"

"Three thousand landed at the Industrial Canal this morning," he pointed on the map. "Another two landed just before lunch time to back up the first wave. We have reserves to send in if we need them."

"Why not send them all, and overpower the enemy?"

"We don't want to shoot our wad too soon," he spoke, and then realized to whom he was speaking. Donny's eyes widened as he looked at the general, and then to his wife, afraid of how she would react. "I'm sorry, Madam President," he close his eyes and shook his head. "I'm used to talking to grunts."

"It's fine, General," she waved it off. "Continue. You were talking about shooting wads?"

"Well, yes, ma'am. If we land all our boys...and girls...at once, and something unforeseen happens, we're left with nothing. Our reserves are an insurance policy."

"Okay, so how are they doing? Where are they?"

"Mid-city," he said. "We run a north-to-south line from the river to Interstate 610, pretty much in line with Elysian Fields Avenue here," he pointed out. "Artillery started blasting the holy hell out of the industrial port at about three this morning, and didn't stop until the troops came by on the landing craft. So landing was easy. There were some five hundred casualties closer to the river upon landing, but they quickly took control of the landing zone, manned the existing cannons, and took out the West Bank enemy cannon."

"So it's lunchtime, and you're already half-way to the CBD," she smiled. "Excellent."

"Yeah, we're happy with our position," he nodded. "They're going to set the line where they are. Most of the troops are setting up camp, while a few platoons probe ahead."

"So they're taking a half day," she sneered slightly.

"We can't push them too hard," his hands opened as he explained. "They've had a rough day. Prepping, nerves, landing, and then the skirmishes they've already had."

"How heavy has the resistance been?" DeLaune asked, chiming in between bites of her pasta salad.

"It's been heavy in places," he admitted. "We've lost a few hundred since the initial landing. But it's been strange."

"Yeah? How so?" Chandler cocked her head to the side.

"It hasn't been a full-court press," he used a basketball analogy. "Reports from the field have been that they've humped whole neighborhoods with complete tranquility, and then come to a major street, and hit very heavy resistance. So we started thinking, and we did some satellite reconnaissance to confirm."

"Show me," Chandler's undivided attention was in the hands of the general as everyone leaned in to see what he was pointing to on the map.

"New Orleans is laid out in a strange set of grids, partially due to the curvature of the river, but also because of the age and heritage of the city. It's grown out from the center of the city—the French Quarter—in a strange, haphazard kind of way. It's grown like old medieval cities in Europe. Whole sections pop up adjacent to the heart of the city as time goes by, usually set up in its own grid, and separated from the older sections by some major road that used to skirt the city. So what you get is a weird jigsaw puzzle of a city, and every piece is uniquely different from the last. These are the oldest neighborhoods, aside from the Quarter—Treme, the Seventh Ward. These are almost as old at the Quarter—set up by freed slaves and Creoles. Then there's the Garden District, another old neighborhood."

"Get to the point, General," Cindy became bored with the history lesson.

"They're all pieces to the jigsaw puzzle, separated by major streets and boulevards. They're not defending every corner—just the main streets. They're defending in a grid. Each major street is a fall-back point, and it gets heavier and heavier the closer you get to downtown."

"So they let you walk through a whole neighborhood untouched, and then hit you hard at the edge of the grid?" Donny puzzled.

"Precisely," the general nodded. "You know what that tells me?"

"What?" Cindy asked.

"They're undermanned. They're playing it smart, or at least deceivingly," he smiled.

No one said anything for a moment. They sat there, ignoring their lunch, and contemplating the situation. They were not sure if this was a good thing or a bad thing. None of them were military strategists, but on one hand, them being undermanned was a good thing. But on the other hand, they were concentrating in particular areas with ferocious might, and they were defending a very important city. It seemed that they would not pull any punches.

"I want to run something by you, and being the Commander in Chief, you need to make this call," General Bates began again.

"Okay, shoot," Cindy nodded.

"I'd like to lighten the load a bit for the ground troops," he continued.

"I'm all for that. How?"

"We have a satellite locked in on the Big Easy now. It's real time. We're following every move. We just can't say definitively how many ground forces the enemy has. We're not so much worried about the area north of I-10—Metairie. There are a few small pockets of troops camped up there. We're going to take care of that with a few Apaches and Blackhawk choppers."

"Okay," Cindy agreed.

"But since we know where the concentrations of all of the enemy ground troops are in the city, we can hit them without endangering our Marines—thin the crowd like the Brits did with bowmen in the middle ages."

"With what?" Cindy was intrigued.

"Predator drones. They can fly by remote for four hundred miles, hover for hours, and then fly the four hundred miles back on the same juice. And we can use satellite imagery in conjunction to bomb the shit out of the Reds along these streets, minimally damaging civilian homes. We can launch them out of the airfield in Mobile, fly them from a command base there, and take out possibly half of the enemy before our Marines even see them."

"With a remote control?"

"Yup."

"Okay, General," she nodded. "Make it happen. Is that all you have?"

"No, Madam President," General Bates shook his head. "I have some complaints from the fronts."

"Oh?"

"Yes ma'am," he replied. "We've never had problems in the way of personnel numbers. We have plenty of troops, which is more than I can say for the Reds, but they seem to have something we don't have. Unlimited weapons and vehicles. Intelligence is saying that they've begun using an old GM plant in the Dallas area to build Humvees and other vehicles. We're running out."

"Running out of vehicles?" she gaped.

"Not particularly in the Gulf South. We've had the biggest loss of Humvees on the northern fronts," he nodded in confirmation. "That's part of the reason the efforts there are so slow-moving. Tanks we're fine on, but all those Humvees and transports we had stockpiled from before the war are running out."

She hung her head in thought and stress. She could feel her heartbeat quicken and her muscles constrict. The fine lines of graceful aging seemed to deepen in an instant, almost adding years to her age in moments.

"And vehicles aren't the only problems our troops are complaining about," he continued. "We're running short on weapons—guns. Not ammo. That's made right here in the US. Only a small portion of the firearms we've used for the military in recent decades have been made in the States. The rest we import. The few arms companies that have a military contract can't keep up with the demand. Our boys...and girls...are running short. We keep getting new recruits out of basic, and some end up with no gun to fight with."

"How are they continuing to fight?" she puzzled. "How are we making the best use of our soldiers if some don't have a gun?"

"They're making due," he frowned. "They're scavenging. They recycle the rifles dropped by those who fall dead or wounded. They're also picking up enemy weapons and ammo and confiscating enemy stockpiles wherever they capture a major command depot."

"Are we ever going to catch a break?" she lamented. "The Republicans thought I was going to bankrupt the country with the stimulus plan, but this fight they picked is going to do that all by itself! Where are we going to get the money to import more guns and vehicles? We're broke. We can't go much further into debt. Congress is already getting antsy about spending as it is."

"Maybe we don't have to," Donny interjected. "Just ramp up manufacturing here."

"That's the problem, Donny," she argued. "We're not the manufacturing giant we were even fifty years ago. Everything's service industry. We don't actually make anything here anymore. We've got the rust belt and the Reds have the oil belt."

"Just because we don't make anything here anymore doesn't mean we can't start doing it again out of necessity," Donny said. "Finance and service is hurting. That's our recession. But what if we started actually building things for ourselves again?"

"It would create jobs," Delaune added. "When we were in Iraq and Afghanistan, we went into a lot of debt because we had to import a lot of our war needs. But military spending right here in the States during the 1940s is what got us out of the Great Depression."

"We could draw up new contracts with GM for vehicles, textile companies for uniforms, arms companies that make hunting rifles for weapons, and whatever else we need for the war effort," General Bates said, liking the idea.

"And then after the war is over, we might see a resurrection of manufacturing in the U.S. and improve the economy and unemployment rate," Donny added.

"Kill two birds with one stone," Cindy nodded. "Win the war and fix the economy. I like it. I'll call an emergency session of Congress and present the idea. This is going to work. I can feel it," she smiled.

"You're going to replace Lincoln on the five dollar bill," Donny joked.

"Hopefully I don't have to get shot for that to happen," she smiled.

Chapter 48

Marines and tanks were now moving into the areas to the west of the French Quarter and the CBD. Claiborne Avenue was a wreck. The street and the grassy median were torn to pieces by drones, leaving craters filled with Red soldiers and downed trees ablaze. St. Charles was just as bad. The once elegant old street, canopied by centuries-old live oaks was in ruin. Most of the old mansions still stood—drone attacks were notoriously accurate—but the median, locally called the neutral ground, was destroyed, along with the men and the old streetcar tracks.

The Marines, reinforced that morning, pushed around to the north of the CBD to surround the remainder of the southern part of the city. They pushed up the widest of streets whose heavy defenses had been decimated by early drone attacks. Tanks and Humvees found no use for their hefty fire power. Troops rode on transport trucks, dropped at key points along the way to take care of small bands of surviving enemy troops, and to hold the line until Metairie, Jefferson, and Kenner could be conquered later.

The city was all but in United States military control. The battle was nearly won, save one last pocket of resistance—downtown. The force of Marines moving west to secure the Garden District and Uptown was relatively small. Most of the resistance was neutralized. But in the CBD, any losses suffered during the drone attacks were reinforced by Republican Guardsmen squirreled away inside the command center within the Superdome. From Calliope to the southwest to Canal in the northeast, and from I-10 in the north to the Riverwalk, Republican troops dug in deep, ready for the onslaught.

"Damn it!" the Republican Major General slammed his fist onto the table before him, his staff looking on with expressions of doom and gloom.

“I’m sorry, sir,” a colonel shook his head. “Those drones screwed us pretty hard. The enemy is pushing out into the Garden District as we speak. We’re surrounded.”

“How bad is the damage outside in the CBD?” the general calmed himself.

“It’s not pretty,” a major spoke up. “Drones hit our defenses on Poydras, Loyola, Canal, Claiborne, and Convention Center Boulevard. On top of that, they’ve got a cannon on the Westbank they’ve been using to shell the city. No residences, so they don’t have any problem firing blind. Harrah’s is burning to the ground as we speak. Hotels and corporate buildings are wrecked. And as you’ve seen yourself, some destroyers have been shelling the Superdome,” he pointed upward to the gaping holes blown in the roof of the giant stadium.

The general looked around at his staff, all silently imploring him to surrender. No one believed there was any hope left. They were outmanned and outgunned. He looked beyond his staff, positioned around the plastic tables set atop the “A” in the “Saints” painted end zone. Troops were busy using powerful fire hoses to extinguish small fires on the field and in the stands. They worked to clear hulking pieces of steel that had fallen from the dome’s frame.

“My duty is to hold this post,” he insisted to the dismay of his staff. “I was ordered to hold this city. It’s one of the most important cities in the Republic. I don’t give a shit if Austin undermanned us. I don’t give a shit if they send us two dozen to do it with. I was given a job. We still hold this CBD. Get those men out there and tell ‘em to fight. Tell ‘em to claw eyes out if they have to. Tell ‘em to use broken beer bottles if they have to. But hold those lines while I try to get some reinforcements in here from Baton Rouge.”

Derek was in a good mood, though he was kept awake most of the night and early morning by the sounds of explosions all over the city. He knew what that meant. He would have an easy day, and it had been so far. His trek from the Seventh Ward into the French Quarter was an easy one. There had been small exchanges of fire with a few enemy troops, but it had been relatively bloodless, except for the sight of burned and bleeding enemy corpses along their ravaged defense lines.

He walked Bourbon Street with his comrades, Alex to his side. He had entered some strange nexus that the battle had forgotten. The old, historic buildings bore no bullet holes. There were no craters or fires. Derek smiled in this revelation. The history of this district was preserved. His heart had ached over the decimation he saw befall downtown Mobile.

Here, there actually were patrons strolling the sidewalks. The city did not bear the extra influx of tourism for obvious reasons, but locals had opened their shops, eateries, and bars as if it were any other day. It was surprising. The French doors gaped, and the opportunity was open to walk in for a cold afternoon beer. It would have been nice, too. Derek had long desired to visit the Big Easy. He had an opportunity to do so a few years back, when Jake and some other friends took a trip for Mardi Gras, but Derek had not the money or time to partake.

As he clutched his rifle, and gazed around at the ethnic and historical vibe emanating from all around, he smiled to think of what it may be like to visit this street during Mardi Gras, or even on a random Saturday night. The neons would reflect from pooling water, booze, and urine in the gutters of the street. The smell of drunkenness would mingle with that of gourmet Creole cuisine. The street would be an endless sea of giant plastic cups filled with beer, and yard-long plastic containers of Bourbon's strongest intoxicating concoctions. Jazz, zydeco, and hip-hop would battle for the dominant decibel levels, while the crowds along the street and the crowded balconies would be dotted by the exposed breasts of drunken women hoping for a fifty-cent set of plastic beads. Forget Vegas, this was America's original Sin City.

But alas, he was not on vacation. He was walking Bourbon Street for the first time, not as an inebriated patron, but as a soldier, decked out in urban camouflage, and carrying an automatic assault rifle. But the city was doing its best to still make him feel as if he were on vacation. Perhaps it was southern hospitality—something the Republican Guard had failed to show him since his deployment had begun.

On the corner to his right, a trombone player blew some classic New Orleans jazz line. The culture filled Derek's ears. The older black man paused, and lowered his instrument. He smiled at Derek, his trombone case open for any donations to his livelihood. It would never come, but something told Derek that it did not matter. That big, toothy smile was enough to let him know that the jazz man was in gratitude of the invading force. He nodded at Derek, and then lifted the mouth piece to his lips. He blew, sliding with his right hand and allowing the classic "When the Saints Go Marching In" to flow from the horn.

A block away, Derek could see four, five, and six-story Victorian and 1920s shops and department stores rising above the palms of Canal Street. Beyond and amid those transition buildings from the colonial to the modern, lofty twentieth century hotels and office buildings towered above most buildings in the city. They were filled with fiery holes. Canal Street smoldered. Gaping craters in the concrete and pavement riddled the wide boulevard. Steel street car tracks twisted up from the ground, engulfed by palm trees and light poles that had fallen in the barrage.

Through the smoke, muzzle flashes pierced the haze. The Marines strolling down the French Quarter streets were taken aback, believing that the resistance had been eliminated. Those closer to Canal Street had not a prayer. They began falling to the asphalt and stone sidewalks, their blood pouring into the gutters normally reserved for beer and vomit. Others further back ducked around the corners at Iberville Street and into the open doors of bars or restaurants. Derek and Alex crouched behind a parked SUV, swinging their rifles from around the hulking piece of steel machinery to return fire.

It was a bad situation for the U.S. Marines. They were confined to the narrow French Quarter streets with little cover, yet needed to advance. The only other option was to push out into the wide open spaces of Canal Street, ensuring casualties would be great on both sides. That was suicide. But something had to be done. The Marines were bottlenecking in a way, only able to move a certain amount of troops down the narrow streets at a time. In an all-out charge, they could keep bombarding Canal Street with an endless stream of soldiers, but with only a few at the opening from Bourbon, it would be limited fire power.

"What the hell do we do, sir?" Derek screamed to Captain Andrews inside the bar to his right as an enemy bullet punctured the left front tire of the SUV, lowering the frame closer to the ground. "Charge? Charge Canal?"

"What?" he screamed back, peering out the window and trying to gain his bearings. "No! No, are you crazy?" he thought for a moment. "Mortar squads! Get your mortar squads about a block to our six, and start putting some shells into that line!" He thought for a moment as he watched a few Marines fall wounded. "You guys," he told a few privates in the bar with him, "run back to the munitions truck a few blocks back. Come back with RPGs, and get up on this roof."

The mortar squads hiding around the corner of Bourbon and Iberville scurried from their comfortable shelter, and ran in terror back down the sidewalks of the bullet-swarmed street. They were desperate to reach shelter behind the corners of Bourbon and Bienville Streets. Bullets ricocheted off of the brick walls and asphalt streets around them as one man was hit directly in the back. The rest of the men had no time to stop and carry him off the street, as he was probably dead already.

Three teams reached the corner, quickly ducking behind the walls on each side of Bourbon, and immediately searching for a suitable place to set up their tubes. Two teams set up in the middle of Bienville, setting their tubes to fire toward Canal Street, while the third took refuge behind a delivery truck parked along Bourbon. The spotters yanked binoculars from their bags, and peered from behind their shelters, judging the distance and instructing the others to adjust the trajectory.

The numbers were locked in, and the squads were set. They began pulling the first shells from the boxes, dropping them into the tubes. The spike at the bottom punctured the percussion cap, and sent the round hurling through the air, the first overshooting its mark, exploding in an off-Canal bar. The spotter watched through his binoculars as glass and brick flew across the street, bouncing off the other building.

"Too far," one spotter told all of the squads. "Back it up a little," he said as the tubes were adjusted.

The next test-fire shot from the tube, and plummeted to the ground, sending defenders flying from the intersection. A smile shot across their faces, as they had found their range. The three squads varied their trajectories slightly from one another, and shot in slightly different directions, varying every few shots to cover more of the heavily defended street as they could.

A few men ran down the deadly Bourbon Street carrying a couple of large boxes. They ran past the mortar squads happily shelling the defense line, and down to the corner of Iberville Street. They tumbled in through the open doors of the more modern-renovated building, which starkly contrasted with the Spanish-style architecture of most of the buildings on that end of the street.

"Get up there," Captain Andrews pointed to the stairs from his position near the Bourbon side window.

The men carried the boxes, each of them on one end, to the back where a hallway led to the restrooms and to the staircase. They climbed the steep stairs to a wide-open upper room used for storage, yet may have housed bedrooms a century and a half ago. There, they found an iron ladder leading up to the roof. A soldier climbed up, and pushed on the hatch to open up to the moist Louisiana air.

"I'm gonna get on the roof first. One of you guys get up on the ladders, and help me get the boxes up here," Queens said, hoisting himself onto the tarred rooftop.

"Alright, hand it up," Queens ordered as another soldier took position on the ladder and took hold of one end of the crate. "Push!" He struggled to lift the box to the man on the roof.

"I'm trying," the soldier beneath grunted. "This is a heavy son of a bitch!"

They all used every bit of strength they had to lift the munitions crates up and onto the roof. They thought they were stronger than that. Being a Marine came with a level of pride. It came with a belief that one was stronger, somehow, than anyone else—at least in the military. Perhaps under normal circumstances, this exercise would not have been a problem, but getting shot at can take a lot out of a man.

Having finally lifted the boxes to the roof, they all climbed up, and began lugging the equipment across the rooftop. New Orleans was an old city, and over time, the citizens began utilizing every bit of space in the French Quarter that could be used. From its founding in 1718, New Orleans was a planned community with squares laid out in a certain grid to be occupied by business owners and residents alike. Over time, fires, hurricanes, and sheer neglect ruined most of the original buildings, and new ones took their place. Spanish era structures mingled with French and newer nineteenth-century buildings, creating an architectural anomaly present in few American cities. The old structures were crammed together, often with rooftops uneven with one another. Steep French rooftops towered above flat Spanish ones.

But on the Canal end of Bourbon Street, the buildings were much newer than in the center and eastern parts of the Vieux Carre. They were flat and tarred; dotted with aging air conditioning units. The men hustled past an opening into a once grand courtyard, which was now used as the pool area of a hotel. The gunfire became louder as they approached Canal Street, and they could see concrete and asphalt burst into the sky from the explosion of mortar rounds.

"Hang back," Queens said as they dropped the crates a significant distance from the Canal roof edge. "Let's load here and fall back again to reload. Fire and run. Maybe they won't see where the RPGs are coming from, and maybe you won't get shot."

They opened the crates, grabbing RPG launchers and rockets. They each loaded a round, and crouched as they approached the edge of the roof. Taking a knee, they locked in on targets that bore larger amounts of enemy troops.

"Ready," one said. "Fire!"

The four rockets left a light trail of smoke as they zoomed toward their targets. Three exploded in the street's median, while one hit the drug store where half a dozen men crouched, firing at the Marines on Bourbon Street. The windows burst with fire and glass as the concussion of the blast threw the defenders cut and burned into Canal Street.

"Shit, yeah!" one Marine exclaimed in excitement as they all fell back to the ammunition crates to reload.

They repeated the actions several times, each shot adding pressure to the Republican Guard below, but each time drew more attention to themselves. The Guardsmen below could see where the rockets were being shot from, and with each launching, the Marines became targets. Once more, they loosed their rockets to the street below, creating mayhem as bullets threw chunks of stucco and stone up from the side of the building below.

"Look at this," one Marine pointed to the opening of Carondelet Street across the way. "They just keep coming," he languished as a bullet struck him in the torso, and he fell to the street.

The remaining three RGP launchers fell back to the crate another time, taking a few more moments to enjoy not being shot at. They breathed deeply in terror, gazing back at the edge of the building where they had seen their man fall to his demise.

"We gotta go back," Queens shook his head. "We gotta keep pressure on that line, and fire off of our guys down there," his thick New York accent dominating his speech.

They reloaded, and took a deep breath before scurrying up to the edge again to take aim. This time, they barely even took aim, pulling the triggers, and attempting to fall back. Before he could fully pull the trigger, another man was hit in the neck. He fell off the roof as his finger jerked, and released the RPG from its launcher while he was upside down. The RPG crashed into the third story of the nineteenth century hotel, blasting stone and stucco into the street while the Marine hit the ground.

The remaining two went back to the crate, and began loading once again when they began to hear a new noise over the sounds of battle. It was low and rumbling—very mechanical. Before they could guess what the sound was, their answer was presented. A deafening blast echoed across the Quarter, and the sound of rubble hitting the ground brought a smile to their faces. They each rushed to the edge, RPGs loaded to see Abrams tanks rounding the corners of North Rampart and Decatur Streets. There were over a dozen, all taking positions along Canal Street, and blasting into the defense lines that extended the entire length of the French Quarter. Skirmishes that were taking place at virtually every street that led from the Quarter to Canal suddenly were disrupted, adding tank fire to mortar rounds and infantry bullets.

Marines yelled in glee, receiving a second wind. The enemy lines were being thinned, and they were beginning to fall back to their defense lines at Poydras Street. The Marines began emerging from behind the corners, the parked vehicles, and bars to chase the resistance back between the much taller hotels and office buildings of the CBD. Tanks pushed across the boulevard to provide cover and help push the Guard back into the city. The west side of Canal Street was in rubble, very much resembling Berlin or some other European city at the end of World War II.

Within the Superdome, the Major General in charge of holding the city stood once again around a set of plastic tables, surrounded by his subordinates. He stared down at the map of the city, as if in a trance. His eyes were transfixed upon the CBD that his men now defended. He noted how relatively small the area still held by the Republican Guard was in comparison to the rest of the US-occupied city. He felt sick. This was his duty, and he had failed, however undermanned he was to complete his task.

"They're closing in, sir," a Colonel broke the silence. "The front has fallen back on all sides. The tanks rolled in, and that was it. No doubt," he continued, motioning all around him, "you can hear the fight right outside to the north."

"And we're not getting support from Baton Rouge," he hung his head. "They say they can't spare anything or anybody. And I believe it."

He looked around at staff members and brass scurrying around the command center within the dome. They shut down computers, erasing plans and orders, and burned anything printed in an attempt to keep it out of enemy hands. He had lost hope. He felt broken and aged ten years in a matter of a few days.

"Call it," he said. "Call surrender. Nobody else needs to die."

Chapter 49

"Breaking news coming in from the war front," the sleek brunette anchorwoman grinned, clearly pleased with the news.

Sherry noted this. She had seen in the past few months a growing lack of concealment of the media's bias. It had always been understood that certain news channels were politically biased, often in line with the viewpoints of the network's CEO and board. Yet, in the past, there had at least been an attempt to dupe the public into believing that the stories were looked at and reported from a balanced perspective. Of course, almost no one bought it, but at least they tried.

Since secession, and certainly since the war began, more newsmen and newswomen openly reported in a way that reflected the network's political standpoints, and even their own. Why hide it now? It was clear that there were two definitive sides to the conflict—left and right. Some people on the continent straddled the fence in the middle, but most stuck to their ideology, whether it was their own, or the views they had been instilled with from family all their lives. The United States-based liberal-leaning media covered the war from the U.S. perspective, touting lines like, "winning the good fight." They felt that they were in the right, but so did the other side. Republican news stations were now raising their own money by selling local advertisement, and broadcasting within their own realm. And now they were beginning to network and syndicate according to propaganda streaming from Austin.

"In just two days, the U.S. Marines have taken control over the vast majority of the city of New Orleans," she continued. "We're told by the Pentagon that the defenders there have been overpowered, and that the city's command center surrendered this afternoon. There are still Republican troops in the western and northern suburbs, but they are expected to be neutralized within a few days."

"Carly!" Sherry called to her future daughter-in-law, who parted with the dishes to join her, a pregnant belly bulging from beneath the orange maternity tank top. "I just know he's there. He's in New Orleans."

"We are winning this war," the screen cut to Cindy Chandler giving a press conference on the victory. "We're sending a strong message to Austin and Mr. Davenport that this Union will be preserved."

"The Republic is not sharing the sentiment," the anchorwoman continued. "They are still calling the United States a bully; forcing themselves on the sovereign nation for the sake of power. The Pentagon would not give us a total number of Marines lost in New Orleans, but it was considerable."

"Oh God, I hope he's okay," Carly gasped, rubbing her belly.

"In other news, the Pakistani capital of Islamabad has been overrun by militants," rare scenes of fighting in a far away street filled the television screen. "The exiled Pakistani government is blaming the U.S. government for a change in foreign policy that removed U.S. forces from Afghanistan and Pakistan. Taliban and Al-Qaeda have taken responsibility for the invasion, and are promising that the western world will feel the effects of this very soon. They are expected to set up a more militant government in Islamabad."

"Okay," the anchorwoman changed the topic. "We've talked a lot on this program about the war front, but what about the homefront? We all know what it's like dealing with the stresses of war here in the United States, but few of us know what life has been like for citizens in the Republic. We know they have experienced a lack of syndicated TV, but what about the policies the government has enacted? Crackdowns and deportations of undocumented aliens, laws resembling Jim Crow laws for Hispanics in the southwest, the banning of gay and lesbian relationships, and streamlining of Christian religion built into their Constitution are just a few things," she said as Sherry used both of her decaying hands to grasp the remote control. "But it seems that in the past few months, they have begun to ignore their own policies on immigration for some reason."

"I don't want to watch this crap," she scowled, struggling to press the power button with her right index knuckle. "Who cares about those Red bastards? Who do they think they are?" she muttered to herself as she finally clicked the television off.

She leaned back in her power chair, and reached over for her pack of cigarettes, disregarding the young woman in the kitchen carrying her first grandchild. She grasped the pack with her left hand, able to lift it with minimal grip due to its light weight. She set the pack upright in her lap, and lifted the flip top before using two knuckles to extract a long, slender smoke. She lifted it to her lips, puckering and positioning it just right, and then raised her new torch lighter. It was a butane torch, capable of lighting in a single press of the button. It was easier for her. Jake had picked it up for her the last time he had come over. She fired the end of the cigarette, and inhaled the first drag, closing her eyes and sighing in relief.

She opened her eyes and turned her head to the right, gazing at Carly, busy cleaning dishes in the kitchen. She had been wonderful in Derek's absence. She visited regularly, never becoming frustrated with Sherry. She was happy to help. She always smiled, taking to her as if she were already her mother-in-law. There were certain things she couldn't do, like lift Sherry into the bed or onto the toilet seat, but she was often the one to clean her pubic area after diaper changes—something that absolutely humiliated Sherry.

"Thank you," Sherry smiled at Carly. "Thank you for everything you do for me. You are going to be a wonderful daughter-in-law."

"And you are going to be wonderful mother-in-law and grandmother," Carly smiled back.

But on the inside, Carly wept. She had watched Sherry deteriorate so much in the past few months. She wondered how long she would survive. It hurt to think that her baby may not remember her grandmother, or even meet her at all. As always, she hid those emotions until she left the house. Sherry was already becoming depressed as it was. Carly did not want to add to the pain by showing those emotions. And she certainly did not want to discuss it. Surely, Sherry had been lamenting the possibility of never meeting her grandchild in her own mind.

"Shift change!" Jake burst in through the door.

"Hi, Jake," Sherry smiled. "Just in time. I'm getting tired. I need to go to bed."

"Hey, Jake," Carly smiled, still drying a few dishes and utensils. "I'm almost done with this."

"Okay, you do that, and I'll take care of the rest," he said. "Any word from Derek?"

"No, not yet," Sherry finished her cigarette. "But the news said that they won in New Orleans. I'm sure that's where he is."

"I'm sure he'll call soon," Jake was optimistic. "Come on, let's get you into bed."

"Okay, baby," she pushed the joystick to steer herself into the hallway, followed by Jake. "He's fine, I'm sure," she called out to Carly. "He's a tough kid—full of honor and integrity. I'm sure wherever he is, he's doing good things."

Chapter 50

"You're an idiot!" Alex cringed, wincing and shying away from the man standing aside from the black wrought iron table.

Next to him was Derek and two other Marines, all sitting around the table. Carter and Phillips, two strapping young soldiers laughed hysterically, slapping their knees and gulping large quantities of Scotch from pint glasses they found behind the bar. Aside from the table, Queens juggled three live pineapple grenades. He hurled them into the air, catching and alternating them, a goofy look on his face as if he were imitating a clown.

"See," he grinned as he caught all three and slammed them onto the table, "I told you I could juggle," his New York accent filling the courtyard.

The five men were engulfed in red brick and darkness with the nearly full moon providing the only light through the opening above. The Bourbon Street bar was likely a majestic abode some two hundred years before. Now it was a Mecca for the New Orleans drunken masses who wanted a lower-key break from the stumbling crowds and packed neon-lit clubs of Bourbon. Fountains imitated the sound of rain, and combined with small palms and ferns along the four brick walls to add to the Big Easy claim to being the northernmost corner of the Caribbean. A large, stocked bar sprawled down the length of one wall next to the entrance to the covered area of the building. Once a home, there was an upstairs, but who knew what was up there now. All rooms and toilets were on the ground level. The space was filled with black wrought iron furniture. Gas-lit sconces, commonplace in the Quarter, illuminated the hallways and entrances, characteristic of the city's cultural essence.

Something told Derek this was the kind of place that one would want to arrive at early to beat the crowds. It did not have the dinginess of some of the other establishments. It did not reek of vomit and urine. Someone earlier in the day told him that the place was a French Quarter icon—one of the most famous places on Bourbon.

"What the hell, dude?" Alex continued at Queens as the bulking New Yorker sat down.

"What?" he raised his hands. "I was just juggling."

"Live grenades," Alex railed him, half smiling. "You were juggling live grenades."

"They have the spoons and pins in 'em. They wouldn't have gone off. Let me make it up to you. Let me buy you a drink. Waiter!" his voice echoed within the empty courtyard.

The men began laughing. A few blocks away, a heated battle had taken place earlier in the day. The Quarter was not open for business. In fact, it was under martial law. There was a strict curfew for all remaining citizens, and all who were out after that time would be shot. That bar, and every bar, was empty.

"Guys, guys," Derek said softly, imbibing a healthy gulp of bourbon whiskey. "Keep it down. If the Captain finds out we broke in here, we're in deep shit."

"Whatever," Carter shook his head. "We're heroes. We just whipped the shit out of the Republican Guard and captured the most important city on the map, other than Austin."

"I agree," Phillips jumped to his feet, and trotted to the bar.

He grabbed a bottle from behind the bar, stumbling slightly. With his elbow, he shattered the glass case beside the bar, and reached in to retrieve a handful of finely crafted cigars. He then trotted back to the table with the contraband, and set the cigars down on top.

"Here are your victory cigars," he smiled as he opened the bottle of eighteen-year-old scotch. "And here are your medals!" he began pouring shots of the fine liquor into every gaping mouth at the table as if it were the middle of Spring Break.

"Bwaah!" Derek grimaced and shook his head, having swallowed. "I hate scotch!"

"Well, this is the good stuff," Phillips looked at the label. "So at least you hate it for the right reasons—not just because of the cheap-ass blended stuff."

The men passed around a lighter, all taking turns warming, rotating, and finally sucking in the smoke of the fine maduros. Their cheeks dimpled as they sucked, the thick, rich smoke filling their mouths before releasing the toxic goodness.

"Jackson would've dug this," Alex sipped his drink. "Night with the boys; cigars—he loved cigars."

"Yeah, and Hubert," Queens nodded. "And Johnson, Tony T, Blondie."

The table fell silent. Each mind was filled with memories of their friends. The memories were sweet, mixed with tragedy. They were memories of boot camp, R and R, brotherhood, and then ultimately witnessing that comrade's violent demise. Suddenly, it seemed everyone silently and simultaneously drank a little heavier. The men had seen things that no man should ever have to see. They had done things that most people could never imagine doing.

"To the ones who didn't make it," Derek lifted his glass as everyone else followed and drank to the dead.

"Do you think God hates us?" Derek randomly asked as he stared at the smoldering end of his cigar.

"Why?" Carter puzzled.

"For killing people," Derek responded. "Thou shalt not kill."

"What the hell kind of question is that?" Carter continued. "We're at war, bro."

"God's all about war in the Bible," Queens said between gulps. "Genocide, even. Joshua and Jericho. There you go."

"That's the Old Testament," Alex chimed in. "The New Testament is totally different."

"I'm not gonna have a theological debate with you Protestant bastards," Queens smiled jokingly. "Those old wars with David and Gideon were fought for a good cause. They were morally-backed. Ours is a good cause, too."

"But according to who?" Derek argued. "The government? Like they're the equivalent of God?"

"Look, even so," Queens opened his hands, the smile fading into seriousness, "you're in a situation where you either kill or be killed. God can't fault you for that. We all killed people. It's war," he motioned around to the men sitting around the table.

"I shot a guy in the face," Alex stared at his drink, and then took a sip. "Back in Daphne."

"You *might* have shot him," Phillips corrected. "With everybody else firing, you can't know it was you."

"No, I do know it was me," Alex said. "It was at the bridge, right after Jackson bought it. There was a short lull in the shooting. Some crazy Red bastard charged to the middle of the bridge, and I shot. I watched him lose half his face and hit the ground. I did that."

They all sat in silence, the only sound coming from the burning of cigars and clinking of glasses replaced onto the iron table. They had become almost obsessed with death. Some were hardened against it, like it was second nature. It was no longer immoral. It was almost fun in the heat of battle, but when all of the weapons silenced, they were left alone to reflect on the day.

"The Reds are only human," Queens said softly. "They've got a job to do just like us. Can't fault those guys for it. You just do the same, but quicker and better than that guy."

"I do fault them," Derek sneered with malice, looking up from his drink with pain in his eyes. "I hate them. I hope every last goddamned one of them dies."

The statement was shocking to the rest of the guys. They either stared at him or purposely stared away, unsure of what to say. They all reached silent consensus—the fighting was getting to Derek. Perhaps it was normal. Neither of them felt very far removed from that sentiment themselves.

"You need to get laid, dude," Alex broke the silence as all men, even Derek, erupted into sudden laughter.

"Yeah," Queens regained his status as the New York loudmouth. "Which one of you geniuses forgot to invite the broads in Echo Company? Dipshits! We're drinking on Bourbon Street, and not one of us is gonna see any tits!"

"Having fun, boys?" a voice boomed from the shadows of the main entrance.

They all jumped, knocking a bottle off of the table, and sending it crashing to the bricks below. As it shattered, sending the glass scattering across the floor, a figure emerged from the darkness. Captain Andrews strolled easily up to them, his face neutral of any expression. Each of the five inebriated men, hurried to their feet, staggering and struggling to properly stand at attention.

"At ease, boys," he raised his hands as the men relaxed only slightly. "You decide to throw a party without inviting your captain?"

"No sir," Carter stumbled over his words. "I mean, yes sir. Sir, I can explain…"

"What he means to say," Derek smirked slyly, "is that we figured that a man of your upstanding moral fortitude and good Christian demeanor wouldn't be caught dead around us poor, drunken sinners."

"Save it, Putnam," the Captain smiled, raising his hand to silence the Marine. "Save the ass-kissing for when you really screw up. You boys fought hard today. You did good. You deserve it. But with all the racket you're making, you could wake up those Republican Guardsmen laying in Canal Street out there. If command catches you, you'll be out cleaning tanks all day tomorrow. Now get the hell out of here and get some sleep."

"Yes sir," they all said, and staggered by him.

They filed out of the courtyard, one by one. Phillips still clutched a bottle of top shelf scotch in his hand. As he passed the Captain, the superior officer snatched it from the private, and turned to see them all out the front into Bourbon Street. He shook his head, and lifted the bottle to his lips, taking in the flavorful spirits. He then sat in one of the vacant wrought iron chairs, and continued to drink the scotch straight from the bottle, staring in admiration at the men exiting the bar.

Chapter 51

August, Ten months before the bomb

Angela Perkins could not stop herself from smiling. She clutched the steering wheel of her little white crossover SUV precisely at ten and two, the way her driver safety manual instructed when she was in high school. She purposely kept the radio turned off so that she could converse with her oldest son, but he was not obliging.

He sat in the passenger seat with no expression, alternating the direction of his eyes from the road in front to the window to his right. He had barely said a word since he got off the bus. He obliged his mother's will to hug him continuously for a good five minutes. He even let her kiss his cheek. But he was no longer the innocent, and even naïve young man he had been. His demeanor had changed as much as his appearance.

"I'm so happy you're home," Angela giggled with a giddiness reserved for young girls, but he still did not respond. "Look at you. All grown up in your manly fatigues."

It was awkward. He would not respond to her. She worried, as would any mother. She had never seen him like this. She knew what it was, but she felt that it was too soon to bring it up. Yet, she had to get him talking about something so he could have some sort of release.

"How long are you home for?" she tried to ask a question that he had to respond to, but he remained silent for a few moments.

"Don't know," he finally spoke, while his expression remained unchanged. "I don't even know where I'm going. A few of the guys think they're getting sent to Missouri or Arkansas. But who knows," he stared at the street.

"Maybe you'll get something here in Texas, away from the fighting," she said.

"I don't know if I want that," he shook his head. "I went through basic. I went through with it. So I'd rather fight than hang out on some base doing nothing. Besides, whoever said the fighting won't come to Texas someday?"

"I just don't want anything to happen to you," she lost her smile.

"Like Ryan?" he finally looked at her for a brief moment. "That happened in basic—not on the front. A lawnmower could fling a damned rock and hit me in the temple tomorrow. It doesn't matter."

If it had not been awkward before, it surely had become so. It was silent. Angela wanted to say more; ask more, but she did not know what to say. She could not tell if he wanted to talk about Ryan or not. She opted to say nothing else. He would open up when he wanted, which came pretty soon.

"Have you seen Ashley?" he asked, taking his mother aback.

"Um," she thought, knowing that her next sentence would tread on fragile ground. "Yes. I saw her once at Ryan's funeral," she watched him nod. "She didn't speak or come say 'hi'. She stood in the back, and when it was over, she left."

Kyle remained silent as they turned onto the street leading into his neighborhood. He looked around with interest. It had only been a couple of months, but it seemed as though everything had changed drastically in the neighborhood. The trees looked taller. The grass looked greener. Perhaps he had just become used to military housing and scenery. Even his own house looked different, or even new as they pulled into the driveway next to his covered muscle car.

As the garage door opened and his mother set the parking brake in the driveway, Kyle noticed his father's car in the garage. He was home. Kyle expected him to be at work on a weekday afternoon such as this. He did not anticipate having to deal with that immediately after returning home. It was difficult enough dealing with his mom.

They both opened the doors to the SUV, and stepped out. Angela made sure to swing her purse over her shoulder, while Kyle did the same with his duffel bag. His black boots clapped the concrete on the driveway and in the garage as he moved toward the entryway leading from the garage into the house. He stepped into the ecstasy of central air conditioning, and turned the corner into the hallway to see his father sitting on the couch watching the news. Kyle's heart fluttered, while anger that he had released through endless PT flooded back to him in an instant.

"Hey, hey!" Drew jumped up from the couch, turning off the television. "There's my son! Private Kyle Perkins of the Republican Guard," he attempted a shoddy salute, only defiling the gesture, to Kyle's mind.

Drew rushed over to embrace his son, wrapping his arms around him in a genuinely proud embrace. Kyle did not reciprocate. He did not even drop his duffel bag as he had countless times with his backpack after coming in from school. He let his father hug him, but kept his arms at his side, neither smiling, nor frowning. Angela watched in pain for her son.

"So," Drew let go, and smiled widely at his son. "Tell me about boot camp. How was it? What all did you do?"

"Drew," Angela attempted to prevent him from stepping into this line of conversation, but said no more for fear of entering it herself.

"Oh, you know, Dad," light filled Kyle's eyes as he had found the inspiration to speak more now than he had during the whole ride home. "I ran, did a year's worth of push-ups, got dehydrated a few times, learned how to kill people," Kyle watched the smile fade from Drew's face. "You know they even let me practice on my best friend."

Drew's head hung. He stared at the floor in silence. He had been so excited to see Kyle that he did not even think before he spoke. He looked back up to witness the pain in his son's eyes, masked by a military façade of hardness.

"Son," he spoke lowly and softly. "I..."

"You're sorry?" Kyle shook his head in anger. "Sorry for what? Sorry for Ryan? Sorry for his parents? Sorry for me? I don't need your sympathy. I'm dealing with it."

"I just mean..." Drew tried to explain.

"Or are you sorry that you pressured me to go off to join the army?" Kyle interrupted.

"I never forced your hand," Drew finally completed a sentence.

"Might as well have," he fired back. "Could've fooled me. You had me convinced that you wouldn't have been proud of me if I didn't. You seemed pretty ecstatic. I'm sure that would have been true. Just because you didn't do it when you had a chance."

"I didn't want you to regret not answering the call when your country needed you," his father said.

"It wasn't my calling, Dad!" He raised his voice. "My calling was college. I should be signing up for classes right now. I should be packing up my shit and looking forward to going off to A & M with a girlfriend who still spoke to me! But no, I get to spend weeks in a house with you, moping around with nothing to do—no girlfriend to kiss, a brother that just sits on his ass all day, and I don't even have a best friend anymore! But no, instead of getting ready for college, I have something better to look forward to. I get to wonder which losing front I'm gonna get shipped out to. I get to look forward to how I'm gonna get killed!"

He turned from a speechless father, his duffel bag still thrown over his shoulder. He walked away from his parents as his mother placed her hand over her mouth, tears beginning to roll down her cheeks. He made his way up the staircase, the hollowness thumping beneath his combat boots.

"Don't bother coming up to get me for dinner," he said as he climbed the stairs. "Not hungry, and when I get hungry, I'll take care of myself," he spouted before he disappeared into his room and slammed the door.

Drew just stood, staring toward the front door. He did not anticipate anything happening there. It was just a focal point as he thought in regret. But part of him did not regret. In his mind, he was still right in some way. Angela, however, simply stared at her husband with disdain—a fleeting love replaced by growing anger and hatred.

Chapter 52

It had already been a long morning. The Marines had shipped out from New Orleans before dawn, and headed out on Interstate 10. There was very little resistance on the way. The Republican Guard was saving their limited resources to focus on the defense of Baton Rouge. Why waste men on slowing the enemy down, when you can build a rock-solid defensive wall around the city?

Upon reaching Highway 30, just before the town of Gonzales, the single line of military transport broke into three prongs. The main force stayed along the interstate, while two detachments exited to the highway, one east and one west. The eastern detachment reached Airline Highway, moving then to the northwest, parallel to the interstate, while the other detachment proceeded in the direction of the river. Derek's detachment moved parallel to the Mississippi along Nicholson Drive, beginning near the town of St. Gabriel.

This was a land of many refineries, both north and south of Baton Rouge, and a major source of income for the state and for the Republic. But the day's objective was not yet to capture the refineries. It was to take control of the city and the port, and worry about the refineries later.

The southern sections of Nicholson Drive were rural. To the east, swamps and bayous lay filled with alligators and egrets—the quintessential ecosystem of south Louisiana. To the west was the river, traveled by the United States Navy, who shadowed the Marine advance. From time to time, Derek and Alex could hear the cannons blast as the Reds tried to sink the ships, but were promptly foiled.

It was not until reaching the area of Gardere, south of Baton Rouge, that Derek's unit began to encounter heavier resistance. Gardere was a small pocket of lower income housing inhabited greatly by the impoverished and by college students. But that morning, it had become a killing field. The infantry had little action in it. That day's assault was spearheaded by tanks on the ground and Apache and Blackhawk helicopters in the air. Each time the Republican Guard was encountered, the tanks blasted their defenses, and the helicopters' rockets and chain guns cleaned up the rest. It was sort of pleasant. Derek began to think that this might be the easiest fight yet. They sat back in the transports relaxing for the trip and trying to guess what was happening ahead with each blast and explosion.

He and his unit looked rough. Their hair was shaggy, and three days' worth of stubble covered their faces. Their clothing smelled of weeks of sweat and urine, depending on the intestinal fortitude of the soldier. Showers were rare. Real cooked meals were virtually non-existent. Battle-hardened veterans such as Derek and Alex possessed an appearance and a look in their eyes of hardness, and even cold hatred. There was a very real and visible difference between the veterans and the new replacements. The reinforcements were often straight out of boot camp. They were clean-cut and shaven, often drawing ridicule from the veterans as "baby Marines." There was no ill will toward them—just the "holier than thou" sense that the veterans had been there and done that, while the new soldiers, still full of Marine Corps rhetoric, were all talk and no experience.

The troops had now exited the transports in anticipation of heavier ground resistance. Derek looked around to see civilization, finally. There were bars and apartments frequented and inhabited by college students. They were probably vacant at the moment, given the ensuing invasion. They were approaching Louisiana State University to the north. They could see the prominent and imposing Tiger Stadium, nestled between clumps of centuries-old oaks, and rising above the endless buildings filled with classrooms and professors' offices. It looked almost like a castle, a stark contrast to the lack of buildings leading up to it. It was nothing but university golf course and parking lots marked by a few small buildings and businesses.

"Keep your eyes peeled," Captain Andrews said. "We've got to go through LSU to get downtown. We're in the open—the perfect opportunity if the Reds want to…"

He was hushed and interrupted by the whoosh of a rocket. It found its mark with one of the Apaches above and ahead of Derek's men. The wreckage flamed to the ground aside from Nicholson Drive, while its blades, still turning, cut into the soil.

"Shit!" Alex crouched, flinching from the sudden blast.

The helicopters began firing their guns toward the university, shattering windows in classrooms, and sending orange bits of the clay Spanish tiles flying into the air. They could not yet tell where the rocket had come from. They were firing blindly, disoriented and afraid. The pilots could finally see the rocket launchers in a parking lot to the south of the stadium, but it was too late. The tracking system had locked on, and the rockets flew in the direction of their targets. The remaining five helicopters exploded above the horrified infantrymen. Shrapnel crushed a few of the Marines, while other large chunks of the craft began littering the fields, roads, and parking lots.

With the menacing aircraft neutralized, the Marines began to be pelted with heavy machine gun fire and lighter personal arms. The Republican Guardsmen teemed from between and within the campus buildings, launching a positively deadly assault on the invaders.

"Find cover!" the captain yelled as bullets whizzed by.

"Where, sir?" a private looked around. There was nothing but open parking lots and fields. The field they were in, used often for football tailgating, had a few trees but nothing else. It was like a return to the archaic methods of warfare in a day when men marched against men in the open fields, prey to fate and wherever the volleys fell. The survival of most of the men in the fields south of the university would now depend largely on luck.

"A ditch! A roadside! A tree! Whatever!" Andrews yelled back. "Just hit the friggin' deck!"

Marines fired from upon their bellies, hoping their bullets met their marks. It was a frantic scene. Mortar squads scurried to set up and begin shelling the enemy, but struggled as their men began falling dead. Gunners set up their tripods and bipods, attempting to place the heavy machine guns upon them and fire back, but the hail of gunfire was too heavy. Tank operators spotted gunners at the top levels of the stadium, and began firing, taking large chunks of concrete out of the upper seating of the hallowed football venue.

For Derek, this was the end. He and Alex remained upon their bellies, firing from behind the lip of a road. Bullets flew overhead and ricocheted off the concrete before them. Mortar shells exploded to the left and right, killing some of their comrades. There was no cover. There was no way to move forward, nor back without certain death. And then there came the unmistakable sound of jet engines.

"Oh yeah!" Derek cheered. "Come and get 'em, boys!"

"I don't think they're ours!" Alex pointed to the jets flying in from the north. "They're coming from the wrong direction. Looks like they're coming out of England Air Base! Those are Red jets!"

The jets rushing in from the north began firing air-to-surface missiles, but not at the Marines on the ground. Explosions rocked the banks of the Mississippi—direct hits devastating the battleships and destroyers cruising the muddy waters. But a ray of hope shined through the mist of uncertainty. U.S. jets moved in from the south, and began losing Tomahawk missiles, sending one enemy jet crashing into the grandstands of the baseball field. All jets climbed into the clouds, engaging in a deadly, invisible dogfight overhead.

The battle on the ground raged on as Marines and Republicans fell everywhere, but the Reds kept coming as if they had an endless supply of reinforcements. The university was a citadel. It was a deadly hydra of a military force. For every head that was lopped off, another three appeared as the Marine infantry force continued to thin. Brick and mortar were blown from university buildings with every tank blast. A jet fell suddenly from overhead. The anonymous clump of wreckage crashed into the golf course in a brilliant flash of destruction.

"Fall back!" some commander yelled, as it was echoed from officer to officer.

The Abrams tanks and Humvees moved up ahead of the Marines, providing cover fire as the troops jumped up from their positions and retreated southward. The Guardsmen were slightly thinned, and many of the gunners were neutralized, yet the fire continued, sending many in the Humvees to their demise. Some retreating soldiers took rounds in the back, and fell lifelessly to the ground.

Alex and Derek ran harder than either of them had ever run—even in basic training. Their lives now depended on it. It was adrenaline and the basic fight-or-flight instinct. Suddenly, Alex fell behind, and Derek could no longer see him to his right. He panicked. He stopped, his leg muscles beginning to cramp, and looked for his friend. He turned to see Alex lying on the hot pavement. His first thought was that Alex was dead, but he saw him move. Blood poured from a wound in the back of his left calf. Alex writhed and grunted in pain as Derek instinctively hoisted his friend, and interlocked shoulders. They ran as fast as Alex could hobble, leaving a blood trail behind on the pavement until reaching one of the transports bound for St.Gabriel to the south.

A thousand miles away in Washington, DC, Cindy Chandler hung her head as she received the news. The Situation Room was filled with the usual advisors, including the Joint Chiefs of Staff. The faces were sullen. They were a collective cocaine addict crashing after an endless high of victories. This was the first major defeat, and they were sore losers.

"Every part of the attack has been halted," Bates pointed to the large map projection. "We moved up Airline Highway all the way to I-12 here. That's where they were driven back—heavy casualties. We didn't get even that far on I-10. We were stopped here at Siegen Lane, ambushed from both sides of the interstate. That force was destroyed—all killed or taken prisoner. And then the downtown attack. They were hit with a wall of resistance at LSU campus. We lost air support. We lost some ships. We lost some planes. And we lost a lot of men and women."

"Damn it!" Cindy shook her head.

"They were dug in deep, Madam President," he remarked. "They sacrificed New Orleans to hold Baton Rouge, basically. More refineries. They may not have many ports to ship refined products abroad, but they can still produce for their own people, and they need the fuel for the war effort."

"So what's going on now?" she asked.

"Those troops at LSU are falling back to the south to St. Gabriel and Geismar. They'll take control of the refineries there, and hold the position."

"Do the Reds have the resources to pursue?" she glared.

"Don't know. I don't think so. I hope not, but ultimately, I don't know."

She paused, breathing deeply inward, and then releasing slowly through her nostrils. One could tell by the look in her eyes that she was deep in thought, trying to reach some sort of acceptance, and simultaneously strategizing the next move.

"Abandon the Baton Rouge campaign," she looked up at her staff. "We have New Orleans, so we control the river, and that's enough."

"Are you sure, Madam President?" Bates tried to argue. "We could send in some air strikes and some reinforcements."

"We're short on troops. We're short on money. Abandon Baton Rouge, and move straight to the Houston campaign. I want Texas. I want Austin and Dallas!"

"Are you sure?" Bates sounded baffled. "Skip Lake Charles?"

"Lake Charles is small potatoes," she argued. "Texas has the capitol and the financial centers. We take those, and everything else will fall into place."

"Yes, ma'am," Bates said, and the meeting was adjourned.

Chapter 53

October, Eight months before the bomb

Kyle strolled along the pavement, crossing the faded yellow lines of the shopping center parking lot. The weather was still relatively warm, and the sun heated the asphalt to the point that the air above it refracted the natural sunlight. He watched as shoppers entered and exited the stores, oblivious. The people visiting the strip mall acted as though the state of affairs in the country were completely normal.

He was decked out in full black camouflage from his fatigues to his helmet. He wore a .45 caliber sidearm and full gear. He was loaded with flashlights, grenades, plenty of ammunition magazines, and other various combat gear. His face was stern and his eyes hidden behind silver mirrored wrap-around sunglasses. He strutted, carrying his rifle with a level of anger while shoppers tried to pretend not to stare.

The staff sergeant in the portable trailer around the corner had pointed him in this direction, but Kyle doubted. He was unsure of where he was going. He could not imagine that there would be an outpost here in the middle of a commercial center, complete with throngs of shoppers. But then he saw the outpost.

He approached with perplexity. He would scratch his head if there were no Kevlar strapped to it. In the back corner of the parking lot stood a chain link fence enclosure. It was quite spacious, including dozens of trailers, machine guns mounted on tripods, Humvees, and of course, men. He approached the gate as another soldier walked up to meet him.

"Orders?" the soldier asked as Kyle handed them over to be read. "Alright, you're in the right place. Come on in," he opened the gate. "Hey, Okie! Got a new guy!"

He was yelling to a young man lying in a pool recliner behind a large machine gun. He lounged, unmoving, stripped down to a gray tank top and his fatigue pants. His hair was spiked. His silver-framed, black aviator sunglasses glared in the sun and loud rock music blared from the MP3 earbuds in his ears.

"Okie!" the guard yelled even louder, finally binging the man from his trance.

"What?" he removed the earbuds and sat up.

"New guy!"

"Alright," he waved toward himself with a lack of enthusiasm. "Send him over. What's your name, private?" he asked as Kyle approached.

"Kyle Perkins," he said, setting down his backpack and saluting the Private First Class.

"Knock it off," the man said. "You don't have to do that," he smiled. "And you don't need all this crap," he pointed to the various gear and helmet.

Kyle unstrapped his helmet, and laid it beside his backpack. He then shed his vest and gear belt. He laid down his weapon, and then rolled up his sleeves.

"I'm Dwayne," the man shook Kyle's hand. "But everybody calls me Okie, obviously having to do with where I'm from."

"Where are you from—I mean what city?"

"Broken Arrow," Okie replied. "How 'bout you?"

"Fort Worth, not half an hour from here."

"No shit? How long you been in?" Okie was curious.

"Just out of basic. I was down at Fort Hood. This is my first post."

"Ah, you're a patriotic boy, huh? I was a Marine stationed out in San Diego. I got booted in the secession, and here I am."

"I wouldn't call myself a patriot," Kyle said. "Confused, maybe."

Okie laughed, helping Kyle pick up his things. He was a moderately-built young man with dark features. His face was shaven and his black hair was well-groomed. His muscles were defined and his tan darkening. It led Kyle to believe that, being from Oklahoma, perhaps he had a lot of Indian blood coursing through his veins.

"So whose ass did you kiss, my friend?" Okie spouted as they worked their way back toward the trailers.

"Huh?"

"You had to have kissed some ass to get this assignment. We call it candyland. It's the easiest combat assignment in the Republic, he laughed. They need a lot of guys on the front lines. You're lucky you got this gig."

"What do you do here? Protect the Best Buy?" Kyle joked.

"We form the DFW Metroplex perimeter," Okie explained. "See that overpass? We guard the infrastructure and the city against invasion and siege."

"And how many times had that happened?" Kyle smiled.

"Exactly," Okie laughed. "That's why I asked you whose ass you kissed to get this as your first assignment. Most of these guys have seen action. Get wounded, get reassigned to minimal duty."

"And you?"

"They had me up in Memphis," he said. "An RPG hit a Humvee near me, and I took a piece of shrapnel in my outer thigh. They sent me in, got me fixed up, and I guess they figured I'd done my combat time. So they sent me here."

"Sounds like you got lucky," Kyle smiled.

"Yeah, I guess," he shrugged. "But sometimes I do wish I was back out there with the guys. They're getting their asses whipped. I feel like I need to help."

Kyle was silent. He could not relate. He had never seen combat, and did not know what it was like. But perhaps he could sympathize with that statement more now than he could before basic training. He had experienced brotherhood. He made a lot of friends. He had lost one. Surely, he would lose many more with some of those guys shipping off to Oklahoma, Houston, and Arkansas.

"But whatever," Okie smiled. "The Guard needs me here, and I oblige. The grunts on the front lines do all the bleeding, and we sit here and reap the benefits. We've got air-conditioned bunk trailers and three squares cooked for us. No MREs here. All home-cooked meals. Sometimes the restaurants and pizza joints bring over food. Hell, sometimes the people living in these neighborhoods bring us barbecue and shit. The Guard rations us smokes if we want 'em. We soak up rays in the day and play cards at night. We can't drink on the premises, but we each get a pass one night a week, and there are some bars nearby where the regulars buy you drinks and there are plenty of women looking to bed a defender of the Republic."

"I'm only eighteen," Kyle shook his head.

"I'm twenty. I'm not old enough, either," he laughed. "Doesn't matter. And the cops tend to turn a blind eye when you do something stupid. They don't want to hurt the war effort. Some of the bartenders will give you drinks on the house. I just have to tell a few Memphis stories from time to time. You'll just have to make something up."

Okie grasped the hot metal handle of the bunk trailer, and swung it open, releasing a refreshing blast of cool air into their faces. Kyle peered into the large trailer where he saw about a dozen double bunks. The walls were plastic and the sole window had an air-conditioning unit placed in it, running on full blast. The fluorescent bulbs flooded the single room with unnatural light, something that always gave Kyle a small level of anxiety.

"Pick a bunk," Okie helped carry in Kyle's gear, and dropped it all in a pile on the floor. "There are a few open. I'm gonna go over to the Big Lot's over there and take a piss."

"There aren't any toilets here?" Kyle panicked slightly.

"Oh, there are some port-o-lets out back, but there's a cute cashier in the store that I'm trying to bang. She don't know we have toilets," he chuckled.

"Happy hunting," Kyle laughed as his new friend exited the trailer.

He smiled as he looked around at his new home, thinking that perhaps this would not be so bad after all.

Chapter 54

This was certainly not the kind of scene Derek had seen in movies. When he imagined walking into a military hospital in war time, he pictured nurses in white dresses and funny little white hats with an equal-armed red cross on them. He envisioned soldiers laid up in beds positioned in rows—dozens of them in the same room. But this was a modern war. It was not World War II or some film set in the 1860s where surgeons were sawing off gangrenous limbs. It was the first war on American soil for over a century and a half. Why set up some make-shift field hospital when New Orleans had state of the art facilities ready to commandeer.

Derek walked down the hallways teeming with military doctors and nurses of all genders. His fatigues, boots, and matching cover gave him unquestioned access to the floor. No one stopped or questioned him, yet seemed annoyed by having to share the hallway with a visitor, as hastily as they moved about.

The rooms, most of them built for two civilians at a time, had no placards by the doors. He had been in hospitals before, usually visiting a friend who had been stricken ill or injured. Usually, there were names of inhabitants placed under the room numbers. But these were not normal circumstances. This was a war, and surely, there would be no visiting family members on the front lines. In the absence of name cards, Derek peeked his head into every open doorway, attempting to locate the correct room.

At the end of the hallway, on the left, he finally spotted the person he was looking for. In a bed closest to the window, he saw his friend clicking through the channels of the room's television using the multipurpose controller wired to the bed. He looked frustrated, although the only source of pain seemed to be his cast-wrapped leg hanging from the ceiling.

"Hey, hey!" Alex smiled as he saw Derek enter the room. "How did I get so lucky? I was hoping for that cute nurse that's been coming to change my IV bags, but you'll do."

"You don't think I'm cute?" Derek smiled.

"The cutest," he replied, "but I'm not going to let you give me a sponge bath."

"Looks like you're doing alright," Derek continued to smile. "Got a room to yourself," he nodded toward the vacant bed to the right.

"Yeah," Alex lost his smile. "That guy checked out a couple of days ago, and not in a good way," he said as Derek nodded sullenly. "But yeah, the doctor says I'll be out of this room, and walking around with a boot in a week or so."

"A boot?" Derek lifted a single eyebrow. "For a gunshot wound?"

"The bullet fractured my shinbone," he said. "And it doesn't help that *somebody* picked me up and made me run on it," he smiled. "Thanks, bro. You saved my ass."

"Aw," Derek swatted the air. "You would have done the same for me."

"Hell, no! I would have run like a scared little girl! You would've been on your own!"

There was a silence as Derek sat upon the uncomfortable plastic chair near the window. He peered across the room at all the machines and IV fluids. He hated hospitals. They smelled like sickness and death. They were too cold, and made him uncomfortable.

"Nothing on TV in this place," Alex frowned, and then clicked the television off. "All reruns of *Judge Mathis* and *Friends*. What are you doing down here in New Orleans? I figured you'd be up in St. Gabriel holding the line."

"I should be," Derek hung his head. "They've got another amphibious attack coming up, and they're pulling as many Marines with amphibious experience as possible."

"Probably at least half the guys that were at Mobile are dead now," Alex shook his head. "It's a damned shame. You know where you're going?"

"Houston," Derek looked up. "Well, Galveston Bay, and then Houston."

"That's going to be hell," Alex looked to his friend in sympathy. "Good luck. I'm sure it will be fun. Back in the action. I wish I could go. I'm tired of sitting around here. I know after my leg gets better that they'll just keep me around New Orleans to enforce curfew with all these stupid new recruits."

"Yeah, I'm sure it will be fun," Derek replied. "But all I want to do is go home to my kid."

"Your kid?" Alex perked up. "Carly had the baby?"

"Yeah," Derek smiled, digging in his pocket at retrieving a photograph to hand to his friend. "There she is. Olivia Grace. Beautiful isn't she? Carly sent that a few days ago. Of course the Marines opened the envelope and looked through it before I got it. And of course, I can't write back, but I called a few days ago. Carly put Olivia to the phone, and all I got was some kind of gurgling noise."

"She is a cutie," Alex smiled, holding the picture. "Must not have any of your DNA. Look at that full head of brown hair!"

"Carly had heartburn the whole pregnancy," Derek smiled. "They say that's an indication of a full head of hair. Carly bought huge bags of peppermints and gallons of ice cream because she said it helped with heartburn."

"Well, congratulations, Papa," Alex smiled, and handed the photo back to his friend. "I'm sure you'll make a great dad."

"If I survive long enough to get back to her," he hung his head, his mind on the upcoming invasion of Texas. "And then if I survive, will I ever be the same guy? Will I be too strict or impatient? Will I try to escape every time things get rough?"

"You'll be fine," Alex reassured. "God's going to make sure that little girl has a father—a good father."

"I don't think I believe in God anymore," he shook his head. "You know how many good fathers I've seen lying on the ground with their guts hanging out? How many kids I've watched orphaned on both sides? God doesn't let shit like this happen. What kind of God would?"

"God gives man free will to start wars and blow each other's brains out," Alex spoke softly. "Sometimes we have to live absent of Him to be reminded of why it was good to have Him around in the first place."

"Visiting hours are over," a female nurse walked into the room. "PFC Jasper needs his rest," she said sternly.

"Better go," Alex looked over at his friend. "She outranks us. That's a direct order. Hey, it was great to see you. Thanks for coming to see me. Nobody else has."

"Who else do we know very well that's still alive?"

"True. Hey, take care," Alex watched his friend out the door. "Maybe you'll get shot in the ass and get sent home to see your daughter."

Derek just smiled, and exited the room, his mind full of thoughts about his mother and his child. He was bitter that he had to ship out again, once again laying his life on the line. And why? Because a few senators and sore loser political candidates wanted to start a new country? That selfishness was keeping him from his newborn and dying mother. He was angry.

Chapter 55

Thanksgiving Day, Seven months before the bomb

Derek was once again on a landing craft. There were no nerves. There was no anxiety. He did not even experience fear over whether or not he would make it through the battle alive. It was now familiar—second nature. He inwardly scoffed at the young, inexperienced Marines on the craft. They were as he was several months ago—scared and unsure. They vomited and prayed, while Derek and the few veterans smiled and prepared themselves mentally for the assault. They prepared their game faces.

As they sped up the San Jacinto River, leading in from the bay, Derek saw a monument towering above a well-manicured sort of park. It was a bit of an obelisk, similar to the Washington Monument, yet much smaller. Still, he wondered what it was.

"Anybody know what that thing is?" he called out nonchalantly, a silence ensuing for several moments.

"San Jacinto Battlefield," one of the veterans spoke up. "That's where Sam Houston beat Santa Anna after the Alamo. That's where Texas won independence."

"Holy shit, Deacon, you're a Texan?" Derek turned around, a slight tone of disdain in his voice.

"No, man," Deacon responded. "I lived in Cloverleaf for my freshmen year. Dad worked in the refineries until he got hurt and we moved back to Philly. We went on a field trip to this place once."

"You weren't born in Texas, and you got out of here as fast as you could, huh?" Derek joked as the rest of the men laughed.

The men passed the portside chemical plants to the left. They watched as Marines began landing and filing off the boats unopposed. They all knew that it would not last. This was a major stronghold. Just because the Reds were not on the dock waiting for them, did not mean that the counterattack would not come, and with fury.

Derek's boat rounded a point where a separate channel meandered to the northeast, and back to the south to rejoin the river, creating a large silt island, around which industrial docks were built. They bypassed barges and tankers and landed upon a bank beside a decaying subdivision. The Marines rushed the shore as the ramps fell, and rallied in a small clearing amidst a clump of trees.

"Alright, Marines," Captain Andrews yelled as men from several boats rallied. "Start pushing into this neighborhood. We've got to get to I-10 and take control of the road coming in."

Already, Channelview reminded Derek of home, or at least his home neighborhood. As they pushed through the trees and onto the first street, he could tell that this was not a ritzy town. The homes were run-down and crumbling. Scraps and broken-down vehicles sat parked in the front yards and driveways. Most of the houses were badly in need of paint, and wild wooded lots separated estates. Clearly, the proximity of this blue collar neighborhood to the industrial areas was no accident.

All was quiet, as it usually was before the storm. The new recruits seemed to be getting used to it, as if this experience was not as bad as they feared it would be. Yet, all the veterans knew better. They were anxious. They had seen this before, and knew something was coming.

The side of a house exploded to the right as other bits of soil and pavement burst into the air from other locations. Gunfire was unleashed from the green belt clearing ahead, dropping Marines left and right. They dove into ditches, behind houses and sheds, and into the brush of the wooded lots as the barrage started.

Derek crouched behind the corner of a decaying old house, intermittently swinging around to fire shots toward the enemy's defenses. The other veterans also returned fire, remaining cool under the pressure. They watched the new Marines wet themselves, and watched others cry. They froze, unable to remember their training. Other new guys took their last short breaths in pools of their own blood.

"Oh shit. I don't want to die!" a young man cried to his left behind the house.

"Get in the fight!" Derek yelled. "You fight or you will die! Mortars! Get some mortar fire on that green belt until the choppers get here!"

The captain smiled, on his belly across the street and firing from a ditch. He was proud of this young Private First Class he had grown to know and had fought along-side of for so long. He was turning out to be the kind to take initiative and make decisions. He was a born leader. He had no business as a PFC any longer. It did not suit his experience and ability.

In Washington, Cindy Chandler, her husband, her daughter, and various members of the extended family held hands around the beautifully carved and stained dinner table. Their heads hung, and their eyes were closed in reverent prayer. They smiled without a care. They were happy to be with one another on Thanksgiving.

"Oh dear Heavenly Father," Donny chanted. "We thank you on this Thanksgiving Day for the ability to have and be around one another. We thank you, not just for food, but for family. We thank you that we are all safe and sound. We thank you for solace. We thank you for guiding our leaders in such a time of crisis. We ask that you watch over our soldiers, sailors, and pilots on the war front. Keep them safe and strong. Guide them in our noble cause. We pray to you that they someday reach safety, whether it is back home or in your loving arms. We pray that this war will be over soon and that our American brothers and sisters can once again grasp hands with us and share Thanksgiving again united. In Jesus' name we pray, Amen."

"That was wonderful, Donny," Cindy looked up. "Thank you. Okay, let's eat."

"Man, I wish we had some football to watch," Donny smiled.

"Yeah, Cindy," her father laughed. "Hurry up and win this war, so we can have a season next year."

"Guys," she smiled. "This is the one day I don't want to talk about the war. But yes, I'm missing football, too. I'll do what I can."

"This turkey looks amazing," Donny gushed.

"Where did you get this turkey, Cindy?" her father asked.

"Um, I don't know. The store?" she smiled.

"It must have come from the projects," he dipped some mashed potatoes on his plate.

"Why do you say that?" she was puzzled.

"Well," he explained in his aging tone, "you pardoned one this morning. And if normal American justice system protocol applies, he must have been the white-collar turkey. But there's still a crime, so someone still needs to do the time. So you pin it on the low-income turkey, and he ends up on the dinner table."

"Dad," she chuckled, as did everyone else, "can we have a nice Thanksgiving dinner without socio-political discussion?"

"Aw, don't mind him," her mother spoke up. "Ever since he retired from the university last year, he's been itching for somebody to teach and debate with. Usually it's me, so I'm just glad he's got you all to target."

Everyone laughed. It was a nice dinner. Everyone helped themselves to heaping piles of green beans, mashed potatoes, sweet potatoes, cranberry sauce, stuffing, and of course, turkey—projects turkey. They continued playfully enjoying one another's presence until the dinner was rudely disrupted by the ringing of a cell phone.

"Julie?" Donny began to scold. "Couldn't you turn that thing off at least while we eat?"

"It's not mine," she defended.

"It's me," Cindy pulled her smartphone from her pocket, and read General Bates' name across the banner. "I have to take this. Excuse me."

She walked away from her family, and into the next room. She hated that this call had to come at such a terrible time, but it was important. That was the price of planning a major assault on Thanksgiving Day. Her anxiety mounted, as she was unsure whether or not she wanted to hear this news. With hesitation, she pressed the 'answer' button, and lifted it to her ear.

"General Bates?" she greeted.

"Yes, Madam President," he said over the sounds of his own family in the background, complete with running and yelling grandchildren. "Sorry if I'm disturbing you and your family, but I just got the first reports."

"Is it good news?" she winced.

"Yes, ma'am. We're on-target, at least," he began. "The bay is secured, and all of the ports, refineries, and plants."

"Good. Go on," she smiled and nodded.

"The Marines have taken control of the Channelview area and I-10, so we're in position to ward off counterattacks from the east. We have successful landings from Baytown all the way to Seabrook, and now that it's secure, we're going to spend the next week or so surrounding the city all along Sam Houston Parkway so we can choke them off."

"Good, general," she smiled and nodded. "Good work. Keep me posted."

"Will do, President Chandler," he smiled. "And Happy Thanksgiving."

"You, too," she smiled, and looked back at her family. Happy Thanksgiving, indeed.

Chapter 56

"Damn, I'm missing New Orleans right about now," Derek tossed around his beef macaroni MRE pouch, blazing hot as it came out of the heating container.

He looked around as the sun slowly sank closer to the western horizon behind him. The fleeting light gave everything a glow. It shimmered on the wide San Jacinto channel water all around. The concrete of the I-10 bridge took on an almost pink hue. There were neighborhoods across the channel, but he could not see them over the elevated land, covered in dying fall grass. All around him was an abandoned shipping yard. Dust covered everything—weapons, clothing, boots, ammunition, and even their food.

"What do you say, there, Queens?" Derek searched for support in his statement.

"Yeah," Queens replied in his heavy New York dialect. "This place sucks. I could go for a visit to that bar in New Orleans," he chuckled.

"Only we'd invite Echo Company and hope we don't get busted by the Captain again," Derek laughed.

"What was it like?" a younger, man with a baby's face asked Derek.

There were a lot of young men like him. They were closely shaven, and their hair retained that classic "jarhead" look. They often seemed aimless, as if they had not a clue what they were doing. Derek sometimes found himself being followed by packs of these kids, trying to pick up a clue as to what was going on. They sat around the veterans as if it was story time and Grandpa was going to recount an old tale of the glory days.

"What was what like, Private?" Derek had sort of an added confidence in his tone, having been promoted to corporal a few days before by the Captain.

"New Orleans," he clarified. "The famous Canal Street Charge. The fight. The experience. The booze—all of it."

"How old are you, Private…" he fished for a name.

"Kirkham, sir," his eyes were wide with reverence. "I'm eighteen, sir. Fresh off the Island."

"Jesus, you're a baby," Queens munched on some crackers from his MRE pack.

"Why do you want to know, Kirkham?" Derek took a sip from his canteen. "What do you mean famous?"

"It's inspiring," another young soldier contributed to the conversation. "We heard all about it on the Island."

"Are you hearing this, Queens," Derek laughed, food shooting from his mouth as he tried to cover it up.

"Yup," Queens smiled. "I guess we're famous."

"I want to know what it was like at Mobile and New Orleans," the first young man insisted. "I can't wait to see some action—tear those Red bastards a new asshole."

"Uh huh," Queens smiled, shaking his head. "Here it comes. The Marine Corps brainwashing. You're all indestructible. You're mean-ass Marines ready to kill. Ever killed anyone, private?"

The young man, as well as others, shook their heads. But they did not get it. They were cocky, wearing their smirks with pride and convinced that battle was easy. They would be ready to kill upon command. They were straight out of boot camp, and did not even participate in the landing at Galveston Bay. They were trucked in to fortify the position. Derek knew that, and Queens could see the pain and fury building in his eyes.

"You want to know what it's like, private?" Derek stood up, lifting his weapon to his shoulder. "Run."

"Sir?" the young man jumped to his feet, falling back in shock.

"You heard me, private. Run!" Derek pointed his gun at the soldier as the young man ran a few yards.

He was terrified. The look in his eyes was one that the veterans knew quite well. It was the look that every single one of them had in their eyes at one point or another—their first time in battle. They smiled, but they were fearful. Even they did not know for sure whether or not Derek would actually shoot at the young man. He took aim, and then he pulled the trigger, allowing the action to click in the absence of ammunition being loaded into the rifle.

"Come here, boy," Derek threw down his rifle as the young man hit the dirt in fear. He walked briskly to the young soldier, and picked him up from the ground by his collar. "It may all be guts and glory to you, private; but that's not the reality! You wanna know what it's really like? You wanna know what it's like to watch a buddy of yours—a guy you went to basic with—get shot through the throat? To watch somebody's father or brother get blown into a million pieces by a mortar shell? To watch a friend take a body full of grenade shrapnel and beg you for help as he bleeds to death? To watch a saveable wounded man or woman get crushed under the tracks of an Abrams? Wait for it! And then come back to me and tell me how cool it was—how much glory there was!" he threw the man back to the dirt and walked away as the group fell silent. "Stupid-ass rookies!"

The young man just laid there for a while, deep in thought. The other new soldiers were in shock. Queens and the rest of the veterans just smiled uneasily and hung their heads, nodding in agreement. Yet, secretly, they were worried about Derek. He had lived through more than most of them. They worried he was losing his edge.

The sound of a roaring engine perked everyone from their almost dream-like state. They all quickly and sporadically whipped their heads back and forth to see where it was coming from. They all silently prayed that it was a friendly, driving in from the west. There should have been no traffic. It was a siege—the highway was shut down. And then Queens spotted a Humvee barreling across the bridge from the east with three more in tow.

"Humvees!" Queens yelled, grabbing his weapon, and alerting everyone else to do the same.

The gunners atop the Humvees began firing off rounds, sending projectiles to kick up dust, ricochet off the empty metal shipping containers, and rip through bodies of the Marines defending the bridge. They all grabbed their weapons and attempted to find some sort of cover before firing at the armored vehicles coming their way.

"More of them!" Derek pointed to the stretch of road across the bridge. "Blow the road! Blow the road!"

A soldier fumbled in panic to pick up the remote detonator to his side. His hands shook, and his nerves were overloaded. He could see the red button on the remote, but actually struggled to place his thumb on it. Finally, his thumb found its mark, and he applied pressure, causing the device to beep, and a monstrously loud explosion went across the bridge. Humvees were ejected from the pavement, and into the air, ripped to pieces by loads of C-4 placed as a defense.

But the four Humvees that made it through were still racing toward the men. They furiously shot round after round at the vehicles, finally hitting one of the gunners on top. A veteran with menacing eyes beaming from his stubbled face picked up an RPG, crouched, and fired a rocket into the front end of the lead Humvee, tearing it to pieces.

A thick net of bullets were continuously fired at the other vehicles, most of which bounced off of the armor, leaving barely a scratch, yet, many more rounds eventually pierced the windshields of the Humvees, massacring the men inside, and sending them crashing into the old cargo boxes.

The Humvees had been neutralized, yet fire was still coming. No one knew how long there had been Republic soldiers firing from across the bridge. It must have blended in with the fire from the Humvees. Dozens of Republican Guardsmen fired their rifles from the banks and the other end of the bridge as mortar shells began exploding all around the Marines.

"Cannons!" the captain yelled. "Get on those cannons!"

Two-man squads began manning the heavy artillery. One soldier would load the shell and turn his head, as the other fired the weapon, sending exploding shells across the channel. They ripped apart the soggy, marshy opposite embankment, uprooting the few trees there, and inhumanely ripping men to shreds.

Both sides battled furiously, exchanging shots and shells for several minutes. However, the skirmish was lop-sided greatly in the Marines' favor. This attack was a shot in the dark. It was a desperate attempt to punch a hole in the line and take control of that bridge. It was not meant to win the Battle of Houston. It was meant to gain some footing, or at least thin the numbers in the process.

The latter, it had done. As the gunfire died down, and the east bank fell silent, littered with the dead, the Marines began to stand from behind their scrap machinery and cargo crates to assess the damage. Derek looked around in pain to see about two dozen of his compatriots either dead or seriously wounded. His eyes stopped scanning, and became transfixed upon one of the young Marines to ask about his combat experience. He was lying in the dust completely still. His eyes were wide and mouth open. Two giant fifty caliber holes gaped in his torso as the last of his blood spilled in a pool around him to create a maroon mud hole. Derek shook his head in anger as his eyes shot across to the young private that he had, a short time ago, tried to teach a lesson. The private sat on the ground in horror and dismay, just sweating and staring at the first dead body he had ever seen.

Chapter 57

December, Six months before the bomb

The cordless phone on the end table of the Perkins' family room began chiming with its irritating and piercing ring. Drew sat in his usual spot on the couch, the same as he did every afternoon upon returning home. He ignored the ringing, glaring at the early news broadcast in a zombie-like state.

The room was decorated in all the usual Perkins-style festive holiday spirit. A Christmas tree, bought from a local tree farmer, stood majestically in the corner of the room. It sparkled with brilliant white lights and was hung with silver balls beneath streams of deep red and silver ribbon from top to bottom. Ornaments made by the kids when they were in grade school intermingled with the more classy store-bought decorations. The staircase railings and mantelpiece were draped with piney garland and red ribbons. Stockings bearing the names of all four members of the family hung over the gas-lit hearth in the corner. Even a bone-shaped one for the dog hung at the end of the row.

"Nearly a month into the siege of Houston," the anchorman reported on the television, "the city is still holding out. There are still no shipments of food going in, but President Davenport insists that there are enough supplies and food already within the city to withstand and outlast the siege. Meanwhile, attacks on the U.S. lines still continue to occur all around Sam Houston Parkway, but have had no luck in punching through."

"I feel bad for the kids in Houston," Drew spoke loudly so that Angela could hear him in the laundry room. "They're not going to have much of a Christmas."

"Well, at least the two presidents have come to an agreement to have a Christmas Day cease-fire," she yelled back, stuffing wet clothes into the dryer. "I hate that so many people had to spend Thanksgiving under attack."

"It's pointless, though," Drew shook his head. "Houston's not going to last much longer. Davenport is full of shit. A city that size is already almost out of food. I have a buddy down there that knows people who are already butchering their pets for dinner. Nobody knows how to get along without the conveniences of grocery stores, fast food, and electricity. Hell, most people living in cities wouldn't know where to begin to light a fire in the back yard for heat or cooking."

"Are you going to get that?" Angela walked around the corner, motioning toward the ringing phone on its cradle. She finally just picked it up herself. "Hello?"

"Mom," Kyle greeted his mother.

He sat on his bunk where there was no heat, but no wind chill, either. His heavy military-issued coat kept him relatively warm, but he could see his breath condense in the air, and his hands ached with cold.

"Perkins," Okie peeked his head in with a whisper. "Hurry it up. That phone is contraband. If Lieutenant Owens catches us with it, we're in deep shit. And the department store girl is gonna be pissed!"

"Okay, just a few minutes," Kyle motioned him away.

"What, honey?" Angela misunderstood, still smiling.

"Oh, nothing, Mom," he said. "I just wanted to call you while I had a chance. I don't think I'll be able to call on Christmas Day."

"Well, I'm glad you called. How are you doing?"

"It's hard work," he lied. "We don't get much time away."

"Oh, that's okay, honey," she smiled. "We understand."

"How are you, Mom?" he asked.

"Fine."

"And Dad?"

"He's the same," she looked over at her husband, who refused to move from the couch. "He misses you. We both do."

"I miss you too," Kyle smiled. "Have you…" he stopped, unsure of whether or not he wanted to ask the question.

"Seen Ashley?" Angela finished for him with an uneasy smile. "No, I haven't. Your father says he saw her last week, home from College for the holidays."

"Really?" his eyes widened. "What did he say? Did he talk to her?"

"Um…I," she hesitated.

"What?"

"Does she have a brother or anything?" Angela asked.

"No, she's an only child," Kyle looked worried. "Why?"

"Your dad saw her with another guy at the mall," she hated to deliver the news, but felt he needed to know.

Kyle sat on his bunk without a word. A whirlwind of thoughts and possibilities filled his head. It was cold, but he was sweating, suddenly. Perhaps the boy in question was a cousin or just a friend, but he could not think of one to speak of.

"I'm sorry, son," Angela broke the silence.

"It's cool, Mom," he did not have to hide the emotions in his face. "Alright, Mom. I just wanted to wish you all a Merry Christmas. I've got to go."

"Okay," she muttered, not wanting to hang up. "Um, Merry Christmas. Stay safe!"

"I will, Mom," he smiled, and then hung up.

There he sat, heartbroken and at the verge of tears. But he had to learn to fight his emotions. He was a soldier. He used his scars to harden himself. He could not let his comrades see what he was feeling.

"This is all your fault," Angela tossed the cordless phone at her husband, and stormed back to the bedroom in tears.

"What the…" he jolted, staring in the direction of his bedroom with shock. "Jesus," he turned the TV back up. "I'll be glad when she finally hits menopause, and we're done with this crap."

Chapter 58

January, Five months before the bomb

The mood was droll and the faces were sullen around the long, rectangular table in the Texas State House conference room. Heads were hung and no one spoke for several moments. President Davenport seemed sad and frustrated all at once. He was shaven and well kept, his tie tight and his suit pressed, but around the eyes, one could see the lack of sleep. The lines on his face were testament that he had aged seemingly decades in the past year alone.

"What are the reports from Houston," he rubbed his temples and his eyes.

"Not good, sir," General Weaver shook his head, the rest of the Joint Chiefs in concurrence. "Little Boy Blue has the city sealed up tighter than Tupperware. No food or supplies in, and no one out. About a thousand troops, as you know, were trapped inside Sam Houston Parkway, and they keep raiding the line, trying to find a weakness."

"And nothing?" Davenport opened his palms. "I thought the Blues were spread thin."

"They are, sir. But they've got a lot of artillery. Every time we get close—from the inside or outside—they just pound the hell out of us," Weaver hung his head. "Our boys on the inside are wearing down. They're pretty much out of ammo. They're badly nourished. I don't know if they can hang."

"And the civilians?" Davenport began to look worse.

"Anarchy, Mr. President," his face was somber. "The food stores are pretty much out of supplies. There have been some riots—fighting over food and the last drops of fuel to run generators. Power has been cut, and this is a particularly cold winter, even for Houston."

"The people are proud Texans, sir," Admiral Haskell chimed in. "They're patriots, and they want to do their part to tough it out. They've been sharing what little food there is with our boys on the inside, but it's getting thin."

"There have been some reports of slaughtering pets," Weaver continued. "Some of the more resourceful residents have taken fishing poles to the ponds and streams. Some weekend hunters have been going to the more rural outskirts to hunt deer, squirrels, rabbits, and whatever else. But they're getting too close to the Blue lines. Some guy last week was seen as a threat to some Marines on the east side of the city, near the San Jacinto, and got himself killed."

"Jesus," Davenport muttered, shaking his head.

"There are a few resourceful people in the area, but most of them are city folk," Weaver continued. "I don't know how much longer they can hold on."

"Can we run a balls-to-the-wall offensive on the line from the outside?" Davenport suggested.

"We can," Weaver's tone was not enthusiastic. "But Hitler tried that in the Ardennes in '45, and that ended up being the beginning of the end for him—not that I'm comparing you to Hitler," he saw a surprised scowl on the president's face. "I'm just saying that we don't want to burn through a huge chunk of limited personnel in one operation that may or may not go our way. We're throwing so many troops into the Carolinas, Northern Alabama, and Oklahoma, we don't have many guys to spare. Others are trapped and surrounded in various areas of the South or guarding the last strongholds. We can maybe spare some troops guarding Austin and Dallas."

"Not an option," Davenport quickly shut down the idea. "If we lose Austin or Dallas, we're truly screwed."

"I'm afraid it's that or, well, you know..." Weaver admitted.

There was a long pause. Nothing was said, as this was clearly the time that Davenport had to make a decision. All had been debated and weighed. The cards were all on the table. It was now up to him to make his play, and be the decider.

The president thought long and hard. The options and scenarios filled his head. He did not want to make a rash decision before he was absolutely sure that all other options had been examined. He kept thinking that maybe there was something they were not thinking of. But alas, his mind kept drifting to the thoughts of Republic citizens starving, sick, and cold. He thought of the head of a household having to make the decision to kill his kid's dog in the back yard so his family would not starve.

"Do it," Davenport finally closed his eyes and spoke. "Instruct General Wolfe to surrender Houston."

"Yes sir," Weaver said softly and sympathetically.

"Gloria finally left me," Davenport sullenly stared into nothing. "Couldn't look at me or even think about me and not picture me with that slut I was banging. Seems like everything I touch falls apart. My country. My marriage. Let's hold this together, boys. Do what you have to do."

Chapter 59

The baby cried without pause, her piercing wail resonating within the Putnam living room with a fierceness that would drive grown men to find refuge. Her white little face turned bright red as the blood filled the vessels in her cheeks. Her tiny mouth was fixed in a gaping position, her tongue curled and flickering. Her blue eyes were hidden by the tightly shut lids.

It was annoying for anyone. Even her mother, Carly, paced and patted her back, aching for her to stop. But there was one soul in the world that the incessant crying did not seem to bother. Sherry sat in her power chair, smiling with all her deteriorating face muscles could handle. She loved that child—her first and only grandbaby. Olivia could have cried all day—and she mostly did—and Sherry would only love her more. She knew that she would never see the little girl grow up. She was enjoying every moment that she had.

Love filled Sherry's nearly lifeless body. Her legs were now completely immobile, and her hands were nearly there. Her breathing was labored, and her facial muscles twitched. She had developed an impulse to stick her tongue out and wet her increasingly dry lips. She could not even smoke anymore, which was fine by Carly because she was there with her daughter almost every day.

"I wish I could hold her and comfort her," Sherry slurred with a saddened tone.

"I don't know that you'd want her like this," Carly jested, still pacing with the wailing child. "Colic day and night."

"Well, at least you're breastfeeding," Sherry commended. "There's no better way, and no better food. It's tailor-made for your child."

"And free," Carly added. "Have you seen how much formula costs? Diapers are expensive enough. But I think my diet is giving her colic."

Sherry continued to watch Carly pace across the living room over and over, patting the baby to try and loosen up any build-up gas. She could not help smiling and doting on her grandchild and on her daughter-in-law to be.

"Have you tried Mylanta?" Sherry asked.

"Mylanta?" Carly puzzled. "Seriously? That won't hurt her? That's for adults."

"It's an old colic trick," Sherry nodded and smiled at her opportunity to provide advice. "You just give her maybe a quarter of a teaspoon. It's an antacid, and it breaks up the gas bubbles. It's very mild, so you can use it on babies."

"I guess it's worth a shot," Carly shrugged with intrigue. "Mylicon and Gripe Water doesn't work on this kid. Do you have any Mylanta?"

"Check the bathroom medicine cabinet," Sherry tried to lift her left arm to point.

Sherry began to take a more heightened interest in the evening news as Carly left the room with the crying baby. She had heard the nurses that sometimes come by to help out complain that the only news was about war, and that they were sick of seeing it. For once, they would like to see some more positive news. But Sherry did not mind. She wanted to know what was going on with the war. She wanted to listen for any news that might pertain to her son.

"The stars and stripes shine big and bright, deep in the heart of Texas," the aging anchorman smiled, making a cheesy Texas joke. "The fall of Houston to the United States armed forces is only the beginning. This is the heart of the Republic, and there is more work to be done. According to our sources, there have been at least two engagements in the last week involving our forces moving north from the occupied Houston area, a story confirmed by President Chandler. A U.S. Marine force moving north along Interstate 45 ran into a pocket of resistance in the town of Huntsville, home to the infamous Texas State Penitentiary. The engagement has been described as a smaller skirmish, resulting in very minimal U.S. casualties, yet much heavier losses for the Republican side. A bigger story is an apparent attack on Austin early this morning. We do not yet know the extent of the U.S. casualties, but we are told that the joint Marine-Army assault has been halted some sixty miles to the southeast of the Republic's capital. Here's a clip of what President Chandler had to say about it late this morning."

"We have made a lot of headway in preserving our union," the screen cut to a presidential press conference. "We have secured major ports and oil-rich areas of the Republic south, and we have continued to press the lines in the Carolinas, Arkansas, Oklahoma, and Missouri. But to bring this horrible conflict to an end, we must strike at the heart of the Republic. Houston was an important victory in breaking down the economic machine within the Republic. It is also a stepping stone to moving on to the capitol in Austin, and to the major financial center of Dallas and Fort Worth. Currently, I can confirm rumors of recent engagements in Texas. I cannot disclose specific battle plans, as it may undermine the integrity of our military strategy. However, I can confirm the allegations of a failed attack between Houston and Austin."

"And there you have it," the anchorman returned. "Directly from the horse's mouth. We are moving on Austin."

Sherry zoned out, thinking about her son and what he may be doing at the moment. Where was he? Was he safe? She fell deep into her own thoughts. Her eyes became blank, and she grew sullen. She hoped that the war would be over soon. She had no clue how long she would last. She had no clue if she would ever see Derek in the flesh again.

Hundreds of miles away, he sat upon the back of a transport vehicle, his helmet next to him. He puffed on a rare cigarette to help calm his nerves. He looked out across the area surrounding I-45 and the town of Huntsville. Smoke rose from the town as homes and buildings lay wrecked and ablaze. Enemy vehicles were overturned, blown to pieces, and littered around them were the bodies of the Republic's dead. Derek smiled, happy with the results of his division's destructive power. Malice filled his eyes, along with a pain that he recently delighted in.

Chapter 60

March, Three months before the bomb

Dull booming sounds rolled across the pre-dawn sky. It echoed from hallowed monument to priceless museum. It crossed the rooftops of homes and important landmarks alike. The average citizen in the area was trying to squeeze out every minute of sleep that they could before their alarm clocks began to chime and they had to roll out of bed for the work day. They lay dreaming of on-the-run coffees, sipping them on their commutes. In their subconscious mind, they heard the menacing noises. They did not wake, but were aware, sure that a springtime storm was rolling in from across the ridges of the Appalachians.

But if one were to awaken from that slumber, they would see that the stars were twinkling overhead without a single obstruction. No thick rain clouds were drifting in, reflecting the orange glowing streetlights back onto the city. Not a drop of precipitation fell. Flashes did, however, fill the sky. They flashed not to the west, but to the east, toward the coast.

Still, the people of the Washington, DC, area dreamed and rested, believing that a rain storm was bringing the sweet, nourishing moisture that would assist the cherry trees to blossom along the pools and basins of the city's most picturesque areas. But as the sun rose over the Chesapeake, blanketing buildings and homes with light and warmth, the thunder continued, and it became apparent that something was certainly amiss.

"More activity out there?" Chandler sipped her coffee, and set it back into the saucer beside a plate of various pastries. "Scone? Danish? Have some coffee."

"No thanks," General Bates hobbled in and sat down beside the president at her breakfast table. "Ma'am, there's been a change."

"Yes?" she did not seem concerned as she took another sip. She had become accustomed to the sounds of naval battle far off in the Atlantic.

"There are more of them," his face remained unchangingly concerned. "More Republic ships. I don't know where they came from, but there are more cruisers and subs in the area. They've been fighting all morning—since before dawn. And our defenses are wavering."

"What do you mean?" the cheer drained from her face.

"Our ability to defend the Chesapeake and the mouth of the Potomac is weakening," he said. "I haven't been updated in about an hour and a half, but there's need for concern."

"Don't we have batteries to keep them out?" she seemed reassured at the thought.

"Plenty along the Potomac," he said, "but they're far inland from the mouth. And there basically are none in the Chesapeake. The navy is the battery in the Chesapeake."

"If their ships get into the Potomac and the Chesapeake, can their guns reach DC?"

"I don't know," he winced, unsure. "The biggest naval cannons can reach about twenty-seven miles. It depends on how close they can get. That range is just outside of our batteries, and the Chesapeake shore is about thirty miles away from the center of DC."

"So can they reach us or not?" she sought clarification.

"It's hard to say," he still held to his uncertainty. "It's possible. And if they destroy our Potomac batteries, it's certain."

Cindy Chandler said nothing for a few minutes. She was thinking. She did not know how to handle a situation that fell so close to home. She had always operated under the presumption that Washington was impenetrable. It was the capitol. If it was captured or destroyed, the game would be over.

"What do you think?" she looked up at the general. "Do we evacuate? Do you think it's that urgent?"

"I think we should be cautious," he said with reservation in his voice.

"Well do we, or don't we?" she sought advice from a military perspective. "I don't want to send this city into a panicked shit-fit if attack isn't a real possibility. So is it?"

He paused to think it through. He knew her concern, and he agreed. He had overseen hurricane evacuations and had seen the chaos that can ensue. There was no need to start that kind of turmoil over nothing.

"I think it is," he responded. "I think we should give people the option."

"Optional evacuation?" her eyebrows raised. "Not mandatory?"

"Optional downplays the issue without taking away from the urgency," he explained. "People will hopefully do the responsible thing."

No sooner did the words escape the general's mouth did a loud, startling boom rock the space in which the two were conversing. The breakfast table shook, moving plates and saucers a few inches from their original placement. Small amounts of dust accumulating along the ceilings and the tops of the walls were shuffled loose, and fell downward in a light cloud.

"What the hell was that?" Chandler sprung to her feet, flinching as if the walls would cave in on top of her.

"Oh Jesus," the general looked around in fear. "They must have punched through the lines."

"I thought you said they couldn't reach us!"

"I said I didn't know," Bates argued as more thunderous sounds were heard further away from the White House.

They were both in shock, looking around within the room and at each other, neither having a clue as to what exactly they should do. The White House was filled with hundreds of people from advisors to kitchen staff. How were they reacting? Two Secret Service members entered the room. They were concerned and hasty, but they appeared astoundingly cool under the given pressure.

"Madam President," one of the black-suited men said. "We have to get you to safety."

"Where?" she looked around, smiling with disbelief. "The bathtub, underneath a mattress? It's not a tornado! It's an attack!"

"There's a bunker underneath the White House we will take you, your family, and your top staff members to," one of the Secret Service men said, approaching her.

"Bunker?" her face wrinkled with perplexity. "What bunker? I didn't know we had a bunker. Did you?" she turned to Bates as more booms echoed across the capitol city.

"Yes ma'am," he nodded and shuddered as another closer shell exploded. "I think it's been there since the Eisenhower years."

"Why didn't I know about this?" Cindy seemed annoyed. "That wasn't on the damned tour on my first day! Don't you think they should have told me about it?"

"Madam President," the Secret Service man's voice increased in urgency.

"Okay, okay," she allowed them to escort her out as General Bates followed. "But bring as many people down there as you can—not just my top staff."

"I don't know how many it will hold, ma'am," one of the bodyguards stated.

"I don't give a shit," she fired back. "As many as you can. We're not going to be living down there. We're just going to wait out this shelling, and when it's over, we'll evacuate the whole building."

As the president and her staff made their way toward the underground bunker, the city was in panic mode. Shells were hitting areas of the city as far to the southeast as Congress Heights, and as far to the northwest as Dupont Circle in the center of DC. People trampled one another as they stampeded from within crowded shopping malls, shops, and grocery stores. They piled into motor vehicles, dropping everything they were doing in an attempt to get out of the city.

Shells began bursting in the middle of the crowded and jammed streets and highways, sending twisted metallic remains of civilian vehicles flying in all directions, accompanied by flashes of flame and bits of pavement. Giant holes were blown into the National Mall, the grassy strip of land lined by the Smithsonian museums between the Capitol building and the Washington Monument. The tidal basin, skirted with blossoming cherry trees and presidential monuments, burst with water into the air like a geyser. A few homes and businesses alike were ripped to shreds by single shells making their direct hits.

An outer wall of the House of Representatives sustained a direct hit, blasting marble outward as the front steps of the Capitol Building took another shell. Other projectiles felled trees between the Supreme Court and the Library of Congress. A single shell struck the top one-third of the Washington Monument, causing the upper portion of the obelisk monument to burst with marble, and crumble in huge chunks to the ground. At the White House, the gatehouse, west wing entrance, and the walkway to the Oval Office was hit, while several craters were blown in the mansion's expansive, green lawn.

The Secret Service and other armed military guards at the White House worked feverishly to herd as many people into the underground bunker as they could. The concrete walls were rough and poorly lit, giving a cold war feel to the whole event. The bunker was large, but not large enough for every person in the White House. Some employees had decided to flee the house altogether, heading home in a desperate attempt to get to their families. Still, the bunker filled to capacity, and Chandler, refusing to enter until everyone was in, still waited by the doorway.

"It's almost full, ma'am," one of the Secret Service agents yelled over the vocal commotion. "You have to get inside!"

"There are still people left outside!" she argued with the bodyguard. "I'm not going in!"

"Don't be foolish! You're the President! We have to get you to safety!"

She looked around at the frightened faces of the White House janitorial and culinary staff. They sat upon the concrete floors, their heads buried between their knees and their hands placed over the backs of their heads like a 1950s bomb drill. Some cringed. Some cried. Others prayed. A few even urinated. Chandler took one look at that, and sat down amongst them, mimicking their actions, and placing her arms around their shoulders to promote feelings of safety and solace.

"Lock it down," she ordered the guards.

They rolled their eyes, yet reluctantly closed the heavy, steel bunker door and waited outside. The barrage lasted another ten or fifteen minutes as tensions ran high and fears ran amuck. The people in the bunker and in the basement could only imagine what the city was beginning to look like, and of course their imaginations ran wild with the possibility of a direct hit on the White House.

As the explosions faded in frequency, anxiety began to fall. The president and those in the hall opened their eyes and slowly stood erect, shocked that they were alive. Slowly, the guards grew more confident that the bombardment was over, and decided to open the bunker. As streams of people filed out of the fallout shelter and made their way upstairs, Cindy pulled Bates and the Secret Service agents aside.

"Get everyone out of here immediately," she ordered without falter. "Get them home and get them out of the city. I don't care what you do, but make sure the whole DC area is evacuated north."

"Will do, Madam President," the Secret Serviceman nodded. "And we'll start arranging for you and your family to be flown up to Camp David."

"No," she closed her eyes and shook her head. "Get my staff members out of here, aside from those who choose to stay on their own accord. God knows I could use some help. But I'm staying. I have a job to do, and I'm not leaving here when my country needs me the most."

Chapter 61

It was a cool West Texas morning, which was not that uncommon, especially in the spring. The sun had not hung in the eastern sky for long, giving little chance for solar radiation to heat the sandy landscape and bake its inhabitants. The air was dry, and without humidity, it did not hold the heat of the previous day overnight. Mornings tended to be quite nice in El Paso.

To the untrained eye, or for someone blindfolded and transported to El Paso, it would look as though there were a river passing through a singular city. But upon closer examination, one could tell by border stations and the vast differences on either side of the Rio Grande, that these were two separate cities and two separate demographics.

El Paso, a city of the Republic, was protected by the freedoms of its new Constitution. The standard of living, though not even close to the greatest in the county, still was not bad. It was dirty in places, and had its own crime and economic problems, but really it was simply a small West Texas town that had grown up a bit. City problems were nothing compared to the city of Juarez across the river in Mexico.

Poverty there was much more rampant. Gangs and drug cartels often dominated the streets, rather than law enforcement. Children starved and were often orphaned, and most people were highly unskilled and uneducated. Yet, the two cities could easily have been part of the same, separated by a river. They were like opposing mirror images separated only by a few hundred yards of bridge, border, and check stations.

There were two main bridges that connected the two cities and the two countries, and they were separated only by the equivalent of a few city blocks. The main border crossing was to the west, a highway becoming South El Paso Street upon crossing into Texas. The other was known as the Good Neighbor International Bridge.

The main western bridge was beginning to bustle with the usual traffic. Luxury SUVs and minivans carried families home into the Republic, returning from vacation road trips into Mexico. Freight trucks transported cheaply manufactured goods in from the maquiladores just south of the border. Republican Guardsmen with weekend passes, packed into a single car, lined up to re-enter the country, reeking of cheap tequila and even cheaper prostitutes.

Guardsmen stood at the gates and patrolled the area. They were clad in the usual black combat garb, complete with Kevlar helmets and assault rifles. Each vehicle that arrived for entry into Texas was searched and every passport, military ID, and visa was examined. Nothing got by. If one could not prove that they had citizenship or business in the Republic, they were shunned away.

The highest demographic of people crossing the border was that of Mexican citizens entering El Paso for work. Republicans touted for years before the secession about cracking down on immigration—and not just illegal immigration. The battle cry was always about immigrants taking jobs and benefits away from already unemployed U.S. citizens. Even in the first days of the birth of the Republic, the first intention was to halt all migrant workers. What they realized early on was that the Mexican people crossing into El Paso every day were doing jobs that most people north of the border usually would not do. They were working as maids and nannies. They were working with roofing companies and construction companies. The Republic began allowing carriers of valid work visas to cross over, but they did crack down on illegal border crossings with a deadly force.

The Good Neighbor Bridge had always been primarily for these migrant workers. Four lanes, before the secession, were fixed as southbound only, herding the migrants southward more quickly than they were brought in. Only the fifth lane was a northbound lane. However, since the establishment of the Republic, there was a change in the protocol. Two lanes now flowed north, and two flowed south, while the fifth lane was now designated for traffic with a special tag and purpose.

The Good Neighbor Bridge was just as heavily guarded as the main bridge. Soldiers carried their weapons and checked identification on every migrant worker. The fifth lane usually carried civilian pickup trucks, most often old and beat-up ones. In the bottom left corner of the windshield, a decal depicting the twenty-nine star flag of the Republic was stuck on every pickup. The trucks pulled up to the gate on the Texas side of the Rio Grande. They were stopped, and first examined for the decal. Often, confused motorists entered the wrong lane, and were turned away.

After checking for the flag decal, the driver rolled down the window and presented a special ID card for every soul in the vehicle. It was high-tech, complete with holograms, bar codes, and microchips aside from the photograph of the person and the typically Spanish names. Upon presentation of the identification, the guard walked around to the rear of the truck to examine the cargo, usually covered by some sort of tarp. The tarp would be lifted, and beneath, crates and boxes carrying German-sounding company names like Heckler & Koch lay in the bed of the truck. The lids would be lifted, revealing stacks of side arms, assault rifles, submachine guns, mortars, and even rockets.

When the guard was satisfied, the driver would be waved along past the gate and onto El Paso's Stanton Street. Another guard waved each truck carrying precious military cargo into a parking lot to the right where a dozen or so other soldiers unloaded the crates onto military transport trucks bound for Fort Bliss a mere five miles to the northeast.

Just to the south of the international border, a pickup truck sat in an empty parking lot surrounded by a grassy area with a few trees, and the remnants of an old playground and basketball court. It was a light blue, late 1980s Ford barely held together by its rusting nuts and bolts. Paint chipped in several areas, leaving scars of rust in the steel body.

Two caramel-skinned men sat in the single cab of the pickup. The windows remained rolled down while the engine did not run, not that it mattered since the air conditioning did not work anyway. They eyed the border checkpoint with intensity from beneath their ragged cowboy hats. The driver donned cowboy boots, and both featured thin,

Mexican-style mustaches to compliment the plaid western button-down shirts.

The air outside was cool, but little air flowed through the open windows of the truck. Sweat glistened on their cheeks and foreheads as they stared at the border and frequently gazed at each other in worry and anxiety.

The driver, without saying a word, motioned for the passenger to open the glove compartment and hand him what was inside. The passenger silently obliged, pulling the small lever on the front to release the cover. It hinged downward with a scraping sound, and the man reached inside to extract a small pint bottle filled with cheap tequila. He handed it to the driver, who twisted its thin, aluminum cap with several snaps and pops. He removed the cap, cringing in disgust at the very smell of the noxious liquid. Reluctantly, he poured a small amount on his hands, rubbing them together as if he were washing after a bathroom break. He then wiped the liquid on the front of his shirt, covering himself in the stench of severely impure tequila. He then handed the bottle back to his cohort, who replaced it in the glove box.

They watched the border for several more minutes, waiting patiently for precisely the right conditions to move. At the moment, there were too many special trucks in the far right lane. They did not want to take any chances. This was far too important.

"Hey!" the soldier in charge of directing trucks into the unloading parking lot yelled to one of the gate guards. "Hey, Hamm!"

"What?" he turned and yelled back.

"I've got to hit the head!" he said.

"The what?" the other soldier was confused.

"The head! The shitter!" he clarified with an amused smile. "Those breakfast burritos this morning messed me up!"

"Alright," he replied, somewhat disgusted. "Hurry up!" he yelled as the man trotted across the street to find a toilet.

The man in the passenger seat of the blue pickup nodded to the driver, indicating that it was time to go. He turned the key, and shifted the automatic transmission into drive. They circled the cracking and decaying lot and exited onto the highway. They had hoped that there would be perhaps one, or even no other trucks ahead of them, and at present, there were two. They could not miss this chance, though. It was the perfect opportunity.

It did not take long for the two trucks ahead of them to pass inspection. The guard taking IDs and examining cargo was tired of doing so already. He was getting sloppy. Within five minutes time, the blue Ford advanced to the checkpoint, and the soldier approached. He said nothing. He simply used his angled index finger and thumb into half of a rectangle to signify the universal sign for identification. They two men understood, as would anyone. They quickly offered their Republic IDs, passed through the open drivers' side window.

"Jesus," he crinkled his nose as he looked at the cards through his dark sunglasses. "No, not your cousin, Hey-sus. You've been hittin' it hard already this mornin', haven't you, boy?" he referred to the stench of cheap tequila on the driver.

"Si," the driver smiled and nodded while the soldier continued to examine the IDs.

"Alright," he gave the cards another look, and then back at the uneasy men. "Here you go, Jose and Carlos," he passed them back to the men in the truck, and began walking around to the back of the truck.

He took his time, seeing no other delivery trucks coming. He reached the bed, and slowly lifted the tarp. There was an ever-present worry that someone might try trafficking humans under the cover. But this time it was only a load of crates. The first box was opened, revealing boxes of handguns manufactured in Germany. The next box was the same, and another box was full of ammunition. A large crate, about the same size and color as the others was pushed against the cab of the truck at the front of the bed. The soldier looked at it, and in his head, told himself that he should check it just to be thorough. Yet, the laziness in him told him that it was clean—it contained the same as the other crates. He neglected to check it, and then backed out of the way, motioning the truck along as three more tag-bearing trucks approached the border.

A sigh of relief escaped the two men's lungs as they passed the gate and the point where the absent guard was to direct them into the unloading lot. They steadily carried on past it. The soldiers in the lot were busy lifting other boxes and crates of munitions, and did not even look in the direction of the wayward truck. They took Stanton Street north into the solace of downtown, and then ramped onto Highway 62, headed east into the desert of West Texas and the Guadalupe Mountains and toward Interstate 20.

Chapter 62

April, Two months before the bomb

Walking out the front door of the White House, Cindy Chandler, guarded by her Secret Service Agents, felt like some kind of creature or mutant. She felt like a cave hermit that rarely saw the light of day. She imagined that her skin had paled to the point of super-sensitivity to the blazing sunlight. The ultraviolet rays hurt her eyes. She quickly placed one of her pairs of dark, oversized sunglasses on her face, and then ducked into the car awaiting her.

As it pulled out of the driveway, she did not know what to expect. The city had been shelled by the Navy of the Republic on and off for two weeks. The frequency decreased each day, averaging five times a day to maybe once every other day by the end of the second week. Close, earth-shaking explosions and booms were replaced, over time, by similar sounds miles away in the Chesapeake.

Since the first shelling of Washington, DC, U.S. Navy forces began steaming their ships from positions on the blockade. They moved north from their stations from the Carolinas to Miami, breaking their necks to get to the Chesapeake in time to save the capitol.

In retrospect, the attack on the U.S. capitol was a suicide mission. The bay and the Potomac were narrow waterways with only one clear entrance and exit. Entering those waters with intent to attack, especially without support of a full-sized fleet, was a death sentence. Surely, they understood that eventually, the superior United States Navy would hit them with the full fury of their wrath, destroying every ship they possessed. And that is exactly what happened.

It was finally safe for President Chandler to put behind her the subterranean home for good, and emerge from the ashes of Washington as a phoenix. She wanted to get a good look at her beloved nation's capitol first-hand. Her protection agents advised against it, fearing more attacks or even some unforeseen ground force that would take her prisoner. Yet, she insisted, as hard-headed as she was.

She never expected to see such a thing in her home country. Americans were raised to believe their country was invincible. Even the terrorist attacks of September 11, 2001, did nothing to damage that belief. In a way, that was a good thing. It meant that the whole point of terrorism as a means to strike fear into the hearts of every American was a failure. Yet, at the same time, there was a false sense of security.

Chandler, along with many other Americans, grew up seeing destruction all over the news, only not in her home country. Decimated cities across the Middle East were commonplace on the evening news. So were places such as Mogadishu, Somalia, Beirut, Lebanon, and Sarajevo, Bosnia and Herzegovina, but not Washington, DC.

Some streets were hardly navigable. Craters dotted many streets and brick and stone piled high, once a part of the unique architecture of Washington. Now it just blocked streets and avenues. It really did not matter anyway. The city was empty, except for a few who weathered the storm, and now they too, were cruising the streets, gawking at the damage.

Tears formed in the eyes of the President of the United States as she took in the sights, still unable to tell whether or not she was dreaming. She hoped to wake up soon, but she could tell the difference. The smell of smoke and the emotions she was feeling were too real.

Shells exploding in the middle of city blocks broke natural gas lines, burning apartments, stores, hotels, and countless other structures until they were charred, gutted shells of their former selves. Landmarks and administrative government buildings were in ruin. The J. Edgar Hoover FBI building was ready to be condemned. Ford's Theater was no more.

The Treasury Department and Supreme Court crumbled to the ground with only a few of the Greek Revival columns standing. Cindy felt as though she were driving around the edges of the Roman Forum. The House of Representatives had a giant gaping hole in it, and the Capitol's rotunda dome had caved in. The National Mall looked like the cratered surface of the moon, while several of the Smithsonian Museums had been blasted and maimed. The Vietnam Memorial wall was missing two large sections, surrounded by broken concrete and chunks of black marble.

The President wept as she absorbed the ruin. She did not just see it. She felt it. It permeated her skin and soaked into her bloodstream like a drug. It intoxicated her. It brought her back to those moments of experimentation in college when she had drank too much at a fraternity party or had smoked pot—moments in a fun night where she truly wished she were sober.

But then, there was a sobering moment—a ray of hope. As she wept for the shortened Washington Monument, surrounded in its own crushed stone, she looked out across the tidal basin to the south near the river. The Jefferson Memorial, in its homage to the third president's home Monticello, stood gleaming and unscathed. Lincoln's iconic memorial, though surrounded by artillery craters, stood majestically. And then, as they drove back up Constitution Avenue beside the damaged Smithsonian buildings and the crater-filled White House lawn, she burst into a torrent of joyful tears. For there, slightly bruised and scratched, stood the stately National Archives building, home to the United States Constitution, the Declaration of Independence, and every important document that made her country pure and great, despite its flaws and the flaws of its people and leader. Small pieces of its stone, columned façade chipped, and it was covered in many layers of smoke and dust. It stood in the face of impossible adversity, surrounded by felled monuments and landmarks, and it endured.

Chapter 63

The Texas sun was nearing the western horizon, blocked somewhat by a few plumes of continuously rising smoke pouring upward from destroyed Humvees and tanks. Derek and his division of Marines had been ambushed in a wooded patch lining both sides of the interstate just to the north of Centerville. It was not a large force. In fact, the ambush was futile. They lost a few dozen Marines and a few vehicles, but that was a drop in the bucket in comparison to the total numbers of the U.S. force. The error that the Republican Guard made was that they did not wait until enough of the Marines had been engulfed in the woods lining the highway. They struck too early and did not inflict enough damage.

The result was wholesale slaughter of the Guardsmen. It was not a long skirmish, but it was brutal. Some fighting became quite close-quarters. Men had to resort to side arms, emptying magazines of .45 caliber ammunition into the enemy within ten yards of one another. Others had to draw blades, slashing and stabbing until their own fatigues were soaked in blood. Some soldiers even used their bare hands to strangle their enemies, crushing their tracheas until dead.

Derek did it without thinking now. He killed indiscriminately; with impunity, even. When he shot a man to death at point plank range or fired a rocket-propelled grenade at a Humvee, he did not see a man. He saw an enemy that was almost less than human. They deserved to die. It was callous and heartless, and he wished it were not personal, but it had become as such. He was tired of people trying to kill him. He was tired of killing, and he could not believe the selfishness of the separatists. The way he figured it, the more people he killed, and the quicker, the sooner the war would end and he could get back to his family. The problem was that he had begun to enjoy killing.

"Son of a bitch!" he shook his head in frustration, sure to melt the platoon cell phone with his angry gaze. "Is anybody going to pick up?"

A lit cigarette hung and fumed from between his lips. The stubble on his face and disarray of his hair gave some indication of how long it had been since he was in a civilized area with access to bathing and grooming. He was oily and sweaty, and stunk of body odor and death. He tried to keep a low profile, ducking away from the other troops so that he could place his private phone call. He feverishly, and even violently, redialed, hoping to finally get an answer.

"Hello?" a male voice answered his mother's phone.

"Jake?" Derek recognized his friend's voice.

"Derek," his voice sounded nervous. "How's it going?"

The tone in Jake's voice was strangely droll. He was normally cheery and his voice burst with energy. He was a happy guy, but he did not seem happy. He sounded tired and depressed. It worried Derek. He was silent for a few moments, trying to make sense of it. His mind churned with anxiety and questions. He frankly was unsure of what to say next.

"Jake," he finally asked, "you okay?"

"Um, yeah," he replied nervously.

"Where's Mom?" Derek finally asked. "Where's Carly and my daughter?"

"Um, well," he staggered. "Carly and Olivia are at her parents' house."

"What about Mom? Is she awake? I wanted to say 'hi' while I have a few minutes."

"Derek, there's something I have to tell you," Jake finally came out with it.

That was all he had to say. It hit Derek in the chest, as if someone had punched him, knocking the wind out of him. He knew this day would come. He hoped that it would be after the war was over. He hoped he could have gotten home. He just closed his eyes and waited for the rest of the statement.

"Your mom," Jake began, "died last week."

Derek still shut his eyes and rubbed his forehead, as if to help the news soak in a little more easily. He was not yet emotional. He was in shock. He expected this to happen eventually, but not yet. Anyone with a loved one that had a terminal illness will tell you that they know it is coming, but on the day that it happens, it is still a shock.

"How did it happen?" Derek spoke softly, choking to fight back his tears.

"Last Wednesday," he replied, still nervously speaking, "Carly was over here with the baby, and I came by on my lunch break to put your mom in bed for a nap. I put her in bed, put on her bi-pap mask, and she was cool when I went back to work. Carly called me a few hours later. She went in to check on her because she had been sleeping for a little longer than usual, and she wasn't breathing."

"Oh my God," Derek shook his head. "Carly had to find her?"

"She called me up, and she was just hysterical. The baby was crying in the background. She was frantic. So I rushed over. Carly had already called 9-1-1, and so the ambulance came and picked her up, but it was just too late," Jake's voice cracked as he began to cry. "Derek, I'm sorry."

He did not reply for quite some time. Derek tried to fight it, but it was no use. Emotions overcame him—the natural psychological and physiological response to a negative stimulus. Tears rolled from the corners of his eyes and down the curvature of his cheeks. They wet the bottom end of the phone and glistened in his facial stubble.

"Come on, Putnam," the captain ambled up. "Hurry it up. We have work to do," he said to Derek, but then saw the emotional state that the young corporal was in, and backed away, his hands held up in front of him. "Take your time, corporal," he said, and then walked away.

"The doctors said she likely didn't suffer," Jake spoke again, trying to console his friend. "She died in her sleep."

"What's going to happen to her body," Derek finally spoke, trying to calm himself. "Is she just lying in the morgue somewhere? I'm not even there to make any decisions!"

"Your mom had been talking about that kind of thing for months," Jake said calmly. "We tried to avoid talking about it because it was so morbid. We didn't like talking about death with her because we didn't want to accept that she was going to be gone someday. But for her, it was a way of coming to terms with it—accepting it. She's been saying she wants to be cremated. It hasn't happened yet. I wanted to confirm that it was okay with you."

"That's what she wanted?" Derek nodded, his eyes closed.

"That's what she said."

"Okay," he nodded again. "Go ahead and have it done. Tell the mortuary that I'm in the war and see if they will let me settle with them when I can."

"Sure, buddy," Jake became a little more relieved. "Sure."

"How's Carly?" Derek asked. "I can't believe she had to find her that way. It's not fair to her. God, I hate not being there for this!" he sounded angry at himself and the situation.

"Carly's okay," he replied. "She's still a little shaken. She cries when she thinks about it. But she's coming to terms with it like the rest of us."

Derek was silent again, lost in his own thoughts and acceptance process. This was so much to take in. So much death surrounded him. It was not difficult to imagine his mother dead when he could see dead bodies lying around the highway and off to the side. Some were men he had personally killed. He was resistant to the emotions dealing with taking an enemy soldier's life. But when it came to his mother, he was ill-prepared.

"I'm never going to see her again," Derek finally spoke, shaking his head.

"I know, bud," Jake turned even more sympathetic. "But you'll remember her as a healthier Sherry Putnam. You didn't have to see her as she got sicker. She loved you, man. That's all she did was talk about you and how proud she was of you. Fighting for the good of the country. Taking care of your family. The nurses that came every day got an earful non-stop about you."

"But I couldn't be there for her physically," he shook his head in remorse.

"Don't feel bad," Jake reassured. "She knew you wanted to be here. She knew what you were off doing. Her biggest joy was that she got to know her granddaughter before she died," Jake heard his friend begin sobbing audibly. "She talked about that a lot. She adored your little Olivia. She was just happy to have seen her, and so was Carly. That's what's getting Carly through this."

"Yeah," Derek sniffled, trying to draw the mucus attempting to escape his nose back into his nasal cavity. "I know."

"What you need to focus on is Carly and Olivia," Jake spoke forwardly. "They need you now, and they're not going anywhere. You get back here safe for them."

"I will," Derek nodded. "I swear to God, I will come back home. I've got to go," he said abruptly. "I've got a foxhole to build. We're digging in for the night."

"Take care, buddy, and I'm sorry," Jake said.

"Thanks for letting me know," Derek said. "Tell Carly I'll call her as soon as I have a chance."

Chapter 64

May, One month before the bomb

Kyle approached his front door as a stranger. It was the first time in his life that had been the case. He had never stood on the front steps of his own home and hesitated to go inside. He had not been home in nearly a year, although he had been less than an hour's drive away. He did not know how to connect to his father, or really even his mother. He had changed. He did not really want to even see his family. He, of course, blamed it on limited leave passes, but that was a lie. He instead spent his very abundant passes on frequenting bars near his post and chasing women. He was a stranger, and now he stood at the door of his parents' home deciding whether to knock or just go on in.

He thought about it for much longer than most people would. He raised his right fist a few times, bringing himself to the brink of knocking, and then lowered it. He finally settled on turning the knob, but upon doing so, found that the deadbolt had been latched, and he no longer carried the key. So he raised his fist and knocked, waiting for the eventual sound of the deadbolt turning and for the door to crack open.

There, emerging from relative darkness in the small opening, his mother's face appeared. Angela first was hesitant. She started eyeing the visitor from the unmistakable combat boots upward to the fatigues, and then eventually settled on the face of her first-born child. Kyle watched his mother beam with joy. Her mouth gaped with a smile, and her eyes squinted with the raising of her cheeks, marked by the appearance of more defined crow's feet in the corners.

"Kyle!" she flung the door open, immediately embracing her son tightly. "You didn't tell us you were coming! It's so great to see you!"

"Hi, Mom," he smiled as she backed away to look at him.

"Well, come in!" she led him inside. "You're just in time for dinner."

He stepped in without a word, hit in the face with the smells of home cooking. He had home cooking and good food at his post, but it was not his mother's. There is something special about mother's cooking to every young man. The aromas were not just pleasing to the nose, it was almost tangible. He could see and feel it.

Smell is the strongest sense tied to memory, and it did its work well. Images filled Kyle's head of happy times in his house. They were memories of laughter-filled family dinners and special holidays of his youth. There were summer barbecues and baking cookies for church bake sales.

The more the memories transported him back to simpler and happier times—before the war—the more at home he felt. The apprehension melted away and fell onto the floor. He walked down the hallway toward the kitchen, family room, and dining nook with no hesitation or awkwardness. It was more like he was returning home from school on a random afternoon, ready to have dinner with the family.

But then he approached the dinner table, and the comfort turned sour. He saw his father sitting in his usual dining spot. Drew's eyes widened in surprise to see his son. A smile formed on his face, truly happy that Kyle was home. Kyle, however, did not share the sentiment. In an instant, the negative memories of late returned in a whooshing torrent, yet he sat down anyway.

It was a little tense. Drew was happy to see his son, and smiled uncontrollably, yet did not yet know what to say. He tried a few times, even opening his mouth to allow the words to flow, but he stopped each time. Kyle had a hard time making eye contact with his dad. He did not know if he wanted to even look at him for threat of becoming angry enough to storm out. At the same time, why would he go through the trouble of catching a ride to his parent's house if he did not want to settle things?

"It's great to see you," Drew finally said without a smile, but instead, a look of genuine sincerity.

Kyle finally looked at his father, still unable to speak. Frankly, he did not know what he would say. He did not frown, nor did he smile. He just stared, thinking and taking it in.

"Son, I love you," Drew continued. "I don't like not being close to you. I don't like you being angry at me. But I understand why," he paused for a moment to contemplate how to say what he had rehearsed a thousand times. "I should never have pressured you. You are not me, and I had no right to pressure you into doing what I wasn't in a position to do."

"Dad," Kyle finally replied, "this has been almost a year. You're just now realizing these things? You're just now apologizing?"

"You know me, son," he calmly explained. "In my own mind, I know everything. I'm always right. But I'm not always right, and I know that. And when I'm wrong, I don't like to admit it. It's hard for me to admit when I'm wrong. Your mother and I have been through some rough patches in our marriage over the last year because I'm so damned hard-headed and stubborn," he said as Angela smiled and clutched her husband's hand. "I've had to learn to take a step back and swallow my pride a little to keep from hurting the people I love."

The statement did not fall on deaf ears. Angela was proud of her husband, but feared that Kyle may still be too hurt and angry to accept the apology. He sat there staring at the table and nodding with a blank look on his face. He was soaking it in, deciding whether or not to forgive and whether or not to respond.

"You once told me something that has always stuck with me," Kyle looked up at his father. "You said that when you make a decision, whether it's right or it's wrong, there are consequences. Even if you're sorry about it, you can't undo it. All you can do is hope to learn from it. You made your decision to pressure me to go into the service. And now I'm out there on the line. The Marines are headed for Dallas and Fort Worth, and I'm gonna have to get dirty now. I might get killed, and you're going to have to accept it."

"I know," Drew nodded sadly, fighting back a tear. "I know. I've thought about that more than you know."

"The truth is," Kyle continued, "I've accepted it. I'm happy where I am. I know that when Little Boy Blue gets to the Metroplex, it's my home that's at stake, and I have to defend my home whether I believe in the cause of the Republic or not. I'm actually grateful to be part of it," he paused for a moment. "I forgive you."

Drew smiled wildly as his son began to grin with the relief of no longer bearing the burden of hating his own father. They each stood up, and rounded the table, finally clutching each other in a masculine father-son hug. Angela began to cry with joy as she watched her wounded family healed before her very eyes.

"Mom, can I borrow your car?" Kyle looked over at Angela as he and Drew released each other.

"Um, yeah. Sure," she was surprised. "You're not going to stay and eat?"

"Save a plate for me," he grabbed the keys off of the kitchen countertop and started for the door. "I've got somebody else to make amends with."

Kyle found it strange to be driving again. He had not done it in so long that it was almost foreign to him. Of course, it was just like anything one learns to do. It came back quickly, but it did not help that he was driving his mom's crossover SUV. He had always had trouble with it. The pedals were very sensitive. He found that when he pressed the brake, he tended to stop abruptly, unable to gradually slow before stopping. Then, when he accelerated from a stopping point, he rocketed from that position, sometimes even spinning the wheels a bit.

He did not have a plan for when he reached Ashley's house. He had no idea whether or not she would be there with a new boyfriend, or if she would even be home. He knew that she would not be at school. College Station was in southeast Texas, which was an area overrun with U.S. troops. The school had shut down and sent everyone home until further notice. In fact, the dormitories there were likely being used to house enemy soldiers. It occurred to him suddenly that if he had gone to college, rather than enlisting, he would probably be missing out on school anyway. However, he would still have Ashley, and he would not be making this drive.

Amongst similarly designed and similarly priced large houses in the planned community, he saw the familiar two story home down the street. It was the crown jewel of the high-end neighborhood. It felt like it had been decades since he had visited the house. It almost seemed as though the place would have changed, but the light stone and exposed beams of the house were exactly as he remembered.

He pulled up to the curb, paralleling it before stopping just shy of the driveway. Relief came over him as he saw the red convertible in the driveway. She was home. Then in an instant, the relief became tension that he felt deep in his gut. He walked up the exposed aggregate driveway toward the front door, all the while increasingly grappling with the fact that he had no plan. He had no idea what he was going to say. He was going cavalier with all guns blazing.

He crept up to the front door, and stared at it for a moment before finally ringing the doorbell. He considered running away like the scared little nerd boy in teen movies. But he was a trained Republican Guardsman. He was trained to stand his ground, and that he did, waiting and bursting with anxiety for an answer.

"Can I help you?" a man answered, poking his head through the crack in the ajar door.

It startled him. He did not expect a male voice, and he certainly did not expect a male head. Initially, his animal survival instincts took effect, as he was prepared for a confrontation with some new beau that Ashley had been seeing. But with a closer look, he realized that the hair atop that aging face was deep silver. Kyle had never met her father, adding to the anxiety of the visit.

"Um," Kyle was unsure of what to say. "I'm here to see Ashley."

"Are you David?" he opened the door a bit more, allowing to be seen, his light blue polo tucked into almost-white khaki shorts.

"No sir," Kyle shuddered a bit at being called by the wrong name. "I'm Kyle," he added as the man quickly looked him up and down, clearly analyzing the strange, soldierly young man before him.

"Kyle," the man grinned and nodded. "She's upstairs. I'll go get her," he closed the door.

Kyle waited at the door, trembling inside, yet attempting to maintain the air of composure and confidence. He had not seen Ashley in nearly a year. He was unsure of how she would react to him even being there. He was sure she had written him off. She had never tried to contact him or his parents. How would she react when seeing him in his military garb?

The door opened. She was as beautiful as the last day he had seen her. She was wearing her trademark little pink cotton shorts and a tank top in celebration of the warmer weather. Her hair was rolled into an upward ponytail, as silky as dark velvet. Kyle did not know how she would react to his being on her doorstep, and clearly she did not either. Her face was of shock and bewilderment, unable to speak as she stepped out and closed the door.

"Kyle? What are you doing here?" she puzzled. "I thought you'd be shipped off to Oklahoma of Missouri by now."

"I'm not. I'm in Carrolton, actually."

They both took a moment to soak in the moment, saying nothing, but eyeing each other analytically. To Kyle, she was still the most beautiful creature he had ever known. To her, she was trying to figure out who this drastically transformed version of her former boyfriend was. She had to admit, though, he looked sexy in his uniform. It was draped over his filled-out body, now giving some masculine structure to cage his extraordinary brains. She may have grinned a little, but not much.

"I miss you," Kyle spoke up.

"Oh God," she sneered. "Give me a break. I cried every night for a month thinking of you and whether or not you were safe. And then Ryan..."

"I was there when he..." he snapped, and then paused to maintain composure. "And I hear you were dating someone else."

"Yeah," she nodded with disdain. "You were off with the boys playing 'war', and left me behind, along with all of your personal beliefs. And I moved on," tears began to show in her eyes.

"My father pushed me," he admitted. "I didn't know what to do. I caved beneath the will of someone who is very influential to me. And I regret it. And he regrets it. And now we've made amends. I've had to learn some acceptance—consequences of my choices and actions."

She said nothing. She looked off to the side, and might as well have been peering into another dimension of existence. She was thinking and stewing. She did not know whether to get angry, to forgive, or to walk away.

"I've accepted my role now," he continued. "I'm not just some soldier fighting for a cause that I won't champion. I'm a defender of my home city. And I love you."

"What?" she could not believe he had inserted the emotional statement into the rhetoric of his soldier's mentality.

"I love you," he repeated. "Even after all this time, I still love you, and I'm pretty sure I always will. The Marines are coming. I won't get another chance to say this. I won't be back until after all of this is over."

"If you come back at all," she wiped tears away.

"That said," he continued. "I can't go back to my post without at least telling you this. I love you. I can't be with anyone else. I can't love anyone else. If I die in the next week, I will have died knowing that I loved someone with all of my heart, and I will be a complete man."

She once again said nothing. Tears still rolled down her soft cheek. She was frozen, unable to move or speak. He had said his piece. Her silence was all he needed to hear. He nodded, and turned, walking back to the SUV with the beginnings of a broken heart all over again.

"How many times did you rehearse that speech?" he heard her call out.

"Probably hundreds," he stopped, turned, and grinned. "But it's true."

"It was pretty sappy and cliché," she rolled her eyes.

"Did it work?" he implored.

"Yeah," she smiled as they rushed toward each other.

They embraced, making up for months of being apart. Their lips locked together as if cemented together. Passion oozed from their grip. They beamed with rays of true love—the kind that is unbreakable in any circumstance. Her father watched from his study window, smiling with happiness for his daughter.

"I love you so much," she looked into his eyes. "I missed you. I was just praying that one day you would show up here. I love you, and nothing can change that."

"So you'll be here when I come back?" he smiled.

"Come back to me, Kyle," she became very grave. "You sure as hell better come back to me, damn it!" she squeezed him, resting her chin on his shoulder.

Chapter 65

June, Two weeks before the bomb

The rifle fire and tank guns booming were deafening, as usual, but Derek was accustomed to it. The older officers who had pervious combat experience often said that he should count on having some permanent hearing loss after the war was over. He did not care. He was having fun. It was fun to kill the men that he aimed at across the parking lot and field of dirt. He watched with joy as they dropped to the ground, dying a deserving traitor's death.

The heat was radiating upward from the concrete beneath his feet. He preferred fighting in the fall or spring. Here, there was plenty of cover. He and the rest of the Marines around him were positioned amid buildings at the Mesquite Convention Center in Mesquite, Texas. They had reached the Dallas area. In fact, downtown Dallas was only about ten miles to the west. But they would not be moving on Dallas, nor would the troops to the south and west be moving on downtown Fort Worth. The objective was the same as in Houston. They would surround the two metropolitan areas, decimating the outer defenses positioned around the interstate loop highways, and then strangle them.

It was a turkey shoot. They had taken the Convention Center easily. It was not like a large city's convention center with a huge domed area and adjacent hotel building with conference rooms. It was a small, Mexican-looking structure with stucco and arches resembling an old Spanish mission. It was the site of an annual rodeo, so to the north of the main buildings was a large dirt area that the Republican Guardsmen were attempting to cross. There was no cover for them, and Derek fired mercilessly. A few times, he almost lost his footing, rolling on the dozens of his own brass shell casings beneath his feet.

"Jesus, these boys just won't quit!" Derek smiled, yelling to his beloved captain across a space between buildings.

"This is one of their most important cities," the captain yelled back. "They're not giving up without a fight."

Finally, the returning Republican gunfire began to waver. Derek could see the enemy troops retreating back across thc field and into the solace of the shopping centers, neighborhoods, and even toward the high school nearby to the north and west. Derek was pleased, and Captain Andrews was pleased with the performance of his men. Feeling that the coast was clear, he stepped out from his cover.

"Good job, guys," he praised the Marines. "It looks like we're going to get Mesquite. From here, we'll leave a lot of you behind to hold the position, and some of you will move up north toward Richardson and Carrolton."

"What about me?" Derek asked.

"You're getting a promotion to sergeant, Putnam," he smiled. "You're a born leader. These new guys need a leader. You'll move out under Lieutenant Jacobi, and help him out up north. I'm proud of you," he laid his hand on Derek's shoulder.

Without much of a sound, Derek felt warm liquid pelt his face and clothing. It startled him. He had no idea at first what it could be. But he quickly understood as he saw his captain's knees buckle and the color drain from his face. In his right side, just beneath his armpit, blood poured from the captain's body. It was a stray bullet fired randomly by a Red soldier retreating across the field, and it had found its mark in the body cavity of one of Derek's role models.

Derek's face displayed horror and shock at first, and then sadness. As quickly as the bullet had struck his captain, his emotions turned to anger and rage. His face turned bright red, and his entire body shook.

"Medic!"

Just one hundred and ninety miles away in Austin, President Davenport was receiving the news from General Weaver. He was visibly distraught, hunching over his desk with his fingers interlocked and hands resting on top. He had not shaven that day and he looked very tired. On nights that he was not poring over endless documents dealing with not only the war, but normal governmental business, he could not bring himself to get any sleep. He would just lie there, eyes wide, thinking of any way that he could turn the tide of the war.

"They're in, sir," Weaver delivered the news about the Dallas area. "There are U.S. forces stretching from about Kennadale, in Tarrant County, to Mesquite just east of Dallas. They're going to try to surround the whole Dallas and Fort Worth area, and then choke it off. They're also coming in from the north. You know the U.S. Army crossed the Red River last week. Well, General Dylan is moving down I-35 as we speak. He's at about Denton, which is where we've been able to keep him for now."

"How strong are the forces in the northern part of DFW?" Davenport looked at his little map.

"We're undermanned," Weaver answered. "We're looking better, as a whole, than we did in Houston. But if our estimates on the Blue numbers are correct, it may not be enough."

"And General Dylan?" Davenport asked. "What are we doing to keep him out of the Metroplex?"

"Everything we can, sir. We've got a fairly large tank battalion up there giving him all kinds of hell, but he keeps getting more and more reinforcements. Once they punched through into Texas, it's like they focused everything they had on I-35 and headed south. We have tried to send out air support from Carswell Naval Air Station in Fort Worth, but the Blue boys brought their fast movers, too. We've lost seven planes in just the last week."

"So he's gonna get through," Davenport nodded. "That's what you're telling me?"

"I'm afraid so."

"Damn it!" Davenport erupted in anger, slamming his fist down upon his desk. "I've got half the Republic bitchin' at me for losing this war! And I'm doin' everything I can! So are you and your boys. The people are looking to me to protect them and their rights from these power-hungry socialists that want to come in and take all their freedoms, but we're losing," he paused for a moment to regain composure.

"It all comes down to numbers. They've got more. I can't seem to pay young people enough to enlist. I've got kids going to Canada, Mexico, and the whole west coast US, dodging the draft. This generation is just too damned liberal! If I had more troops to work with, we wouldn't be having this conversation."

He sat behind his big desk, shaking his head in dismay. He stared into space, contemplating his plight and wondering where things may have gone wrong or what he could have done differently.

"Why would anybody want to be a president?" he thought aloud. "You run for office with all these ideals in your head. You're a man of vision and you make all these promises to the people when you're running. And then you get elected, and it's all out of your hands. You've got the legislature that can't agree on anything. Then there's lack of personnel to send into battle. It's impossible to make good on all the promises. If you're a person of vision, you're better off as a Martin Luther King, Galileo, or Gandhi—somebody with no restrictions in bureaucracy. Nope. The presidency is no place for someone who truly wants to make a difference in the world."

"On the bright side, we're holding them off far from Austin," Weaver said. "We lost New Orleans, Houston, and now possibly DFW, but we're holding Austin."

"True," Davenport nodded. "If we can hold out, we can try to pool greater numbers from our western states. They haven't seen a bit of this war. Then, maybe we can start launching some counterattacks."

"Sounds good, Mr. President," Weaver nodded.

"Keep me posted," Davenport dismissed the general, and he left the room, and left the president to sit in silence, brooding over the difficulty of his situation.

Chapter 66

Days before the bomb

The night was humid, and though the temperature was in the eighties, it was still unbearable. The rain came at just the right time during the day. It was mid-afternoon, so when the hour-long shower cleared out, the sun began scorching the North Texas earth once again and evaporated everything into the air. With a few more hours of the most devilish of rays left in the day, the moisture in the air absorbed and kept the heat of the day, carrying it on into the night. It was the kind of night where one may walk outside for just a few moments and still sweat profusely.

Heavy wheels generated tiny tsunamis in the leftover puddles dotting the concrete parking lot that housed many Porsches and high-end BMWs. They glistened in the street lights, most of them with fresh coats of wax. And amid these executive and lawyer-owned status symbols came a new addition—a mid-sized moving van. It was ugly and worn, definitely not meshing well with the existing vehicles. Yet, it was acceptable. It was a moving van not unlike the ones any of the tenants of the high-rise apartment building used when they moved in. No one would ask questions.

The two men opened the doors and lowered themselves from the elevated cab. They had changed from their simple Mexican garb and now wore higher-end clothing as to not be stopped by any patrolling and profiling police officers in the area. They closed the doors and locked the van. As they walked away from the van, they looked back and up at the high-rise apartment building. It was glamorous and stately, yet dwarfed by the towering Dallas skyline very close by. They each smiled. This was the perfect place. The expensive deposit on an apartment here was money well-spent.

Chapter 67

The Dallas and Fort Worth area was somehow caught in a time warp. It was as if it had crossed into an alternate dimension; a veritable parallel world. It seemed to have fallen prey to the same unfortunate fate as so many other deserted ghost towns of the American west.

One would never be able to tell that it was a weekday. Normally, the streets and highways bustled with life. But now, there were no commuters in stand-still traffic. No minivans carried children to baseball practice and dance lessons. No pickup trucks loaded with supplies and workers made their way to construction sites. Traffic lights changed from red to green with no hurried travelers to accelerate through the intersections. Aside from occasional military vehicles and policemen patrolling the streets, the roadways were dead.

It was as if humankind had spontaneously vanished from existence. Plastic shopping bags and straw-impaled cup lids rode the wind currents, tumbling down the asphalt. Stores and restaurants, dark within, crowned empty parking lots. Quiet was the loudest sound.

The sprawling double metropolis was not, however, vacant. For those who had the money or friends and family to stay with elsewhere, it was feasible to leave. They took the opportunity for a family vacation, packing up the kids and pets for a long get-away. Monied residents stayed in hotels far from the Metroplex, while others had to rely on kin. Some tried to cross over US-held territory or into the United States itself, only to be turned away. Others looked to the west, either to western plains and deserts of West Texas, or to other western states that were untouched by the terrible tentacles of war.

But the vast majority of the people living in Dallas/Fort Worth were, indeed, present on this day. A unilateral mandate had been issued by the mayors of Dallas and Fort Worth, as well as every suburban city in between and surrounding the region. No one was to be on the roads. They were to stay indoors at all times. It was a shut-down of the fastest-growing metropolitan area in North America.

At least the power was not cut to Metroplex homes. The ranks of the invading U.S. forces were not filled with monsters. The mounting heat of a July day could be unbearable. No one wanted the heat-related deaths of small children or the elderly on their hands. Food, while it lasted, could be cooked and homes could be cooled.

Television sets only displayed static. Stations had been deserted, their transmitters silenced. Many families revisited their collection of DVDs, rewatching movies they owned and loved, yet had not viewed in ages. On-Demand service with the cable, satellite, and fiber optic providers had become too easy. Some radio stations, before becoming unmanned, looped their computerized playlists so that the entire area could enjoy the music. Many families chose to dock their MP3 players in their stereo systems, rather than listen to what the radio stations dictated. It did not matter. The point was to somehow drown out the terrifying sounds beginning to echo across the cities.

For people in the inner cities, the sounds were faint. There were occasional distant booms of cannons and explosions of mortars, but it did not feel threatening—only eerie. But for the families living further out into the suburbs and outskirts, the sounds were nightmarish. People huddled in the interiors of the houses, crouched to the floor or taking refuge in bathrooms as if there were an approaching tornado. Children cried and screamed as bullets shattered their windows and shot across their once peaceful living rooms and bedrooms, puncturing the sheetrock walls. Mortars destroyed their non-paid-for SUVs and sedans sitting in the driveways. Chunks of their well-manicured lawns were missing and decorative trees had been felled.

Though no bullets flew across their household, the Perkins family could hear most of the action. They were close enough for it to be frightening. The three of them sat on the floor around the family room coffee table, playing a game of Scrabble. They never played the game because Angela always seemed to win. They hated playing her. She started out slowly, and then began building a lead by placing only two or three tiles onto the board, building on other words in multiple directions. And she always seemed to be able to find ways to do it on a triple word space. She knew ridiculous words that were frequently challenged, only to be proven valid—a word no one had used in conversation in a century. This day was no different. She was beating her son and husband by a comfortable thirty-three points.

It felt nice to her to have her youngest son Dylan actually participating in being part of the family, although the circumstances were shameful. Nevertheless, he was there, finally free of his nexus of digital music and antisocial behavior. Angela and Drew tried to pretend that he was genuinely enjoying the family time, but the truth was that he was terrified. His eyes were wide and his heart felt as though it would leap from his chest. He was clinging to his parents in his time of fear, jumping each time he heard an explosion in the distance.

Games and companionship were meant to ease their minds. It was meant to take their thoughts from the reality of an invading force at their doorsteps. It was meant to divert their thoughts from the fact that an immediate family member was out on those front lines. He was witnessing the horror first-hand. He was likely being shot at. It was a very real possibility that he would not return. It was a terrible feeling, and it was beyond their control. But at the moment, the focus was trying to build a word, but having five vowels, a Q and an S to work with.

Suddenly, the three of them could barely see their letters or the board. Bright, white light poured in from every window, seeming to permeate the very walls. It was blinding, as if one stepped from a dark room, directly into a brilliant day-lit parking lot. Each of them instantly raised their hands over their eyes to shield their retinas from the brightest light that they had ever witnessed. And then it slowly dimmed. They had not even the chance to be fearful. It was sheer wonder, rather than fright.

But then fright did set in. As the mysterious light dimmed, the Perkins home began to shake. Windows and doors rattled against their frames. Unseen dust was shaken loose from the upper walls and ceilings. The strange vibration resonated through the house as the very boards and beams that gave the home structure were shaken to the last molecule. Angela's prized decorative plates and glass figurines toppled from shelves and wall hangers onto tile floors, crashing and shattering into a thousand glistening pieces. Then it stopped, leaving the Perkins family in awe, in terror, and in puzzlement over the cause of the uncanny experience.

Miles away, soldiers stood in wonder and in horror over what they were seeing. Masses of combatants gazed into the southern sky in something akin to a trance. It became silent. Men struggled slowly to their feet, completely in disbelief. This was something they had only seen in movies and old World War II reels. No one could ever have imagined that they would see something like this in their lifetime. No one knew quite what to do. Fighting and killing was no longer a focus. The objective and mission was washed away by the cleansing power of mass destruction. Minds were blank. Anger was neutralized, at least for most.

Kyle continued to watch the mushroom cloud rise into the sky, billowing and rolling in a ghastly fashion. The once mild-mannered intellectual began to waver in the insecurity of his feelings toward the enemy at the gates. He was starting to feel emotions—raw and uncontrollable emotions. He could feel the brief terror of Dallas residents shortly before their fiery demise. He could feel their screams ripping out his insides. He thought of his family and beloved Ashley in Fort Worth. It could easily have been that side of the Metroplex, and he would have no one left. There was anger, and it built to a level that he had never experienced. It overflowed, and had to escape.

He turned, facing the men still mesmerized on the battlefront. His eyes might as well have glowed as embers in a dying fire. The emotion emanated from every pore on his body. No one paid attention, but Kyle disregarded his fallen rifle, reaching instead for his .45 caliber side arm. He drew it from the holster and pulled back the slide, his face grimacing in sheer fury. He then pointed it.

"You sons of bitches," he calmly stated. "You fucking nuked Dallas?!" he then shouted in fury.

He trained the sights of his pistol on the first soldier he saw. The Marine was not even paying attention. He was still staring at the monstrous cloud of debris lifting into the Texas sky. But he was brought out of the trance by the very familiar sound of a weapon discharging. Then he felt it. A bullet struck his left shoulder, immediately causing the man to grasp his wound in reflex. Then another shot was fired, and this time the round perforated his lower abdomen, sending him to the ground.

"Kyle!" Okie grabbed his friend, wrestling for his gun. "It wasn't them! Are you crazy? They wouldn't do a shitty thing like this!" he finally freed the pistol from Kyle's hand, sending him to the concrete in tears.

As Derek Putnam sprawled onto the ground, blood pouring from two wounds, he still could not take his eyes off of the mushroom cloud in the sky. He did not whimper or even grunt in pain. He found the sight strangely peaceful and comforting. He drifted, slowly losing consciousness. His eyes became heavy, as if he were unable to stop himself from dozing off to sleep.

"Medic!" was the last word he heard before losing consciousness.

Chapter 68

July, One month after the bomb

Every television set across the United States and the Republic was tuned to the same program. It was on in every home, bar, office break room, and airport. It was a view of the White House rose garden. A stage was set with two podiums facing a large crowd of journalists and camera operators. Behind each podium stood a president. Presidents Chandler and Davenport faced the crowd with expressions of solemnity and composure of somberness.

"The two of us stand before you today, not as enemies," Chandler began to speak. "We stand before you as Americans. Though we remain separate in political vision and separate as leaders of two separate countries, we stand before you as members of a common nation and heritage. Democrat or Republican, we are brethren."

"A month ago," Davenport contributed, "in the midst of a battle for the cities of Dallas and Fort Worth, an event of unprecedented proportions occurred in downtown Dallas. A hydrogen bomb was detonated, killing countless thousands of innocent civilian residents. It is not known the strength of the weapon, but experts are saying that it was a small one. But it was strong enough to destroy many lives and much of a great American city. It was also strong enough to get our attention."

"The detonation of this nuclear warhead," Chandler began again, "is believed to have been an attack on our home soil, planned and executed by an Islamic terrorist group. Taliban has already claimed involvement, and it is believed that the warhead was taken from a Pakistani silo shortly after fundamentalists overthrew the democratic government there."

"It was a sucker punch," Davenport picked up. "And it came at the most opportune of times for them. There's a lesson in this tragic event. The best time to throw a sucker punch is when the guy is distracted.

And that is something that has plagued us for more than a year. It is now time to focus on what is most important for the people of the Republic and of the United States—our security. It's time to focus on the security of our people, blue and red. The cease-fire will continue and our nations will remain at peace, while peace talks and negotiations will continue here in Washington."

"In the meantime, we will begin planning to bring to justice those who would do our people harm, and President Davenport has assured me that the Republican Guard will be right there alongside the U.S. Army and Marines. Thank you," Chandler said as reporters fired questions at the two of them.

In Texas, Ashley and Kyle sat on the edge of her bed, watching the TV address. They grasped each other's hands, lovingly caressing with their thumbs. Ashley looked into his eyes, sympathetic in detection of the lingering pain and trauma there. They released hands, and gently placed their arms around each other, saying nothing, but letting their embrace do all of the talking.

In Cleveland, Carly sat in the living room of the Putnam home, the glare of the television illuminating her face. Beside her, Sherry's power chair still sat, now gathering dust in her absence. She turned her head and smiled, watching Derek lovingly cradle his nine-month-old baby girl in his arms. The sling that supported his left arm was not an obstacle. He held the child to his chest, sitting in his mother's once favorite chair. Olivia knew this was her daddy. She nestled her tiny head into his chest, finding comfort in his warmth and love. Derek smiled, having never felt this kind of adoration for anything in his life. In that moment, the pain seemed to fade away.

About The Author

J.M. Richardson is a native of southeast Louisiana where he studied education and social sciences, earning his degree from Louisiana State University. He has been writing for leisure nearly all of his life, wrote competitively in high school, and had intensive writing coursework in college. He now resides in the Fort Worth, TX, area with his wife and two daughters where he teaches geography, history, and sociology.

Follow J.M. Richardson:
jmrichardsonbooks.com
Twitter: @jmrichardson1
Facebook: J M Richardson - Author

Made in the USA
Monee, IL
20 October 2026

66035298R00249